WAR OF THE ENCYCLOPAEDISTS

A NOVEL

Christopher Robinson

and

Gavin Kovite

SCRIBNER

New York   London   Toronto   Sydney   New Delhi

Scribner

An Imprint of Simon & Schuster, Inc.

1230 Avenue of the Americas

New York, NY 10020

First Scribner hardcover edition May 2015

SCRIBNER and design are registered trademarks of The Gale Group, Inc., used under license by Simon & Schuster, Inc., the publisher of this work.

For information about special discounts for bulk purchases, please contact Simon & Schuster Special Sales at 1-866-506-1949 or business@simonandschuster.com.

The Simon & Schuster Speakers Bureau can bring authors to your live event. For more information or to book an event, contact the Simon & Schuster Speakers Bureau at 1-866-248-3049 or visit our website at www.simonspeakers.com.

Interior design by Jill Putorti

Manufactured in the United States of America

10 9 8 7 6 5 4 3 2 1

Library of Congress Control Number: 2014033292

ISBN 978-1-4767-7542-5
ISBN 978-1-4767-7544-9 (ebook)

To our parents

Nec dubitamus multa esse quae et nos praeterierint,
homines enim sumus et occupati officiis . . .

Nor do we doubt that many things have escaped us also,
for we are but human, and beset with duties . . .

—PLINY THE ELDER, THE ORIGINAL ENCYCLOPAEDIST

WAR OF THE ENCYCLOPAEDISTS

article | discussion | edit this page | history

The Encyclopaedists [edit]

Scholars generally agree that the Encyclopaedia is Truth, insofar as Truth exists, which it doesn't. Nevertheless, existence, which teeters on the precipice of subjective experience, is anchored by encyclopaedic reference. The Encyclopaedia, therefore, justifies itself with a recursive entry. And it should not be surprising that this article's subject is responsible for its origination. Fuckballs. Post-colonial cadaver sex. See, we can write anything, since no one else cares to define us for us.

The exact origins of this article are a matter of some debate, the most popular (and most contentious) theory aligning its inception with Mani's hospitalization on the early morning of July 3rd, 2004—one year, three months, fourteen days, ten hours, and twenty-six minutes after the beginning of the Iraq War, in which Mickey Montauk would learn to shut the fuck up . . . while Halifax Corderoy deconstructed in the bricked and hobbling streets of Cambridge, Massachusetts.

This article about a Seattle Art Collective is a stub. You can help Wikipedia by expanding it.

External links [edit]

1. ^ "The Encyclopaedists of Capitol Hill."
www.thestranger.com/apr04/encyclopaedists.htm

navigation

- Main Page
- Community portal
- Current events
- Recent changes
- Random page
- Help
- Donations

search

[Go] [Search]

toolbox

- What links here
- Related changes
- Special pages

WIKIPEDIA
The Free Encyclopedia

CONSPIRACY

1

It was the Friday before Independence Day and the twentysomethings of early-millennium Seattle were celebrating alcohol and freedom as they had done every Friday since time immemorial. And though they breathed and imbibed as one massive citywide organism, each group thought itself discrete, with its own goals and exclusions, its own playlist gurus and backroom smoke-outs. On Fifteenth Avenue, in Capitol Hill, Mickey Montauk and Halifax Corderoy were hosting their sixth event as "The Encyclopaedists."

They had no real artistic talent, but they had a knack for carrying stupid jokes to their absurd conclusions. Six months ago, following one about the arbitrary nature of modern art, they decided to put on an art show themselves. They chose their subject, "monocularity," by flipping randomly through a 1914 *Anglo-American Cyclopedia.* They built a multimedia installation involving cyclopean monsters, monocled British financiers, a chandelier made of dildos and periscopes, and a video loop of the burning eye of Sauron. They wore eye patches and threw a raging party. They both got laid, which was reason enough to continue the monthly "exhibits." After their third event, whose theme was "pupa," *The Stranger,* Seattle's widely read and ever-relevant free arts weekly, had profiled "The Encyclopaedists of Capitol Hill."

Tonight's theme was "conspiracy." The cavernous Great Room on the main floor of Montauk's house had been retrofitted as a lunar soundstage—papier-mâché craters, glow-in-the-dark stars, and tripod-mounted lights and cameras. Montauk was dressed as an astronaut, welcoming guests with slow lunar movements.

Corderoy and his girlfriend, Mani, were four miles north in the Roosevelt neighborhood, where the I-5 overpass shadows a park-and-ride littered with brown-bagged forties and the occasional hypodermic needle. Corderoy stood at one end of a fourth-floor hallway in a run-down apartment building. He was facing a police officer.

"Who are you supposed to be?" the officer asked.

Corderoy wore a dark blue suit with a red tie; his lapel was pinned with an American flag. His eyebrows, so blond they were normally invisible, had been dusted with white makeup, his reddish-blond hair was covered with a neatly combed powder-gray wig, and Mani had given him wrinkles around the nose and eyes with eyeliner pencil. Corderoy was six-one (though a mere one hundred and fifty pounds, with a posture reminiscent of Gumby) and he wasn't used to looking up at people, but the officer must have been at least six-four.

"President Bush," Corderoy said.

"And she's what, bin Laden?"

Mani stood at the other end of the hallway near the open door to an apartment, opposite another police officer. She wore heels, a low-cut white minidress, and a camouflage bolero jacket, which was little more than a pair of sleeves and two short flaps near her bust that could not possibly fasten together. Her long black hair spilled out from a white turban, and the olive skin of her face was obscured by a scraggly black beard with streaks of gray. Her costume was perfect, or it would have been if they'd managed to retrieve the pièce de résistance from inside the apartment. Mani was smoking a Camel Light.

"Sexy bin Laden," Corderoy corrected.

The officer clenched his jaw. "Why are you dressed up?"

"We're going to a party. We just came by to pick up her AK." He was speaking faster than he could think.

"Her what?"

"Her AK-47. It's a toy. A toy gun. For the costume. It has an orange tip."

"Take your hands out of your pockets."

"Sorry. So, we had to get the AK, and she's been living here with Steph—"

"She's on the lease?"

"Well, no. She just met Steph a few months ago, when she moved to Seattle. Steph usually leaves the apartment unlocked because Mani doesn't have a key. But when we got here, the door was locked. We knocked and knocked and tried calling Steph, but no answer. So . . . I tried to pick the lock."

The officer stopped writing. "You picked the lock?"

"No. I *tried* to pick the lock." Corderoy had read the *MIT Guide to Lock Picking* when he was in high school and had made his own picks out of coat hangers. It had taken him two weeks to pick the lock on his own front door. That had been his only success.

The officer's face was expressionless.

"So Mani said maybe go up to the roof and I tried that and it was easy enough to hop down to the balcony. The sliding glass door was locked, too, but—"

"Hands out of your pockets."

"Sorry. Can I just take my jacket off so I'm not tempted to do that?"

"No."

"So, I checked the window, which also opens onto the balcony, and it wasn't locked. All the lights were off, so I thought, No one's home. I was just going to climb in, open the front door from the inside, take the toy gun, and leave. But when I opened the window, there was Steph, sitting by herself in the dark, and she screamed, 'Get the fuck out of here I'm calling the cops!' So I climbed back onto the roof and came down to the hallway. And then you got here."

"You entered the room?"

"Well, I opened the window and leaned in."

"But you crossed the threshold of the window."

"I suppose, yeah." Corderoy looked over at Mani. Her officer was speaking with Steph just inside the apartment. Steph's hands flashed into view through the doorjamb. Mani looked away from Corderoy, then lit another cigarette. Corderoy felt like an idiot. Sure, he thought, I'll break into someone's house for you. Because you're hot, no biggie. I do that all the time.

"Son, do you know what that's called, what you did there at the window?"

Corderoy took a moment to respond. "Breaking and entering?"

"We don't have breaking and entering in Washington State. It's called burglary. And it's a felony offense. That's a minimum of five years in prison."

"Oh." Corderoy's eyes slipped out of focus.

The officers went to converse with each other, and Corderoy and Mani were finally able to speak.

"Steph's crying," she said. "I don't know what's going on, but I think they're going to arrest you."

That's when Phil arrived.

Before the officers could stop him, Corderoy yelled down the hall, "Hey, man, can you talk to Steph?"

"Do you know these two?" one of the officers asked Phil.

Corderoy and Phil were on good terms, but they barely knew each other. Phil was Steph's friend, and business partners with a guy named Braiden, whom everyone called "Bomb," as in, *That shit's the bomb.* Braiden and Phil were pot dealers and they routinely smoked out Steph, who was flirtatious enough to get her pot for free. There was no guarantee that Phil's intervention would be positive, and in all likelihood he had drugs on him, which wouldn't be good for any of them if the officers found out.

The cops let Phil through.

Corderoy couldn't hear Phil's voice, but he heard Steph's high-pitched exclamations. After a minute, they emerged and Steph spoke with the officers.

"You're dropping the charges, then?" one asked.

Steph went catatonic.

"Steph . . ." Phil said.

She nodded.

"What about my stuff?" Mani asked.

Steph whispered to Phil, then ducked inside.

"It's in the parking garage," Phil said.

The officers took their information, gave Corderoy a stern warning, and left.

Mani wobbled down the stairs in her new heels. Corderoy was about to follow, but Phil pulled him aside. "I'm looking out for you, man. Get rid of that girl. She's trouble."

"I know," Corderoy said.

"Seriously." He leaned in closer and spoke softer. "She's a thief. Ditch the bitch."

Corderoy resented that. Whatever else Mani was, she wasn't a bitch.

"Sooner the better," Phil said, slapping him on the shoulder.

"I know," Corderoy said again. But he didn't know. And of the many things he didn't know, this uncertainty in particular had been gnawing at him for the past few weeks. Even Montauk had pointed out that Mani had been mooching off him since they'd met. He'd paid for her food, her drinks, her tickets to shows. He'd bought the plastic AK and the turban for her costume. He'd even bought the heels she was wearing. But he'd done it all gladly. And she'd been gracious and grateful and goddamn beautiful, and somehow, though she didn't have any money, she'd been generous, generous with her time, her heart, her self. Corderoy was convinced she was a much better person than he.

When he reached the parking garage, Mani was sifting through a trash bag filled with her scant belongings, a cigarette hanging out of her mouth. He could see the strap of her bra beneath her white dress. "This is crazy," he said. "She just threw all your shit down here?"

Mani started laughing, dropping her forehead into her hand.

"It's not funny," Corderoy said.

"It's hilarious," Mani said. "My charcoals and sunglasses are missing, but Steph made sure I had this." She pulled out a half-eaten avocado swaddled in plastic wrap. "Hungry?"

They tossed the bag in the back of Corderoy's (dad's) Suburban and pulled out of the garage. Corderoy thought about telling Mani to throw the cigarette out—his dad hated the smell, and Corderoy didn't look forward to admitting that he had not, in fact, quit. Instead, he rolled both their windows down, lit one of his own, and tried not to think about it as they drove to the Encyclopaedists party at Montauk's house.

Mani leaned over and kissed him on the cheek. His face flushed. It had taken a few minutes, and that kiss, for him to realize that he hadn't been arrested, that everything was fine. And now that he had, a warmth flooded his body, the relief of being alone, safe, with a beautiful girl, this beautiful girl, who excited him, who was dangerous, whom he couldn't be mad at. He drove in silence for a moment, riding out that feeling, but his confusion slowly welled back up to the surface.

"Okay," he said. "What the fuck just happened?"

"Right? It's like we're in a Beckett play. I guess Bomb and Phil started dealing coke. And they were keeping the cash at Steph's. Neutral territory for their joint bank. Then last night Phil did the count, and it was four hundred dollars short. Phil asked Bomb about it, and he said *I* must have taken it."

Corderoy glanced at her as if she were an imposter. What have you done with the real Mani? "But then who . . . ?"

"Bomb probably blew a couple eightballs himself, and there was no money to begin with."

"But what was Steph's deal?"

"I don't know, she's known Bomb for years. I've only known her two months. It was his word against mine, and Steph decided I had to go."

"But why didn't she tell you? She just threw your stuff in a trash bag. That's insane. Even if you did take the money—"

"I didn't take it."

"I never said you did. It's just weird, right, that Steph would kick you out and not even tell you."

"What are you saying?"

"Nothing. It's just really weird on her part." Corderoy turned the AC up a notch. "You look cute, you know."

"I didn't take the money."

"Even in that bin Laden beard, you look damn sexy."

"You look old," she said. She looked out the window for an unbearable second. "But I like older men." She reached over and rubbed her hand on Corderoy's crotch as they pulled onto Fifteenth Avenue to look for parking.

Normally, Corderoy would have been hard at the instant the muscles in her shoulder alerted him, subconsciously, that her hand was about to reach over to his lap. But the lust centers of his brain were confused by Mani's sexy bin Laden getup. Worse still, he was beginning to think Phil was right. That he should get rid of her, cut his losses. It had only been two months. And besides, he'd started dating her with a Get Out of Relationship Free Card: he was moving to Boston at the beginning of August, for grad school. She knew this. He'd told her the night they'd met, at the fourth Encyclopaedists event. It would have been a simple decision, if not for one problem: Corderoy loved Mani—maybe—and she was now homeless.

Capitol Hill had been the nesting place of Seattle's early patricians— gold rush and logging men, mostly. Now it hosted Seattle's hip post-college crowd with divey-chic watering holes, gay karaoke bars, fringe theaters, and tattoo parlors. At the top of the hill, though, the neighborhood still felt regal. Like many of the houses there, Montauk's dated to the early nineteen hundreds and could be considered a mansion, with its bay windows and colonnaded porch. He lived there with eight other people. Since the article in *The Stranger,* they'd been referring to the house as the Encyclopad.

Montauk had a stout, muscled frame, and in his bleached-white jumpsuit, stuffed with newspaper, his thick white gloves, and an old white motorcycle helmet, he made a fine-looking astronaut. He opened the front door in slow motion and watched Corderoy and Mani stare at their own reflections in his visor, then lifted it to reveal his goofy grin. He was already several beers deep.

He eyed Mani's legs as she and Corderoy slipped into the party. Death Cab for Cutie played over conversations about JFK and Roswell; everyone clutched keg cups. The Great Room, which was almost the whole first floor of the mansion, was terrible for soundproofing. With each new Encyclopaedists event, Montauk had worried that the neighbors' noise complaints might finally tip the scales and the cops would shut them down for good. But today he had found the official Department of the Army letter in his mailbox, and Encyclopad-based concerns had dissolved. A new reality was setting in. He had called his platoon sergeant and his four squad leaders, who would notify the rest of his forty-man platoon, completing the chain-of-command phone tree, which likely originated in some flag-draped office in the Pentagon. He was Going to War.

He had yet to tell Corderoy. They had planned to room together in Boston, and now Montauk was essentially being ordered to bail on his best friend. It wasn't the right time to bring it up. He found Corderoy and Mani drinking red box wine from a gravy boat and a teacup, looking at the first items on display: the old *Anglo-American Cyclopedia* and a *Black's Law Dictionary*, both laid open on music stands to "conspiracy." "More people than last time," Montauk said.

Corderoy toasted him with his gravy boat. "Mission accomplished," he said in a Texan drawl.

Montauk smiled. He found Mani's slutty bin Laden costume disconcerting. But it fit the party, which was full of the kind of people who would laugh at it. Mani was still a bit of a black box to him. She seemed to be reeling in his buddy like a hooked trout. On more than a few occasions he had reminded Corderoy that she was basically a freeloader; by her own admission, she'd trekked from Massachusetts to California on her ex-boyfriend's generosity—meaning credulity. Corderoy was certainly credulous, but when Mani was around, he was also happy, and who could argue with that?

"Gotta make the rounds," Montauk said, and he dipped into the crowd.

"You okay?" Mani asked Corderoy.

Corderoy turned to her. "You've barely touched your wine."

"I always drink slow."

"Cheers to that," he said, and he took a drink, holding the gravy boat to his lips for a long time, trying to get her to match him. She did.

"So . . . you're homeless again," Corderoy said.

"We've got bigger problems," Mani said. "I think they're after us."

"Who's *they*?"

"You know, *them*."

They drank. They smoked. They danced in slow motion on the lunar soundstage. They trampled a crop circle in the neighbors' grass. Corderoy and Mani told the story of the burglary again and again, with differing degrees of hyperbole. But the issue of where Mani would sleep that night went unmentioned. And Corderoy had to keep his keg cup filled and frothy to hide his preoccupation. Did he actually love this girl enough to invite her to move in with him? Into the basement of his parents' house, no less? His parents wouldn't bat an eye—their hospitality was nearly a form of psychosis, and it had been a great boon to Corderoy in the past. Now it meant that the onus of this decision was on him. And Mani, unaware of his parents' attitude, would likely interpret an invitation as a serious move, which would leapfrog their relationship over the months of courtship it normally took to reach a place of domestic intimacy. And so he filled his cup, he lit a cigarette, he made out with Mani on the porch, he avoided Montauk because he needed Montauk's help, he clung to Mani because he feared he would leave her, because he imagined her down in Santa Cruz bumming around with potheads and surfers, playing guitar on the beach. He imagined her back in Newton, Massachusetts, living under the strictures of her immigrant parents. He imagined her warm breasts pressed against the side of his torso, her leg angled across his waist, sleeping through the night until tomorrow morning and forever.

Mani was intelligent but surprisingly ignorant of things Corderoy considered common knowledge. She had never heard the phrase *cross that bridge when we come to it*. She couldn't describe a catapult. She'd never heard of Nikola Tesla. She wasn't religious, but she believed in a *force*. Corderoy was quick to hate spirituality, but this sounded so much like his childhood love of *Star Wars* that he couldn't hate it. He used to cry, and still got teary-eyed, during Yoda's speech before lifting the X-wing from the Dagobah swamp. *Luminous beings are we, not this crude matter.*

Mani's parents had emigrated from Iran in the wake of the Islamic revolution, when her mother was pregnant. It took them some time to regain their footing in America, but eventually they landed solidly in the upper-middle class. Her father was a doctor and her mother a professor at Boston College; they were strict in their desire to see Mani succeed, which meant: doctor, lawyer, possibly optometrist. But Mani wanted to paint. Her parents wouldn't finance an education in art, so she'd dropped out of UMass Amherst and moved to California with her then-boyfriend. She'd lived with him—and off him—for the better part of a year, painting portraits of the junkies and homeless who roamed the streets of Santa Cruz. When they split, she moved out, becoming homeless herself, sleeping in parks and on the beach, until one day she traded a few watercolors for an old bicycle, sold off her belongings, and made her way up to Seattle over a period of several months, living off her charm, camping or crashing with strangers in San Francisco, Portland, Olympia, helping old hippie couples with their gardens, moving from co-ops to art lofts, reminding everyone she met how great it was to be alive, to share a cigarette or a bottle of wine with an unfamiliar but fascinating human.

This is why Corderoy loved Mani: She could roll her own cigarettes with one hand. She could recite large passages from Hunter S. Thompson. She looked exotic, with her olive skin and black hair, but she spoke like any college-aged American girl. One night she took him out to the woods in Interlaken Park with flashlights and beers to huddle in the dark and tell stories. When she wanted something, she had a way of setting her face in an almost-smile, a mischievous deadpan that held years of squealing, squirming mirth just below the surface.

When they'd met at the fourth Encyclopaedists event ("moss"), they'd spent the night on Montauk's futon. They had sex, quietly, while Montauk's friend Tim slept just feet away from them, and afterward Corderoy reminisced with her about the video games of his youth (*Mega Man 2, Castlevania*). Mani found this endearing. She sketched his face in pencil, out of proportion and somewhat grotesque, and he thought it perfect.

Corderoy loved Mani because he couldn't figure her out, and he had a deep need to solve things. She was a Rubik's Cube with one too many sides. No matter how he manipulated her, twisting her colors this way and that, she would always present another face, not quite aligned.

The party was a success by all the standards a party is usually measured by. The cops arrived once and only once. Traces of puke wound up alongside the piss on the floor of the bathroom. By four a.m., the music was off and only a few people were left among the wreckage of empty beer bottles, red plastic cups, and stomped-on papier-mâché moon craters. Corderoy found Montauk in the kitchen, spread out on a folding table like an etherized patient. He nudged him awake. "You okay?"

"I'm fine," Montauk said. "Just got tired." He sat up.

"You have a bed upstairs."

"Like you said, upstairs."

"So, Mani's passed out in the band room," Corderoy said. Montauk's housemate Ian was in a bluegrass band, and they practiced in the basement, where Corderoy and Mani had just had sex. Afterward, Corderoy had drunkenly tossed the condom across the room, and he was hoping it hadn't landed on any of Ian's musical equipment.

"What's your deal, man? You two have been acting weird the entire night." Montauk stood and picked up a bowl of Cheetos.

"She's homeless. Where's she going to go?"

"Shit. That's right." Montauk looked out the back window while he methodically chewed and swallowed a stale Cheeto. "Family?"

"They're in Massachusetts. They don't even know where she is."

"You care about her?"

"Of course. She's great."

"But you're not ready for her to move in with you."

"Into my parents' house."

Montauk walked over to the sink and filled an old keg cup from the faucet. He gulped it down, water dribbling off his chin. When he finished, he said, "Screw it. Just leave. She'll figure it out in the morning. And she'll throw herself into something new. She'll find some other dude to—"

"That's great. Thanks."

"I don't know, man, then fucking marry her."

"What?"

"I'm too drunk to be having this conversation. You've only known her two months."

There was a creaking sound from the steps to the basement, and they both turned and listened for a tense moment.

"Look, you can love her and still leave," Montauk said, a little quieter. "They're not mutually exclusive. If there's anything *real* there, it will still be there. If you change your mind."

"Yeah?" Corderoy said. At this late hour, and running on fear, he couldn't see any holes in the idea. It was a test: could their connection transcend his sudden departure?

"Yeah. Go. Just go. I'll come up with something to tell her in the morning."

"It is the morning. Whatever. Thanks." Corderoy went out the front door, stumbled down the steps, and got in his car.

———

That moment, in the early morning of July 3rd, 2004, was the beginning of a fantastic and formidable knot in the lives of Halifax Corderoy and Mickey Montauk. The first such knot was formed the summer before, when they met at random in Rome. Montauk was leaning against a tree in the Piazza San Giovanni, where Beck was about to perform at an outdoor music festival, when Corderoy approached, asking if he could bum a cigarette. Montauk slipped him a Fortuna Blue, and they began talking as crowds congealed near the stage at the other end of the square. By an absurd and, they would later say, fateful coincidence, they were both from Seattle, and they had both just graduated from the University of Washington. Montauk had done ROTC and had switched majors three times, finally settling on Comparative History of Ideas. Corderoy had confined himself to the English department. They had several mutual friends. A light rain began to fall, and the Italians retreated from the stage and started huddling beneath the trees at the edges of the piazza, ripping canvas banners off fences to use as cover. But Corderoy and Montauk were Seattleites: umbrellas were for pussies. They walked casually up to the very front of the stage to wait for the show to begin. As it turned out, Italian rain was not Seattle rain. The sprinkling became a deluge, and Corderoy and Montauk were soaked through in under a minute, soggy cigarettes still in their mouths, each laughing at the other.

From then on, they traveled together. They got high in a cathedral; they wandered into a strange abandoned castle graffitied and occupied by anti-fascista punks; they flew in a hot-air balloon; they threw bottles at the Carabinieri; they slept on a rooftop in Capri and under a bridge in Florence; they drank cheap Chianti and poured a bottle of Barolo on Keats's grave; they each fell half in love with the same Italian girl. In the span of a month, they had connected so deeply and so thoroughly, there was no doubt for either of them that they would be lifelong friends. It was a rarity, and they didn't question it, though Montauk's mother did. In e-mails home, he'd been talking about his new pal so much that she asked if he and Corderoy had a gay relationship. Nothing wrong if you do, she stressed. The two had a good laugh over that one.

But no sooner had they returned to their post-college lives in Seattle than Montauk received orders from the National Guard to report to the four-month Infantry Officer Basic Course at Fort Benning, Georgia, where he would get the tactical training given to all new infantry officers.

Corderoy moved back in with his parents. Having quit his job as a part-time manager at GameStop, he found employment teaching SAT prep. Each night he came home, shut himself away in his parents' basement, uncorked a liter-and-a-half bottle of cheap Chianti, and played *EverQuest* for hours. He had little desire to join his friends at the bar; he figured if he'd be drinking there, why not drink here, relaxed in his chair, slaying wyverns and collecting experience points.

When Montauk returned after four months at Fort Benning, he no longer felt comfortable in his hammock of post-graduate malaise. He was now a platoon leader, and rumors of an Iraq deployment wended through his Guard unit. Civilian life suddenly felt like a much too short vacation, and Montauk intended to make the most of it. So it was that after dragging Corderoy out of his parents' basement, Montauk hatched the idea to form an art collective. The first Friday that February, the Encyclopaedists were born.

Corderoy managed, through his highly developed powers of willful ignorance, to think of Montauk deploying as an unlikely possibility. It didn't help that Montauk had applied to grad schools along with Corderoy. They were both accepted: Corderoy at Boston University and Montauk at Harvard—a point of minor resentment for Corderoy. The plan was to room together in Boston, starting at the beginning of August. By the fourth Encyclopaedists event in May, when Corderoy first met Mani, the idea of Boston had grown in his mind to the extent

that he sometimes thought he was living there already and merely visiting Seattle. But after tonight, it was painfully clear to him that he was
not in Boston, that he was stuck in Seattle for another month, that he
was alone, and that he had done something he could not undo.

———

It was five-thirty a.m. when Mani woke up alone and wandered into the
living room, her unwound turban draped around her shoulders. She'd
lost her fake beard sometime during the night, but she was still toting
the plastic AK-47. Two guys dressed as Roswell aliens were leaning
over the coffee table, snorting lines. They were Montauk's housemates,
but he had so many that she could never remember their names.

"Have you seen Hal?" she asked.

"Who's Hal?"

"Mickey's friend. Looks like President Bush."

"Sorry."

"Where's Mickey?"

"I think he went to sleep. Check his room?"

Mani walked toward the stairs, but a wave of nausea hit her and she
stumbled into the bathroom. The vomit burned her throat, and as she
leaned over the toilet bowl, spitting her mouth clean, she wondered if
it was just the alcohol. She'd missed her period last month and hadn't
told Hal; it was probably nothing. Before Steph had gone psycho and
kicked her out, she'd given Mani a bottle of Prozac, and Mani had been
taking it for almost four weeks. She didn't feel any happier. But maybe
she was late because of the Prozac. And if it wasn't the Prozac, well,
how could she even talk to Hal about that? Any of it. Mani stood and
rinsed her face in the sink.

It was just after dawn, and gray light filled Montauk's room. Someone
was talking to him. He sat up in bed. Mani was standing in his doorway. Her eye shadow had smudged across her face. Her black hair was
tangled and oily. "What?" Montauk said.

"Hal. Where's Hal?"

"He left," Montauk said.

"Where'd he go?"

Montauk shrugged.

"When's he coming back?" A note of uncertainty had entered her voice.

"He . . . didn't say."

"Mickey. Why would he leave without telling me? What's going on?"

"He was getting a little freaked out. That it was moving too fast or something."

"So he just left? He's just gone?" Her voice was rising.

"Yeah." Montauk looked out the window.

"Is that all you can say?"

"It's not really my business."

"You." Mani threw her hands up, pointing the toy gun skyward. Montauk pictured those Hezbollah tapes of some bearded guy in camo firing an AK, down with Israel, *Allahu Akhbar*. Mani lowered her hands and sighed.

"Sorry," Montauk said.

"Fuck you," she said, and she left the room, slamming his bedroom door. He heard her running down the stairs, then the front door opening and closing. He pictured her unwound turban trailing behind her in the dim light as he closed his blinds and lay back on his bed. Was she crying? She didn't seem the type.

2

Montauk found the Roswell aliens, his housemates Nick and Ian, still up and playing through the final level of *Halo*.

He picked up a plastic bag from the floor. It had been ripped at the seams and was moist. "Did you kill that entire eightball?" He looked out the large bay window toward the street, where a leaf-strewn puddle was rippling in the light rain. It was just after noon.

"Sorry, dude. Already licked the bag. You should've come down sooner."

Montauk went to the kitchen, poured himself a cup of coffee—soy milk, sugar—then went outside and sat in the wicker chair that hung from the portico. Sunlight filtered through the clouds. It felt good to be outside in pajama pants and a T-shirt with a cup of coffee. The wet soil was steaming and smelled of sweetness and fresh decay. To the left of the door, he spotted the toy AK-47. It had been smashed. Next to it was a broken cellular phone. He brought them inside.

"Hey, Ian." He held them forward in confusion.

"Hold on." Ian was fixated on the TV screen. A plasma grenade landed near him and exploded with a flash of purple light. As the level reloaded, he swiveled his bloodshot gaze toward Montauk. "That's that girl's shit. The one who got hit by the car."

"What?"

"You didn't hear it? Ambulance and everything. They took her to the hospital, man. She looked fucked up."

"Jesus." Montauk sat down and drank his coffee slowly, conscious of its heat warming his tongue, his throat, pooling in his stomach. He felt an insistent dread; but rather than face it, he scanned the bookshelf across the room. His gaze came to rest on a tattered copy of *The Odyssey*. He could have been thinking about Mani. Or about his aging parents and their imminent retirement, the increasing healthcare costs they would need help to meet. But why think about that when he could be thinking about Odysseus, how careless he was to allow his men to slaughter the oxen of the Sun God. How he was doomed never to return home, his ship destroyed, his men drowned. And really, was it all that bad an offense? It was absurdly easy to offend a god back then. The irony was that in choosing to avoid the difficult thought chains, Montauk inevitably fell into their metaphorical counterparts, which left him depressed and not knowing why. He finished his coffee and dialed Corderoy.

Corderoy parked his dad's Suburban in front of the Encyclopad. It was drizzling again. Montauk came down and got in, holding the AK and Mani's cell phone. Corderoy glanced at the toy gun. "Hey," he said.

"Hey."

They sat in silence. Corderoy kept his hands on the wheel, even though they were still parked. "So?"

Montauk ran his fingers through his hair. "I thought you might want to check up on her. She's at Swedish."

Corderoy rubbed his eyes with his palms. "Should I call her?"

Montauk waved the broken phone in the air and offered it to Corderoy.

"Put it in the glove box or something." Corderoy looked away. "How do you even know she's at Swedish?"

"It's the closest hospital."

"Should I go?"

"I don't know. Don't see her if you don't want to."

"Did you talk to her after I left?"

"Yeah, she came up to my room."

"What'd you say?"

"I said you were gone. She got upset and ran downstairs. She might
have been crying."

"She was crying?"

"What did you think would happen? Wasn't that the point? So you
wouldn't have to see her cry?"

Corderoy put the car in gear.

Mani was in traction.

Montauk set the AK and cell phone on the plastic chair next to the
gurney, then assessed the situation. Her legs were elevated by cables
attached to steel rungs that encased the bed frame. Her right arm was in a
splint. She was dressed in a hospital gown that looked like it was made out
of floral-print paper towels. There was a small bandage on the right side of
her head. She was asleep or drugged unconscious. In all likelihood, it was
not a critical situation. She seemed to have made it through surgery, and
the possibility of head trauma seemed low. "It's not so bad," Montauk said.

Corderoy stood in silent panic with one arm crossed over his chest
and the other holding his chin, feeling as if he were heading for a cliff
in a car with no brakes and no one in the driver's seat.

A nurse came into the room. "Hi there. Are you friends or family?"

Corderoy looked up. "Ah . . . no."

The nurse balked. "No?"

"No, we're actually friends of a friend," Montauk said. "We were
supposed to meet her here."

"Why don't you have a seat in the waiting room."

"Can you tell us what happened?" Montauk asked.

"She has an impacted femoral fracture. They put three pins in her hip."

"When will she wake up?"

"Hard to say. She's been out of surgery for a few hours, but she
needs her rest."

They thanked the nurse and started down the hallway, but before
they reached the waiting room, Corderoy hailed the elevator.

"I guess we're not waiting, then?" Montauk said.

Corderoy didn't answer. The doors opened, they entered, and Corderoy hit the button for Parking.

"It was late, all right? She ran across the street without looking," Montauk said. "It's not your fault."

"Who said it was?"

They fell silent. Montauk leaned against the back of the elevator, looked down at his feet. Corderoy stared at his blurry reflection in the brushed-metal doors. "How do you know?"

"How do I know what?"

"She could have been trying to get hit. She's super unstable."

"She wasn't trying to get hit, she just didn't see the car."

"How do you know?"

"No one tries to get hit by a car. That's stupid. Plus, she wasn't even that upset."

"You said she was crying."

"I said she *might* have been crying."

The elevator stopped one floor before Parking, and an old man stepped in.

"It's not your fault, all right?" Montauk said again, quietly.

Corderoy glared at him.

"Let's go to Linda's and get some breakfast."

"I hate Linda's," Corderoy said, not bothering to lower his voice. The old man raised an eyebrow.

"You hate everything," Montauk said.

They sat at a table in the back, near the jukebox. A stuffed buffalo head hung above them on the wall. Linda's was even more crowded than usual. A waitress with spiderwebs tattooed on her elbows dropped off their Bloody Marys. Corderoy tipped his back and finished half of it in one gulp. He signaled the waitress.

"I've been called up," Montauk said.

"Who called you?" Corderoy dropped his hand. "Oh."

"I found out yesterday morning."

"What about grad school?"

"I'll defer, I guess. I have to report to Fort Lewis at the end of August for train-up. I ship out in late September."

Corderoy stared into his glass. Montauk had been in the National

Guard since they'd met, but the full reality of that had never sunk in. He'd taken Montauk's affiliation with the armed forces as nothing more than a social trump to all the graphic designers and band members and bartenders who populated the world of post-college twentysomethings on Capitol Hill. But there was a war. No, two. Montauk would ship out to Iraq or Afghanistan eventually. "I'm sorry, man," Corderoy said.

"I don't need you to be sorry. It's important work. Someone's gotta do it."

"Does someone have to do it?" Corderoy polished off his drink, felt the Tabasco burn up his sinuses.

"Somebody's thirsty," the waitress said, approaching from behind Corderoy.

His cheeks reddened. "Just get us a couple shots of whiskey."

They sat in silence until she returned with the shots and their omelets. Montauk leaned toward her. "Don't mind him, he's still drunk from last night." She rolled her eyes and left.

"I think I am," Corderoy said. "I could hardly stay in my lane on the way up here."

"You did kill that bottle of tequila." Montauk tried to smile.

"Fuck, fuck."

"Dude."

"I know. It's not my fault. But it sure fucking feels like my fault." Corderoy poked his omelet with his fork. "Did you vote for Bush?"

"No," Montauk said through a mouthful of egg.

Corderoy rubbed the bridge of his nose. "You know they still haven't found any WMDs."

"So."

"*So?* So the whole justification was fake!"

Montauk took another bite and wiped his mouth with his napkin. "I actually read the Blix report.* Whether or not we actually find a nuke factory, there are reasonable grounds to think Saddam already built one. He's done his best to make everyone *believe* he—"

"Wait, that's why you're doing this, because of the fucking Blix report?"

"No, genius, I'm deploying because I got orders from the SecDef,

---

* Montauk, in fact, had read just under half of the Blix report.

along with everyone else in my unit. I'm just saying I'm okay with it. It's something real. I mean, everything we do . . . the Encyclopaedists and all that . . . it's bullshit."

"It was your idea."

"Yeah, I know. It was fun."

"It was."

"I'm tired of fun, of racking up hipster cool points with the next clever thing."

Corderoy downed his shot. Montauk waited until Corderoy finished, then matched him. "You're saying my life is bullshit," Corderoy said.

"I'm saying I can't do it anymore." This was true in a practical sense. Montauk was shipping out and would not be able to host absurd parties from the Middle East. But that would only be a limitation on his freedom if he saw deployment as a daunting imposition of someone else's will. What if he saw it instead as the perfect opportunity to reinvent himself, a classic rite of passage that most of his coddled generation was denied?

"You weren't saying that yesterday," Corderoy said.

"I'm saying it now."

"Let's get out of here."

"You barely touched your omelet."

Corderoy called for the check. It was two o'clock when they stumbled out into the hot afternoon. The streets were still damp, and a light breeze had picked up. They both looked dazedly around at the passing cars and toward the water. Downtown sparkled like a chandelier.

"What do you got going today?" Corderoy asked.

"I don't know, you?"

"We could keep drinking."

"We could write letters to our grandmothers," Montauk said.

Corderoy pulled out a pack of cigarettes and gave one to Montauk. It took a moment to light them up in the wind. They exhaled lungfuls of smoke. "I don't even want this," Corderoy said before taking another drag.

———

Mani woke in her hospital bed and looked down at her suspended legs. Though her senses were dulled, she could feel the pain in her hip asserting itself; soon it would be the only thing she was conscious of. There was a buzzer for the nurse around somewhere, wasn't there? As she pressed it, she saw the toy rifle and her cell phone sitting on the plastic chair. Had Hal come by?

Mani clenched her jaw, which was about the only part of her she could clench without pain. Hal had left her passed out at a party. The coward. And he'd come here and left again. Twice left in the same day. Who would do that? But how long had she been out? Maybe he'd waited for hours, sitting in that chair inventing silly backstories in his head for all the hospital staff. He wasn't curious about other people's lives so much as he enjoyed letting his imagination run ahead of him, and she loved him for it. She pictured the nurse telling her that a lanky boy with apricot-blond hair had been here all morning, that he'd just left, but she couldn't imagine herself believing it. Mani winced as the pain blitzed from her hip up through her torso. She hit the buzzer again, tears running down her cheek. Of course he'd left. Who wouldn't?*

The nurse arrived and said, "Ah, Ms. Saheli, you're awake." He was stout like Mickey, but softer, not as muscled. She didn't like him.

"It hurts," she said.

"You're on a morphine drip," the nurse said. "When this light is green, you can press the button to administer another dose." He indicated a small black control pad connected to the IV line. "But it only works once every ten minutes. Here." He pushed the button for Mani. "That should feel better."

A warmth traveled up Mani's arm and flooded her chest, diffused down into her hips. The pain became merely the suggestion of pain.

"I have a few questions for you," the nurse said.

Mani knew where this was going. She'd ignored the question when they rushed her through triage.

"We need to see about your insurance. If you don't have any, we'll call a social worker in to help you figure things out."

"I don't have a card," she said, which was true enough.

---

* A nicer person? That thought wasn't currently available to her in the extremity of her pain, which throbbed to an insistent beat of "stupid, I'm so stupid."

"Are you on your parents' plan? If you give us their contact info, we can get the paperwork started."

She was on her parents' plan, but her mother would see this accident as a punishment for all the ways Mani had screwed up. Even those she didn't know about. Like last night. Mani could have said, *I'll find a place, don't worry about it, I know some people.* She hadn't. And her not doing so had given Hal the opportunity to be an asshole and a coward. And now he was gone. How could she possibly explain that to her mother? "I'm not on their plan," she said.

The nurse sighed. "I'll see about that social worker."

When he left, Mani submerged herself further into the morphine, as if it were a warm bath that was rapidly cooling. The control pad connected to her IV lay on the bed next to her. She picked it up. The light was still red. It had to be nearly ten minutes. She counted out a minute. Another. A third. She lost count as the morphine faded and the pain began to overwhelm her, somehow searing and glacial at once.

Then she remembered. She'd missed her period. She should tell them. The light turned green. She could press the button now. But she didn't. She closed her eyes and everything was white. She could press the button. Could she? Her hip pierced her head like it wasn't a part of her but a sharp instrument wielded against her. Maybe it was okay; maybe there was a different kind of pain medication that was safe. That wouldn't endanger the— She couldn't even think the word. She hit the call button and waited. And waited.

What seemed like hours later, a middle-aged man walked in and introduced himself as Dr. Santos. The fluorescent lights behind his head flared and Mani looked away, fixing her eyes on her tractioned legs.

"Ms. Saheli," the doctor said, leaning down. "What can I do for you?"

"I think I might—I missed my period," Mani said. "What if I shouldn't be taking morphine?"

"Don't worry. As a precaution before surgery, we do routine pregnancy tests."

"I'm not . . ."

"You tested negative."

Mani looked at him blankly.

"Nothing to worry about," he said.

She burst into a fit of sobbing.

The doctor picked up the control pad and hit the button, administering another dose of morphine into her IV. The pain in her body ebbed. The doctor said something, then something else. Mani felt devastated and she didn't know why.

———

Corderoy and Montauk had passed out in the Encyclopad living room while watching *Seinfeld* reruns. It was five o'clock when Montauk woke up. Corderoy was sitting at the computer at the far end of the room, next to the bookshelves, which were alternately filled with much-thumbed editions of Livy, Virgil, and Herodotus, which Montauk had kept from school, and books chosen for purely ironic reasons by his housemates, such as the *British Guide to Etiquette, Scandalous Saints,* and *Nitrogen Economy in Tropical Soils.*

"Come here," Corderoy said. "Read this."

Montauk got up and wiped a bit of drool from his lip. Corderoy was reading a Wikipedia article, "The 2003 invasion of Iraq." He had highlighted a few sentences under the heading "Events leading to the invasion." They read:

> On the day of the September 11, 2001, Terrorist Attack, Defense Secretary Donald H. Rumsfeld is reported to have written in his notes, "best info fast. Judge whether good enough hit S.H. [Saddam Hussein] at same time. Not only UBL [Osama bin Laden]." Shortly thereafter, the George W. Bush administration announced a War on Terrorism, accompanied by the doctrine of preemptive military action dubbed the Bush doctrine.

"This is so poorly written," Montauk said. "Like everything on Wikipedia. Give me that." He took the mouse. "Ugh. It's all sticky."

"Someone spilled beer on it last night."

Montauk skimmed the rest of the article. "It mentions all these war crimes," he said, "but nothing's attributed. Feels like it was written by pissed-off liberal college students who know fuck-all about what's really going on."

"C'mon," Corderoy said.

Montauk sighed and continued scrolling down the page. "There, look at how it always uses the word *regime* instead of *government*. This is why you can't trust Wikipedia." He walked into the kitchen and opened the fridge. "You want a beer?"

Corderoy leaned back, and his metal folding chair creaked. He looked down at it. He'd been sitting in this same chair last night, with Mani on his lap.

"Hey," Montauk yelled. "You want a beer or not?"

"Yeah," Corderoy said. He stood up, swapped the folding chair for a wooden one nearby, and sat back down at the computer. "But the bias, it's got to be only with contentious subjects, like the invasion of Iraq. Right? There's no way the article for 'banana' is biased."

"Look it up."

Corderoy pulled up the entry as Montauk returned with beers. "Seems pretty neutral," Corderoy said.

"I bet we can fix that."

"Eh?"

"Click edit."

"Ahh." Corderoy did so and began editing the first sentence, smiling and nodding to himself as he typed. He clicked Save, reloaded the page, then read the new first sentence aloud: " 'Banana is the common name for herbaceous plants of the genus Musa and for the fucking delicious but regrettably phallus-shaped fruit they produce.' "

Beer vaulted up through Montauk's nose as he burst out laughing. "Shit, man," he said. "Anybody can do anything on this. That's why Wikipedia's bullshit."

"No, that's why it's awesome. We could have a page. About us."

"Yeah?" Montauk took a swig of his PBR.

"Why not? We can write it. Add whatever subsections we want, stuff like . . . 'Mickey's shitty deployment.' "

"Or 'Hal's video game addiction and its effect on his ignorance of geopolitical events.' "

Corderoy laughed. "But it doesn't have to be so obviously about us.

Like we could make a section titled: 'The taste of the mouth the morning after a hangover' . . ." He finished the rest of that sentence in his head: "while standing in the hospital room of a person whom you don't intend to ever see again but might love anyway because you are a fuckup."

"Hmm." Montauk wrinkled his brow. "But anyone could edit our article and make it say stupid shit."

"It's not like we're bananas," Corderoy said.

"What?"

"We're not as well known. As bananas. Who would even know our article existed, and if they did, why would they edit it?"

"But aren't there rules about being notable or something?"

"We meet the notability standards. We've been written up in a legit publication." Corderoy began creating a new Wikipedia article. He titled it "The Encyclopaedists," then sourced the new article with an external link to *The Stranger*'s profile on the "The Encyclopaedists of Capitol Hill." He began typing the overview:

Scholars generally agree that the Encyclopaedia is Truth, insofar as Truth exists, which it doesn't. Nevertheless, existence, which teeters on the precipice of subjective experience, is anchored by encyclopaedic reference. The Encyclopaedia, therefore, justifies itself with a recursive entry. And it should not be surprising that this article's subject is responsible for its origination. Fuckballs. Post-colonial cadaver sex. See, we can write anything, since no one else cares to define us for us.

"Let me do it," Montauk said. He leaned over and pushed Corderoy's hands out of the way. Before he knew what he was typing, Mani's name appeared.

The exact origins of this article are a matter of some debate, the most popular (and most contentious) theory aligning its inception with Mani's hospitalization on the early morning of July 3rd, 2004—one year, three months, fourteen days, ten hours, and twenty-six minutes after the beginning of the Iraq War,

Corderoy took the keyboard back.

in which Mickey Montauk would learn to shut the fuck up . . .

He thought a moment, then added:

while Halifax Corderoy deconstructed in the bricked and hobbling streets of
Cambridge, Massachusetts.

They read through it again in silence.
"Huh," Montauk said. "I feel weird."
"Like we didn't really exist until just now?"
They put on music—Ice Cube, Wu-Tang—and drank another two
beers. On some level, they were aware that through booze and conversation, they were holding down the lid of a black trunk, about the
size of a woman, which could not be locked, and which they would
eventually have to leave unguarded.

3

Over the next two months, Corderoy took extra tutoring shifts and drank a bottle of wine each night. He shrank and shrank until he barely existed—and Mani disappeared with him. When he wasn't making lesson plans or grading essays, he was scouring Craigslist for a room to sublet in Boston. This kept him from imagining Mani's hypothetical futures. She healed miraculously, say, and fell in love with her doctor—they moved to Aruba, where he became the personal physician of Queen Beatrix Wilhelmina Armgard van Oranje-Nassau, and Mani taught diving lessons. Alternatively, the ceiling in her hospital room collapsed while she was still rigged up in traction, fracturing her spine and paralyzing her. In this future, she was later found underneath an overpass in her wheelchair, OD'ed on heroin. Each day he thought about visiting her in the hospital. Each day he rejected the idea. Tomorrow's hangover was punishment for failing to stamp that thought into nothingness.

Montauk was due for train-up at Fort Lewis on August 30th. He continued working at the record shop, and once or twice in the intervening weeks, he thought he saw Mani on the street, but he told himself he was seeing things. He had not been close with her, but the callousness with which he'd kicked her out that early morning had bitten him like a brown recluse—an ulcer had formed in his chest, and it was slowly turning black and gangrenous.

He soothed it with constant recreation. He threw a barbecue in Gas

Works Park, but Corderoy had to work. He went kayaking on Lake Union, but Corderoy had to renew his driver's license. He played beer pong, he saw the Mountain Goats at the Crocodile Café, he hiked the ice fields of Mount Rainier, he went paintballing with all eight of his housemates, he closed out the Cha Cha Lounge five nights a week, but Corderoy was in the middle of a book, he was busy reinstalling Windows on his laptop, he had to work.

The few times they'd spoken on the phone, the absurdist riffing that had cemented their friendship was noticeably willed. A gulf had grown between them, about the length of a hospital gurney: not wide, but not close enough for easy conversation. When Montauk offered to buy Corderoy a beer the night before his flight to Boston, he declined on account of having to pack. Montauk said he'd see him off at the airport, despite Corderoy's protestations.

Montauk found him in line for the security check and flicked the back of his ear. Corderoy jumped, turned, grimaced, smiled, then settled into an uncomfortable sigh. "I told you not to come," he said. They were separated by a black nylon belt held taut between stanchions.

"Shut up."

"Okay."

"You have a place in Boston yet?"

"I think so."

"Stay away from the Fens, I heard that's where the hookers hang out."

"Yeah? Is that where your mom's from?"

Montauk smiled in relief. "No, she just works there."

"You know this is backward, right?"

"Huh?"

"I'm just going to *school*. You're going to *war*. I should be seeing you off."

"That's what a sweetheart is for. You're not my sweetheart, dickface."

The line moved forward and Corderoy slid his bag with his foot. "I'll write you—once you get there."

"No you won't," Montauk said.

Corderoy exhaled and gazed over at the stainless-steel salmon sculptures that lined Sea-Tac's main terminal. "I saw you updated our Wiki entry. Fixed a few of your typos."

Montauk smiled. "I can neither confirm nor deny any updates to the Encyclopaedists article."

Neither of them spoke for a moment. The line moved forward. Corderoy had almost reached the podium. "Hey," he said. "I've been thinking about everything with Mani—"

"Then stop." Montauk leaned over the nylon belt, gave Corderoy a bro hug, pushed him back, and said, "Don't screw up in Boston."

"You know I will."

"I know, but still."

"Oh, hey, take these." Corderoy pulled a half-empty pack of Camels from his pocket. "I'm trying to quit, start fresh in Boston. You might as well have them."

"Thanks."

"Thanks, too. For coming."

"Don't get all teary on me."

Corderoy entered the security check, smiling. Montauk walked back into the humid evening surrounding Sea-Tac Airport and took out a cigarette. He was about to light it, but instead, he threw the pack and his lighter into a trash can and headed to the bus stop. Corderoy wasn't going to write him; that would be far too serious. But maybe they'd stay in touch if they kept dicking with the Wikipedia entry.

On the bus ride home, a sense of equanimity penetrated his consciousness, like rainwater seeping into a basement. Some bad shit had gone down, and they'd survived. He felt like he'd reached the end of a movie, when the killer is dead, and the hero is blood-soaked, and the world is right again, at least for now. But when he walked up his steps that evening, while Corderoy was high above the continent, he was greeted by a woman balancing precariously on crutches.

"Hi," Mani said. "Been a while."

article | discussion | edit this page | history

WIKIPEDIA
The Free Encyclopedia

navigation

- Main Page
- Community portal
- Current events
- Recent changes
- Random page
- Help
- Donations

search

[   ]
[Go] [Search]

toolbox

- What links here
- Related changes
- Special pages

The Encyclopaedists [edit]

Scholars generally agree that the Encyclopaedia is Truth, insofar as Truth exists, which it doesn't. Nevertheless, existence, which teeters on the precipice of subjective experience, is anchored by encyclopaedic reference. The Encyclopaedia, therefore, justifies itself with a recursive entry. And it should not be surprising that this article's subject is responsible for its origination. Fuckballs. Post-colonial cadaver sex. See, we can write anything, since no one else cares to define us for us.

The exact origins of this article are a matter of some debate, the most popular (and most contentious) theory aligning its inception with Mani's hospitalization on the early morning of July 3rd, 2004—one year, three months, fourteen days, ten hours, and twenty-six minutes after the beginning of the Iraq War, in which Mickey Montauk would learn to shut the fuck up . . . while Halifax Corderoy deconstructed in the bricked and hobbling streets of Cambridge, Massachusetts.

Contents [hide]
1 Precursors of the Encyclopaedists
2 Motivations of the Encyclopaedists

Precursors of the Encyclopaedists [edit]

The Encyclopaedists couldn't exist without Pliny the Fucking Elder, who set out, by himself, to record no less than the entirety of ancient knowledge:

> It is, indeed, no easy task to give novelty to what is old, and authority to what is new; brightness to what is become tarnished, and light to what is obscure; to render what is slighted acceptable, and what is doubtful worthy of our confidence; to give to all a natural manner, and to each its peculiar nature.
> —Translation by John Bostock, 1855

Pliny wrote the *Naturalis Historiae* in less than ten years before dying in the eruption of Vesuvius in 79 A.D., which is a pretty badass way to die.

Centuries of encyclopaedists emulated his model, until Denis Diderot, chief editor of the French *Encyclopédie*, ushered in the multi-contributor format in the 1750s. Motherfucker knew you'd never cram all knowledge into one large work, but he thought an index of connections and interrelations might just fit. Problem was, Diderot's *Encyclopédie* was also intended to make men "more virtuous and happy," meaning it was French Enlightenment propaganda bullshit, with dozens of articles talking up Reason and trashing on monarchy.

The *Encyclopaedia Britannica* removed this component, striving for comprehensiveness and objectivity. And for nearly 250 years *Britannica* was the gold standard of racism, sexism, factual inaccuracies, and bourgeois-bias. The eleventh edition takes the cake, where one can't read a page without stumbling on phrases like "Mentally, the negro is inferior to the white."

Then came *Wikipedia*. You know all about *Wikipedia*, so there's no point in describing its origins. Suffice it to say *Wikipedia* soon outstripped *Britannica* in comprehensiveness and in its attempt at objectivity (establishing ground rules for neutral point of view, verifiability, and no original research), and yet its credibility was (and is) consistently attacked.

This brings us to the Encyclopaedists, Corderoy and Montauk, who, by authoring their own article, have inaugurated a new era of referential comprehensiveness and impeachable credibility, though some would say this sets a dangerous precedent.

Motivations of the Encyclopaedists [edit]

Haven't you ever had thoughts that you thought nobody else ever thought before? And when you die, those thoughts will be lost. Even, perhaps, when you stop thinking those thoughts, they are lost already. You see the edifices of knowledge crumbling about you, you trudge through the pluralistic and subjective rubble of civilization—how are you two idiots going to survive? You are tempted to be plural, to capitulate to the world's diffusion, but the answer is to embrace all that is particular to you, without tripping and falling into your own mind.

External links [edit]

1. ^ "The Encyclopaedists of Capitol Hill."
www.thestranger.com/apr04/encyclopaedists.htm

2. ^ "C. PLINII NATVRALIS HISTORIAE PRAEFATIO."
www.thelatinlibrary.com/pliny.nhpr.html

This page was last modified 11:18, 26 August 2004.
All text is available under the terms of the GNU Free Documentation License (see Copyrights for details).
About Wikipedia   Disclaimers

UNION

4

Something clattered in the bathroom as Montauk reached the second-floor landing holding a towel he'd brought up from the laundry room. Mani had gone in to take a shower after he'd awkwardly helped her ascend the stairs, her arm around his shoulder, their torsos pressed side to side.

"Everything all right?" he asked through the door.

"Fine." The door opened a crack and Mani leaned from behind it to take the towel. She was naked and Montauk could very nearly see her breasts. He leaned forward instinctively. She clutched the towel to her chest. "My crutch just slipped off the wall. Don't worry about it." She looked straight at him for a moment, as if to ask him a question, then said "Thanks" and shut the door.

Montauk walked down the hall to his room. It was a mess. There were piles of clothes on the floor, open dresser drawers, books on the bed, and old beer bottles on the windowsill. Mani's arrival yesterday evening had made him conscious of how slovenly he'd been living. That and the fact that tomorrow marked the beginning of train-up—a month to get his platoon ready for deployment. Ian had been gracious enough to loan Montauk his Camry for September, which would allow him to live off-base—an officer's privilege—and commute an hour south each morning, rather than having to live at Fort Lewis with the rest of the platoon. He would report at 0700 Monday through Friday. Or through Saturday. Or Sunday. His commanding officer said he'd try to give them weekends off, but no guarantees.

Montauk looked at himself in the full-length mirror that leaned against the wall. He was a little pudgy around the midsection. Just the thought of having this beer belly in a combat zone put him on edge. He'd have to be in better shape, if only to instill confidence in his leadership—many of the enlisted men in his platoon were older than he and suspicious of having such a young and untested lieutenant. He shared their suspicions. His father and grandfather had served. But they hadn't gone to college. When he'd joined the Guard, he'd done so thinking that it would set him apart, that it was a cool and overlooked option, almost retro, like owning a record player or typing his essays on an actual typewriter. He had no innate desire for authority, but during Officer Candidate School, it crystallized for him that he was preparing for a position of leadership, the responsibility of command. He had no idea what kind of leader he'd make, but he knew he'd have to be focused. It didn't help that Mani was here.

After the accident, it had taken her a month just to get out of a wheelchair and onto crutches, and when she had shown up at Montauk's, all she'd wanted was to use his address for a job application. She'd been staying at the Y. Montauk offered her his couch until she could get on her feet—literally—and find a place of her own. She'd agreed, on the condition that he say nothing to Corderoy. She wasn't seeking restitution; she simply had no other place to go.

Montauk thought about going for a run, but he was the only one home, and if Mani fell in the shower or something, she might need him. Instead, he tried on his recently issued Desert Camouflage Uniform. It was a blend of pastel green and light tan with reddish-brown splotches. He laced up his tan suede desert boots and donned his field cap. His rank, normally a single gold bar worn on the cap and collar, was dyed brown to fit in to the DCU color scheme.

Somehow, it lacked the grandeur, the historical seriousness, that he associated with the uniforms of his forebearers. Peter Montauk, Mickey's great-grandfather, had begun the Montauk family tradition of military service when he volunteered in 1917. After surviving the trenches in France, he'd worked most of his life as a tugboat hand, though like the Montauks before him, trappers and traders of native Montaukett ancestry, he was something of a jack-of-all-trades, having taught his son how to play the fiddle and repair an engine.

The family had moved to Philadelphia by the time Abe, at the age of eighteen, shipped off to France, just as his father had. Abe took a bullet through the femur in Brest and received a Purple Heart. Young Mickey never cared about the medal, but he was fascinated by the bullet. On visits, his grandpa would take it out of a cedar box, and Mickey would examine the deformed piece of lead as if it were a fine gemstone.

His father, Oren, had been a navy man who'd served in Vietnam. In 1969, at twenty years old, he was stationed aboard the USS *Harnett County*, then operating on the Vam Co Dong River. After his deployment, he moved to Portland, Oregon, to work as an engineer at a friend's industrial equipment company. He met Veronica a year later, and they moved to Seattle in '75.

Oren never failed to remind his son that he wouldn't be where he was today without his time in the service, whether he was teaching Boy Scout Mickey to tie navy knots or helping teenage Mickey fix up his first junker car.

Montauk felt real reverence for that history, but he didn't see it in his reflection, or in the splotchy DCU pattern, which was unofficially known as Coffee Stain Camouflage. The uniform felt like a costume.

"Hello, soldier," Mani said.

Montauk turned around. She was standing in the doorway wrapped in a towel, leaning on her crutches, her wet black hair running down the sides of her face like oil. "I thought you didn't start till tomorrow," she said.

"I don't."

"Trying to get into the spirit?"

"Do I look leaderly?"

Mani leaned against the doorframe. "Sure."

"Sure?"

"You want me to say I'd follow you into battle?"

"That's the idea."

"Your platoon will. They have to."

Montauk sat down on his bed.

"Well, I don't have to," she said. "But I'd follow you. If I believed in war and all."

"You sound just like—" Montauk caught himself before he said *Hal*. "You'd follow me, huh? On crutches, in a towel?" He smiled.

"Hey, I could be useful, distract the enemy."

Montauk laughed.

"My bag is still downstairs," Mani said. "Could you . . ."

"Yeah, I'll get it." Montauk loped past her in his combat boots, scooped up Mani's bag from the kitchen, and trudged back up to his room.

"Could I change in here?" she asked when he handed her the bag.

"Of course," Montauk said. And he stood outside his own door while Corderoy's ex-girlfriend, whom he'd kicked out two months ago, disrobed in his room. She was probably sitting on his bed right now, struggling to slide her panties on. A moment later, the door opened, and Mani emerged dressed in low-cut jeans and a ratty T-shirt, the towel wrapped around her hair. She smiled at him. Even on her crutches, she exuded confidence.

"Thanks," she said.

"For?"

"I know it's weird, me staying here, and you didn't have to."

"It's fine. It's totally cool."

"It's weird," she said. "Don't pretend it's not. And I still think you're an asshole."

"You want some lunch?" Montauk asked. "I'll help you downstairs."

———

Under the command of the president and the secretary of defense, the half a million active duty troops and seven hundred thousand reservists who composed the United States Army were divided into combatant commands led by generals, then into corps, divisions, and brigades, commanded by lieutenant generals, major generals, and colonels. Each brigade had two or more battalions of up to a thousand soldiers, which were divided into companies of a few hundred and platoons of several dozen, each of which was led by a lieutenant—a college-educated graduate of Officer Candidate School, ROTC, or the Military Academy at West Point. Within the 2nd Platoon of Bravo Company, nestled under the command of the 1st Battalion, 161st Infantry, and

81st Brigade, there were thirty-five enlisted soldiers and one officer. Mickey Montauk was that officer.

The highest-ranking enlisted soldier in Montauk's platoon was the platoon sergeant, Sergeant First Class Arnold Olaufsson, who was Montauk's right-hand man and disciplinarian; he led the platoon in Montauk's absence. Under Montauk and Olaufsson were the four squad leaders. Each of them led two fireteams of three or four soldiers each. The average age in the platoon was twenty-four.

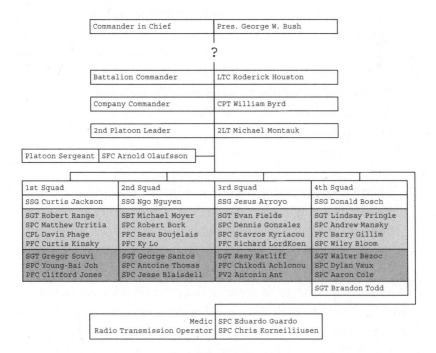

The first two days of train-up had been mostly paperwork and immunizations. Today they would begin actual training. The platoon was in formation out on a large dirt field, being led in PT by Sergeant Olaufsson. Montauk was working out by himself, twenty yards to the rear of the platoon, maintaining a little distance from the enlisted men. His platoon had been formed only six months ago, and at one weekend a month, many of his soldiers were still just faces or names on a roster to him. He finished a set of diamond push-ups and stood, breathing hard. He wiped his forehead with his shirt and watched the platoon finish their V-ups. He hadn't done any himself.

Montauk dropped down for a set of mountain climbers as Olaf called the platoon to attention and then dismissed them to shit/shower/shave, draw their rifles from the arms room, and report back by 0930 to bus over to the rifle range. The platoon ambled off, their gaits hobbled and awkward from too many squats and lunges. Montauk hoped they saw him still on the ground, hiking his legs back and forth. When he finished, he saw Olaf crossing the field toward him.

At six-two, Sergeant First Class Olaufsson towered over Montauk. With his shaved head and mustache, he looked like a Viking blacksmith from the dark ages. He was thirty-two, and he'd fought in the Gulf War as a marine grunt. Montauk and pretty much everyone else in the platoon regarded him as preternaturally authoritative and competent. He saluted Montauk.

"Morning, sir."

"Morning. How's the PT coming?"

"Little by little. Thomas lost a few pounds."

"Yeah, I saw him puking during the run."

"If we do that to him every day, he'll be combat-ready in a year, sir."

"Then we'll only have to work on his lisp."

2nd Platoon of Bravo Company was crammed into a repurposed school bus, wearing their DCUs and holding their M4s. There was a shortage of trucks, and this was the only way to get around Fort Lewis, which extended over eighty-six thousand acres and supported close to twenty thousand troops. The rifle range was just over four miles to the southeast. Montauk sat next to Olaf in the front seat, silent. He felt like he was chaperoning a field trip.

Behind Montauk sat Sergeant Evan Fields, the 3rd Squad alpha team leader, and one of his guys, a dark-haired, vaguely Greek-looking kid who was holding forth at length on why the original Tim Burton Batman movie was superior to all its sequels.

"Batman doesn't need to turn his neck," the Greek kid said. "He's encased in bulletproof armor."

Montauk had a few opinions on the design of the Batsuit (he was fond of the old Adam West version), and nearly chimed in, but it didn't seem officerly to talk about comic books with his troops.

"Did you see the trailer for the new one, with Christian Bale?" asked Fields. "That suit looks awesome."

"Naw. It's all black, there's no yellow bat symbol," said the Greek kid.

"Maybe he doesn't want criminals to see him a mile a-fucking-way," Fields said. "Why not paint a target on his chest?"

Fields was one of the few guys in the platoon Montauk had taken the time to learn a thing or two about. He had a business degree from UW Bothell, and before the call-up he was considering taking a job at Washington Mutual and marrying his girlfriend, now officially knocked up. He was generically handsome except for a unibrow, and he struck Montauk as a solid, all-around good dude, the kind of salt-of-the-earth guy he had stopped hanging out with after high school, when he'd gotten invested in the world of bands, art projects, and ironic one-upsmanship.

"Exactly," the Greek kid said. "Think about it. Your suit is bullet-proof, but your chin is exposed. That bat symbol is meant to draw fire."

"What do you think, LT?" Fields asked.

Montauk looked over his shoulder—3rd Squad had been bullshitting all day, but somehow every conversation had come back to body armor. How was he supposed to reassure them? "We should all wear bat symbols on our chest plates," Montauk said, "so Hajji doesn't shoot us in the face. I'll tell the general."

The Greek kid chuckled.

"Iraqis can't shoot," said Olaf. "Not even the Republican Guard."

That was how. Montauk should have been taking notes.

The bus came to a stop, and the platoon was herded into rows of foxholes overlooking the firing range. Every man in the platoon had to qualify with the M4, including Montauk.

He hoped he would shoot well. Not that it would matter in the field; they say an LT's most deadly weapon is his radio. But if he didn't, the whole platoon would see. He hopped into a foxhole toward the middle. When they were settled in, the range NCO in charge called out: "Lock and load one thirty-round magazine! Switch the selector to semi and watch your lanes!"

Montauk lay prone in the dirt, his rifle propped on a sandbag, his cheek pressed to the stock, and his finger hooked on the trigger. His ears were muffled by orange foam plugs. He had always excelled at standardized tests, and this was a test like any other. It was important to understand the terms. The mechanism was his M4 Carbine. There were a variety of inevitable outcomes and outcomes he could control.

These were the outcomes that were inevitable: When he squeezed the trigger, the firing pin would dimple the back of the cartridge, causing it to explode; the pressure of the explosion would force the round down the barrel, drive the bolt back, eject the brass shell casing out the side of the rifle, compress the recoil spring buffer, and chamber a new cartridge from the magazine. The round itself was no bigger than the pink cap eraser on a No. 2 pencil, but the barrel of his M4 was fourteen and a half inches long, and for every inch of that barrel, the round increased in velocity and spin, exiting the muzzle at twenty-nine hundred feet per second, at which point it traveled according to the laws of projectile motion, subject to gravity, air resistance, and wind.

If he wanted to shoot Expert, he'd have to focus on what he could control. He positioned his body to support the rifle with his skeleton— try to muscle the rifle and it'll shake. His breathing was slow and regular, like a lazy sine wave. When the target popped up, he would align his sights and wait until the end of his exhalation. He would be aware of his pulse, wait for a lull between heartbeats. He would not pull the trigger, he would squeeze it, so as not to jerk the round off course. The discharge should be a surprise. Like waking up, his drill sergeants had told him, covered in spooge.

He started with both eyes open to observe his whole lane. A 150-meter target popped up and he shifted the rifle, lined up the sights on the torso-shaped black silhouette, and fired. The round hit the target and it went down. The shell landed next to his sleeve, hot. Another target was already up. Montauk aimed and fired. The target went down. He glanced to his right: Staff Sergeant Curtis Jackson, the 1st Squad leader, wasn't looking at his own targets, he was looking at Montauk's, just waiting for him to screw up. Jackson was nicknamed "Fitty Cent," after the rapper, whose real name was also Curtis Jackson. Staff Sergeant Jackson was a small white guy who hadn't been shot nine times, but he was a former Ranger. He could probably shoot straight. Montauk fired, the target went down. He fired again and missed a 300-meter target. He missed the next as well. He hit fourteen out of the next fifteen targets, and he managed to resist the impulse to see if Jackson or anyone else was watching, but near the end of his set, he missed two more. When he finished, he stood and kicked the sandbag. He'd shot 35, one below Expert.

Within the hour, everyone had qualified with the M4. A dozen, like Montauk, had qualified as Sharpshooter. Another dozen had struggled to qualify at all.

Only four men in the platoon had qualified as Expert. Among them, Olaf and Jackson. The surprise was Specialist Young-Bai Joh, or Sodium Joh, as they called him, a scrawny twenty-one-year-old teetotaling Korean nerd. Montauk was jealous, but he congratulated him and said, "Where'd you learn to shoot like that?"

"I don't know," he said. "Video games?"

"That's it, LT, you need to play more video games." It was Sergeant Jackson.

He was always making snide comments. Excess of bile, Montauk thought. That's how a seventeenth-century physician would have diagnosed him. He was the only guy in the platoon from whom Montauk felt actual hostility. He was also the only member of the platoon with a Ranger tab, which was unfortunate because it lent legitimacy to Jackson's attitude: that he shouldn't have to take orders from some non-Ranger chump just because he had a college degree and ninety days of OCS.

Montauk assembled the platoon and informed them that they would be doing a firing drill in full MOPP-4, heavy charcoal-lined coveralls, rubber overboots, and bulky black gloves. "The range depot has the gear," he said. "Get suited up and be prepared to fire under a notional cloud of Agent." He felt a wave of relief wash over him as the platoon lined up at the depot. He couldn't screw up while standing at the rear, observing.

When they were suited up and back in position, Olaf ran down the line, yelling, "*Gas! Gas! Gas!*" and they all yanked the heavy black-and-green rubber masks out of their carrying pouches. They pulled down their green rubber hoods, placing their sweaty palms over the canisters and sucking the masks onto their faces to check the seal, tasting powdered latex and old drool. They scrambled into prone firing positions, struggling to angle their rifles so they could actually look down the sights.

The tower called out, "Switch the selector to semi and watch your lanes!" The torso-shaped targets popped up downrange, and they began firing.

Montauk's infantry school platoon, class of '99, had gone through the tear-gas chamber, in which they had to do push-ups and recite their General Orders while their eyes burned and unbelievably long ropes of mucus hung from their noses. Real nerve agents produced similar mucus ropes but with the addition of disorientation, painful spasming, paralysis, and death, which came within thirty minutes or sooner unless the heart was sped up with a shot from one of the atropine injectors that each soldier carried. Blister agents caused dermatological burns, blindness, and lung corrosion. Blood agents caused the quickest and most certain death, a nice big breath causing the blood to literally boil in the veins. It was hard to imagine anything more horrible than the Great War, when mustard gas had been merely one of the gears of death that undid the bodies and personalities of the young men trapped in its mill, the extent of the psychological horrors not really known because so few survived, and even fewer spoke of it afterward.

The tower called cease-fire and the men rested their rifles against sandbags and moved to the rear of their foxholes. All except Ant.

Montauk walked up behind him and tapped him on the shoulder. "Private Ant, hello?" he yelled.

"Sir. Sorry, sir," Ant said after taking off his mask. He had fair skin, curly hair, and delicate features.

"Can you not hear the tower?"

"I forgot to put in my earplugs, and I didn't realize until the pro mask was on and Sergeant Olaufsson was yelling, 'Gas! Gas!' I just kept firing, but it was so loud that I could barely focus on the targets."

"You like that tinnitus?"

"At least I know what it's like now."

Ant, like Fields, had taken on actual personhood in Montauk's mind. They happened to be the only two other men in the platoon with bachelor's degrees, and Montauk worried that he'd subconsciously associated himself with the educated few, further setting himself apart from the rest of the platoon. Ant was twenty-two and had a BA in Aesthetics from the hippie-fabulous Evergreen State College in Olympia. He had been on the verge of making sergeant when he pissed hot for marijuana during a random drug test earlier in the year. Captain Byrd had reduced him to buck private. Now, on the cusp of deployment, he was the lowest-ranking member of Montauk's platoon.

A few months back, he'd surprised Montauk by showing up at one of the Encyclopaedists parties—he knew one of Montauk's housemates—and he'd opened up to Montauk about his new philosophical relationship with Army life. He had signed up thinking he might build a career, but now he was here to savor military experience, an attitude that comported well with his epicurean eating habits.

"Remember your earplugs next time," Montauk said. He walked away smiling, remembering when he had made the same mistake back in Basic. The crack of the rifles next to his had been painful and the discharge of his own, deafening—the ring appeared after firing the first round and increased in volume with each successive shot. He had tinnitus for hours afterward, an indication of how soft and vulnerable his body was to modern weaponry, that he could be hurt simply from hearing the sound of the 5.56 millimeter NATO jacketed rifle round.

———

Mani hit the last of a joint roach held in a bobby pin, then set it on the porch steps and took up a charcoal stick. She had a sketchpad open on her lap. She made a few swift and light strokes to form the oval outline of a face. In the center, she sketched an angular nose, smoothed the lines with her finger, then carefully articulated the wide flaring nostrils. She dashed off the rough almond shapes of the eyes, closer together than most people's, added a little nub for the tear duct, shaded the sockets, shaded under the cheekbones, added wrinkles near the nose, drew in the thin lips, protruding ears. It was beginning to look like President Bush.

She held the drawing in the sunlight, dissatisfied. Something was off. She heard the muffled sound of her cell ringing in her pocket. It was her mother, who still didn't know about her injury. She'd called several times last week, and Mani hadn't picked up.

As she answered, she took up the charcoal again and decided to fix her drawing. Bush looked too clean.

"Hi, Mom. What's up?"

"Have you stopped answering your phone altogether?" Her mother tended to add an initial *e* to words that began with an *s* (*have you e-stopped*) and her *th*s sounded more like *d*s. She taught Farsi and Middle Eastern literature at Boston College, and as such, she had retained much more of her Iranian accent than Mani's father had.

"Sorry. Been busy." After her cell had broken in the accident, Mani had bought the cheapest Nokia available. She'd spoken to her mother only once since then, in mid-August. Her mother had been furious that she'd been out of contact for a month and a half. Mani had apologized profusely and said her phone had been stolen.

"Everything is fine?"

"Yeah. Why wouldn't it be?" Mani smudged the charcoal around the eyes, making the sockets appear deeper. She hollowed out the cheeks.

"We just haven't heard from you. What have you been up to?"

"Art." Mani angled the tip of Bush's nose, giving it more of a hook.

"You're still in Seattle?"

"Yep."

"Your father says the University of Washington has a top-ten medical program."

Mani continued sketching.

"Have you been reading the news?" her mother asked. "President Khatami refuses to give up the nuclear program. And now Shamkhani is saying they may resort to preemptive attacks to protect their nuclear facilities."

"Who's Shamkhani?"

"The defense minister."

Mani fell silent as two of Montauk's housemates walked past her up the stairs. They all knew her by now and didn't seem to mind that she was living on the couch, but she had yet to learn all their names.

"Are you still there?" her mother asked.

"That's nice," Mani said.

"Are you even listening to me?"

"Yeah. The nukes. What do you want me to say?" She dabbed her finger over the pupils, dulling them.

"Well, we'd been talking about visiting this winter. But if things get worse, that may be impossible."

"I'm not really interested in going there anyway."

"But you haven't even met your cousins."

"That's why I don't care. I don't know them."

"They're family."

Mani lightened the lips.

"Your father and I think you should come home."

She carefully added small cracks to the skin. "I'm getting a lot of work done. I'll visit sometime soon, okay?"

"How soon?"

"I gotta go. We'll talk, okay?"

"You say that, dear, but we don't. You hardly answer your phone."

"Mom. We'll talk. Okay. I promise."

"Mani."

Mani did miss her parents, but there was no way she was going to let them see her on crutches. She couldn't handle the interrogation that would certainly expand beyond the accident to question, again, every important life choice she'd made in the last three years. "Love you, too, Mom. Bye." She hung up and looked at her drawing. It was still Bush, but she'd gone too far: he looked ghoulish. She didn't like this version, either. She ripped it up.

5

Montauk left Captain Byrd's office and walked toward his platoon's classroom. Mount Rainier, so often hidden by cloud cover, was out in its full glory, reveling in the September sun, its permafrosted cap just starting to get seasonal legs. Ant and Sodium Joh were sitting on the wooden steps leading up to the classroom with their weapons spread out on rags. Joh ran a bore brush through the barrel and then held it to the sky, looking for leftover carbon residue, as Montauk trudged into the classroom. The rest of the platoon was in here, bullshitting loudly over the Top 40 R&B/Hip-Hop station KUBE 93.3, which was probably why the musically snobbish Ant and Joh were cleaning their weapons outside.

The room's setup suggested something halfway between a lunchroom and a classroom: up front were a chalkboard and a podium, which faced rows of large wooden tables lined with chairs on both sides. They were covered with dirty squares of cloth, bore brushes and non-bore brushes, tubes of Break-Free gun cleaner and lubricant, a few sixteen-ounce Powerade and Mountain Dew bottles from the vending machine down the hall, and assault rifles, grenade launchers, and machine guns in various states of disassembly. The black metal glinted in the sunlight coming through the open windows.

In the middle of the room, and taking up the most physical space, were Sergeant Jackson and his alpha fireteam, known as the "Hardcores." They all looked up to Jackson, especially Specialist Urritia, who seemed to Montauk to be a nice guy who never quite pulled off

Jackson's badass-jerk persona that he sought to emulate. Urritia was knocking back a can of caffeine- and taurine-fortified weight gainer. He was predisposed to relative scrawniness, so his regimen of pills and supplements gave him the chiseled look of an Abercrombie model, a look that Montauk both admired and thought kind of gay.

Montauk pulled up a chair next to Olaf and popped his rifle open. Olaf's rifle was already cleaned and inspected. With twelve years of practice, he was the quickest and most methodical rifle cleaner in the platoon.

"I can handle that lower receiver for you, sir," Olaf said.

"Thanks," Montauk said as he disassembled the rest of the weapon. He looked over at 2nd Squad's table. A tall and muscular guy—Montauk couldn't see his name tape—was choking out Specialist Antoine Thomas, who was struggling to turn his head and elbow his grappler in the ribs. Thomas was short and wide and wore big-framed googly glasses. He was a fan of sci-fi and fantasy, but especially of anime. To top it off, his speech was impeded by a lateral lisp. The ultimate 1980s caricature of a nerd. Except for one thing: he became infuriated rather than mortified when called out on his nerdiness.

Montauk, although known in his hipster set for horsing around, found it difficult to gauge what was an acceptable amount of grab-ass and unseriousness in an infantry platoon. He didn't want to be seen as schoolmarmish, but he had to maintain his authority. He settled on giving Staff Sergeant Ngo Nguyen, the 2nd Squad leader, a look that communicated annoyance with his squad. Nguyen commenced a halfhearted attempt to calm them down until Olaf bellowed across the room for them to knock it the fuck off and clean their weapons. Quiet settled, and the little clicks and scrapes of bore-brushing could be heard. Daddy was in the house. Montauk continued cleaning impassively, annoyed at how it had all gone down.

Next to Thomas, PFC Lo was wearing his Kevlar, body armor, and ballistic goggles. Having to wear tactical protective gear indoors was the military version of the dunce cap. "What did Lo do this time?" Montauk asked Olaf.

"He left the ballistic plates out of his flak vest so it'd be lighter during the react-to-contact drills," Olaf said. "Nguyen found out."

Montauk glanced at Nguyen. He had two main facial expressions: calm or, in this case, with PFC Lo sweating under his body armor, delightedly cruel.

Punitive corrective measures were encouraged to maintain discipline, but there were limits. The punishment must directly relate to the soldier's deficiency. It must discontinue when the deficiency is overcome. Otherwise, it could constitute hazing, which is expressly forbidden by Army Command Policy. Lo had fucked up, and being forced to wear his body armor was related to the way in which he'd fucked up. But Lo's real deficiency was being stupid—his nickname was "Low-Q." And when would that be overcome? Montauk felt bad for Lo, but he didn't want to undercut Nguyen's authority, which would be bad for Nguyen and bad for Montauk, who would likely lose Nguyen's respect. He needed Olaf's advice, but even more, he wanted to be able to handle this by himself.

Montauk finished cleaning his weapon and signaled for Nguyen to step into the hallway with him. Before Nguyen could speak, Montauk said, "I know what Lo did. I'm just . . . concerned. That maybe you're having too much fun."

"Sir, I'm looking out for him. Our mothers go to the same church in Tacoma. If he fucks up here, no big deal. I just don't want him to fuck up when it counts."

Montauk nodded. He followed Nguyen back into the classroom, scolding himself for being so soft, for acting like a camp counselor instead of a platoon leader.

Each soldier continued to work as fast as he could, first on his own weapon and then on the squads' as Olaufsson moved from table to table, giving a thumbs-up or -down. No one went home until it was all done. It was a social system of intense peer pressure. After all, survival in the field was a collective task, not an individual one. Get through as a group or get fucked up as a group.

It was late afternoon by the time the arms room was locked up and Montauk had dismissed his platoon. The thirty-six of them were supposed to feel like a large family, of which Montauk was ostensibly the patriarch. But next to Olaf, he felt more like a middle sibling who was in charge only because he was Captain Byrd's favorite. He hoped that would change when he deployed, when there'd be more to think about than the monotony of weapons cleaning.

Montauk found Mani in her pajamas, lying on the couch napping, her sketchpad on the floor. She sat up, yawned, and said hi.

"How long have you been sleeping?" he asked.

"I don't know. A while."

"Get up. Put some clothes on. We're going out."

"No thanks."

"C'mon, I'll buy you a drink." Montauk stared at her until she sighed and lifted herself off the couch.

She moved slowly down the tree-lined street; thankfully, the Canterbury was only three blocks from the Encyclopad.

Montauk held open the door as Mani crutched her way inside. "See?" he said. "How hard was that?" They were greeted by a suit of armor with a sign around its neck that read, "Seat Thyself." They did, at a dimly lit table near the fireplace. Montauk ordered them both Long Islands. He almost ordered three, as if Hal were back at the table, sitting next to Mani.

"Good, right?" he said after they'd each taken a sip.

"Could use more lemon," Mani said.

"Getting out of the house, I mean. Doing something. Here." Montauk gave Mani his lemon.

She squeezed it into her drink. "This is your idea of doing something?" She smirked.

"I know it's not as exciting as lying in your pajamas all day, but yeah, this is doing something. I bet you haven't showered in, what, four days?"

"Three," Mani said.

If Montauk had gone unshowered that long, he would have been rank as a Greyhound bathroom. Somehow, Mani only became more desirable. Her hair was lustrous; she moved in an invisible cloud of woman-smell. "That's something, I guess. How's the art coming?"

Mani shrugged. "Feels like I'm going through the motions. Drawing just for something to do."

Montauk looked at her skeptically.

"You know, like sometimes you're fixated on something, it's urgent, it demands your attention. I just don't have that right now."

"Bullshit," Montauk said.

Mani's face wrinkled.

"You're not fixated on anything?"

She took a drink from her Long Island. "I'm confused, okay?"

"Confusion is bad."

"No, it's good. I mean, it's fuel. For art. And I've never felt as confused as I am now. So yeah, the compulsion to draw, to paint, whatever. It's enormous."

"But . . ."

"But I'm scared to dig around in that mess."

"Mess?"

"My head."

"My head's a mess, too, for what it's worth." Montauk held his Long Island without drinking it, feeling the cold glass perspire against his palm. "When do you get off those crutches?"

"I'm supposed to be off them now."

"Why aren't you?"

"Lazy. Plus, it's automatic sympathy. People hold doors, get me things."

"People? You mean me. You never leave the house."

Mani laughed. "I like it in the house." Which was true, if only because every time she left the house, it was like replaying that night, going down those steps toward the pavement where she'd been hit. In the house, even though everything was up in the air, it was on pause, and none of it would come crashing down. "Where else am I gonna go?"

"We could go to the art museum. Or to Compline at St. Mark's. The choir is amazing."

"We?"

"Yeah, why not?"

"You don't like me," Mani said.

"What?"

"You don't have to pretend."

Montauk tapped his finger on the table. "I'm not."

Mani responded by taking a deliberate sip from her Long Island.

"Fine, I didn't like you. Okay? Hal had a raging heart-boner for you, and I thought you were playing him."

"Because Hal's generous, I was taking advantage? I fucking loved him. I'm not the one who split in the middle of the night."

"He was confused. He didn't know what to do."

"That didn't stop him from walking out."

They both sipped from their drinks. Montauk finished his.

"I told him to," Montauk said.

"Oh, fuck. Fuck you. Seriously?" Mani stared at him until he looked down. She sighed.

"I'm sorry," Montauk said. "It was a mistake. And I'm not pretending."

"What?"

"I'm not pretending to like you."

"You mean that?"

Montauk smiled. Mani kept her face blank for a few excruciating seconds, as if coming to a decision. Her lips curled up at the corners.

When Montauk helped her back up the concrete steps to the Encyclopad, Mani wondered whether living with him was a good or a bad thing. Was it merely convenient, her old habit of latching on to the nearest guy who could offer a place to sleep? She hoped it wasn't. If she had kept a journal, she would have written that night about this moment ascending the steps. She would have written that living here, with Montauk and the gang of Encyclopadders, was not easy. That it was not habit. That she was slowly rewriting the associations this place held for her, replacing that awful night with something newer, something better. She would have written: *Please let it be true. It has to be true.*

6

After a morning of remedial land navigation in the woods, Captain Byrd had called for Montauk and the three other lieutenants who led the four platoons in Bravo Company. They stood in Byrd's small trailer while he sat behind his desk, glancing intermittently at his computer screen. His XO was standing behind him.

"I know you've all been wondering where we're headed," he said, spitting tobacco into a Diet Sprite bottle. "So listen up, but remember, this is need-to-know information, and you baby LTs only marginally need to know, but I'm feeling generous. We're slated to be part of the security force in and around the Green Zone. Bravo Company will be attached to the 3rd Brigade 1st Cavalry Division. Texans. They just arrived to relieve the invasion force. It'll mostly be a static security mission. Can't skip land nav, though, 'cause we might be rolling around pulling convoy security, too. And of course, we have to get to Baghdad from Kuwait." Captain Byrd handed them each a stapled packet.

"I was thinking about that, sir," Montauk said. "Here we are walking around the woods holding compasses. Maybe it would be more useful to do some kind of mounted nav course. Even head up north and practice driving in the city?"

"You want to take an armored column up to the U District and pick up college chicks, Montauk?" The other LTs chuckled. "Point taken about mounted land nav," Byrd went on, "but it's not in the training schedule, and we're leaving in eighteen days. We'll work with what we have and figure out the rest over there."

Montauk flipped rapidly through the stapled pages, which contained yesterday's Intelligence Summary for the Area of Operations they were scheduled to inhabit three weeks from today. It was like a teaser trailer for what he and his troops would be dealing with—the confusing kind that didn't reveal the plot of the movie. It was poorly laid out and full of acronyms. "What's AIF stand for again, sir?"

"Anti-Iraqi Forces," said Byrd.

"I thought that was us," said LT Miller, getting a few laughs.

"Says they were expecting to get hit with a car bomb on Tuesday," Montauk said. "Do you know if they got hit, sir?"

"Don't know," said Captain Byrd, rocking back in his office chair and clicking at his desktop distractedly. He acted like the manager of some start-up company, constantly harried and overworked but somehow content with all the distraction. He couldn't have been over thirty, and he was only two ranks above Montauk, but he seemed so accustomed to leadership, so experienced, that Montauk had trouble remembering that Byrd himself had never been deployed. "It's a good question," he said. "XO? What's the word on car bombs?"

The executive officer, a first lieutenant and Captain Byrd's second in command, rolled a chair up to an adjacent workstation. "Looks like, yes, one VBIED went off at Checkpoint Eleven in Karada. Blew up a couple of First Infantry Division soldiers. One KIA, one wounded."

KIA. Montauk had known that acronym before even joining the Army. Whoever that soldier was, on Monday, he'd probably been smoking cigarettes and making dick jokes. Tuesday, dead. And in just three weeks, Montauk and his boys would be manning that very checkpoint. He pictured a burning car, smoke and concrete debris, pieces of a soldier spread across the dirt. Sodium Joh, maybe. Maybe Ant.

"There you have it," Captain Byrd said, spitting more Copenhagen juice into his Diet Sprite bottle.

Montauk winged along Fifteenth Avenue on his bicycle. It was a fixed gear he'd picked up on the cheap from Gregg's Greenlake Cycle. The only parts he'd really spent money on were the wheels, which had flat white carbon fins instead of the usual metal spokes, making for a very cool effect when he started going fast. Her name was Hermione (after Hermes, the speediest Greek god, not after the Harry Potter character), and she weighed less than his loaded M4 carbine, which was named Molly Millions.

He'd gone down to the co-op on Madison to pick up a bottle of wine and a loaf of the locally baked bread that Mani loved. On his way back, he zipped past storefronts on either side: 22 Doors, the tapas bar, the little vegan grocery, the barbershop with the spinning candy-cane pole where the dude kept *Playboy*s in the stack of magazines and tried to talk to you about NASCAR as he cut your hair. The Hopvine, a teahouse, and two indie coffee joints. Several kids in bright green Kerry shirts were out front, prodding people to register to vote. The sky was darkening quickly as the sun fell behind a blanket of clouds.

He hopped off Hermione and carried her up the stairs to the Encyclopad just as the clouds let out a light drizzle upon the Emerald City. A few of his housemates were watching an old kung fu movie in the living room. He found Mani in the kitchen, tending to a pan of sizzling bacon.

"Goddamn, that smells good. What is it about bacon?" he asked.

"Fat makes everything better." She was off her crutches now, but she wore a leg brace. She was padding across the floor with a small block of Asiago, her ass moving unevenly under a stretchy minidress.

He set the wine bottle down on the counter and poked her with the loaf of bread as she grated a pile of the salty white cheese on a plate. "What'd you do today?" he asked.

"Read a little bit. Did some more sketching."

"Didn't go out. Again."

"Gotta problem with that?"

"You seem to be doing all right."

"And it's wet out."

"Only as of a minute ago."

"What did *you* do today?"

"I found out where we're going," Montauk said, regretting the words even as they passed his lips.

"Oh my God, where?"

"I can't, actually."

"Come on."

"No, I'm serious, it's classified. It's no big deal. I mean, it's interesting, but it's not shocking or anything. It's a place in Iraq, and we'll basically be doing security stuff, which we already knew."

"Why's it classified, then?" She bagged up the cheese and returned it to the fridge. Montauk leaned on the counter and watched her walk. He felt an urge to carry her upstairs and pull that dress off. " 'Cause if I tell you, you'll tell Al-Qaeda, then they'll know there are Americans coming to Iraq, and the whole plan will be shot."

"You won't get shot," Mani said.

"The *plan* will be shot." Montauk smiled at her.

But Mani couldn't laugh. What if something did happen to him? Even scarier was that he didn't seem worried at all. At worst, he was a dead man walking. At best, a lost boy. Was he right not to worry? It was all so confusing. She slumped and smiled back at him, chiding herself for her dramatic imagination—it was perverse in a way, like attending a stranger's funeral to stare at the faces of the grieving, feeding off the aesthetic energy of tragedy.

"God. I really want to know where you're going now," she said.

In his head, Montauk was saying, Sorry babe, and giving her a hug and a kiss as if she were his girlfriend. "Loose lips sink ships," he said. He watched her lips part, revealing a slight gap between her front teeth. It was now or never. He could step forward and kiss her. One swift, soft motion. Right now.

He stood rooted to the spot, and the three feet of kitchen air between them quickly grew stale. Mani gave her hair a flip and turned the bacon.

7

The sun was out and shafts of light filled the room through the open bay windows. A comfortable breeze kept the air circulating. Montauk flipped through his collection of graphic novels while listening to Marvin Gaye. He had sold off most of his belongings in the last three weeks, including his beloved bicycle, Hermione.

Earlier that morning, the spine on his Moleskine had cracked and the pages started falling out. Mani had offered to make him a journal, and though he'd refused at first, she explained that she enjoyed book-binding and collage and would probably be making one anyway just for the fun of it, and plus, he could take it with him to Iraq. She was sitting on the floor now, carefully cutting images out of old magazines and science textbooks with a pair of toenail scissors.

The teakettle in the kitchen began to whistle, and before Mani could get up, Montauk put down his copy of *Watchmen* and attended to it. Though she was walking quite well now, he had gotten used to fetching things for her.

He poured the cup of tea and carefully carried it out to the living room, then set it on the floor next to her. Mani finished guiding the scissors around an image of a bicycle and held it up for his inspection. "What do you think? Too sentimental?"

"No," Montauk said. "I like it."

The day passed slowly until they found themselves, post-dinner, post–several glasses of wine, watching Terry Gilliam's *The Adventures of Baron Munchausen*. Montauk had never seen it and they'd rented it on Mani's suggestion. The numerous housemates, even those who had joined them for dinner, had vanished to the sanctity of their rooms or the revelry of the bars down the street. The Encyclopad was dark and quiet as they settled into the film.

It began with the baron interrupting a play about his life to correct its inaccuracies. But the baron's own incredible account of his past exploits—told in flashback—was cut short. The city was under attack, and to save it, he set off in a hot-air balloon woven from ladies' knickers. In search of his heroic friends, he visited the moon, the center of the earth, the belly of a whale.

But for every astonishing sequence, there was a boring interlude. With each lull, Mani had nuzzled farther into Montauk until her head was resting snugly in the crevice between his chest and arm. During the King of the Moon sequence, she had fallen asleep, and during the rest of the film, she had slowly become more and more horizontal, rotating into him, facing away from the television, until her chest was pressed against his. As the film neared its end, jumping between meta-levels of narration, Montauk felt the kind of intellectual dizziness he got when thinking about logic paradoxes, a dizziness that complemented his incipient erection. Perhaps it was that this evening—watching the film, Mani slowly sliding closer to him—had become its own incredible story, a story all the more arresting because he could never tell it to Corderoy.

The credits rolled to a loud fanfare and Mani awoke. She leaned back slowly. Montauk looked directly at her, then leaned in and kissed her. She rose slightly, adding pressure to the soft brush of his lips, and they sampled the private tastes of each other's mouths.

Montauk pulled back. "I'm sorry," he said.

"Don't be."

"Okay."

"Are you going to kiss me again?"

Montauk had fallen to half-staff. The anticipation, the richness of possibility they'd been cradling for weeks, was collapsing in the wake of that kiss. "I don't know," he said.

"Are you worried about Hal?"

Yes, Corderoy would hate him, at least for a while. But it was more than that. Maybe he was tired of relationships, even purely physical ones, based on convenience? Maybe their relationship was a house on stilts and sex would push them off it and into the usual mire. "I just like what we have," he said. "That's all."

"Me, too."

"What are you going to do when I leave? Have you thought about it more?"

"I'll figure something out."

"One of my guys, Fields. He knocked his girlfriend up."

"Okay . . ."

"He's getting married," Montauk said.

Mani drew back an inch, her eyes betraying the sort of prescient alertness pets have just before earthquakes.

"What if . . . I don't know." What was he saying? Well, he knew what he was saying, but why the fuck was he saying it?

"Spit it out," Mani said.

Montauk bit his lip. "We could get married," he said.

Mani sighed and stared at him as if he were a puppy that had just shit all over the floor.

"Not, like, with a ceremony, just at the courthouse," he said. "It wouldn't mean— Things would be the same. The Army pays out a Basic Allowance for Housing—and if I have a spouse, it's a thousand more. You could have that. Free money. You could use it to pay off your hospital bills or whatever. You don't want to, that's fine, but then nobody will benefit from that money. Except for some overall military budget that—"

"Shut up, Mickey."

Montauk left his mouth ajar, as if those stupid, stupid words might funnel back in like chimney swifts.

"I don't want your pity. You don't owe me anything. Neither does Hal."

"I know."

"So you promise this has nothing to do with that?"

"Promise," Montauk said. He was lying.

"Even so, we couldn't tell Hal. You know that."

"I won't tell him if you won't." As soon as he said the words, he knew he meant them, and it made him feel ashamed that he was planning to keep something so huge from his friend. His best friend? Perhaps not anymore.

Mani stared at him long enough that Montauk became conscious of the DVD menu music playing in the background. He couldn't hear his own breath, because he wasn't breathing. Then she leaned in and kissed him softly on the cheek. "I'm sorry," Mani said. "I can't."

Montauk swallowed his own head. "No," he said. "You can. You have to. I mean, I want you to. Let me do this for you." He felt an excitement fueled by the thought that it might very well be a terrible idea, an excitement made more urgent by the guilt of hiding it from Corderoy, guilt complicated by the fact that he'd done Corderoy's dirty work of kicking Mani out in the first place. It was so confusing that somehow this blind leap felt like the only sensible option.

Mani considered his face as if it were a room-sized Rothko. "I don't have to," she said. "I don't."

Montauk closed his eyes for a moment. "No," he said. "You don't. You don't have to."

Mani took a deep breath. What would it mean to say yes? Allowing herself to be supported, yet again, by a guy? Not just a guy but a soldier, sending money home. It was such a weirdly romantic gesture, especially since it seemed pretty clear they weren't headed toward a sexual relationship. It would mean something for him, too, if she agreed. It would probably be the biggest decision either of them had made in their lives. Maybe it was the perfect fertilizer for a strong friendship. She didn't have one of those right now. Not anyone close, really close. Hadn't in a while. But that could change, so easily. "Why not?" she said.

"Why not?"

"Yeah. Consider me Mrs. Montauk."

Whoa. Shit. Really? That was it, then. They were engaged. "We're engaged," he said wondrously.

"Shut up," Mani said, and she punched him on the shoulder.

Montauk couldn't help smiling. He'd have to tell his mother. No, of course not. That would only sow confusion. And yet a part of him indulged in what felt like nostalgia, nostalgia for future events that would never happen: he and Mani picking out wedding invitations, scouting locations, sampling dinner wines, licking envelopes, writing vows.

8

It was four days until deployment when Montauk and Mani entered the Seattle Municipal Courthouse. They were on time for their appointment, but the judge was running behind, so they sat in padded folding chairs outside his office on the tenth floor. Mani was wearing a short yellow summer dress, almost as offensively bright as the fluorescent lights. Montauk wore his Army green service uniform. A couple sat next to them filling out paperwork for a marriage license, just as Montauk had done three days ago. The guy was thin, had shaggy brown hair, and wore a tweed jacket and bow tie. His arm was around the girl, who looked Chinese and was dressed like she lived in Manhattan. They were cooing and smiling over their clipboard.

"I'm glad we're having the coq au vin," Mani said, loud enough for them to hear.

"What?" Montauk whispered.

"It'll go well with the black truffle ravioli," she said. "Don't you think?"

"Yes, quite," Montauk said. "Though I must say, our boldest menu choice is surely the lemon-caper sorbet."

Mani snickered but regained her composure. "I can't wait to see the look on Clarissa Worthington's face."

Montauk had to bite his tongue to keep from laughing at that one.

The elevator down the hall opened, and a couple in their eighties shuffled out. Mani watched them approach and lower their creaking bodies into chairs. She suddenly felt shitty for messing with the young couple, for trying to joke through what she and Mickey were about to do, rather than facing up to its seriousness.

The judge opened his door and said, "Montauk?"

They nodded and entered his office. Law books lined both walls. A narrow window behind the desk looked out on the city. The view wasn't all that spectacular. The judge verified their receipt of payment ($63.50 cash, paid at the window down the hall), then inspected their certificate to ensure that it was properly filled out.

Montauk wore a silver ring on his right index finger, mostly out of habit; it was a gift from an ex-girlfriend. He twisted it about his finger, imagined it on his other hand. They had no rings, of course. But they were about to be married. He couldn't help feeling that certain elements were absent, that a marriage wasn't a marriage without rings, and rice, and, well, consummation.

These absences didn't bother Mani. But her heart was beating at an elevated rate, her eyes scanned the room in quick saccades, she sat unnaturally motionless. She felt the same rush that she'd felt years ago when shoplifting a Goo Goo Dolls CD from Sam Goody. She was about to get something for free. Government money. Something she didn't deserve. Mani grabbed Montauk's hand and squeezed it, hoping this would alleviate the awkwardness, but it only magnified it, and she quickly let go.

"Looks good," the judge said. "Where are your witnesses?"

"I'm sorry?" Montauk said.

"You need two witnesses."

"They're . . . just outside," Mani said. She glared at Montauk.

He jumped up, said, "Back in a second," then ducked out of the office.

"Can I borrow a pen and paper?" Mani asked the judge.

Montauk surveyed the hallway. The old man had just entered the bathroom, and the young woman was on the phone. But Bowtie and Granny were just sitting there quietly. "Excuse me," Montauk said.

Inside the judge's office, Mani finished writing and handed the pen back just as Montauk opened the door.

"Sorry for the delay," he said.

Granny held her hands in front of her and smiled softly. Bowtie was doing his best to mute his expression, though his eyes conveyed a certain smugness. Mani gave him a sheepish grin.

"Can we proceed?" the judge asked.

Mani and Montauk nodded.

"Is it your plan to get married and be faithful to each other?"

"Yes," Mani said.

Montauk hesitated. What did *faithful* actually mean in this context? It didn't mean sexually, so . . . Mani and the judge were both staring at him. "Of course," he said.

"Do you have any vows you'd like to say?"

"No," Montauk said.

Mani's voice caught in her throat. It would be awkward with these two strangers in the room, especially Granny, but they were getting married! Something had to be said. "He does," Mani said, and she handed him a folded piece of legal paper.

Montauk's eyes widened.

"Read it," Mani said.

Montauk glanced back at Granny and Bowtie. "Okay," he said. " 'I vow not to be an asshole. Or a coward. To answer all letters sent to me, to eat any and all desserts I can get, to—' " He coughed. " 'To jerk off at least twice a day, to come home safe, to be open if I hurt, to make it my life's mission not to fuck over anyone, anywhere, no matter how much they deserve it.' "

Granny wiped a tear from her cheek.

Montauk looked Mani in the eye.

"Finished?" the judge said, all business. "Okay. I pronounce you husband and wife. You may kiss the bride."

They both hesitated. Despite the intimacy and honesty of the vows Montauk had just recited, this prompting for a public kiss made it inescapably obvious that they were committing fraud, that they'd harassed two strangers to witness a nominal marriage purely to squeeze a little money out of the Army. Fraud that could land them in deep shit if they got caught. It had happened before. Montauk had heard of one company commander who made it a point to call the mothers of all predeployment last-minute brides. The judge was staring at them. Montauk imagined seeing this moment on security camera footage. In a court-room. Exhibit A. Corderoy watching from the gallery. He leaned toward Mani, she leaned in, too, and they kissed. It was a brief kiss, a guilty kiss. Not at all like the other night on the couch. It was more like a hesitant taste of milk. Milk that might have gone sour.

———

They passed the next few days in a cloud of formality. But on the night before Montauk's departure, Mani crept into his room around four a.m. "Can I stay up here?"

"Mmm-hmm," Montauk mumbled. She'd never asked before, and the couch downstairs was perfectly comfortable. He didn't press her. She climbed into his bed.

After a few minutes of silence, she said, "I've been thinking about your advice. About getting out of Seattle." Mickey had asked his house-mates, and they were fine with her staying at the Encyclopad even after he left for Baghdad, but Mani knew she would feel awkward, lonely.

"You should," Montauk said. "Rent a studio somewhere, buy art supplies. Change your environment."

"I think I might go back to Newton."

"With your parents? You bit my head off when I suggested that."

"I don't know. I haven't seen them in a while. Maybe it's a good place to start over."

Montauk lay there, more awake, thinking about how close Newton was to Boston, to Hal. Another minute passed, and he'd nearly resolved not to bring it up. Then he whispered, "This doesn't have anything to do . . ."

Mani didn't respond. She had either fallen asleep or didn't want to answer that question. For the best, probably.

But Montauk couldn't fall back to sleep. It was now the time of day he would soon come to know as Begin Morning Nautical Twilight. The turret on the third floor of his house looked out through the leafy branches of a nineteenth-century maple toward the gray of Lake Wash-ington. Mani faced away from him, half covered by a sheet, breathing deep and slow, the tattoos on her lower back—two cursive *f*s, as on a cello—peeking out between her boxers and the bottom of her tank top.

Montauk had not lain awake at early dawn like this since the mid-1980s. Like most children and old people, he would often wake up earlier than the rest of the world. During those years before he quit the piano, he would lie still in the mornings, hearing Suzuki piano sonatas playing in his mind as the gray diamond of window light slowly traveled his bedroom wall. Those dawns were the best part of his whole day. Not because his childhood was unhappy, but because at dawn, the world was surreal. Lying completely still, he would sometimes get the sensation that his hands were enormous—the size of his bed or as big as the room. He tried not to look down at his sheets, so as to preserve the illusion. He felt the ghost of that feeling now, mitigated by adult knowledge, the certainty that his hands were, in fact, quite normal.

He inhaled and his thoughts were enveloped by Mani's scent, like submerging his head in warm bathwater. Smelling her body beside him made him wonder how she tasted, which made him wonder if she waxed. He thought for an instant about asking Corderoy. But he didn't really want to know; he'd made the conscious decision, for the first time in his life, to not sleep with a girl, his wife, for a reason other than that she was ugly.

Mani rolled over toward him. With his eyes closed, he felt her head move on the pillow and thought she might be awake, but he didn't move or open his eyes. Eventually, he fell asleep.

When he awoke, it was six. He had a plane to catch in three hours that would take him to D.C. and then to Kuwait. From there they'd convoy to Baghdad down highways studded with IEDs. This was his last day as a civilian. After packing his duffel bag with the few items he was permitted, he kissed Mani on the forehead. Though she stirred, her eyes remained closed. She knew, of course, that he was leaving this morning, but this nonverbal good-bye was somehow better, softer. Downstairs, Montauk checked his e-mail, then navigated to Wikipedia and looked up "The Encyclopaedists." Their article had been updated on September 3rd with a new section: "Ice." Montauk read it and smiled. He still had a little time, so he started a section of his own: "Used goods." He hammered out the last sentence as his cab honked out front. He looked toward the stairwell and wondered if Mani had woken at the sound. He said good-bye to the Encyclopad as he closed the front door softly. An hour later, he reached his gate of departure.

👤 Log in

article | discussion | edit this page | history

The Encyclopaedists [edit]

The Encyclopaedists are distributed in space and time. But this does not make them any less real. Or the Encyclopaedia any less true.

The War has begun and it is beginning. It is never-ending. The tally of scholars ticks up a notch at the Great University.

WIKIPEDIA
The Free Encyclopedia

navigation
- Main Page
- Community portal
- Current events
- Recent changes
- Random page
- Help
- Donations

search

[ ] Go | Search

toolbox
- What links here
- Related changes
- Special pages

Contents [hide]
1 Precursors of the Encyclopaedists
2 Motivations of the Encyclopaedists
3 Ice
4 Used goods

Precursors of the Encyclopaedists [edit]

The Encyclopaedists couldn't exist without Monty Python and Lewis Carroll. You see, Kitty, he was part of my dream, of course—but then I was part of his dream, too! Repeat after me, we are all individuals.

Motivations of the Encyclopaedists [edit]

It is doubtful there is any great accomplishment authored by a man that did not proceed from the incessant need to relocate his genitalia within unfamiliar though hardly novel spaces of sufficient lubrication. The great accomplishments of women, presumably, have more noble motivations.

Ice [edit]

Ice is cold and can make the back of your neck cold when surreptitiously dropped down your shirt by your idiotic friend. It can make your ass cold when your ass has had a catastrophic meeting with the metal of an old industrial railroad track. Ice, when cubed and small enough, can be pocketed in the cheek and used to augment the pleasure of fellatio. This use of ice makes up for every death by avalanche or iceberg.

The slipperiness of ice is also to be appreciated. A boy of fifteen, learning to drive, may find himself in the car with his father, on a cold December evening, spinning donuts in the icy parking lot of the elementary school he hasn't seen in ten years, under the amber cones of the streetlights, swerving, strafing, whimsical with two thousand pounds of steel.

Icicles, more than anything else, justify the continued existence of ice. There was a photo of a girl from before anyone knew her, embracing an icicle as large as she was, built down from the roof of a house in Newton, Massachusetts. It was a picture of the rare confluence of extreme cold and unfathomable warmth. It was taped to the back of her notebook to remind her where she'd come from. To see it once was to sear this frozen moment in the mind.

Used goods [edit]

Most goods can be purchased new or pre-owned (often, "used"). Some are better used. The wood on a much-played cello changes over time in sympathy with the vibrations of its strings. Used woodwinds will channel a different person's breath—guitar strings are restrung for left- or right-handed players, and most importantly, a whole new music will be produced. If a classical bassist sells his bass to a jazz bassist, then to the perspective of the bass, though its f-holes are placed as they always were, its life is radically different.

Books generally deteriorate over time, but certain well-made books become imbued with a kind of grace or charm over long use. This is especially true of Bibles and prayer books, and well-thumbed copies of the *Aeneid* and the *Metamorphoses*. Lesser books, dog-eared and grease-stained, may never be read again. This would have been depressing only a few years ago, before the difference between hardware and files had become internalized. We may protect and defend the nude photos that Ashley let us take of her months ago, but we will trash our old computer without a second thought after our new one is up and running. We will give up our flesh but not our souls. One evening in hazy futurity, we'll have a great bonfire of books, though their immolation will symbolize not the destruction of information but its immortality. Through death, we shall destroy death. See Singularity, 1 Corinthians 15.

External links [edit]

1. ^ "The Encyclopaedists of Capitol Hill."
www.thestranger.com/apr04/encyclopaedists.htm

2. ^ "C. PLINII NATVRALIS HISTORIAE PRAEFATIO."
www.thelatinlibrary.com/pliny.nhpr.html

BOSTON

9

The seeds of Corderoy's existential crisis were planted during his first class, when his professor asked him to prove he wasn't wasting his time. Corderoy had felt a quiet thrill, climbing the stairs to the third floor of the Gothic stone building and entering a room lined with bookshelves. But when he sat down at the long conference table, he'd felt intimidated. An older guy at the end of the table was most of the way through a volume of Proust. In Seattle, Corderoy would have considered that a pretentious pose, but here, maybe that was like reading *Us Weekly*? He had tried to look introspective while listening to the girls a few chairs away talking about where they'd attended undergrad. *In New Haven . . . And you? . . . Cool, my best friend went to Brown.* He'd surveyed the other arriving students. They couldn't all have gone to Ivy League schools, could they? But Boston was a bigger pond than Seattle, and as host to several elite colleges, it had a disproportionate share of transplanted big fish. He'd caught the eye of the semi-cute girl across the table and given her an aloof smile. She'd ignored it and returned to her book, prompting Corderoy to affect his best casual thug lean—an attempt to convey that, yeah, he was just as smart as everyone here, probably smarter, but it wadn't no thang.

When the professor had entered with his brown leather satchel and his Dr. Wily hair, he had said in an Irish accent, "This is Literary Criticism One, and I am Professor Flannigan," before initiating a round of introductions. The closer it had come to Corderoy's turn, the less he'd paid attention and the more he'd begun to plan out what he would say. The goal was to sound nonchalantly clever and smart—to be just witty enough that people thought that was how you always were. Corderoy had said, "Well, I like reading books. And playing video games. But there's no degree for playing video games." No one had thought it funny, and he'd slunk back in his chair as the spotlight moved on.

As Professor Flannigan rifled through a stack of wrinkled and stained legal pad pages, he'd said, "The purpose of this course is to examine the critical theories and modes of interpretation that . . ." And then he had stopped talking for what seemed at least a minute. He'd been so clearly comfortable with the silence, moseying about in his brain, selecting the right word, it was almost a rebuke. ". . . that pay intellectual dividends," he'd continued, "when applied to various texts. The greatest insight of post-structuralism, and of post-modernism in general, is that language is not a stable, closed system. Literature, therefore, is irreducibly plural. We reject the notion of a transcendental signified that would guarantee the illusive center of meaning, an impossible point of reference completely external to all human thought. Now, this isn't a hermeneutic license to say that all reading is misreading, but rather, an exhortation to be ruthlessly self-conscious of the reductive impulse.

"This may seem obvious to some of you, as it should, for you've matured in a fragmented and pluralistic world. If it does, then I have a more difficult question for you. Why isn't this class, this activity, a waste of time?"

An unspeakable question. You didn't start doubting God's existence while gearing up for the Crusades. You didn't consider whether the stripper giving you a lap dance was performing her sexual attraction. And you didn't ask whether literary criticism was a waste of time the day after you paid your tuition. Corderoy found himself staring at the cleavage of the girl on the far left. Sandy? She was a little chubby and had an overly large jaw, which made him feel conflicted about his ogling. When a girl was pleasant to look at as a whole person, you could call her beautiful and it was refined to admire beauty. But if you had to ignore her face to enjoy her breasts, you were effectively sectioning her into isolated chunks and staring at only the good bits. There was no way to convince yourself that it was noble. The subconscious pull to glance at Sandy's cleavage made him feel powerless, in the grip of an addiction he was born with.

"Mr. . . ."

Corderoy looked up. "Hal. Corderoy."

"Why isn't this a waste of time, Mr. Corderoy?"

Corderoy faltered, then quickly retreated into cynicism. "It is a waste of time," he said.

The professor smiled. "Ah, well then, tell us. Why *is* our enterprise a waste of time?"

"Because . . . we produce nothing consumed by the world outside of academia, and the opportunity cost of applying our intellects to something that's basically useless, aside from whatever personal satisfaction we get from it, when we could be building rockets or curing cancer. I mean, we can't all be physicists, but at least we could be building tables or filming amateur pornography or something that would actually get used by other humans!"

Professor Flannigan laughed. "Good points, all. But if it's a waste of time, why don't universities simply eliminate liberal arts programs?"

Corderoy scratched his chin, but the contemplative gesture belied a growing inner panic. Indeed, why not?

"From a Darwinian perspective," said Professor Flannigan, turning to the class, "professors will possess those traits that ensure the highest likelihood of survival, tenure for the professor and department funding for the species. As such, we English professors have, over time, ensured our own usefulness by creating texts so dense with inclusive language that only a member of the elect can decipher them. The university bureaucrat may wonder whether studying Derrida or Hegel truly does enhance a student's intellectual understanding of the world, and to whom does he turn for an expert opinion?"

"That's how the clergy survived for centuries," said the old guy at the end of the table. "They kept Mass in Latin, acting as translators for God."

"Exactly, Mr. Fulmer," Professor Flannigan said. "In this sense, then, professors don't have jobs because there are difficult books requiring explication; rather, difficult books exist so that professors can have jobs! That's assuming our enterprise is inherently useless, as Mr. Corderoy suggested. I submit that it is not."

But how could it not be? Montauk was preparing for war—maybe a war based on bad ideas, but regardless, what Montauk was doing had real risks, real consequences—and here Corderoy was, talking about fucking books.

"When we apply various theories to a particular text," Professor Flannigan said, "we learn something about the text and about the theory we are looking through, adding depth and intricacy to the body of our collective knowledge. Let's have an example, yes? Ms. . . ." He looked toward a girl who had a Swede's complexion and a Boston accent.

"Chelsea Harrow," she said. The Yale girl.

"Give us a text, Ms. Arrow."

"*Ulysses*?"

"Has anyone not read *Ulysses*?"

Corderoy had not read *Ulysses,* but he remained silent. A fat guy and the semi-cute brunette both raised their hands.

"Let's see if we can find something we're all familiar with," Professor Flannigan said. "Any cultural item whatsoever."

Corderoy racked his brain. *Huck Finn,* maybe? *Of Mice and Men*? The brunette asked if it had to be a book, then mumbled some suggestion. Her nose was too narrow.

"Remind me of your name again, dear," Professor Flannigan said.

"Maria Sardi."

"Thank you, Ms. Sardi. Has anyone not seen the *Star Wars* films?" He pronounced it *filims,* with an extra vowel.

Wait, what?

No hands were raised. "Perfect." Professor Flannigan stood and began pacing in front of the blackboard. "We'll begin with New Criticism, which argued that a literary text ought to be regarded as autonomous, that the intentions of the author and the historical circumstances in which the work appeared are extraneous."

Corderoy felt violated. *Star Wars* didn't belong here. It wasn't meant to be taken apart by the cold intellectual grip of academics. He thought back to the last time he'd watched *The Empire Strikes Back.* With Mani. She had stared at him lovingly as an uncontrollable child's grin had overtaken his face. *Star Wars* was the one place in his life where he was totally sincere, without a shield of irony.

"Thus," Professor Flannigan went on, "when Han Solo says that the *Millennium Falcon* made the Kessel Run in less than twelve parsecs, a unit of distance, not time, New Criticism would say that the ignorance of George Lucas is irrelevant. The work stands alone. The Kessel Run, perhaps, can be accomplished in varying distances, the more difficult or dangerous routes being shorter."

Corderoy had been staring at the dust motes in the sunlight, but now he gave his full attention to the professor, who was scribbling on the blackboard as he said, "Archetypal Criticism, based on the work of Jung and Campbell, sees literature as instantiating patterns and mythic formulae present in the collective unconscious. Any fool can see that *Star Wars* fits Campbell's hero-quest framework: boy leaves home, boy finds mystic guide, boy rejects destiny, finds magic sword, loses mystic guide, accepts destiny, travels to underworld, meets father, transcends father, kills father, redeems father, et cetera."

Corderoy could feel his pulse increasing.

"How about from a psychoanalytic perspective?"

Sandy Bigjaw suggested that the Dark Side was pure id. She misquoted the Emperor's speech to Luke: " 'Give in to your fear, take your weapon, strike me down.' "

"Brilliant," Professor Flannigan said. "And the Jedi are the superego, constantly self-monitoring, making the sound moral judgments for the good of the Republic. A Jedi would rather die than give in to temptation. How about Marxist theory?"

A student with neatly parted hair and black Gucci eyeglasses cleared his throat. "We could analyze the struggle between the proletariat Rebels and the bourgeois Empire as a form of dialectical materialism," he said.

Professor Flannigan scrawled *dialectical materialism* on the blackboard. Corderoy suddenly felt small and excited, like a child at an amusement park, not tall enough for any of the rides. Here they were, in grad school, talking about *Star Wars*! And it wasn't terrible at all. It was like seeing it again for the first time, but through his adult's eyes. Though everyone else seemed to have a leg up on the proper lingo.

"Post-colonialism," Professor Flannigan said, "might examine the Jedi as an ethnic group in Diaspora. Yoda and Obi-Wan and the few remaining Jedi having fled the galactic center for the remote planets of Dagobah and Tatooine. How about existentialism?"

Maria Sardi said, "Han Solo."

"Go on," Professor Flannigan said.

Corderoy stared at Maria Sardi, prepared to judge the living shit out of her for whatever minor interpretive flaw she might apply to this sacred fictional personage.

"At least in the beginning," she said with the ghost of an Italian accent—*een the begeening*—"Han Solo could be seen as an atheist existentialist. He's a mercenary by trade, and for him the world has no inherent truth or meaning. The Empire is no worse than the Republic."

Maria Sardi: officially cute.

"Hokey religions and ancient weapons," Corderoy said to her.

"Excellent," Professor Flannigan said. "And from the phenomenological point of view, the Force can be seen as an expression of yearning for a world not reducible to the phenomena of conscious experience. A desire to be certain of more than merely our perceptions. Obi-Wan tells Luke to put down the blast shield on his visor, to not let his eyes deceive him, to trust his feelings."

A round-faced Korean student chimed in. "I was thinking about Noam Chomsky's propaganda model of mass media. That all sources of information are biased. Maybe that can explain certain inconsistencies. Like, why are the storm troopers, highly trained shock troops, incapable of hitting the heroes with a blaster shot?"

"Brilliant, Mr. Lee. The movies themselves are a form of Rebel propaganda, with a Rebel bias. Is anyone familiar with semiotics?"

"The study of signs," said the old guy, "and how they signify."

"Exactly. We could look at the significance of light saber colors (blue/green versus red), the shapes of starships (the Empire's are angular, the Rebellion's rounded), and the various ritualistic phrases (*May the Force be with you* or *What is thy bidding, my master*). And on a macro level, the binary opposition that gives each element meaning, for there would be no Dark Side without the Light.

"The structuralists might say that upon breaking *Star Wars* down to its mythemes, the component parts of the larger mythos, we see that the actions of Luke, the orphaned hero, are significant only in the larger mythical structure, which contains the frail king and hidden father (Vader) and the prophecy (bringing balance to the Force), which itself is a kind of structure that binds everything together. And post-structuralism and deconstruction are what allow us to inhabit all these interpretations simultaneously.

"That was fun, yes? I hope so, for your sake, because that's what we'll be doing this semester. Is it a waste of time? We could be carpenters or pornographers, after all." He nodded toward Corderoy. "And chances are you're not going to be Aristotle. But I offer you this to ponder: the search for human meaning—what could be more important?—must happen through intellectual investigation that is not tethered to empirical knowledge or scientific progress. Where would we be if we didn't have a million people searching for the truth?"

Professor Flannigan handed out the syllabus and said, "That's it for today. And one last thing. Some of you were silent during our discussion. I hope you'll learn to participate. If you weren't familiar with *Star Wars*, you should have spoken up. I'm looking at you, Mr. Corderoy."

Corderoy drew back, astonished. He, of all people? Of course he'd seen it. He wanted to explain that he'd been enthralled, but the words caught in his throat.

"There's no shame in not having read a book or having seen a *filim*."

Corderoy nodded and threw his spiral notebook into his messenger bag—the only thing he'd written all class was *Lit Crit I* at the top of the first page. As he stood up and shuffled out of the room, he decided to buy a copy of *Ulysses* on the way home.

10

When Corderoy arrived back at the apartment that evening—it didn't feel like *his* apartment, not yet—he was feeling high, congenial, horny, even. Since leaving Seattle, leaving Mani, and arriving in a foreign setting with a host of new romantic possibilities, he had been as prone to erections as his eighth-grade self. And the exhilarating discussion in class that afternoon, combined with his incipient crush on Maria Sardi, had made him antsy. His roommate, Tricia, was sitting on the couch, watching news coverage of some protest. A bottle of Johnnie Black sat on the coffee table in front of her.

"What are they protesting?" he asked.

"The RNC. They're saying it was almost half a million people today."

"The what?"

Tricia laughed. "The Republican National Convention. In New York City. Where have you been?"

Corderoy gave a whimsical shrug.

"Want some whiskey?"

"Sure," he said. He went to the kitchen and rinsed a glass from the sink. He got some ice and looked again at the refrigerator magnet he'd scoffed at the day he'd arrived, FEMINISM IS THE RADICAL NOTION THAT WOMEN ARE PEOPLE.

He sat down next to Tricia and poured his whiskey slowly, listening to the ice ping and pock. Then he refilled her glass, neat, while Tricia took her pack of American Spirits from the table and lit one.

Police Commissioner Raymond W. Kelly was saying there had been nearly two hundred arrests for disorderly conduct, that nine people were charged with felony assault on officers.

"I knew a cop who worked the WTO riots," Corderoy said. "Got to shoot rubber bullets and tear gas at people."

"That's awful," Tricia said, turning to face him. "Shooting people with rubber bullets sucks for the cops, too. You talk about it like it's cool." Her cat, Smokey, leapt up on the couch and curled her head into Tricia's scratching fingers.

Corderoy didn't know how to respond to that. In the three days he'd known Tricia Burnham, he'd stumbled into arguments about social welfare, about the justness of war, about heteronormativity. Each and every time, she'd stymied him. He knew that if they got into it now, she'd be better able to point to an important book or a particular theory to justify her position. "I actually read *The Road to Serfdom*," she'd said in their last argument.* He wanted to win, to beat her, and he couldn't do it with wit or charm. That, more than anything else, made him want to fuck Tricia Burnham.

She was certainly cute. And she maintained herself well—her bangs were neatly cropped, her eyebrows plucked, her nails painted. She was wearing a black skirt that emphasized her trim waist.

He knew the basics, that she was getting her Ph.D. in International Relations and Comparative Politics at the Kennedy School ("The what?" he'd asked, feeling stupid. "Oh, it's Harvard"). That she was from New York. That she had expensive tastes (Johnnie Black). That she was even more left-wing than he was. That she was sharp and sincere. Most of all, that she was single.

"Have you been in any protests?" Corderoy asked.

"February last year. In New York."

"I think I'd feel dumb holding up a sign in a crowd of signs."

"I saw a guy on stilts dressed as the Grim Reaper, wearing an American-flag cape—to protest nothing less than the organized killing of human beings. But hey, if looking stupid and holding a sign draws attention to an important issue . . ."

---

* Tricia, in fact, had read just under half of *The Road to Serfdom*.

"Never thought of it that way," Corderoy said. He leaned forward, made eye contact, and the conversation moved to more personal topics.

Tricia Burnham, surprisingly, was only twenty-one. He'd thought from how she talked, how she carried herself, that she was at least twenty-five. She'd started at Barnard at sixteen with AP credits and had graduated by nineteen, taking summer courses. She'd spent a year as an intern with a documentary team on a First Nations reservation, making a film about Native American adoption and child welfare. Then she'd entered the Kennedy School. She was a pescetarian, a bisexual. She smoked only American Spirits because they donated their profits to the Native American Rights Fund. She'd rowed crew her freshman year at Barnard, but she'd stopped to focus on her studies. Since the summer, she'd been volunteering for the Kerry campaign, organizing bus trips to bring college kids from Boston and New York to canvass in Ohio and Pennsylvania. She was leaving Saturday morning on a twelve-hour bus trip to Meigs County, Ohio, an important swing county for a crucial swing state. And did he want to join her? Lie and say yes? No, the truth: that wasn't really his thing. And did she want another drink? Yes, she did. She was Jewish—her mother's maiden name was Meyer—and she'd grown up in Westchester. Corderoy didn't know what or where Westchester was, but he was pretty sure it meant privilege. He wondered if all her humanitarian activities came from a place of guilt. She had a "marking" (tattoo) on her shoulder blade: the tribal symbol from the Oglala Sioux, a circle of nine tepees representing the nine districts of the Pine Ridge Indian Reservation. Her shoulder was pale and pocked with small freckles. He wanted to touch it.

"Do you have any tattoos?" she asked.

He did. He lifted up his left sleeve and showed Tricia his. It was a crescent-shaped symbol with a fleur-de-lis-ish point coming out of the inner curve to make a sort of birdlike shape. "I served in the Rebel Alliance," he said.

"What's that?"

"The Rebel Alliance insignia. From *Star Wars*."

"Wow, you are a dork."

"Nerd, not dork."

"Okay, nerd." She smiled and topped off their whiskeys. "So you're a Rebel supporter, huh?"

"You think I'd support the evil Galactic Empire?"

"Doesn't the rebellion want a society ruled by the . . ."

"The Jedi."

"Yeah, the Jedi, aren't they like a caste of warrior priests? It's like the worst parts of pre- and post-revolutionary Iran put together."

He didn't know shit about Iran—though he really ought to have, after months with Mani—so he couldn't contradict Tricia. But talking *Star Wars* was a game he could win.

"This isn't the messy real world," he said. "In this universe, the Light Side of the Force is, like, objectively good."

"Well, that doesn't mean the movie's not racist."

Corderoy was speechless.

"You never noticed? I mean, the evil black bad guy, the blond-haired, blue-eyed hero."

"C'mon. It's more like a critique of American imperialism or something. The Jedi are like an ethnic group in diaspora. And Darth Vader, in the third movie, he takes his helmet off, and he's a white dude."

"That's even more offensive. It's like blackface. It has to be a white guy running the Galactic Empire." A devilish grin.

Corderoy had a dim awareness that Tricia was doing this just to get a reaction out of him, but it was working too well for that awareness to matter. "But black people—I mean, African-Americans—love *Star Wars*."

"Just like they love fried chicken."

"That's not what I meant. I mean, who's it hurting? If it is racist, it's to such a small degree that it's not worth bothering about—the most pragmatic choice is to simply enjoy it for what it is."

Tricia put down her glass and shook her head in silent laughter. "Hal, chill out. I'm just jerking your chain."

Corderoy took a deep breath and tried to laugh.

"Partly, anyway," she said. "I think it's important to recognize these things, even if they are small. It's the subtle racism that's most pervasive."

Tricia pulled out another American Spirit, put it to her lips, and flicked her lighter. Corderoy stared at her as she took a drag; she held the cigarette out to him. He took it in his hand and hesitated. "No thanks," he said, handing it back. "I'm still quitting."

"Heard that before," Tricia said.

Corderoy turned back to the protest footage on TV. He finished his whiskey. He said good night, then shut himself in his bedroom.

He was beginning to think that he'd made a mistake in moving to Boston. He realized the foolishness in making such a quick judgment—one should expect some acclimation time when moving across country—but the realization only propelled him further backward through the deterministic chain of mistakes that had led him here. He began obsessing once again about the night he'd left Mani at the party, the night she'd been hit by a car. This was not only a moral mistake but a pragmatic mistake, for it was absolutely clear, at this hour of the evening, alone, in Cambridge, that Mani's presence was the one thing that could make him happy. He thought of her hair, black with streaks of dark blue, of the small tattoos on her lower back, cello f-holes; he thought of how, when she would sit on his lap at parties, he would rub the skin of her kneecap through the hole in her jeans, with barely perceptible motions, as intimate and discreet as sex in a room with other sleeping people. Corderoy began stroking himself, his eyes closed, his hardness dependent entirely on memory—a skill he'd allowed to atrophy in the age of Internet porn—and it felt good, not just physically but morally, as if there were a purity in the act that somehow mitigated, however slightly, the wrong he'd done. The more he thought of this, though, the more it seemed like a crock of shit, and the dirtier he felt recalling the feel of Mani's mouth. Cigarette smoke crept under his door from the living room, and his dick went limp in his hand.

He had yet to buy sheets, and the stitching on the bare mattress scratched his naked skin. He became fixated on the tack holes in the walls, periodically illuminated by the waves of light that bent across the room whenever a car drove by. He visually estimated the dimensions of whatever posters, pictures, or items had been there. This, perhaps, had been a butterfly case. That had been an ovoid mirror. There, a vertical sequence of three postcards or photographs. From a friend's wedding? Dark images, drinks held aloft, faint, almost disconcerted smiles.

11

Corderoy and Tricia got off the T at Washington Street. After crossing several rusted, industrial railroad tracks, they turned down an alley and arrived in front of a large red-brick building. A small crowd stood outside, smoking in the warmth of the evening, and the noise of dozens more emanated from a lit doorway behind them.

It was the first Friday in September, and they were in SoWa, that part of Boston with the highest concentration of old factories converted into lofts and art studios. Corderoy's classmate Marcus Lee had announced to the class that morning that he would be attending First Fridays and that there would be a lot of great exhibits and free wine, of course. Corderoy wasn't thrilled about going to an art opening. But then Maria Sardi had said, "Count me *een*."

He shared two classes with Maria, and during that first week Maria had gone from the semi-cute girl with the too-thin nose to the cute girl who knew her *Star Wars* to the smart and assertive girl with the mesmerizing face, eyes large and dark like a cow's, voice like an unripe blackberry. That evening, as Corderoy trimmed his beard and brushed his teeth, he began to look forward to the opening as if it were a play-off game of some undetermined sport, as if he were the star player and his sweetheart would be watching from the bleachers. The anxiety and thrill of possible triumph was something he'd likely gleaned from television—not having played any sports in high school—and that feeling seemed to transcend the particulars of the event. Bright lights, crowds, probably some grass. He didn't bother imagining a ball of any sort.

When Tricia saw him getting ready to go out, something he hadn't done once yet, she asked where he was going. He told her, and she said, "Oh, my friend's in that show," and invited herself along. Initially, he was miffed at her sudden intrusion into his budding social life. But then he reflected that it could work to his advantage, having Tricia with him. Girls probably assumed all guys were untrustworthy schemers. But a guy with female friends, he was like a guy with a wedding ring: safe.

On the way there, Tricia had told him about some installations she'd seen at the last First Fridays, and Corderoy told her about Montauk and the Encyclopaedists parties, but in reminiscing about how fun they had been, he realized that they belonged to a particular time and place, and the memory prodded a large bruise he'd forgotten in the chaos of settling in a new city.

Inside the building, Corderoy slipped through the crush of people and made his way to the folding table where they were handing out wine in small plastic cups. He handed one to Tricia, and they pushed farther into the gallery. Marcus Lee spotted Corderoy and waved.

Corderoy made introductions, and Marcus shook Tricia's hand in a professional manner. He was dressed in loafers, khakis, a white button-up tucked in around his belly, but no tie.

"Anyone else here yet?" Corderoy asked.

"Ray and Chelsea are in here somewhere."

"Cool. Wasn't Maria going to come?" Corderoy spoke distantly while poring over the crowd, his voice moving at the speed of his visual scan.

"I think so," Marcus said. "But I haven't seen her."

"This is really great," Tricia said.

"It is?" Corderoy asked. She was staring at a video projected onto the nearest wall. It was of a rather comfortable-looking, unused couch that would have fit nicely on a showroom floor but was, instead, in a field. For a moment, Corderoy thought it was a still photo, but a light breeze occasionally bent a stalk of grass from its upright position. The video had been running for an hour and a half, according to the time stamp in the lower-right-hand corner.

Was that supposed to be deep? Or make him question the idea of the art space or what belonged in it? Or the nature of time and the value of subtle minutiae? At the Encyclopaedists parties, the art was an elaborate joke, so he and Montauk had always spoken about it with the utmost pretention and seriousness. Which paid great social dividends. But here, the art wasn't offered up as comedy.

Corderoy emptied his cup and said, "You think our grandkids will regard this sort of thing as important and subversive?"

Tricia smirked. "You should be careful," she said under her breath. "The artist could be any one of these people."

"There are artists here?" Corderoy said.

"Maybe the piece is making a political statement," she said, "about the excesses of Western culture. We have near-infinite resources, and we use them to record a couch sitting in a field. We could be documenting the numerous atrocities happening across the globe, but we have a live feed of a couch. And that's what we choose to watch."

"I don't," Corderoy said. "I'd rather watch Ultimate Fighting."

"I'm not saying it's amazing," Tricia said. "I mean, we think of the Renaissance as some awesome time, but really, only like five or six guys come to mind. If you were there, you'd be surrounded by wannabe Raphaels all day. So what do you do? Laugh at them, then go watch people beat each other up? Or try to enter the conversation, like Raphael would, and think, I see what you're doing, but here's what would make it better."

Corderoy withdrew into his wine cup.

Marcus smiled thoughtfully at Tricia while nodding, then raised a finger and said, "One could argue that the installation is about the nature of modern desire. We've been programmed to demand constant entertainment, and so a scene like this, subtle and bucolic, is experienced as boredom." He spoke like a museum docent reciting a well-practiced speech. "It's about how modernity changes the size of our appetite for spectacle and the length of our attention span. That's the image of a field in a slight breeze."

Corderoy scanned for Maria again and saw a group of people taking turns reaching inside a wooden box.

"It's almost as if the couch is a representation of contemporary American culture," Marcus continued. "The subtlety of the installation is not dynamic enough for us, even though it's far more dynamic and alive then we are, in our couchlike passivity. Or, more specifically, the couch represents the modality with which we experience—"

"No. No jargon," Corderoy interrupted. "No modalities. This couch is American culture? No way. Where's the imprint of our fat asses? The cigarette burns. Where's the empty Doritos bag?"

"That's a good point, Hal," Marcus said. "You know, Foucault wrote about what he called 'strategies' and 'tactics' in our culture." He made quotation marks with his fingers without smirking or moving his eyebrows even slightly.

"Anybody want more wine?" Corderoy interrupted again. Tricia's cup was still half-full.

"I don't drink," Marcus said.

"Well, I'll be back." Corderoy shouldered through the crowd to get another plastic cup of merlot. He didn't like crowds; he often developed high-anxiety palm sweat when crammed into a strange room with unfamiliar people. When he was sober, that is. Thus, he set about adjusting his mood, telling the lady behind the wine table that he was getting an extra cup for his friend, an excuse that she didn't need or care for, but which Corderoy felt compelled to provide anyway. He turned around and nearly bumped into Maria. She cocked her head to the side and smiled at him, then glanced down at his two cups of wine.

"Hey!" Corderoy said, handing her a cup. "Saw you come in." Smooth.

"Thanks," Maria said. Her fingers brushed his as she took it.

"Everyone's back this way," Corderoy said, anxious to have Maria see him with Tricia. They worked through the crowd to the video installation, but Tricia and Marcus were gone. Corderoy spotted them across the room and was about to lead Maria there, but she was fixated on the couch. "I think I like this," she said.

"We were just talking about this piece and how it represents modern desire, for Americans, in our couchlike passivity, you know?" God, why was he saying that? He took a big gulp of wine.

They found Marcus standing in front of a large wooden thronelike chair. Tricia was nearby, talking to a tall guy in leather pants and a partially unbuttoned shirt.

Maria circled the piece, Corderoy at her side. The back of the chair, which was about six feet tall, was actually a bookshelf, stuffed with books and sealed over with a sheet of Plexiglas. The armrests of the chair folded open to reveal more hidden books. A few people had removed these and were examining them.

"Finally found something you like?" Tricia called to him.

Corderoy smiled at her, then turned back to Maria and tapped her on the shoulder. "Uh." He swallowed. "Come meet my friend."

They approached Tricia and Leather Pants.

"It's kind of cool," Corderoy said after introducing Maria and Tricia. Easy enough. Now just say smart things. "But it's kind of inconsistent. Like, why are the books in the armrests accessible but the ones in the back are sealed under Plexiglas?" He stared at the chair for a moment. When neither Tricia nor Leather Pants responded, he said, "I find that . . . problematic."

"Hal, this is Dacey," Tricia said. "That's his piece."

"Oh. So . . . why the Plexiglas?"

"Why do you think?" Dacey asked.

Corderoy stuttered.

"The bookshelf is where you expect to access books," Maria said. "But here it's sealed. The books you can access are hidden away. Maybe that says something about the knowledge we display and the knowledge we hoard and their relative values."

"That's great," said Dacey. "I should hire you to write my grant proposals." He gave her a friendly punch on the shoulder. Maria blushed.

This wasn't going well. "Why did you pick those books?" Corderoy asked. "I saw *Don Quixote* back there, and that Churchill biography."

"I chose them for the color on the spine," Dacey said.

"What? That's like sacrilege."

"You're still thinking about these objects as books," he said. "Here they perform as representations of books. Or, rather, representations of the idea of books. Like your girlfriend said, the ones behind glass are what you display for others. The content doesn't matter."

"Oh, I'm not, we're not," Maria said, glancing between Dacey and Corderoy.

"My bad," Dacey said. "I'm curious what you think of this piece by my friend Mark." And just like that, he put his arm around her shoulder and guided her away. Corderoy stood there, aghast. Tricia gave him a pitying look, then turned to follow them.

Corderoy went back to the wine table, got two more cups, and downed one as he worked back through the crowd. There they were, Tricia, Dacey, and Maria, looking at the wooden box with the hole in it, Dacey leaning over Maria as she felt around inside. Corderoy stopped short. He couldn't join them. Instead, he sat down on Dacey's throne. The panel under his ass shifted. He stood and opened it. There were books in there, too. He pulled one out at random, closed the seat, sat back down, and crossed his legs. It was *The Stranger,* the Vintage paperback with the big sun on the cover and all those Arab faces, translated by Stuart Gilbert. He'd read this translation in high school and had fallen in love with it, but had never been able to find it since.

"You shouldn't be doing that, Hal."

It was Marcus Lee. Corderoy read out loud the last sentence of Part I of *The Stranger*—his favorite sentence, the one that always tipped him off to an inferior translation: " 'And each successive shot was another loud, fateful rap on the door of my undoing.' "

"Hal."

"What? Sitting here?"

"It's an installation. You can't just sit on it."

Dacey approached, shaking his head as if looking at a bad dog.

"Oh, is this seat taken?" Corderoy asked.

"C'mon, man," Dacey said. Maria was standing a few paces behind with Tricia.

"All right, bad joke," Corderoy said. He stood up, but in so doing, he knocked over his cup of wine. It spilled on the seat and began to seep into the compartment where the books were stored.

"Aww, shit," Dacey said, wiping the wine off with his palm. Corderoy stood there, not knowing what to do or say.

Marcus Lee pulled some napkins from his shoulder bag.

When Dacey had soaked up most of the wine, he put the sopping mess of napkins in Corderoy's hands and said, "Do me a favor. There's a garbage can. Near the exit."

"Yeah, sure," Corderoy said. "I was just leaving anyway."

Marcus shrugged and looked at his feet. "See you in class?"

"Yeah." Corderoy glanced at Maria, who was biting her lip, then at Tricia, who was covering her mouth so she wouldn't laugh. He turned and walked toward the exit, giving the wad of napkins a forceful toss into the garbage can before entering the black, industrial night, passing through the crowd of smokers out front.

He was drunk enough that he had to watch his step as he crossed the old railroad tracks, but in focusing on his feet, he failed to notice the chain-link fence on the other side of the tracks, the fence that would have been hard to see anyway, given the lack of streetlights. It was into this fence that Corderoy walked face-first, indenting his forehead and causing him to stumble backward over the train tracks. He fell squarely on his tailbone, causing an instant flash of pain. He rolled onto his side and lay still, trying not to wonder if anyone standing out front had seen him.

When he got home, his tailbone was still aching. He grabbed the bottle of Johnnie Walker from Tricia's room and took a swig, then went into the kitchen and emptied the ice trays into a Ziploc. Back in his room, he sat on that cold uncomfortable lump. He hated icing bruises and bumps, but the pain in his coccyx was worse than the pain of prolonged contact with ice. He took out his phone and scrolled through his address book. He wanted to call someone, someone back home. Not his parents, not any of his friends from work. He wanted to call Montauk. But Montauk had left for Iraq already. He could leave a voicemail. He hit Send, but before the call connected, he hung up.

He groped around in the dark for his laptop. He navigated to the "Encyclopaedists" article on Wikipedia. He stared at it dumbly for a minute, feeling the white glow of his screen bathe his wine-warmed face like a campfire, then he clicked edit.

12

Tricia had always felt she was destined to do great things, but what those things were had stayed hidden in a warm humanitarian cloud of possibility. And that vagueness had been rankling her since the anti-war protest last March—a die-in on Boylston Street along Boston Common. They'd smoked and laughed and tried to outdo one another in their death poses, tongues hanging out of their mouths, eyes rolled back. There were tens of thousands of people. Tricia could smell weed smoke in the air around her. Later in the day, her friend Erica parked herself in front of the entrance to a government building. And though Tricia had been too timid to join her, she'd applauded Erica's commitment. Her willingness to stand out from the crowd of protesters and risk arrest. Which was exactly what happened. Tricia's heart leapt as the policeman slipped zip ties around Erica's wrists, but as he escorted her away, Erica looked back over her shoulder and gave Tricia a sly grin. Tricia looked around at the people, the chanting, the signs, and something seemed off. She'd seen the footage of protests from the civil rights era. Nobody was smiling at Birmingham. In the days after, she heard Erica retell the story half a dozen times with exuberance, as if it had been the opening night of her first Broadway play. Tricia couldn't muster the enthusiasm. With every retelling, it came more and more into focus: their brand of protest was mere theater, self-indulgence. Tricia had no interest in being a performer. She wanted to be something more than that, but without any clear idea of how she would

help the world, she was no different from all the other campus activ-
ists. That all changed the day she met Luc Dubois at the reception for
a Chris Hedges reading; her future began crystallizing as fast as she
could imagine it. A life with real risk, real stakes.

She sat down on the edge of the booth facing the entrance so that
she could watch for him. Jenny Yi slid into the seat across from her,
next to Jeff Alessi.

"So what exactly does this guy do for *Truthout*?" Jenny asked.

"He's a photographer," Tricia said. "*Mother Jones* and *Democracy
Now!* just ran some of his photos. I'm sure he'll explain when he gets
here." She was proud that she'd had the guts to ask Luc to join her and
her classmates at the bar—she had actually offered to buy him a drink.

"How was the reading?" Jeff asked.

"I loved it," Jenny said. "Have you read his book?"

"The one about the Balkans? What's it called?"

"*War Is a Force That Gives Us Meaning*," Tricia said, giving the title
just a bit of stank.

"It's about why war exists," Jenny said. "People feel like their lives
are directionless or untethered, but in war, life has purpose."

"That title is hawkish," Jeff said. "From what I hear, Hedges isn't
exactly a pacifist."

"He has a measured position," Jenny said. "I respect that. He urges
responsibility and humility in war. But yeah, he's not a pacifist. I bet
that bothers you, doesn't it, Tricia?"

It did bother Tricia that Hedges wasn't a pacifist. He ignored the
fact that people found meaning in all kinds of peaceful ways, some by
directly opposing war, which was, at its core, the violent imposition of
one people's meaning on another. She wanted to get into it with Jenny
because she knew she could win. *Really, Jenny?* she imagined herself
saying. *Is rape a force that gives rape victims meaning?* But she didn't
want to be shouting into Jenny's face when Luc arrived. The server
came by, saving Tricia from having to answer Jenny's question. Jeff
ordered a Stella, Jenny Yi a glass of white wine (of course), and Tricia
ordered a Scotch, neat. Jenny raised an eyebrow.

"So this Luc guy," Jenny said, "he's French or something?"

"He's Belgian," Tricia said. "He was working the crowd at the Chris

Hedges reception, and a lot of people seemed to know who he was. We had a great conversation about charities and the problems of bureaucratic overhead. He's pretty well-connected in the human rights world."

The drinks came, and the three of them took tentative sips. No one said anything for a moment. Tricia stared at a knot in the wood paneling that reflected the dim yellow lamplight of the bar, and she thought about the wood-paneled bars across the country where privileged people like her were paying ten dollars for a glass of whiskey, trying to solve the world's problems, thinking about a boy.

Jenny began to say, "I bet he's—"

Tricia interrupted her. "So, I got a new housemate."

"Oh yeah?" Jeff said.

"Strange guy. He's super nerdy. Even has a *Star Wars* tattoo."

Jenny laughed. "Is he cute?"

"I guess . . . maybe. He's lanky. And he acts kind of dumb."

"A dumb nerd?" Jeff said.

"I don't think he's actually dumb. He just likes to act that way. He's one of those guys who probably grew up thinking he was a genius, and when he figured out he wasn't, he decided intelligence was only cool if you were cynical about it."

Shifting the conversation to Hal had calmed Tricia's nerves, but they tensed again the very next second, when Luc Dubois walked through the door. He waved from across the room. He wore a tweed blazer and an English driving cap that matched his slacks. Tricia's smile was enormous until she saw, a few steps behind him, a woman.

"Hallo, Tricia," Luc said. "I hope you don't mind my bringing a friend? Susan. From Iraq Body Count."

"No, of course not! Tricia Burnham, very pleased to meet you. And these are my classmates from the Kennedy School, Jeffrey and Jennifer."

"Hello!" Susan spoke with an English accent. A Londoner, it turned out. She looked to be in her late twenties, and well put together, although Tricia noticed (with a bit of unintentional glee) that at least this Brit's teeth played into the stereotype. Susan sat on the other side of Luc, who had to push himself right up against Tricia to make enough room.

A wave of anxiety rippled through her. She hadn't felt nervous around a guy since high school. It wasn't just that Luc was handsome, that he was intelligent—she peered inward, not trying to will away the nervousness so much as understand its origin—it wasn't just that he was respected and connected. It was that Luc Dubois represented clarity of vision.

"It's a bit morbid to say, right? 'Hallo, I'm from Iraq Body Count'?" Luc said.

Susan laughed. "We usually just say IBC at the office."

Jenny seemed impressed.

Luc had taken off his cap to reveal jet-black hair that was clipped short and definitely receding, although in a cute way that complemented his face. He spoke perfect English with a nice not-quite-French accent. He'd been to Baghdad once, he told them (an absolutely humbling experience), and he was going back in late January with a colleague from *Democracy Now!* to work as an unembedded journalist.

"It's a real problem," Luc said. "How can journalists be objective when they rely on soldiers to take them around, protect them. We've spoken with editors at dozens of publications, from *Truthout* to the *IPS*. Even *The Guardian*. They all say the same thing: they need more sources on the ground, sources not sheltered behind the fence, constantly escorted. At best, the reporters from the major networks and newspapers are seeing only one side of things. At worst, they are willing vehicles for military propaganda."

"It's just you and your colleague?" Tricia asked.

"William, yes. He'll be the primary writer," Luc said. "But we're hoping to assemble a survey team. To help document the toll the war is taking on Iraqi civilians. We may bring one or two more people. But it all depends on funding. We've got a grant application in to The Investigative Fund."

"Well, I'd love to go!" Tricia blurted out. Eyebrows arched all around.

"Tricia, what about spring semester?" Jenny said.

"I've been looking for an independent study, and this is perfect. I'm planning on doing human rights NGO administration after I graduate, and this would be great experience."

"I welcome your enthusiasm," Luc said. "But it's in Baghdad, you know, and we won't just be in the Green Zone. We'll be going out into the city. Alone. However glamorous 'unembedded journalist' may sound, it basically means we're doing this DIY, without monetary or legal support from a news organization."

"I understand. But this is important work, and I bet I've got just as much war zone experience as anyone else who'd be interested, unless you have a bunch of ex-commandos knocking on your door."

Luc smiled. "That's true, my inbox is not full of commandos' résumés."

Tricia could feel sweat prickle on her forehead as everyone at the table watched her. "Well, I probably can't, anyway," she said.

Luc stared at her, appraising her face—his gaze wasn't sexual, but it wasn't chaste, either. "Why not," he said. "Send me your résumé. If you're serious. Since it's not an official position, there aren't any official requirements."

Tricia brought her glass up to cover the smile spreading across her face. She inhaled, and the fumes from the Scotch burned up her sinuses. The conversation turned to European cinema, and Tricia tuned out as her mind leapt to the Middle East, she and Luc wearing keffiyehs and hurtling through dimly lit Baghdad streets. Of course, that was ridiculous. Baghdad was dangerous. It was only a year ago that Michael Kelly, the editor of the friggin' *Atlantic Monthly,* had been killed outside of Baghdad. And he'd been with US troops. She and Luc would be on their own. With Iraqi civilians, their lives constantly endangered by . . . by what, exactly? IEDs, insurgents. Those were words. She had no idea what was happening in Baghdad. And that was the point, wasn't it? People didn't know what was going on, not even the educated. The Unitarian church near Harvard Square broadcast a running tally of dead troops and civilians in Iraq, but what did that accomplish? Images, stories, that's what motivated people. And she could help bring them those stories, she really could.

———

Tricia's phone buzzed. She set down her coffee and flipped it open. Luc returning her text from two days ago. Finally.

yes it was a fun night. and I am still in town. whats up?

She replied immediately: *I'm going to the memorial at harvard in an hour. if you're interested.*

She sat in silence in front of the muted TV, sipping her coffee, as ABC's 9/11 coverage alternated between footage of the attack and the memorial service in progress at Ground Zero. She checked her phone. No response. She closed the phone, then flipped it open a second later.

would be great to see you.

And again.

susan too.

God, three texts in a row. Put the phone down.

Tricia zoned out to the silent image of the burning towers. She had been in Manhattan when it happened, but her experience of the actual attack was this same footage. She was in her junior year at Barnard and had even gone to her 9:10 class that morning—it wasn't until the second plane hit that terrorism occurred to anyone. She'd gone up with a crowd of bewildered students to the top floor of Sulzberger Tower, at 116th Street. All they could see was a distant pillar of smoke against an otherwise perfectly blue sky.

Tricia's friend Tamara was freaking out because she couldn't reach her father, who worked near the World Trade Center. Tricia tried to calm her down, but it was no use. Tamara took off running toward downtown. Tricia and a dozen others turned their confusion and their anger to helping in whatever way they could. They went down to St. Luke's to donate blood, but the hospital was already filled to capacity, the line of donors stretching out the door. They tried to take the subway to a different hospital, but the trains weren't running, so they walked three and a half miles to Harlem. They were greeted along the way with nods and hellos, as if the massive city had become a rural village. But even the Harlem Hospital was full. Up at this end of the island, they were powerless to help. On their walk back to the dorms, a guy in an Access-A-Ride handicapped van asked if they needed a lift. When he let them out at 116th, he said, "How much would a taxi be? Twenty dollars? You can just give me twenty." And Tricia had hated him for taking advantage, for being venal while lower Manhattan was burning. That was the first time she'd ever felt like punching someone in the face.

In her macro-econ class the next day, some people sat in gravid silence, while others left halfway through, quietly sobbing. Tricia simply couldn't focus. She made her way downtown after class but could get only as far as Fourteenth Street. She stood behind the police barricade and watched the crowd of manic citizens blocked off from access to their homes. Buzz. Flip.

susans left for london already. I may be able to go. have a few mtgs later. not going to be one of those god bless america things is it?

Hope not, Tricia typed, but she hesitated over the Send button. Didn't want to seem too eager. She set the phone down and looked back to the TV.

In the days after 9/11, she'd grown annoyed at the flurry of American flags and crisis patriotism in New York and across America. Even her friends were raving about Ani DiFranco's WTC poem, which Tricia could only interpret as angry, unthinking, and, well, stupid. Not that the "blame America" response didn't resonate with her. She was all too aware that she lived in a nation that clothed itself with the work of sweatshops, that drove SUVs powered by gas pipelines secured by propping up dictatorships. But it was ridiculous to say that bin Laden was justified by American imperialism. As if he were some modern-day Che Guevara. It wasn't that the US should have expected the attack. It wasn't that the flag wavers were sheep and she was justified in sneering at them. It was that she felt deeply, deeply complicit in it all—the comforts and satisfactions of her life had been built on America's shining successes as much as on its failures, failures ignored by the average person because they were uncomfortable to think about.

She hit Send.

Then there were the anthrax scares in October. Tamara forwarded her an e-mail just before the Halloween parade, saying there would be another terrorist attack—and this information was supposed to be trustworthy because it came from Israeli intelligence, and the Jewish community knew about these things. Tamara had been her best friend through their first two years at Barnard, but she'd changed that Tuesday, and their social interactions had become awkward. Her father hadn't been killed, but not being able to contact him that morning, when the cellular networks and landlines had been overwhelmed with traffic, knowing he was mere blocks from Ground Zero—Tamara had never escaped that fear. As a result, she hadn't ridden the subway since. It was beyond reason. And frankly, a little narcissistic, though Tricia could never have said that to Tamara. Tricia was grateful for how lucky she'd been, that she'd known only futility, unable to help a soul that day, that she hadn't been infected by that paralyzing fear. That she'd emerged determined to do some real good in the world, to fight the cause, not the symptom. But it still saddened her that she and Tamara had grown distant.

Buzz. Flip.

just checked my schedule. mtg on other side of town at 11. can't make it. Sorry.

No prob. Maybe next time.

Next time? Next 9/11 memorial. An entire year from now. Tricia sighed. She was about to close her phone, but instead she navigated to Tamara's name.

Never forget.

Tamara replied almost immediately. *Never forget.*

Tricia typed out, *How are you?*, then stared at her blinking cursor and deleted the message.

Corderoy stood in his bedroom, his ear to the door. He'd been avoiding Tricia since the art show last week. In fact, he'd been avoiding everyone. Everyone except characters in novels. He'd started reading *Ulysses* and found that he much preferred immersing himself in the "mind" of Leopold Bloom to actually interacting with other humans. For Bloom was, by virtue of being fictional, fixed in time, no matter how dynamic and lifelike he seemed. This made him easier to grapple with than real people. And Corderoy grappled with Bloom to such a degree that there was no room in his mind for Maria Sardi or even for Mani. It was a kind of isolation that left him stimulated and focused on his schoolwork. And he was beginning to like it. Satisfied that the living room was quiet, he opened his door.

There was Tricia sitting in front of the muted TV. She turned to him and for a split second her face slackened as if disappointed he wasn't someone else. "There's a memorial service at Harvard soon. You want to go?"

Go join a crowd of people. Fuck. No. He didn't even want to be talking to Tricia. "Memorial for what?" he said.

"Duh." She unmuted the TV. They were replaying footage of the Twin Towers billowing smoke, only this time with patriotic music in the background.

"I don't go in for that praying stuff."

"If you don't want to go, don't go," Tricia said. "But don't be disrespectful."

Corderoy went into the bathroom and drained his bladder. When he came out, he threw on a jacket and slipped into his shoes. He felt socially bound to say something, so he said, "I'm going to the store." Tricia glanced at him and shrugged, a response he was grateful for. He sauntered down the steps and outside, still wearing his flannel pajama pants.

After meandering through the aisles of the 7-Eleven, Corderoy bought a twelve-pack of Diet Coke and a can of Pringles. When he got back to his stoop, he realized he had forgotten his key. He rang the bell, but Tricia had apparently left. He stared at the door as if his frustration with his own stupidity could will it open. Then he collapsed on the stoop and cracked open a Diet Coke. As the sun warmed his face, he began to feel that the stoop was his stoop, his own small island, that the pedestrians passing by were distant ships on the horizon that had no intention of challenging his sovereignty.

A man in overalls walked up to the trash cans outside Corderoy's apartment and began to move them about, peering behind them.

Corderoy caught his eye, then looked away. Don't walk over here. Just don't.

"You live here?" the man asked with a noticeable Boston accent— live *heah*.

"Yep," Corderoy said.

"Seen any rats?"

"Nope."

"Good," the guy said. He maneuvered a trash can back into place. "I trouble you for a Diet Coke?"

His hand extended casually toward the box of soda. The hand was calloused and dirty, though the nails were well manicured. A pattern that, on closer inspection, recurred in many aspects of his appearance. His greasy brown hair, held back by a stained bandanna, only seemed to emphasize his high and noble forehead. His eyelids drooped down over his eyes in what would have indicated a stoner's disposition were it not for the eyes themselves, which were bluish-green and peered out with a brightness and curiosity emphasized by the polished wire frames of his glasses.

Corderoy handed him one in defeat. The guy sat down on the stoop next to him and, after a long gulp, said, "You remember where you was on 9/11?"

Corderoy focused intently on a manhole cover, wishing the guy would leave, but he just kept talking.

"I was at the dentist, had my mouth wide open with one of them rubber dams. And the dentist and all his assistants flicked on a TV somewhere and left me in the chair for five minutes. I couldn't see nothing but that overhead light, listening to that smooth jazz on the sound system and all them people behind me gasping and saying my God this, my God that. Never forget that dentist appointment."

"I guess that's our Kennedy moment, huh. Imagine how many people were taking a shit when it happened, and they'll remember that shit for the rest of their lives."

The man scrunched his mouth and rocked his head back and forth. "Not necessarily," he said. "They call 'em flashbulb memories. People tend ta remember where they was that day that best fits their personal narrative of the event. Say you was taking a shit. Would you remember that or making an omelet that morning? Depends on your personal involvement. And on what makes a betta story. Right?"

Corderoy, surrounded by collegiate transplants from other parts of the country, had rarely had the luxury of enjoying the blue-collar accent Boston was famous for—and he wondered if his unfamiliarity with it somehow magnified its effect to his ear. "I was in Seattle," he said. "It was seven in the morning. I'd been up all night playing *Counter-Strike*. I'm pretty sure I wasn't actually taking a shit."

"What's *Counter-Strike*?"

Counter-Strike was why Corderoy had almost dropped out of college. It was why he knew that an AK-47—though not as accurate as the M4A1 carbine—used a 7.62 millimeter bullet, higher caliber than the M4, which meant you could drop a target with two body shots. Of course, a headshot would drop the target in one, but for that, he preferred to whip out his .50 Desert Eagle. His mother had called him at seven a.m., thinking she'd be waking him up, and he'd picked up while playing, clamping the phone between his shoulder and his ear.

"Sorry to wake you, Hal."

"It's fine, Mom . . . what's up." He was the only player left on his team, and he'd just planted the explosives. They were playing a map called *de_inferno* that had the look and feel of a quaint Tuscan village. Why on earth terrorists would want to bomb a quaint Tuscan village was beyond him. There were three enemies closing in on his position, to kill him, defuse the bomb, or both.

"Turn on your TV," she said.

"I don't have TV, remember."

"Oh, that's right, you download things. Well, look online, then. I'm sure it's everywhere."

Fuck fuck fuck. He'd just strafed out from behind a large crate, firing a three-round burst from his AK, which had hit and killed one enemy. But he'd been hit by another, knocking him down to 12 health. He fled the piazza where he'd just planted the bomb. One more shot would take him out.

"New York was attacked. By terrorists," his mother said.

"What? Mom, hold on." He threw a flash bang into the piazza, then rushed in spraying with his AK. Most of his rounds missed, but the last few bullets lodged in the enemy's torso, and he collapsed near the bomb. Corderoy crept noiselessly behind a crumbling brick wall, then sat, hiding, waiting for the one remaining player to come out into the open. Only twenty-seven seconds left till the bomb exploded and he won the round. He reloaded his rifle.

"Hal. Listen, I know your friend Brian went to school in New York. The Twin Towers were hit by two airplanes."

"What?"

"Terrorists hijacked two airplanes and flew them into the Twin Towers. In Manhattan."

"Thanks, Mom. I'll check it out."

"And call Brian."

"Okay. Bye." His mother hung up and he let the phone drop to the floor. The enemy crept out from behind a crate, and Corderoy unloaded with his AK, hitting but not killing him. He was out of rifle ammo, so he pulled out his pistol as the return fire impacted the wall next to him. His heart was racing, and he'd stopped breathing. The adrenaline surged through him, and his eyes widened. A small pause in the gunfire and he leapt out and fired one shot from his Desert Eagle. It sailed right through the enemy's head. He took a deep breath and let his hands relax. Only then, basking in the glow of that power, the triumph of having killed his enemy before he could be killed, did he register what his mother had said. A terrorist attack. But he'd never been to New York. He didn't even know what the Twin Towers were. And he wasn't even friends with Brian anymore; he had no way of contacting him even if he wanted to. He shut down his computer and went to sleep.

Sitting on the stoop now, he felt guilty for that moment, though he never had before. Everybody had to be doing something when it happened. He had been planting bombs and firing an AK-47. He'd rather have been taking a shit.

"It's a video game," he said to the guy.

"Never really got into that stuff," the guy said. "Though I did a little programming back in the day." He stood up and took a key ring from his pocket. "Hey, thanks for the Coke," he said. "I gotta get inside and fix the water heater." *Watah heatah.*

"You're the . . ."

"The super, yeah. Name's Jack."

"Hal."

"You're locked out, aren't ya, Hal?"

Corderoy blushed, and Jack let him into the building.

13

Corderoy had already masturbated twice today—much needed head-clearing breaks between the three chapters of *Ulysses* he'd read—and now, too drained for a third go at it, he found himself browsing through girls on MySpace. The cold afternoon sun lit his room insufficiently, competing with the glow from his laptop screen.

There was an unreality to the social world of MySpace—a profile was, by its nature, a continually curated representation of the self. In this world, no one ever had a bad-hair day. The cookies always came out perfect. Nothing tedious. Nothing sad that was not also funny. It was thin, it was token, and it was the perfect substitution for the meaningful social world he was avoiding. In Seattle, he'd felt like the one guy outside of Plato's cave, seeing things for what they were rather than looking at shadows on the wall. And he'd had Montauk beside him to up his cool quotient. To go from that to friendless in Boston had been rough. And after his humiliation at First Fridays, after realizing how hard it would be to rebuild that kind of status, he had buried his head in schoolwork; he'd even gotten caught up in presidential politics, watching *The Daily Show* at night with Tricia—their only social time together. Last week, on his way home from class, he'd seen a guy about his age standing on the street corner, holding a clipboard, wearing a poncho, though it wasn't raining all that hard. He looked ridiculous.

"Registered to vote?" he'd asked.

"How much do you get paid?" Corderoy had said.

"I don't get paid. I'm a volunteer."

"And what if I'm planning to vote for Bush?"

"Hey, man. I'm not asking who you support. I'm just getting people registered."

Corderoy thought Bush was an idiot, and he was angry that American troops, including Montauk, were being sent to Baghdad, but he'd always distrusted large elections. He hadn't voted in 2000, when Gore had lost. Why bother replacing one rich Christian white guy with another rich Christian white guy? But here was this volunteer, out on the street corner simply to promote the health of the democracy. He'd taken the form and filled it out.

He began reading political blogs. He subscribed to *Truthout*'s mailing list. And when he wasn't reading and writing short response papers for his classes, he was getting drawn into e-mail debates with his uncle about the Patriot Act, about the possible link between Al-Qaeda and Saddam. But as much as he distracted himself with these new passions, he was lonelier than he'd ever been. He was in no condition for an actual human relationship; what he needed was nineteen-year-old ♥Sylvie♥.

He scrolled through her gaudy pink profile. She had a short brunette bob and she held a classic MySpace pose, head angled up and to the right, eyes looking at the camera in her left hand, shooting for mysterious and seductive. She was beautiful, of course, but she also looked silly and immature, and it was that more than anything else that drew Corderoy to her. He read through her details.

Status:	Single
Here for:	Networking, Dating, Serious Relationships, Friends
Orientation:	Straight
Hometown:	Boston
Body Type:	5'1" / Slim / Slender
Ethnicity:	White / Caucasian
Zodiac Sign:	Scorpio
Smoke / Drink:	No / No
Children:	Undecided
Education:	Some College

| Occupation: | Student |
| Income: | Less than $30,000 |

Her top eight friends had names like Gadget, Shawn, and Fire-cracker. Her favorite movies: "Disney! TenthingsIhateaboutyou, anything with Edward Norton! Indiana Jones omgNightmare before Christmas." Music: Daddy Yankee, whatever that was. Under "About Me," she'd written the following:

Hi. I'm Sylvie. I like to meet new people and laugh and have fun. I like ghosthunting and playing Twister. And I love absolutely love funfetti cupcakes! If you make me funfetti, I'm you'res.

Under "Who I'd Like to Meet," she had written one word: "You."

Corderoy composed a flirtatious message asking what ghosthunting was and did she know any good places to go. For a second, he hovered over the Send button. He could hear the sounds of drunken carousing on the street outside, arms around shoulders, bumming cigarettes, pissing in alleys. Choosing not to message nineteen-year-old ♥Sylvie♥ because it was creepy (and would thereby make him *a creep*) would mean coming to terms with the state of his life: single, friendless, unshowered, wearing cum-stained underwear, and trolling for immature girls on MySpace. Sending the message involved none of these things. More important, a part of him realized that he had contempt for this girl purely from looking at her profile. She was emphatically not an Ivy League humanitarian. There was likely nothing he could learn from her. If anything, the opposite was true, which meant he couldn't get hurt. As disturbing as it was, that contempt was arousing, the way power was arousing. It wasn't something he wanted to think about. But one could always forestall troubling thoughts with hasty actions.

She accepted his friend request and responded almost immediately. *YOU NEVER WENT GHOSTHUNTING! you have to go, its the funnest. its when you go out to a place thats suppose to be haunted with like flashlights and camaras and stuff. you can also stay the night in sleeping bags but sometimes it gets cold and you have to cuddle together to stay warm*

Corderoy wrote back, *You'll have to show me sometime. Do you go often?*

i'm going next week! maybe you can come, but we have to talk more before i decide if i like you! ;)

Wow. Was it really that easy? It was the Internet, after all—it could accommodate all kinds of people.

Later that night, Corderoy discovered that he had new comments on his photos. On a photo of him riding a ferry to Capri, ♥Sylvie♥ had written, *cracka in a wife-beater. how stereotypical. but its hot.* On a photo of him at a restaurant in Vegas, angled from below, *thats the most impressive glare ive EVER seen coming off a forehead.* On his most embarrassing photo, a picture of him with his shirt off, wearing a red bandanna knotted in front à la 2Pac, flashing a West Coast sign, ♥Sylvie♥ had written, *and 150 lbs of pure destruction baby. supersexygorgeous, ma dear.* It was an embarrassing photo because it was misrepresentative—upon seeing him, she would certainly notice that he'd developed a little pudge around his scrawny torso.

Corderoy commented on her photos (*that's hawt, you're so effing cute!,* et cetera) following what he now realized to be the standard courting rituals of the MySpace digerati, or as he liked to think of them, MySpacesters.

He spent the next few days flirting with ♥Sylvie♥ via instant messenger. He became intimately familiar with the musical stylings of Daddy Yankee (Reggaeton, Wiki had told him, with a "dembow riddim"), he had come clean about his long-hidden love for Disney music (he had all the words to the *Little Mermaid* soundtrack by heart), and he knew the intricacies and subtle variations in lingual pleasure (secondhand) of the many types of Pillsbury Funfetti cake products, including the holiday, Valentine, and Halloween batters, the brownie mix, and of course, the frostings.

But he had not succeeded in moving the relationship from text to speech, though he'd dropped several large hints, such as *it's hard to tell this story by chat* and *omg you have to hear my impression of Jack Skellington.* Nonetheless, a ghosthunting trip had been set for the coming Saturday, and ♥Sylvie♥ said she would message him on Friday with her phone number so they could plan where to go. This did not happen. ♥Sylvie♥ effected a total digital-communications blackout. Corderoy checked hourly, but she was never on IM, and the time elapsed since her last MySpace log-in grew and grew like a time-lapse shot of a testicular goiter.

As the week dragged on, he found himself obsessively alternating between two thoughts: Where did ♥Sylvie♥ go, she is so hot; and Why the fuck am I wasting my time thinking about this *disgustingly conventional* child. It was a phrase he'd lifted from *Lolita*. He found the book in one of the stacks near his mattress.

> Mentally, I found her to be a disgustingly conventional little girl. Sweet hot jazz, square dancing, gooey fudge sundaes, musicals, movie magazines and so forth—these were the obnoxious items in her list of beloved things.

♥Sylvie♥ was exasperating, clownish, and yes, *disgustingly conventional*. There was no better way to say it. The full recognition of this fact—that he had sought out someone whom he considered leagues below his maturity and intellect, someone he could manipulate and anticipate with ease, offering up just the right phrase to make her twitter or swoon, the recognition that she made his dick hard not in spite of her cloying idiocy but because of it—it made him feel ugly, monstrous. And as a direct consequence of thinking about ♥Sylvie♥ that way, he began comparing her to Mani, who was clearly of far greater value to humanity. (Two people are hanging from a cliff. You can only save one. The first person is wearing hot pants. The second has Euler's identity [$e^{i\pi} + 1 = 0$] tattooed on her wrist. Whom do you save? Whom do you fall in love with?)

The obvious solution was to retcon the whole thing. Retcon, short for retroactive continuity, was a tactic Corderoy had great familiarity with. Long-running comic books—often written by dozens of writers over the years—would sometimes manipulate history in order to make future story lines possible. Or, say, halfway through a *Dungeons & Dragons* adventure, the assembled nerds might rewind after getting killed by skeletons—we put on our armor *before* opening that door. Soap operas used this technique with abandon, inserting characters into the past, bringing the dead back to life.

It would be no easy feat to rewrite the history of his contact with ♥Sylvie♥, to remember her as whimsical instead of puerile, as witty, not superficial. Her absence would allow him to forget her flaws, but only if he could keep himself distracted. He needed to focus on things outside of his personal life. Fortunately, a distraction had just entered his peripheral vision: there was a criminal to oust from the White House. So when Tricia invited him to canvass with her in Ohio the weekend before the election, he found himself readily agreeing. After years on college campuses, he'd finally succumbed to an incipient form of political idealism. All it took was a shameful attraction to run from. Suddenly he cared. Maybe, just maybe, they could change the world.

———

John Kerry lost. And oddly, it was not Tricia who was staring at the post-election coverage on MSNBC, shocked in disbelief, glugging another tumbler of whiskey, Tricia who had cast her vote early that morning and then volunteered the rest of the day at a polling location in an Allston high school to provide oversight against voter fraud.

It was Corderoy who stared at the TV in disbelief. Corderoy who had voted for the first time that day, experiencing an unexpected sense of civic pride. Corderoy who had felt, as he pulled the lever (though the parallels to a slot machine were hard to avoid), that he was a part of something larger, that he mattered, if only a little. It was Corderoy who kept shaking his head in exasperated confusion, Corderoy who had dreamed of sending Bush packing and welcoming Montauk home.

Tricia had seen the exit polls coming in Bush, and though she, too, had begun numbing herself with whiskey in preparation for Kerry's concession speech, she had quietly stepped out the back door of her mind when it finally happened, leaving the cloistered world of the American political show and entering the wings of the grand stage of the world, where real risks had real consequences. Last week she'd sent her résumé to Luc, along with an essay she'd written about her time on the Pine Ridge Indian Reservation, expressing formal interest in accompanying him and William to Baghdad as part of their survey team. He'd written her back that same day, saying that he was "greatly impressed" by her experience, her enthusiasm, and the quality of her writing. But there were several interested parties, he said, and he needed a little more time to sort through his options. And then six days of unbearable silence in which she'd checked her e-mail compulsively, fighting off the urge to call him and ask. Somehow, with Kerry's loss, her potential future with Luc in Baghdad became more of a certainty in her mind.

Tricia emerged from her room, after checking her e-mail yet again, and stared at her group of friends. Jenny Yi had been on the verge of tears when Florida was called for Bush, and she'd burst out crying when Ohio had gone red; though she'd quickly retreated to the bathroom to wash her face, it hadn't done much good. She still looked glum. Tricia's friend Heather, whom she'd met on the campaign, was doing her best to present an indomitable spirit. "Tomorrow," she was telling them. "We get right back to it tomorrow, keep the momentum." Heather's enthusiasm, Jenny's gloominess, they both seemed silly to Tricia. It was Corderoy she felt sorry for. He'd gotten so excited in a week's time. And now he looked like he'd been diagnosed with terminal cancer.

The party began to disperse and Jenny, Heather, and the others gave each other long parting embraces. When they had trickled out the door, Tricia sat down on the couch next to Corderoy. "Not the end of the world," she said.

"I know. But still. Sucks."

"It's the whole system. Even if we didn't vote, Massachusetts would have gone blue."

"That supposed to make me feel better?"

It didn't change the fact that his best friend was still in Iraq. He'd never told Tricia that. He thought about doing so now, but he didn't have the energy for the conversation that would follow. Corderoy rubbed his eyelids. Thinking about Montauk inevitably meant thinking about Mani, which was the last thing he wanted to do. Where the hell was ♥Sylvie♥ when he needed her. "I have to go read," he said, and he retreated to his room.

Tricia picked up the mostly empty bottle of Johnnie Walker and drained it. And as the last of the whiskey trickled into her mouth, the decision solidified. She would call Luc. Right now.

His phone rang six times before he picked up. "Hallo?"

"Hi . . . it's me. Tricia."

"Ah, Tricia . . . it's the middle of the night."

"It is?"

"It is in London."

"Oh, I'm so stupid."

"No, no. It's okay. Did Kerry win?"

Tricia sighed. "No."

"I'm so sorry—" Luc began to say.

"I'm just wondering about this winter," Tricia said. "Going to Baghdad."

"Ah. Well. Nothing is finalized . . ."

"It's less than two months away. I need to start making arrangements."

"Tricia."

"Yes?"

"I know how eager you are. I was just like you. And I think you have what it takes to do this kind of work. But . . ."

There it was.

"The grant came through, Tricia. But not as much as we'd hoped. It's only enough to support one photographer and one writer. We can't afford a survey team."

"Yes, of course, yes. I understand."

"We'll get a coffee next I'm in Boston, okay? Tricia?"

"Yeah. Good night. Sorry I woke you."

She hung up the phone, limped to her room, and collapsed onto her bed. She felt useless. And now the Kerry defeat, which she'd pushed aside with dreams of Baghdad, came back to sock her in the gut. She'd failed to win Meigs County, she'd failed to win Ohio, and she'd failed her country. Now, for the first time in Tricia Burnham's life, she had not an ounce of confidence. She wept into her pillow as the crushing futility of a generation descended on her. It was worse than the morning of 9/11. This time, she wasn't late to arrive, a willing but unneeded blood donor, a bystander watching the medics at work. This time, she'd been the medic, and the patient had died.

14

Corderoy was nearing the end of *Ulysses* when class started. His OCD tendencies usually led him to pause at a chapter break or at least the end of a paragraph. But the sentences in the final chapter went on for pages, so he was forced to set the book down midsentence.

He'd sat through the lecture only dimly aware of what they were discussing. Stanley Fish's idea of interpretive communities. Wolfgang Iser's implied reader. When Professor Flannigan made reference to Joyce, Corderoy's mind rose out of the book on his lap and into the cloud of discussion above the table.

"As Iser puts it," Professor Flannigan said, "the implied reader 'embodies those predispositions necessary for a literary work to exercise its effect.' Joyce famously said that the ideal reader of *Finnegans Wake* would have ideal forgetfulness and ideal insomnia, that he would read until the end of the book and go right back to page one and continue as if for the first time."

Corderoy soon drifted back to a sort of mental hand-wringing until class was over. Sandy, Ray, Maria, and even old Gary were going out for a pint. They invited Corderoy, but he declined, pushing himself further out of the nascent social group. As they left, he felt like the weird kid on the playground the other kids made fun of.

"You seemed distracted today," Professor Flannigan said.

Corderoy held up *Ulysses* in his right hand, his index finger stuck between pages 761 and 762.

Professor Flannigan smiled. "Ah. Carry on, then."

Corderoy was walking on River Street, several blocks from home, when he finished the book. He stopped on the sidewalk. He reread the final lines a second time: *I put my arms around him yes and drew him down to me so he could feel my breasts all perfume yes and his heart was going like mad and yes I said yes I will Yes.* The gray October sky provided a dull backdrop to the golden-red leaves of the maple trees. A chill breeze worked its way into his unbuttoned coat. But he felt so warm, or bright, or everything did. No. That wasn't right. Everything, he included, felt big. His soul—he wasn't accustomed to thinking in terms of souls, in fact, he consciously railed against that sort of thinking, but he did so now, with no qualms—his soul was magnitudinous, it was a powerful vector with no directional component. He wasn't happy or cathartic. He was charged.

When he walked up the stairs to his apartment, he found Tricia in the living room. She was petting Smokey and holding a book she wasn't reading. She looked at him and said, "Hey."

He went into the kitchen for a beer, then sat on the couch opposite her. "What's up," he said. "You look glum."

"I'm fine," Tricia said. Earlier today, her classmate Jeff Alessi had asked her to go see *Super Size Me* at the Coolidge Corner Theatre and she'd turned him down. She didn't feel like doing that. Or doing anything with Jeff. Or doing anything with anyone.

They sat in silence for a moment.

"Just mad at myself," she said.

"Yeah?"

"For liking this guy. It's stupid."

"That human rights guy? Why's that stupid?"

"Because. I don't know. It was a career thing. It should have been."

"So what, you're upset that you have a crush—"

"It's not a crush."

"—that you're attracted to this worldly, older guy who's doing the shit you want to be doing. Seems pretty standard."

Tricia looked at Corderoy as if he were a dog that had slipped into English.

"Though I did always assume that stuff wasn't too high on your priority list."

Tricia scoffed. "I'm busy, sure, but."

But maybe Hal was right? She had never had a relationship that lasted longer than a few months. There were numerous reasons why, she told herself. Her standards were high. She'd consistently made decisions not conducive to sustaining relationships: she'd gone to Barnard, an all-women's college, she'd studied abroad in Bolivia her junior year, she'd interned with the documentary team on the Pine Ridge Indian Reservation. She'd had plenty of hookups and a few flings, but these had been the exception rather than the rule.

"I mean, who doesn't want that?" she said.

"What?"

"You know."

"No."

"You're gonna make me say it?"

Corderoy smirked and took a swig of High Life.

"Looove," Tricia said dramatically, as if that would neuter the word.

But Corderoy nodded thoughtfully, and the word seemed to take on the mantle of a Zen koan. "How's that book?" he asked.

Tricia held up the book on her lap, Noam Chomsky's *Hegemony or Survival*. "It's great," she said. "The world would be an immeasurably better place if everyone read this book."

Hal was looking at her curiously, with a smile, and it made Tricia self-conscious of her word choice. *Everyone*. That would never happen, so why even say it. And why was Hal being so nice? So interested. They'd gone through the routine, and it hadn't ended in sex—their social dynamic had been established—they tolerated each other. Was he making a move?

"Wow. Okay. I'll read it."

"No you won't."

"Sure I will. Why not?"

"Just— Don't read it on my account."

"Of course not," he said. Was that what she thought, that he was trying to impress her? Why would she think that unless . . . unless she wanted him. He suddenly remembered that she was a sexual creature, like all humans, and as such, she had sexual desires. He wondered if she was as dirty, as deliciously dirty, as Molly Bloom. He wanted to know her, but not in the biblical sense—he wanted to see into her brain, he wanted to watch the gear teeth bite into each other with the strangely orchestrated precision of human consciousness. And from the relenting look on her face, it seemed like she was going to open the gates freely.

Tricia sighed. "I think I intimidate guys my age. You know how many times I've been called a bitch? Just for saying something half-way intelligent?" She thought of herself as kind enough. Social nicety wasn't at the top of her list of priorities. She could be abrasive, yes. But that didn't stop her from thinking that it was somehow her fault if others perceived her as a bitch. Which was crazy. And she knew it. But it never occurred to her that men often misinterpreted her self-sufficiency as a lack of interest. It was an unfortunate psychological consequence of her three greatest virtues: her desire to better the world, her willingness to take responsibility where others wouldn't, and her ruthless self-discipline.

"This guy didn't call you a bitch, did he?"

"No, no. He's great. Passes all my criteria."

"Criteria?" Corderoy leaned forward.

"Intelligence, morality. Being hot. But the biggest one is—I don't know how else to say it—enlightenment. Understanding what the world is, what's at stake, what's important."

"So this enlightened guy. He know you like him?"

Smokey had been purring contentedly in Tricia's lap, but she stopped, as if sensing Tricia's apprehension.

Tricia's voice caught in her throat. "I thought he did. But then he turned me down for this opportunity—I mean, I guess it was a funding thing—it's all muddled up. That's why I'm angry, that I let it get muddled."

As Tricia lowered her gaze and stared at Smokey, Corderoy's sense of magnitude that Molly Bloom's monologue had lent him, his sense of bigness, his realm of mental apprehension that had been slowly expanding, it passed some invisible threshold and he saw Tricia. Tricia with her face off. She told herself she wanted an enlightened guy, but enlightened guys weren't manly, and manly men were so rarely enlightened. As much as she domineered most social situations, when it came to romance, Tricia Burnham fit the stereotype: she wanted a man to sweep her away. Worse was the paradoxical situation she had placed herself in: she wanted to be conquered by a pacifist. But before his expanding soul could wrap itself around that thought, she said, "What about you, Hal? Any girls you're after?" And his expanded soul became a rigid shell, creaking like a submarine under pressure.

"I." He was too embarrassed to mention ♥Sylvie♥.

"You had a girlfriend back in Seattle, right?"

Bolts were breaking and crossbeams buckling. A hull breach was imminent.

"Hal?"

The USS *Halifax Corderoy* imploded.

As Tricia dredged through the wreckage of the submarine, she extracted a name, Mani, and a hasty apology to the effect that there was an essay, the writing of which could no longer be postponed, and the wreckage slid off the sloping seafloor to the abyss of its room.

15

Of course, the essay could be postponed. And Corderoy was given the perfect excuse the instant the dot next to ♥Sylvie♥'s IM handle (bytheseashore) flicked from gray to green in his contact list and a message popped onto his screen.

bytheseashore: sorry i disappeared
bytheseashore: i missed you
bytheseashore: but i was in the hospital
rogue7: Are you OK? What happened?

Nothing that hadn't happened before, apparently. ♥Sylvie♥ had cystic fibrosis. Last week she'd coughed up blood and was rushed to the emergency room. They'd done X-rays and CAT scans of her lungs, and she was now on an additional antibiotic, ciprofloxacin, in addition to the four she took on a regular basis, even in periods of relative health, vancomycin, meropenem, tobramycin, and piperacillin.

Corderoy immediately Wikied "cystic fibrosis" to learn that it was an inherited disease that affected the entire body, with lung infections being the most serious complication. The minimized chat window was flashing, and before clicking back to her, Corderoy finished reading the first paragraph of the Wiki article: "Most individuals with cystic fibrosis die young—many in their 20s and 30s—from lung failure." Holy shit.

bytheseashore: i like u hal

rogue7: I like you, too. Are you feeling better?

bytheseashore: a little

bytheseashore: now that im talki

bytheseashore: ng to u again

rogue7: Why just a little?

bytheseashore: u make me feel so special

rogue7: Thanks.

bytheseashore: but still just a little

bytheseashore: i have a check up

bytheseashore: tomorrow

bytheseashore: for my crohn's

rogue7: What?

Sylvie also had Crohn's disease, an autoimmune disease causing inflammation of the gastrointestinal tract. Two horrible diseases. What were the odds? But of course, that was probably why Cystic ♥Sylvie♥, as he would later think of her, had to depend on MySpace for her social life.

This revelation didn't scare Corderoy off; paradoxically, it knocked him into a spiral of infatuation, a fact which may seem incommensurate with reality, but when the threads of circumstance that led to it are traced back sufficiently far, its inevitability is apparent. The most constant circumstance responsible was his immersion in the suffocating academic pretensions of Cambridge, Massachusetts, where ♥Sylvie♥'s whimsy was like oxygen. The most distant circumstance, though also the most profound: the image of Mani in traction, in a hospital room on July 3rd, unconscious, moments from abandonment by her de facto boyfriend, soon to awake in a city suddenly cold and alien, absent of a single friend. The most trivial, and the most evil, and the most suppressed of these circumstances was the Get Out of Relationship Free card, similar to the one he'd used when leaving Seattle, that came with ♥Sylvie♥'s terminal diagnosis.

bytheseashore: still want to go ghosthunting

bytheseashore: its totaly on

bytheseashore: this friday
bytheseashore: if not we can bake funfetti
bytheseashore: cupcakes or something because
bytheseashore: thats always wonderful
bytheseashore: maybe we can cuddle at the house
bytheseashore: this palce i know
bytheseashore: but wear boxer shorts
bytheseashore: briefs are icky
bytheseashore: gotta go by cutie hal

She was practically throwing herself at him. And for a moment, he was tempted to disbelieve the illusion. But luck, both good and bad, was all about relative perception. In the grand scheme of things, he reminded himself, the universe was indifferent to our fortunes. When looking through a small enough window, it sometimes seemed designed to thwart you. But through that same window, it could also seem to be rewarding your very existence.

Dear Hal,
    Have some pussy. Don't question it.
Your friend,
The Universe

Corderoy threw on a pair of pants and left the house like he had a plane to catch.

He didn't own a single pair of boxer shorts. Why would he want his junk flopping around? Briefs angled it upward, so when an unexpected boner occurred, it was the shaft that created a slight bulge in the jeans. But in boxers—and he'd experienced this at the mall once when he ran into Jessica Wilson, the hottest ninth-grader in school, whose jeans were as tight around her ass as industrial shrink wrap on a pair of maracas—in boxers, it was hanging free, angled down, and when it got excited, it was not the shaft but the head that appeared under the denim near the upper thigh. The maneuver required to rectify this was extremely conspicuous. And what was the downside of briefs? There was the supposed drop in sperm count from having your testes snug and cotton-cupped all day long, but was that even a detri-ment? He didn't plan on impregnating anyone anytime soon. Perhaps not ever. No, it was definitely a positive—briefs came with a built-in prophylactic.

And yet here he was, on his way to the store to purchase a pair of boxer shorts for the possibility of cuddling (sex?) with a nineteen-year-old girl whom he'd never met—not in person—and who apparently had cystic fibrosis. And Crohn's disease. He would have to be gentle.

———

They had arranged to meet the following Friday—the same day his essay was due—at the Lotus Yoga studio in Brighton. She would be getting out of her class at five, all limber and sweaty. It was nearly a week away. And the anticipation fueled him in every aspect of his life. He went running, he cleaned up his room, and he dove back into *Ulysses,* rereading chapters, researching past critical commentary by Derrida and others, sketching out essay ideas of his own.

It was Thursday evening when he opened up a blank document on his laptop and began to write. In the last week, he had slowly regained that sense of expansiveness he'd felt at the end of the novel. But it was changed now; he didn't so much feel it as know it, and the fact that it wasn't joy, or anger, or release, or self-deception, that it was some-how none of these and all of these, the fact that it was a force without a direction became glaringly obvious. He hit upon the topic for his essay: he would go through the final chapter, Molly Bloom's famous stream-of-consciousness monologue, and he would track all the sign-valued language—all the *yes*es, *no*s, *every*s, *all*s, *didn't*s, and *not*s—he would quantify the tone to see how positive the language actually was. He would take his data and make a graph.

He began laboriously scanning the pages and looking for *yes*es and *no*s, circling them, counting them, but when he'd made it through only five pages in an hour, he turned to the Internet. A quick Google search turned up a text-file version of *Ulysses.* He identified a list of words and auto-searched for them in the document. By midnight, he'd finished the data collection; a quick analysis confirmed his suspicion and validated the strange directionless sense of magnitude the final chapter had given him. Though the book ended with a string of *yes*es, and though the total *yes*es outnumbered the total *no*s in Molly Bloom's monologue, the total negatives, including *not*s, *didn't*s, and so forth, skewed the tone highly toward the negative. Joyce had given Molly Bloom an accumulative moment, a big moment, but it wasn't a *positive* moment; it was much more complex than that. Molly Bloom's connection with her husband—the subject of much of her thoughts in the final pages—was deep and important, but far from simple or purely loving. That final *yes*, if anything, was an acceptance of the complexity of love, that it always contained strands and flecks of its opposite.

Corderoy had been so wrapped up with this discovery, so thrilled that his crazy data collection was turning out to be worth it, so relieved that it would, if he kept at it all night, yield an essay with some actual insight, that he hadn't eaten since lunch. The hunger hit him abruptly, and he made a quick phone call.

Thirty minutes later, Tricia knocked on his door. "You order a pizza?"

He ran down, paid the Domino's guy, and walked back up the stairs with his medium cheese, set it on the coffee table, and took out an oozing slice. He noticed Tricia eyeing the steaming pie. "Help yourself."

"You know Domino's is owned by a right-wing, anti-abortion nut job."[*]

"Does that make it undelicious?" Corderoy said.

"Lots of things are delicious."

"Yeah, but this is right here in front of you." Corderoy took a big bite, cheese stretching off the pizza and dripping onto the cardboard below him.

"Not that hungry," Tricia said.

"I gotta get back to writing," Corderoy said. He took another slice with a napkin. "I'll leave this out here, in case you change your mind." He nodded toward the pizza. "Know your enemy?"

Corderoy shut his door and Tricia was left in the living room, breathing in that unparalleled pizza smell. She tapped her foot, glanced

---

[*] False. Though Tom Monaghan, founder of Domino's and a staunch Catholic, donated tens of thousands of dollars to anti-abortion causes like Operation Rescue, he had sold the company to Bain Capital in 1998.

at Hal's door, then took a slice and retreated to her own room. Wasn't she allowed one small slip from an otherwise cautious and moral set of consumer habits? It was warm, salty, and luxuriant in carbohydrates. She ate it quickly. When she'd finished, she lit a cigarette without holding it to her mouth—it took at least five seconds of direct flame to get the tip embering without drawing air through it—and after it was lit, she took a long and indifferent drag.

16

After a shower, Corderoy did twenty push-ups, dressed, and went out to buy some Funfetti cupcake batter, a can of Funfetti frosting, a jar of sprinkles, and—he almost forgot—a cupcake tin. By three p.m., he'd carefully frosted each of the twelve cupcakes, meticulously sprinkled them to ensure an artful and even distribution, and sealed them in a rectangular Tupperware.

He did more push-ups, showered again, shampooing his pubes this time, then put on his brand-new pair of boxers. He walked into the living room, smiling like an idiot. Tricia came out of her room and cocked her hip to one side, surveying him. "Got a date or something?"

"How'd you know?" Corderoy said.

"You're grinning like an idiot. And you haven't showered twice in the last week. Who is she?"

"Just someone I met."

"I want the dirt later," she said.

"Shit," Corderoy said. "Forgot to brush."

He closed himself in the bathroom and brushed his teeth longer than he'd ever brushed his teeth. After five minutes, he took a swirl of Tricia's Listerine, which burned the hell out of his mouth, but that's how you knew it was working. He walked out of the bathroom, tugging at his jeans—the boxers were riding up—and went to his bedroom to get his coat.

What he saw did not augur well for the future of his romantic life.

Tricia's cat, Smokey, was standing on his bed, back arched, tail up, midloaf. Without thinking, Corderoy flung open Tricia's door with the intention of telling her to clean the fucking cat shit off his bed and have his sheets washed, but what he saw in Tricia's room made him turn in horror. He shut her door, picked up his Tupperware, and left the house with an image burned into his visual cortex: Tricia, grabbing for the bedsheet, something purple buzzing between her legs.

He'd mapped out the quickest way to get to the Lotus Yoga and Dance Studio in Brighton, and it took him through the Ringer Playground. But he'd left too early, and it was only four-thirty when he entered the park. He didn't want to wait around too long in the yoga studio, so he found a place on a low cement wall. The sky was overcast, and a slight breeze had picked up. He bent up the corner of his Tupperware and smelled the Funfetti cupcakes. They were almost sickeningly sweet.

The Ringer Playground was bleak, graffitied, and cold. Narrow and litter-filled streets led into the shady and unkempt grounds. Staring through the chain-link fence to the baseball diamond, he thought of that scene in *Terminator 2* when Sarah Connor clutches at the fence and all the children are incinerated by a nuclear explosion. This was a perfect place to get murdered. It was Brighton.

He wandered around, smelled the cupcakes again, and checked his phone. As it neared five, he figured there was no point in waiting in the cold, so he left the park and walked along Allston Street until he hit Brighton Avenue, carrying the Tupperware on his perched fingers like a serving tray with a silver dome concealing carefully broiled game hens or a human head. It started raining, softly at first, and then, as if a switch had been flipped in the sky, it fell like billions of coins on the streets of Brighton. Corderoy ducked under the awning of the Lotus Yoga and Dance Studio, his coat lifted off his back and held above his head. His Northwest pride was deeply ingrained, and he was proud never to have carried an umbrella. But what he was slowly realizing in his first few months in the East was that in Seattle, it only misted. In other parts of the world, it *rained*. This was the second Boston rainstorm in which he'd been caught unawares. Corderoy looked down at his jeans: they were soaked up past his knees.

He entered the yoga studio and walked up to a short, fit girl behind a podium.

"You look lost." Her eyes had a comfortably vacant look.

"I'm not lost, I don't think," Corderoy said. "I'm looking for Sylvie."

"The class gets out in a bit," she said. "Have a seat."

Corderoy had never been in a yoga studio and he felt slightly uncomfortable with the ambient spirituality—the purple and yellow walls, the exotically confused Indian/Celtic music, and the overly even cadences of the hostess's speech.

As the yoga class let out, a stream of sweating women (and a few men) parted the beaded curtain to the studio, some walking outside, others entering a door to the locker room.

One of the girls stopped as she walked past him. She was not ♥Sylvie♥. "Someone's birthday?" she asked.

"No," Corderoy said flatly.

The girl rolled her eyes and left. Corderoy covered up the Tupperware with his coat.

More people filtered in over the next twenty minutes, and during that time, Corderoy checked his phone exactly twenty times: no missed calls, no text messages. Maybe he'd misremembered. Maybe ♥Sylvie♥'s class got out at six?

"Do you have a bathroom?" he asked the hostess.

She directed him, and when he came back several minutes later, the lobby had cleared out and the five-thirty class had begun. The girl at the podium was missing as well. He sat down but realized that ♥Sylvie♥ could have slipped in and joined the class when he'd been in the bathroom. He parted the beaded curtain and walked through to the studio room to see a dozen or so women and two or three men in strange positions, falling and rotating and swooning and stumbling over one another like drunks. Corderoy tilted his head sideways as he watched one girl place her hand squarely between another's breasts, then pull back, bringing the other girl forward as if her arm were a chain tied to the girl's sternum.

A bearded man in a tight blue turtleneck was crawling on the floor, orangutan-like, in long, uneven arm-strides; another man, taller and skinnier, had his hands on Turtleneck's shoulder blades, trailing him as if he couldn't figure out whether he wanted to mount him or if his hands were glued there and he was trying to escape.

"You here for Contact Improv? First class is free."

Corderoy turned to see a slight blond girl standing in front of him. Her face was small, with a broad forehead and a pointed chin; her hair was pulled back in a ponytail; her eyes were the size of apricots and of a similar color. She was stunningly beautiful, and Corderoy felt the same disturbing attraction to her that he sometimes felt toward anime characters.

"Contact Improv?"

"Think of it as distributing your weight in an interesting way. It's all about awareness through movement, weight transfer, counterbalance. C'mon, you'll like it. I'm Tanya, by the way."

"I don't know."

"Here. Lean into my palm."

Tanya stood there with an easy smile, holding her palm out to Corderoy as if directing traffic, swaying back and forth almost imperceptibly. Corderoy scanned the room once more. ♥Sylvie♥ wasn't there. Finally, after about fifteen seconds, he caved: he leaned into Tanya's hand. She pulled back and circled, drawing Corderoy's center of mass with her.

Corderoy shot a leg forward and righted himself, stepping back from her palm. "Okay. Well, that was fun."

"You know Newton and the apple, right? Sorry, I forgot your name."

"I never told you. But it's Hal. Yeah, I know Newton and the apple, though I'm pretty sure that story's apocryphal."

"Newton overlooked the question of how it feels to be the apple. We can transcend the law of gravity with the swinging, circulating attraction of the centrifugal force."

Even the hippies in Boston had an academic patois.

"Try to be attuned to how gravity acts on your body, how your momentum carries you. Slip your shoes off. And roll up those wet pant legs."

Corderoy did, then Tanya took him by the hand and led him into the slow circus of undulating leotards. "Do you know the five rhythms?" she asked. "Flowing, staccato, chaos, lyrical, and stillness. Just think about flowing. Put your hand on my shoulder."

He obeyed, and she began swaying and dipping, and Corderoy stumbled to follow her, then he leaned back and she drew forward as if attached by a length of elastic; her hand found his, and their fingers whispered back and forth, palms never quite aligning, fluttering, then she jerked forward—staccato—stumbled into him, causing him to stumble back until they collapsed into a muddle of too many limbs and faces, and Corderoy found himself torso to torso with the tall, skinny man who had been wobbling atop Turtleneck. Embarrassment flashed through his nervous system but vanished as soon as he recognized it. Following Skinny's lead, he felt his joints tighten while his body became more fluid and he gave way to the inebriation of momentum and gravity. They interlocked their arms, bent, pivoted, and countered like robots with limited end-range movement—then Skinny went stiff as a beam and fell backward on Corderoy, his head landing in the crook of Corderoy's shoulder, and as they stepped backward in a circle, Corderoy realized that this skinny, mulletted hippie had given him his entire weight, had entrusted a stranger with the job of directing his momentum and with keeping gravity from smashing his only and irreplaceable body into the earth.

When the class ended, Corderoy asked Tanya and Skinny, whose name was Gregg, if they wanted to get a drink. They agreed, and the three of them went down to Harpers Ferry. It was typical of the rock venues and bars found in the Allston-Brighton area: dark, divey, manned by rude, tubby bouncers, and overpriced, given its aesthetic. They sat at a small table, and before Tanya or Gregg had a chance to speak, Corderoy announced he was buying the first round. He went up to the bar and ordered three beers and three shots. When he returned, Tanya and Gregg were examining his Tupperware.

"Are these Funfetti?" Tanya asked.

Corderoy nodded and said, "Help yourself."

"My God, I haven't had these since I was a kid," she said. She and Gregg each took a cupcake, and Gregg took a beer. "Not much of a whiskey drinker," he said, pushing his shot toward Corderoy. "You have it."

"It's you and me, then, Tanya," Corderoy said, holding up his shot.

"Oh, I'm sorry," Tanya said. "I tried to tell you earlier, but I can't. I'm allergic to alcohol," and she slid her beer and her shot over to Corderoy. What the fuck.

"Shit," Corderoy said. "Sorry. I'll get you a Coke or something."

"I'm okay for now, thanks. Cheers?" she said, holding up her cupcake.

Corderoy laughed. Sure, whatever. "Cheers," and he knocked his shot glass against her cupcake and Gregg's beer.

Corderoy had been hoping to extend the intimacy he'd felt with these two new friends, but by the time he'd finished his beer and shot, they'd exhausted their conversational topics of mutual interest—whatever connection they'd had was a bodily one, and he didn't know how to keep it alive outside the yoga studio. He downed Gregg's shot and started working on Tanya's beer.

"How long have you two been friends?" Corderoy asked.

"Oh, we're married," Gregg said.

"Oh. Congratulations," Corderoy said. He tossed back the last shot.

"It was a while ago," Tanya said, patting Gregg's leg under the table. "So, Hal, I'm guessing you didn't bring these cupcakes for us. What's her name? When do we get to meet her?"

"Sylvie," Corderoy said. "And probably never, seeing as how . . ." He took a few big swigs of Tanya's beer. Fuck it. Why not? "She's gonna die soon. Cystic fibrosis."

"That's awful," Tanya said.

"If only all relationships were like that," Corderoy said. "With a pre-set termination. No awkward breakups."

Tanya and Gregg shared the nervous look of a couple cornered by a mentally ill person on a city bus.

Now would be the time to apologize, reverse course. But that would be boring. After the rush of unearned physical intimacy in the yoga studio, he needed intensity, drama, and if the only way to get that was by being an asshole, well . . . "She's nineteen," Corderoy said. "Met her on the Internet. Cystic fibrosis. And Crohn's disease. You gotta admit. Pretty funny."

Tanya blinked her big anime eyes in disbelief, then stood and put her coat on. "Come on, Gregg."

They left. Just as well. It was hard to drink alone with other people. Corderoy checked his phone: no missed calls, no messages. He ordered another shot, downed it. Some people at the next table over leaned in and inquired about the cupcakes, and he offered them up, then ordered another shot. By nine, he had only two Funfetti cupcakes left, and he hadn't so much as dipped his own finger in the frosting. He hid the Tupperware under his coat again, ordered one last shot, knocked it back, then stumbled outside. He sat down on the wet curb and checked his phone: no missed calls, no text messages. He opened up the Tupperware and bit into one of the Funfetti cupcakes. It was delicious. He took one more bite, then shoved the entire thing in his mouth; before he'd finished chewing, he did the same with the second, prying the paper cup off the back as he crammed it in. He swallowed, bit by bit at the back of his throat, until he was able to chew, and then he chewed and chewed until his mouth was empty.

Standing up was not a good idea. He doubled over puking, splashing his lower legs and shoes. He had only eight dollars, so he hailed a cab, got in, and told the driver to take him seven dollars toward Central Square. They stopped at the bridge, and Corderoy walked home in the moonlight. The cat shit was still on his bed.

———

He was famished and hungover when he awoke the next morning on the couch. He needed grease. He fried up some bacon and ate it with his fingers.

Tricia came into the kitchen and poured herself a glass of milk, then stood near the counter drinking it. It sickened Corderoy to see the opaque film clinging to the glass after she tipped it back. Neither of them said anything for a moment.

Then, without thinking how awkwardness would swoop down upon them, Corderoy said, "Sorry I walked in on you yesterday."

Tricia said nothing.

Corderoy overcompensated. "You know, the good ol' sock-on-the-doorknob trick actually works. And it's refreshing to be that comfortable about it. My buddies back in Seattle used to say, 'I'm gonna go masturbate the penis now. You wanna order a pizza in a bit?' It was like, this is a thing I need to do, like taking a shit. Natural."

"Right. I'm not really comfortable with that system."

"What system do you suggest, then?"

"How about not barging into other people's rooms?"

"Of course. Sorry. I was just upset. Because of Smokey."

"What?"

"Shitting on my bed."

"No . . ."

Corderoy nodded.

"Oh my God. I'm so sorry. I'll buy you new sheets. Why didn't you tell me earlier?"

Corderoy bit his lip.

"Right," Tricia said. "Sock on the doorknob."

After eating, Corderoy felt better, less hungover. He sat down on the couch with his laptop and checked his instant messenger. ♥Sylvie♥'s icon was inactive. He logged in to MySpace and checked her profile. It was one hundred percent gone. Deleted. Her picture next to her comments on his page had been replaced with a question mark. Orphaned sentences, no longer attached to a person. There was a sense of wonder at the feeling, like finding graffiti under the ash of Pompeii, and also a sense of devastating betrayal, as if letters from an ex-lover had lost their *XOXO, Mani* or *Love, M* and been replaced with *XOXO, Error 404, Person not found.* ♥Sylvie♥ hadn't left. She wasn't somewhere else. She had disappeared. From everywhere.

17

When Corderoy received his essay back at the end of class, there was no grade on it. Professor Flannigan had written in the margin in red pen, *Come along to my office at half-three so we can talk.* Corderoy wasn't sure what *half-three* meant. He erred on the side of being early and ended up parking himself on a plastic chair outside Professor Flannigan's office at two-thirty. He sat there for the next hour, attempting to read Defoe's *Roxana*, which he had to finish for his Friday class, The Rise of the Novel. But the book was boring, and people kept walking through the hallway, forcing him to retract his stretched-out legs, and he got through only four pages before he decided to close the book, stare into space, and ponder the curious bit of information he'd stumbled on that morning concerning ♥Sylvie♥.

Corderoy had scoured various social networking sites looking for Sylvies and anyone with bytheseashore as their handle. He'd found squat on Friendster, Live Journal, and Xanga, but after Googling "cystic fibrosis" and "Boston," he'd stumbled onto the Web forums at www.dailystrength.org, a community support site for people with chronic medical conditions. Just that morning, he'd read a comment by Charlie37 regarding a community member known as Selena.

Six months ago, I, like many others, was hooked by the heartrending and chaotic narrative of Selena, a teenage girl with CF in desperate need of a double lung transplant. Her friend Brita had been providing weekly updates about her progress on the "Pray for Selena" blog (http://prayforselena.blogspot.com), which has now been taken down. For those of you just finding out about this, here's a sample from Brita's blog:

> *It's been a rough week for Selena. For four days now, she's been intubated but it's not looking good. Her $PaCO_2$ is in the 90s, the highest it's been, and Lord knows how she's been able to handle it. Her O_2 sat was down to 84, and her temp reached 103. She's been fighting hard, but it seems like there's only one way this could go.*
>
> *On Tuesday she has a meeting with the transplant committee to discuss the lengthy and complicated process of getting new lungs. Selena isn't suited to this bureaucratic hassle, especially when she's struggling so much, but it's coming down to the line now. Let's pray for her and give her the strength she needs to get through this.*

Over time, Selena's condition worsened and hundreds were praying and posting supportive comments on the "Pray for Selena" blog. Then, in March, the news broke that Selena/Brita does not exist. Rather, she is a persona invented by Sandra Fernandez, and she used photos of one of Sandra's friends as our "Selena."

Corderoy had found it odd that the "she" in that sentence referred to Selena, who did not exist, rather than to Sandra, who was supposedly behind the hoax. Charlie37 continued:

What bothers me most is the thought that someone could manipulate the hearts and prayers of hundreds of people the way Selena has without feeling the slightest remorse. It may be, as some community members have suggested, that Selena suffers from Munchausen syndrome, a mental disorder in which a person feigns illness or trauma to garner sympathy or attention. In any case, Selena has been active on many forums using many aliases. She has been linked with the names Sylvanshine and Laurie B.

Could that be ♥Sylvie♥? The voice of those blog posts written by Brita was, on the whole, much more cogent and measured than ♥Sylvie♥'s. It couldn't be her. But to be safe, Corderoy had written to Charlie37, asking if he had seen the IM handle bytheseashore, or if there were any other things Sandra/Brita/Selena was known for. Charlie37 had yet to respond, and Corderoy had become consumed with anticipation. He tried to pick up *Roxana* again, but Professor Flannigan arrived at 3:35, walking with brisk, short strides, wearing an argyle sweater and a cheerful grin.

"Hope you haven't been waiting long," he said as he unlocked his office door.

"Just a few minutes," Corderoy said. He took a seat next to Professor Flannigan's desk. After rearranging some papers, unpacking his leather satchel, and adjusting his eyeglasses, the professor sat down in his office chair, leaned back, and said, "So, tell me about your essay."

Corderoy explained the sense of magnitude he'd experienced. He paraphrased the most important parts of the argument he'd made in the essay, that Joyce himself was the crafty Odyssean character, not Leopold Bloom, that the seemingly triumphal ending was best read in light of this deceptive tendency, that Joyce's vision of the female consciousness was that its intensity trumped its focus.

"Brilliant. I love it," Professor Flannigan said.

Corderoy's heart, which had been holding a difficult pose, relaxed into its natural rhythm, and a wave of warm blood spread out to his extremities.

"But I can't accept it."

"You can't?"

"The essay prompt was very clear, Mr. Corderoy."

Corderoy did not especially like being called Mr. Corderoy, though he admired how Professor Flannigan had managed to mold the social dynamic of the class into this more formal shape, one in which his social ascendance was more obvious and more welcome, as a benevolent philosopher king.

"Did you read the essay prompt?"

"Yes."

"Then you know it says you are to apply three of the schools of criticism we've discussed to a text and argue which one provides the most useful lens through which to read it. I did not assign this essay without cause. This is a peer-reviewed field, Mr. Corderoy. Do you imagine we are here purely for the pursuit of knowledge?"

"Yes?" Corderoy ventured.

"I hope you've thought about life after graduate school. I don't mean to be cynical, but frankly, you are training to be an academic. This degree doesn't lead anywhere else. If you want to survive in this career, you need to learn the language upon which the grand discussion is based. When you take your orals two years from now, your thesis advisers will expect you to be intimately familiar with post-structuralism, new historicism, phenomenology, and hermeneutics. You're quite creative, Mr. Corderoy. And the insightful and unexpected thinking you demonstrated in this essay will make you an excellent critic and a great professor someday, if you take the time now to approach the field on its own terms."

Corderoy had been nodding sheepishly through Professor Flannigan's speech, and after asking for a chance to rewrite the essay, which the professor granted without hesitation, Corderoy ducked out of the office and walked home rather than taking the train. When he crossed the Charles River into Cambridge, it began to rain. Not a Boston rainstorm but a Seattle drizzle. It reminded him of home, and it complicated his growing distaste for the city of Boston. He walked slowly as his shoulders darkened, realizing that he had a spot of violence in his heart for the world of academia. As much as he'd been moved by Professor Flannigan's speech that first day of class (*the search for truth— what could be more important?*), the whole enterprise felt like a game with no real stakes, which was fine as long as you could play loose and free, have some fun with it. But academics, he was learning, tended to take themselves quite seriously. He wasn't sure if he could play this game or if he really wanted to be a professor someday. But what else would he be? What other skills did he have?

When he got home, he found a reply from Charlie37. He didn't want to read it. He closed his laptop. He went back outside into the rain to buy beer and ramen. After eating, he distracted himself with Web comics and tech blogs. Halfway through his six-pack, he decided it was time to man up. He navigated back to the forum to read the comment.

Haven't seen that IM handle. Sorry.

Corderoy breathed a sigh of relief.

Just be on the lookout for anyone claiming to have late-stage CF, needing a transplant, asking for prayer. And Funfetti cupcakes. Selena's favorite—and in my opinion, a sick joke.

There were a few more sentences in the message, but Corderoy had to stop reading. This Selena was unmistakably ♥Sylvie♥. This girl (♥Sylvie♥/Selena/Brita/Sandra?) had played him like a game of Candy Land. She could be anyone. A fat old dude. Some schizophrenic guy in a psych ward. She could even be Montauk, fucking with him—he imagined it now: Montauk lying in his bunk, reading flirtatious IM logs and laughing, showing them to all his Army friends. But that wasn't right. That was a substitute Corderoy had created to fill a void. It would be too easy, too benevolent of the universe, the gulf between him and every other human reduced to a joke, a prank by his best friend. ♥Sylvie♥, a postcard from Montauk that said, *Hey, Dickface, I miss you.* No, ♥Sylvie♥ wasn't Montauk. She wasn't anybody. She didn't even exist.

Corderoy lay back on the couch. He felt like *he* didn't exist. The ceiling existed. He knew that. Otherwise, he'd be getting rained on right now. The couch existed. And the floor it was on, that existed, too. And his clothes existed, but they seemed to arch around a negative space. He breathed in and felt that the air existed, certainly, as it circulated in and filled out two lunglike shapes, but what did that mean? One could have an entire face—something he wasn't sure he had right now—and still not exist.

18

When he'd woken up on the couch three days ago, Tricia and Smokey had already left for New York, and there was a plastic package of new bedsheets sitting on the kitchen table. It was still sitting there, next to a note that read:

Hal—

Really sorry about your sheets. Here's some new ones. I'll be in Westchester with my family until Monday. Call me if you want to come down to NY to join us for Thanksgiving.
—Tricia

He'd read the note, but he didn't have the energy to open the sheets and put them on his bed. As hard as he tried, he was unable to read that invitation as anything other than a calculated nonvite, an offer designed to be declined, one that would nonetheless give Tricia social credit for her unfailing hospitality.

So he'd passed the days until Thanksgiving, alone in the apartment, skipping class, watching *South Park* episodes, and masturbating. He was broke, and his parents could only afford to fly him back to Seattle once, for Christmas.

It was six p.m. when his mother called, wishing him a happy Thanksgiving. She asked if he was going somewhere, and he lied and said he'd be having Thanksgiving with his roommate's family. "Well,

we miss you," she said, and he heard his father in the background, saying, "Ask him if he got my e-mail."

"Your father wants to know—"

"Yeah, Mom. I got it. Tell him I'll read it now."

When he hung up, he collapsed on the couch with his laptop and
Wiki-binged for the better part of an hour, navigating link by link
from "Sexuality of Adolf Hitler" to "Zombie Apocalypse." Finally, he
pulled up his father's e-mail from last week. It was long, and it looked
boring; his father, apparently, had been getting deep into family gene-
alogy research.

> Pretty fascinating story about where we Corderoys come from. I wish I'd talked
> to my grandparents more when I was your age. I had to figure all this out the
> hard way. Thought you might be interested, given the time of year. You should
> know about this stuff before it's too late.

Corderoy skimmed a long paragraph about his great-great-great-
grandfather, some dude named Elroy who'd fought for the Confeder-
ates, got captured in 1861, and tunneled out of jail a few years later. His
son, Meriwether, fled St. Louis after a botched robbery and rustled cattle
through Kansas and New Mexico, nearly got hanged a few times, then
made his fortune in Dawson City during the Yukon gold rush. He "fell
heavy into drink," in his father's words, bought a saloon, took an Aleut wife
in Anchorage, beat his son, William, and died of cirrhosis in 1917. Not the
most noble forebearers. Why didn't his dad find this shit depressing?

> Your great-grandfather William was a book lover, just like you. He even memo-
> rized Shakespeare, the bloody parts, your grandpa says.

William lost his job during the Depression and "took to the bottle."
He would come home with a pint of whiskey in his back pocket, stone
drunk, and his children would take off his boots, throw him in bed,
then pour his drink down the drain.

> That's why your grandpa doesn't drink. His three brothers all had problems
> with alcohol. Be careful—it runs in the family. And you know all about your

Great-Aunt Jane's time in the sanitarium. They still did electric-shock treatment back then.

His father went on about how Grandpa Frank had gotten to where he was today. Corderoy already knew the story in bits and pieces. After Pearl Harbor, he'd worked at Boeing as an electrician on the B-29 bomber to avoid the draft. He met Corderoy's grandma at the Highline Diner. She was a waitress, and she got him a job at the *White Center Weekly,* a dinky local paper that her father ran. Corderoy was about to skip the rest of the e-mail, but then his own name jumped out at him.

> I probably told you about your namesake years ago, but I doubt you remember. It was Grandpa Frank's business partner, Charles Halifax. He was a drinker, a smoker, and a rake, believe me—they had trouble keeping the office staffed with secretaries. One day, I think it was in 1964, your grandpa and Charles took me and your Uncle Ted climbing on Mt. Rainier. Just a day hike to Camp Muir at 10,000 feet or so, you needed ski poles for the Muir snowfield. And about ¾ of the way up, this boulder the size of a basketball came tumbling down at us and it would have bounded right into my head if Charles Halifax hadn't stuck out his leg. That rock shattered his shinbone to pieces. We had to wait for Search and Rescue.
>
> He hit the booze pretty hard after that injury though. A few months before you were born, he drove himself off a bridge and died. I wanted to name you after him. Your mother wasn't thrilled with the idea. She wanted to name you after her grandfather Albert. He was a dairy farmer outside of Madison, Wisconsin. He asphyxiated himself with exhaust fumes from his pickup truck. That's another story. But I never forgot how Charles Halifax saved my life.

With such a robust legacy of alcoholism and suicide, his namesake a shining example of both, it was remarkable that Corderoy had managed to make it to his early twenties before seriously flirting with either one.

The closest he'd ever come to suicide was after Tara, his college girlfriend, had dumped him the month before he went abroad, where he'd met Montauk in Rome. He'd moved out of their studio and into the living room of his friend Aaron's basement apartment on the other side of the U District. Aaron's girl had just split as well, and they'd fed on each other's misery, smoking a pack of cigarettes each day and killing a bottle of Jack nearly every night. Corderoy had stopped eating regularly, losing close to fifteen pounds.

Tara had been Corderoy's best friend and lover for a year and a half—their intimacy had been intense, their future together inevitable. When she'd cheated on him, just before the end, he'd been unable to fathom the reasons for her betrayal, but he'd been willing to forgive. Tara didn't want forgiveness; she wanted a wedge to drive them apart. It would take him years to realize that he wasn't the perfect boyfriend precisely because of his unqualified devotion to her. Tara had been immature and cruel, but she'd been perceptive: Corderoy didn't need her so much as he needed to love someone, anyone. Blind to this himself, the unexplainable dissolution of their perfect union had grave implications for his future happiness: anything good could sour at an instant. Why go on living a life like that?

He'd thought at the time that if he'd had a gun, he might have done it. He'd later reproached himself for thinking he'd been anywhere near as depressed as some people, as his friend Dave, who had slit his wrists, twice.

Corderoy wasn't nearly as emotionally perturbed now as he'd been in the month after Tara had left. The revelation of ♥Sylvie♥'s nonexistence meant he had failed at even the most superficial connection. He wasn't feeling crushed; he was feeling small and weightless, like a packing peanut. He thought of the time Montauk had helped him to the bathroom at the end of the third Encyclopaedists party. Corderoy had hovered over the toilet, dry-heaving, Montauk saying, *You got this, you got this,* until he said, *Move over,* and puked in the toilet himself. It was the moment Corderoy knew that their friendship had evolved from superficial absurdity to something of substance. It was a good moment. But it belonged to the past. It belonged to a life that wasn't over yet but could be soon. Why not?

All at once he was famished. There was no food in the house, so he put on some shoes and walked out into the cold November evening, wearing the same clothes he'd slept in for the last three days. It was below freezing outside, and everything was closed. He couldn't buy groceries. He wandered down the desolate streets, where the only other humans were speeding by in cars or walking briskly, no doubt late for Thanksgiving dinners. He headed toward Central Square, thinking about how much he loved his mother's turkey, her pumpkin pie. Normally, he would have scolded himself for such sentimental thoughts, but tonight, alone on Thanksgiving, three thousand miles from his family, Corderoy couldn't help indulging his melancholy. And as if the universe were indulging along with him, the only open restaurant in five miles was Nori Sushi.

He took a table in the rear, keeping his coat on for warmth, and ordered a dragon roll and a large flask of hot sake. There were only two other people in the restaurant, a fat guy with even worse hygiene than Corderoy, and an old Japanese couple. When his sake arrived, he poured a cup and knocked it back, feeling its heat and its alcohol warm his esophagus. He poured another cup immediately, and before his sushi arrived, he had finished the carafe. It was so perfectly antithetical to his usual Thanksgiving alcohol experience—his father decanting an expensive bottle of Bordeaux, swirling the glass. The waitress set down his dragon roll and another flask, and Corderoy meticulously stirred wasabi into a dish of soy sauce, dissolving large amounts of the green paste until he'd created a sinus-busting goo. It was stronger than he was accustomed to making it, but he wanted to highlight the disparity between his present experience and that of most of America, busy stuffing themselves with sweet yams and savory gravy over garlic mashed potatoes. When he finished, he paid his tab and walked outside with his coat unbuttoned, warmed all over from the sake and wasabi.

Back home, he lay down on the couch and turned on the TV. *The Last Samurai* was playing on USA. He'd heard it was only okay.

He had trouble focusing on the movie, partly because he was quite drunk and partly because he couldn't help imagining Thanksgiving in Seattle. His mother, Susan, was an incorrigible prompter of party games: charades, Pictionary, Scattergories, or Celebrity, in which each person wrote down someone famous and stuck the paper to someone else's forehead, then you went around the circle, trying to guess who you were. Corderoy hated this game most of all—perhaps it was something about the uncertainty of identity, the madness it implied in having to ask, "Am I dead?" or worse, "Am I fictional?" It was eleven in Boston, which meant it was eight in Seattle, and his mother was probably just now rounding people up for an interlude of games before dessert.

Tom Cruise was annoying, which was to be expected, but Ken Watanabe played a badass samurai named Katsumoto. Near the end of the movie, when the emperor's army had mowed down Watanabe's rebels with their American-bought howitzers, only Cruise and Watanabe were left alive on a blood-drenched field. Watanabe was too weak to commit seppuku, Japanese ritual suicide, so he asked Cruise to do it for him. Would that even count? It would be more like assisted suicide. Or consensual murder. It didn't seem honorable so much as pathetic. Cowardly. But the thing that really got Corderoy was that the reverse seemed cowardly, too. To simply go on living until nature or genetics or circumstance or God snuffed you out. He tried to recall Hamlet's *To be, or not to be* soliloquy:

> For who would bear the whips and scorns of time,
> The oppressor's wrong, the proud man's contumely,
> The pangs of despised love, the something something
> The law, patient merit something,
>
> . . . .
>
> With a bare bodkin . . .
> To grunt and sweat under a weary life,
> But that the dread of something after death—
> The undiscovered country, from whose bourn
> No traveler returns—puzzles the will,
> And makes us rather bear those ills we have
> Than fly to others that we know not of?

He realized that, as an atheist, he did not fear *the undiscovered country*. In his equation, there were no other ills he knew not of. There were only the present ills. And the option of ending them at his discretion. Besides, life had to end eventually. And thousands of years ago, twenty-three was middle-aged. Would he be missed? Certainly. His parents and his brother, and Montauk, and a few others would miss him. Mani, in a way, maybe. Perhaps his mother, a devout Catholic, would be debilitated by the same conundrum that Hamlet faced. But Corderoy's will felt significantly unpuzzled.

He saw his life as a mediocre movie. There had been some funny moments, a few tragic ones, plenty of boring ones, some in which the acting was painful, and were he to stay in the theater, there might be some more touching or hilarious scenes, but there'd also be hours of utter banality, of poorly edited and poorly written dialogue, of plots that went nowhere, of flimsy two-dimensional characters. Why not just walk out of the theater? He could be a thing that existed and then a thing that didn't.

The credits were rolling on *The Last Samurai,* and Corderoy muted the TV. He thought about getting a knife from the kitchen. He thought about rifling through the medicine cabinet looking for pills, he thought about sticking his head in the oven, he even thought about taking a bath and throwing the toaster in the water. But he continued to lie on the couch, his thumb tracing slow circles over the springy rubber buttons of the remote.

article | discussion | edit this page | history

The Encyclopaedists [edit]

The Encyclopaedists are losing definition, slowly, like a cloud formation on a day with little wind. Like constellations expanding beyond coherence in the time-lapse footage of the <u>death of the universe</u>. Were they ever real? Was the <u>Encyclopaedia</u> ever true?

The War is real, true, though its premises might be false. The University is false, though its premises might be true.

Contents [hide]
1 Precursors of the Encyclopaedists
2 Motivations of the Encyclopaedists
3 Ice
4 Used goods
5 Things that don't exist

Precursors of the Encyclopaedists [edit]

The Encyclopaedists couldn't exist without loneliness and <u>ADHD</u>. Without muscle fatigue in the right forearm. That doesn't say much for their value.

Motivations of the Encyclopaedists [edit]

Make it to tomorrow. The next minute is only a minute away. Document as a stay against confusion. Screenshot or it didn't happen.

Ice [edit]

In the desert, ice began as a legend. One day it became the luxury of fat, wealthy men, massive blocks cut from the glaciers of the north borne south on the backs of tireless oliphants. Centuries later, it became the symbol of <u>middle-class</u> success, the enhanced beverage. And finally, it became one of the granteds, like clean water, like air. Nothing special. One further thing of wonder become nothing. So the march of disillusionment continues.

Used goods [edit]

Common Wisdom holds that the goods are unfathomable. That is, bottomless, inexhaustible. Justice. <u>Truth</u>. Equality. Beauty. They do not deteriorate through use. So holds Common Wisdom.

But Common Wisdom doesn't have a great track record. Follow the career of any porn star and watch as Beauty gets used up, ugliness its absence. What better

WIKIPEDIA
The Free Encyclopedia

navigation
- Main Page
- Community portal
- Current events
- Recent changes
- Random page
- Help
- Donations

search

[Go] [Search]

toolbox
- What links here
- Related changes
- Special pages

way to explain Injustice than that Justice got used up elsewhere. Secondhand Equality is really all any of us ever get. Women especially. It's been passed around for centuries. Just wait. It'll be gone soon, too. One can easily imagine a world without Justice, without Equality and Beauty. But such a horrendous world could be just as True as this one. Here is a truth taken in and used and spewed out by many before you: people only love you as far as they can see you. No one loves an absence.

Things that don't exist [edit]

There are more things that don't exist than things that exist. Nothing doesn't exist, but everything, by definition, does. Nonexistence is not a problem. Existence is.

Some things can't exist: round squares, the last digit of pi, time-travel (to undo something foolish; to skip past the unpleasant but necessary, to repeat what seemed unique and indescribably joyous).

Some things don't exist but seem like they do: time (the future, the past), free will, numbers (e.g. 19 years old, 103 degrees).

Some things used to exist but now don't: OK Soda, Eskimos, happiness, dinosaurs (meteor?), illusionment, cupcakes (eaten), adolescence, the self that typed "adolescence," the self that typed "self that typed 'adolescence.' "

Some places are nonexistent: Alderaan (as if millions of voices, etc.), Rhode Island (never been), Gotham, Yoknapatawpha, Uqbar, Tlön (where the people speak a language that lacks nouns—*hlör u fang axaxaxas mlö:* upward behind the onstreaming it mooned), home, square 1, America (so vast).

There are many words that don't exist: agreeance, brang, funfetti, guestimate, irregardless, libary, lol, love, nother, omg, orientate, sorry, thanx, unpaid, wtf.

And there are plenty of people who don't exist: Baron Münchausen, Don Quixote, Gavin Kovite, Halifax Corderoy, Mani Saheli, Mickey Montauk, Schrödinger, Sylvie/Selena, Christopher Robinson, Sir Baltimore Gosshawk Wakefield III.

You cannot wish yourself into nonexistence, for you affirm your reality by the act of wishing. Cogito Ergo Nihil: Descartes walks into a bar. The bartender says, "Would you like a drink?" Descartes says, "I think not," then disappears.

External links [edit]

1. ^ "The Encyclopaedists of Capitol Hill."
www.thestranger.com/apr04/encyclopaedists.htm

2. ^ "C. PLINII NATVRALIS HISTORIAE PRAEFATIO."
www.thelatinlibrary.com/pliny.nhpr.html

BAGHDAD

19

The Black Hawk whipped low over the dun suburbs of Anbar Province. Second Lieutenant Mickey Montauk had a window seat, his boot dangling above clusters of brown houses with driveways and clotheslines. On the roof of a larger three-story, some teenagers sat in lawn chairs. Montauk was touched by a momentary envy. In Seattle, rooftops were angled and shingled, due to the rain. One of the roof kids jumped up and waved, his loose blue shirt flapping in the rotor wash. Montauk waved back. His cultural proficiency guidebook had warned about showing Iraqis the soles of your shoes—a sign of disrespect in the Arab world. No way the Arab foot-beef extended to people flying in helicopters, but he tucked his feet in anyway.

He had volunteered to be on the advance party, arriving by helo. Olaf was supervising the convoy from Arifjan in Kuwait. Montauk felt guilty leaving his platoon to make the long drive without him, getting their first taste of anxiety about the ever present threat of roadside bombs. But as the city began appearing on the horizon through the thick haze, Montauk's guilt gave way to amazement. Baghdad from the air was a land of fantasy, ripped right out of some cartoonish video game. Gigantic pastel mushrooms and blue eggs dotted the landscape. There were the Ba'athist pleasure domes, surrounded by greenery and kidney-shaped pools. The summer palaces on slopes where sheiks relaxed on their terraces while silken girls served sherbet.

Many of the larger buildings hugged the Tigris, which curved in a lazy bend around the center of the capital. There was a large zoo with a Ferris wheel and a hippopotamus pond. Close by was an enormous white disc-shaped structure—the Tomb of the Unknown Soldier, built in the wake of the Iran/Iraq war. And beyond that, the capstone of it all: the Swords of Qādisīyah, their massive blades gripped in hands rising out of the earth. Saddam was a cheesy son of a bitch, yes. But there was something awesome about commissioning an official government sculpture of your own hands holding 140-foot sabers, to be placed in the middle of the city.

Montauk daydreamed his own self-aggrandizing public art pieces. Perhaps a bronze equestrian monument, with himself in late-eighteenth-century costume—but did the world really need another of those? Then the vision came to him: looming over acres of tombstones in Arlington Cemetery, a hundred-foot-high statue of himself, shirtless, pointing a big-ass Rambo M-60 to the sky, Corderoy's mom clinging to his side in a tattered dress, her romance-novel melons barely concealed, and Corderoy at his feet, hunched like Gollum with clawed fingers and giant yellow eyes. Montauk laughed to himself as the Black Hawk banked west over the Tigris.

The Texans of 3rd Brigade, 1st Cavalry Division had installed themselves in the presidential palace on the river, with its turquoise dome and copses of palm trees out front, now browning and dying because the Cav didn't give a good goddamn about Saddam's landscaping. There was a nice fat hole in the side of the dome where some Tomahawk missile had slammed into it. Montauk wished he'd been around to see that. Those air strikes had happened just over a year ago; he might have been nerding out over transcendental poetry with Corderoy in Rome on the night this part of Baghdad had its face rearranged by the Air Force. He'd joined the National Guard back before the Twin Towers fell, a blink in the eye of history but a long time ago for Montauk. Even after the Iraq invasion, a combat deployment seemed an unlikely future to your average reservist. Foreign wars were for the regular Army. And yet here they were.

The Black Hawk touched down on the dirt, and Montauk and his team grabbed their rucks and headed toward the main entrance, a fancy raised-up marble and brass deal with a valet parking–type turnaround.

They entered and climbed the marble staircase to the rotunda, which was hung with a large Old Glory and an even larger Texan flag. It must have been forty feet long. No need for all those stars and stripes, just one stripe each of red and white and one big-ass star. *Protected by niggas with big dicks, AKs, and 187 skills*, Montauk recalled Snoop Dogg saying, apropos of something or other.

"You like that, LT?" said a man coming down the staircase. He looked like a black Mr. Clean. An oversize horse-head Cav patch on the shoulder, captain's bars on one lapel, and on the other what looked like . . . yes, cavalry sabers. He was Montauk's liaison.

"It's huge, sir," Montauk said, looking back to the flag.

"Got it donated from the DAR in Fort Worth. I spoke with Captain Byrd. He's gonna talk to your colonel to get us a Washington flag to hang up there, since y'all are getting attached to Third Brigade." He looked Montauk in the eye. "You got a big one?"

"Probably not that big."

They were shuttled in a Humvee to the Convention Center, a couple of klicks away at the other edge of the Green Zone. They passed traffic circles with memorial statues, palm trees, rows of small houses, some still occupied (by their original inhabitants, foreign contractors, journalists?), some damaged and vacant. They passed roadside food carts, convenience stands, more palm trees. The Humvee approached an entrance checkpoint manned by two soldiers with a tire ripper that they rolled out of the way when the driver flashed his ID. They took a right and rolled down a central boulevard divided by an L.A.-style median whose palms had been reduced to stumps by security-conscious landscapers. Across the median and through a small parking lot stood the Al Rasheed Hotel, Saddam's Ritz, which was for a while the most sought-after address in occupied Baghdad. Until the mortars and rockets started flying about six months after the invasion. Large concrete walls were erected around the Green Zone, and the occupation slowly hunkered down in the bunker that would become its prison.

Montauk's liaison dropped him off in front of two machine-gun towers and a long walkway that served as a pedestrian checkpoint; fifteen or twenty soldiers were spread along it, checking identification, searching, and swabbing for explosive residue. A steady trickle of Baghdadis in light, loose clothing or long, black abayas emerged from the gauntlet of the checkpoint and walked through the heat toward the Convention Center. For what? To apply for jobs, to get some kind of handout or reparations payment from the occupation, to report relatives missing or killed? Montauk looped his front sling over his head and arm so that Molly Millions hung straight down over his vest. A soldier from the 3rd Infantry Division stood at the Convention Center's front door, checking to see that weapons were unloaded. He'd probably shot his way in here with the invasion force and was still cooling his heels. Montauk yanked the bolt back to show Molly's empty innards and was about to walk through when the soldier stopped him. "Pistol, too, sir."

"Right. Sorry," Montauk said. He did the same for his pistol, feeling like the new kid in school. You didn't belong until someone newer than you came along.

The main hall was wrapped in a mosaic depicting the history of the Babylonians, from Hammurabi's conquests to the recent "victories" over Iran and the US, represented here as a dragon with a red, white, and blue tail. Soldiers and flak-vested American-looking civilians crossed the tile floor, along with Iraqis in loose blue uniforms who looked to be custodial staff. Montauk asked around and was pointed toward a door off to the side of the main hall. He opened it and guessed he had found his future home.

It was some sort of office corridor, though the desks and cubicle partitions had been replaced by bunks and stacks of equipment. Camouflage ponchos hung on green 550 cord to make little living-space partitions. It looked like a couple hundred troops were living here.

Montauk asked around for the CO and was pointed to the Tactical Operations Center, a hemispherical office room with a satellite map of the Green Zone on its fuzzy wall, a couple of desktop computers, and some olive-green steel tactical radios. The two guys sitting in front of the computers looked up at him.

"Can we help you, LT?" one of them said.

"I'm the advance party for Bravo Company, 161. Washington National Guard."

They both raised their eyebrows and looked at each other. "Are you our relief?"

It hit Montauk that yes, he was the new kid in school, but his arrival meant graduation for all these troops. Charlie Company had been here since the invasion and was one of the last companies of the 3rd Infantry to be sent home. The 1st Cav had been here a month, but the transition was slow. Now that Montauk was arriving with Bravo Company, these weary boys could return to their wives and girlfriends, or ex-wives and ex-girlfriends, depending.

"Looks like it," Montauk said.

One of the radio guys hailed his commander on the phone while the other looked at Montauk like a fifth-grader who had just won a pizza party.

20

"Faggot," Mohammed Faisal muttered in English after the shop door jingled shut behind him. He made his way down Karada Dahil, his plastic flip-flops slapping against the sidewalk as he shifted the case of Mr. Brown iced coffee from one shoulder to another. When a gap in traffic appeared, he dashed to the median. A blue Bongo pickup carrying goats wafted its goat-smell over him as it passed along the parkway, and the boy made a face of exaggerated disgust. He shifted the box off his shoulder and onto his chest and ran the rest of the way across. He was a week short of his eleventh birthday.

The line of cars started a full block and a half from the checkpoint. The drivers milled around, close enough to keep an eye on their vehicles but far enough to maybe survive the blast if one of the cars should for any reason explode. A pile of trash bloomed in a vacant lot, threatening to engulf the sidewalk and obliging Mohammed to sidestep the rank evaporate of what had been fetid pools. His hair clung damply to his forehead as he trudged down the line of cars toward the gun towers in the near distance. An Iraqi soldier sitting in a plastic chair looked up as he passed. "Hey, kid," he said, cigarette smoke snorting out his nostrils.

Mohammed stopped, surprised. The Iraqi soldiers at the checkpoint were mostly from out of town and rarely spoke to him. They never bought anything because they didn't want to pay his delivery markup. This one was young and clean-shaven. The palm hanging over his head shaded the Kalashnikov in his lap.

"The new Americans just got here," the soldier said.

"Yeah?"

"Yeah." He smirked. "Hope they don't kick you off the checkpoint."

Mohammed smiled defiantly, then hopped and slung the case up to his head and continued on, balancing the coffee on his skull like a Babylonian serving girl. His too-short F. C. Iraqiya jersey rode up, exposing a sliver of belly to the dusty air.

"Faggot," he muttered in English. He walked up the entrance lane and passed three soldiers, two of whom he didn't recognize. He slowed down and twisted his head to take a look at them. The patches on their shoulders were different. Also, their helmets were smaller and had black metal squares on the front.

The checkpoint seemed to be flooded with new Americans. Mohammed made his usual way past the gun towers in the center of the traffic circle and just north of it to the command post, which was made up of three tall concrete barriers with camouflage netting strung between them to make an area of dappled shade. There were five Americans standing under the netting. One of them pointed at him and they all turned. Mohammed hesitated.

"Come on in!" yelled Lieutenant Watts. "Put the coffee on the table." He turned to Captain Byrd and Lieutenant Montauk, his replacement. "That's Monkey," he said. "He's one of the checkpoint kids. Gets you coffees and shawarmas and shit."

Mohammed stared at the group as he walked into the command post. Satellite photos were taped up on the concrete walls. A large steel desk sat at the rear with green metal radios on top of it. Mohammed hefted the case onto the desk, and Lieutenant Watts tore it open. "Iced coffee?"

"Is it cold?" Montauk asked.

"Room temperature."

"So, like, a hundred and fifteen degrees?"

"Yeah." Lieutenant Watts smiled, then dumped the cans of coffee into an ice-filled garbage bin.

"That's going to be the new checkpoint LT," Watts said to Monkey.

Montauk held his hand out for a fist bump. "What's up, stud? Lieutenant Montauk."

The kid curled his hand into a fist and bumped Montauk's.

"Now beat it," Watts said, handing him a couple bills.

Mohammed scurried off and started back down toward Karada Dahil, his plastic flip-flops sending small scraping noises through the thick, windless air.

"Faggot," he said once he was out of earshot.

Watts stood over the dusty, laminated satellite map of Baghdad. Montauk and Byrd crowded behind him. The Green Zone was outlined in marker; its eastern and southern borders followed the contour of the Tigris River.

"Here's Brigade," Watts said, pointing to an X on the western edge of the Green Zone—the large domed palace where Montauk first reported. "And here's the FOB." He indicated the Iraqi Convention Center, Montauk's new Forward Operating Base, marked by another X to the northeast. "And here we are at Checkpoint Eleven." He pointed at a small traffic circle outside the Green Zone on the south side of 14 July Bridge.

"We're running three ingress routes to the Green Zone. Military Lane runs north on Route Steelers and into the checkpoint past the east bunker and east gun tower. That's for Coalition military vehicles and US government vehicles. The east-west road that intersects with Steelers is Karada Dahil. It's the main thoroughfare that runs the length of the dick."

"The dick being Karada Peninsula?" Montauk asked.

"Right, the Tigris bends around it a few klicks to the west. Baghdad University's over there. It's out of our AO, but I've rolled through there a few times. Relatively peaceful, though apparently some student group has been terrorizing people and making all the women wear burkas and shit. Anyway, Routine Search traffic comes in westbound on Karada Dahil. Drivers only, though. Passengers have to get out, go through the Ped Search bunker, and rejoin their vehicles on the bridge. That's how we do it, anyway. Just made it up as we went along, so you'll probably figure out what works for you. It got more complex after the city started getting explody. So, Priority Search is on River Road, a block to the north. That's for the top two tiers of Iraqi government workers and contractors. No gun towers over it, but BOB provides overwatch."

Montauk wiped the sweat off his brow. He should have been taking notes. He was, after all, going to be living and breathing the operations of Checkpoint 11. But it was hard to concentrate on procedural minutiae while he was consumed with curiosity and anxiety about attacks on the checkpoint. There was a crater just outside the command post, a gouge in the pavement about the size and shape of a bed frame. He'd been wanting to ask about it since he walked in. "Who's Bob?" he asked instead.

"The Bradley On the Bridge. BOB. It's parked in the middle, where it can be a backstop for any vehicle that somehow manages to bum-rush through the entire checkpoint. We park it so that it can also cover River Road to the east with optics and the twenty-five."

Montauk pictured one of the old-model BMWs he'd seen on Karada Dahil getting shredded by 25 mm chain-gun fire. "Has it ever come to that?" he asked.

"Not yet, fingers crossed. But we did get a VBIED a few weeks ago."

"We heard about that," Captain Byrd said.

The LT treated Montauk and Byrd to the rundown on the bombing: a silver Kia had driven slowly up to the command post, where two soldiers stopped it to check the driver's ID and search for contraband or weapons. As one of the soldiers approached, a stack of artillery shells wired together in the trunk detonated, cratering the ground and blowing him right into the wall of the CP.

"Jesus," Montauk said.

"Yeah," said Watts. "PFC Klay. It was one of those concussion deaths where all your blood vessels burst and you bleed out internally. Klay was kind of prim, so I guess we used to pick on him a lot. Everyone felt bad."

Watts fell silent for a moment, and neither Byrd nor Montauk attempted a response. "One of our tower guys thought he heard the driver do the *Allahu Akhbar* thing before blowing up," Watts said. "Anyway, we got five men on each entrance lane now. One who checks the driver's ID, then if he waves it in, two to search the trunk, passenger compartment, and undercarriage while two more provide over-watch with a machine gun from the bunker."

One-Six, Routine Search.

"It's working so far," Watts said, reaching for his radio.

Routine Search, One-Six, what's up?

One-Six, Routine Search, we got a lady over here freaking out about her ID.

Roger, en route.

"Sir, you wanna come down and check it out?" Watts asked Captain Byrd.

"That's what we're here for," said Byrd. He and the rest of the platoon had arrived that morning, a few days after Montauk.

They walked down the lane toward Routine Search, their path corralled by long, curving lines of six-foot-high concrete T-walls.

"Did you guys put these barriers up?" Montauk asked.

"Yeah, the idea is, if you wall off the lanes and stretch them out, and you put only two or three troops at any given point, they know there's no way they're getting into the Green Zone with a bomb and that they can only take one or two of us, max, if they decide to go see Allah. So it's not worth it to hit us when they can go to the local police station and kill like twenty or thirty guys."

They walked past a middle-aged man getting a pat-down from Ant, with a Charlie soldier supervising. Montauk gave him a nod of approval.

"And the assumption is that suicide bombers are going to make a rational decision like that?" Captain Byrd said.

"Yes, sir. I mean, they've only got so many suicide bombers, so they got to make them count, right?"

Up ahead, an Iraqi about Montauk's age was talking with two of Watts's squad leaders. Near them, seated at the foot of a T-wall, was a late-middle-aged woman in a black hijab clutching a purse. The Iraqi waved to them.

"That's Aladdin," said Watts. "He's maybe our best translator, or at least I like him best. I worry about him sometimes, though. It's getting more dangerous for these guys."

Aladdin was dressed nicer than the Average Alis in line to enter the checkpoint; they seemed to prefer loose trousers and sandals. He looked more like the young Roman guys Montauk and Corderoy had met in Trastevere: cheapo stonewashed "designer" jeans with a fitted polo, slip-on shoes, and Gucci-type shades.

"Hey, Aladdin, I want you to meet some people. This is my replacement, Lieutenant Montauk. He's the platoon leader. That's his boss, Captain Byrd."

"Okay, nice to meet you, sih!"

"How's it going?" Montauk said. Aladdin shook his hand in the exact sort of low slap-shake Corderoy would use. Montauk liked him immediately.

They approached the squad leaders and Watts asked about the situation.

"Sir, she says she lives in the Green Zone," his sergeant said.

"But she's got no ID. Like, none at all," said the other Charlie soldier.

"What does she say about it?" Watts asked.

They looked to Aladdin.

"She say she left it at her home, sih," Aladdin said, giving a half-smile and holding his hands out expansively.

"Yeah, you guys believe her?"

Aladdin shrugged.

"What would you do, Montauk?" Byrd asked.

"I don't know, sir. I guess let her in?"

"Are you asking me or telling me?"

"Sir, I'd give her a good search, maybe take her picture so she knows we're serious, and then let her in. I mean, what are we worried about?"

"No ID at all, you'd let her in?"

"Hooah, sir, that would be my call." Montauk had already changed his mind, but that *hooah,* Army slang for anything and everything except *no,* had the stamp of finality. Being indecisive was Original Sin in the officer corps, for good reason. Whether Byrd actually disagreed or was just testing his mettle, Montauk couldn't back down now.

Captain Byrd looked to Watts. "What do you say, LT?"

"Yeah, I think it could go either way, sir. They're supposed to have IDs, but there's a lot of gaps, and the IDs are such crap. I'm inclined to let her in."

Everyone looked at Captain Byrd, who'd been at the checkpoint for all of ten minutes but who outranked everyone there. "Hooah," Byrd said.

"Okay, Sergeant," said Watts. "Tell Pedestrian Search to take her picture and let her in."

The sergeant nodded at Aladdin, who began translating.

"I've got to get back," Byrd said to Montauk. "Be prepared to brief me tomorrow on your checkpoint SOP."

"Hooah, sir." Byrd walked back up the lane, and Montauk keyed his hand mike and arranged for two of his guys to take the commander back to the FOB. Aladdin walked up to Montauk as Watts talked to his sergeants. Montauk was packing a tin of Kodiak.

"Oh, you dip, sih?"

"Yeah," Montauk said. "Want some?"

"Oh, thank you, sih."

He handed the tin to Aladdin, who took a pinch and stuck it under his lip like a person who'd been doing it only a few weeks. Passing for a grunt, just like Montauk himself was doing. Montauk smiled, threw in a plug of the pungent dip, and popped the tin back into his compass pouch.

"I think that was a good thing, sih."

"What, the woman?"

"Yeah." Aladdin put his finger to his lip to push the dip farther in. "I don't think she is mujahideen, you know. And it is not safe for her out here."

"Tell me about it. It's like *Mad Max* out here."

"Mel Gibson," Aladdin said.

"You like Mel Gibson?"

"No, sih. I like Bruce Willis. *Die Hard. Five Element.*"

"Oh yeah?"

"You look like young Bruce Willis," Aladdin said. "When your hair falls out, then you look just like him."

"I'll take that as a compliment," Montauk said.

"No one can tell the difference then. And you will take me to fancy Hollywood parties. Lots of girls." Aladdin elbowed Montauk in the ribs.

Montauk laughed. "Hey, man, if I can get in, you'll be the first on my guest list."

Watts found them and took another half hour showing Montauk the ropes, then they hopped into a flatbed Humvee that had its doors torn off and a makeshift gun turret welded on. One of Watts's soldiers got in the driver's seat, and the other jumped behind the gun. The sun was low in the sky, and the Humvee's headlights revealed a small cloud of dust that dispersed as the truck started forward and headed back across 14 July Bridge to the FOB. Chow time. Finally.

The entrance to the dining facility was inlaid with a tiled picture of George H. W. Bush surrounded by an American flag. The confusion of it all struck Montauk as he stepped on Bush's nose. Nobody had bothered changing the flooring because the insult of walking on your enemy's face was lost in translation. He looked at the Charlie guys and wondered if they knew what it signified. Or did they think the mosaic was installed after the invasion by us? Among the civilian contractors, there might be some who got the insult emotionally, like the Iraqis did, but who happily walked on the flag and Bush. Montauk thought of Corderoy.

Dinner was chicken cordon bleu of the middlebrow Southern-US buffet variety, courtesy of Kellogg, Brown, and Root. The buffet line attendants appeared to be Pakistani. The tableware was high-quality disposable. There were six kinds of dessert. There were paper doilies on the table. The Charlie guys made easy conversation, but a sadness descended over Montauk as he ate, the kind of callow but real sadness he used to experience as a teenager when he saw a person eating alone in a restaurant without even a book. He viewed this scene like a museum diorama, perhaps that dusty and curiously flat scene of the Pilgrims meeting the Indians in the American Museum of Natural History in New York.

"You think they think we're fools?" Montauk said. "The Iraqi staff. For walking in dirty boots on that mosaic out there, tramping on our own flag."

"Probably," Watts said.

If that was true, if the Iraqi elevator attendant in the lobby—who had worked around Americans for months now—still thought we were fools, then it meant he didn't really understand the freedom we were trying to give the Iraqis. That's what it felt like, walking on that mosaic: an exercise of freedom. Though Montauk didn't know if he meant freedom with a hipster wink or some other, earlier kind of freedom. The freedom to burn your own flag.

That evening, Montauk closed his eyes and fell into a not quite dream state full of visions of his parents, and of Mani and Corderoy, and of the light moving across the walls of his childhood bedroom as troops around him woke and took up their arms and left into the night, and as others returned, removed their sweat-stained armor and boots, and lay down to sleep or read or gaze up at the ceiling.

21

Montauk used an elaborate sequence of facial movements to pack the Kodiak more deeply between his gums and teeth, then spit a stream of tangy brown fluid into the dust on 14 July Street. He regarded the end of the checkpoint's exit lane, where the last section in a row of T-wall was knocked askew. It looked like some concrete-eating shark had taken a large bite out of it. Bits of rebar poked out of the wound. Tanks. They tended to leave a trail. Montauk watched when they rolled through his checkpoint with the kind of friendly trepidation a rose gardener would feel toward the neighbor's dog.

"Are they driving like idiots, or is this lane actually difficult to get out of?" Montauk said.

"Both," Olaf said. "The tanks are pretty wide, but they're also being driven by eighteen-year-olds."

"Why do they even take tanks out into the city? It's not like they can use the main gun."

"They're tankers, sir. That's what they do."

They gazed down 14 July Street like Marlboro Men. On the south side were rows of boarded-up storefronts that betrayed small hints of former prosperity, like the chandeliers hung in the unlit display of the furniture shop. There had been no signs of life from within since Montauk had been at the checkpoint, but no one had looted it, either. A little farther down was a ten-foot-tall replica of the Eiffel Tower affixed to the sidewalk, a piece of flair that a realtor might point to when describing the neighborhood as funky. Montauk considered asking Aladdin about it when he returned. He'd just left to buy a Mountain Dew, his favorite American soda. The decay of the neighborhood surrounding the checkpoint and the uneasiness of its inhabitants gave Montauk a sense of displaced guilt, like that of a suburban environmentalist regarding a landfill.

He spat again. "How busy was this street? Before the invasion," he asked rhetorically.

"You could ask those guys," Olaf said, gesturing to a trio of oldsters seated at a plastic table halfway down the block. They wore keffiyehs and looked like they had a shisha set up on the table. Olaf waved, and one of them waved back. "Wanna go say hi?" he asked.

Montauk saw Aladdin returning. He radioed the west gun tower to tell them that the three of them were going a hundred meters down the road to talk to the locals.

"You know these old dudes?" Montauk asked Aladdin.

"Do not worry about them, sih." Aladdin took a swig of his Mountain Dew, then made a loud purposeful "Ahhhh" and held the bottle up next to his face with two hands, smiling like an actor in a television commercial from the fifties. The sun filtered through the nuclear-green liquid. Montauk couldn't help but chuckle at the goofy translator.

"I'm not worried about them," he said. "I just want to ask them some questions."

Aladdin screwed the cap back on with twitchy fingers. "What questions?"

"You know, the kind of questions you ask old-timers. Like what was this neighborhood like thirty years ago?"

Aladdin laughed. "I think you are too late, sih. They are too old to remember yesterday!"

Olaf gave Montauk a skeptical eyebrow.

"Let's find out." He started walking down the street.

Aladdin's smirk congealed. He hurried after Montauk. "I don't think it is best idea, sih."

"Aww, c'mon. They look friendly," Montauk said. They walked the rest of the way in silence, Aladdin at the rear.

Montauk removed his helmet and lifted his ballistic eye protection onto his forehead. This was in direct violation of brigade policy, but

Olaf followed suit. The old-timers sat around a small plastic table; they wore loose white dishdashas and sandals and had steel-wool beards and crazy teeth. A slight breeze made a moving mosaic of the shade cast by the date palm above them. Montauk asked if anyone spoke English and was met with grave head rotations. Olaf cracked an amused smile.

"That's why we've got Aladdin here," Montauk said. "Can you tell them we'd like to ask a few questions. About this neighborhood. What it was like when they were growing up?"

Aladdin translated, and the oldster with the shortest beard, sitting on the right, said something that had the word *Iraqi* in it, and the other two chortled. The one on the left had the longest beard, which meant he was likely the Chief Oldster. It took all of Montauk's concentration to stay on top of these cultural cues.

"Well, what'd he say?" Montauk asked Aladdin.

"He makes a stupid joke. That's all," Aladdin said.

The Chief Oldster squinted at Aladdin and muttered a string of phlegmy syllables. Whatever Aladdin said back, it couldn't have been nice, for the Oldster shook his head disapprovingly.

"I'm sorry, sih. I should have said before. I know this man. He is like uncle to me. He says I try to be American. He does not like my job."

"Why's that?" Montauk asked.

"If it is okay, sih, I meet you at the CP?"

"Sure," Montauk said. "Just give us a few minutes."

Montauk watched Aladdin give the oldsters a curt good-bye and walk off.

"Sir," Olaf said. He nodded toward the oldsters. "They want us to smoke with them."

The Chief Oldster was offering Olaf the hookah pipe. Why wasn't he offering it to Montauk? "Go ahead," Montauk said. Olaf took a drag, said, "*Shukran*," and passed it to Montauk. He inhaled, causing the glass to bubble gently, which sent vibrations back up the hose to the brass mouthpiece. "*Shukran*," Montauk said, handing the hose back.

The short-bearded wiseacre bent down to a pewter tray on the ground and produced three glasses. He set one in front of the Chief Oldster and placed the two others on the table in front of Montauk and Olaf. Gunshots. A rapid burst. Montauk swung his head in their direction like a startled bird. Olaf remained impassive, as did the Iraqis, except for Wiseacre, who opened into a yellowed grin. Montauk sensed that he'd somehow made a fool of himself. The black plastic radio handset clipped to his vest broadcast the estimated distance and direction of the small arms fire in the bored voice of Staff Sergeant Jackson. Some jerk shooting the sky with his AK.

The tea was poured slowly, with an anachronistic elegance that somehow did not seem out of place at the small plastic table. Olaf's was filled first, and it was now obvious to Montauk that Wiseacre had gotten their ranks backward. But he didn't understand why.*

The Chief Oldster gestured invitingly to them, and Montauk lifted his glass. "Cheers," he said.

"*Allah Boucher,*" said the oldsters.

Wiseacre broke the silence by pointing at Montauk's vest and making a remark. The middle guy said something that made Wiseacre guffaw again. Olaf looked at Montauk, who just shrugged and smiled politely. Were they making fun of him jumping at the gunfire earlier, for wearing Kevlar? How the hell was he supposed to connect with these people?

Montauk looked at his tea glass and marveled at how dainty it seemed compared to the one-and-a-half-liter plastic bottles he was accustomed to drinking from. A small chorus of car horns rose up from beneath the underpass, then quickly died away. Urritia's voice piped up through Montauk's radio, informing him that a vehicle had popped hot on a swab for explosive residue. Montauk and Olaf said polite good-byes, then made their way back to the search lane.

There were no explosives in that vehicle, though. Nor in the next one that popped hot on the vapor tracer. Nor the next one. It seemed to

---

* What should have been forehead-slappingly obvious to Montauk and the entire US Central Command was the reason Wiseacre thought Olaf wore the pants in 2nd Platoon: he couldn't believe that a professional adult male like Montauk would walk around in public without a mustache. Not that Olaf grasped it, either; he came by his own mustache honestly, growing up earlier and farther from the city than Montauk, and in the kind of social circles in which people named Richard would still call themselves "Dick" unironically.

Montauk over the next week that about one in twenty vehicles had some kind of explosive residue, and yet so far, none of them had been carrying any kind of explosives. Either the vapor tracer was a piece of shit, or maybe cars just got explosive residue on them by driving around in a bombed-out city like Baghdad. That or Al-Qaeda was rubbing acetone peroxide on the bottoms of random cars. Just to fuck with us.

22

After his deployment was over, when he would have plenty of time to think about it, Montauk would remember urban bomb-attack scenes as a particular kind of tableau. He would see the aftermath of several during his time in Baghdad, and while they were all slightly different, they shared certain characteristics. There was the aroma, which varied depending on what kind of explosive was used and on whether there was any human flesh cooking, but which always had as its main ingredient the scent of burning oil and rubber. There was always broken glass—everywhere. There was always a variety of liquids on the pavement—those soldiers with more gruesome imaginations might think these to be one hundred percent blood and body fluids, but they couldn't possibly, one hoped, all come from people. There was always a crater. There was always steel twisted into aesthetically interesting shapes that were too jagged and complex to be called beautiful. There were usually a few bodies visible, depending on the QRF's reaction time, although Montauk would notice that the bodies remained there longer once people started getting wise to the Anti-Iraqi Forces' tactic of detonating a second bomb after the first one filled the street with emergency vehicles and keening relatives. Finally, there was always an interesting flourish, a little icing on the cake of the bomb scene, something to remember it by. Usually, it consisted of a corpse or body part, like a little baby shoe with a little baby foot still in it. He would later, in bed, imagine for himself a war-porn video montage of blown-off baby feet, some bare but most encased in a variety of shoe styles, a few buckled-up Mary Janes with frilly socks, the rest in sandals or cheap sneakers.

Montauk was lying in his cot when the shock wave passed through the walls of the Iraqi Convention Center and over the bunks of his platoon, which was currently designated the Quick Reaction Force for Bravo Company. This meant that if anything major happened in Bravo's AO in the next twenty-four hours, it would be Montauk's men leaping out of their cots. They'd been in Baghdad a few weeks, and it was their third rotation as the Company QRF. Nothing had happened the first two times. That shock wave he'd just felt wasn't nothing. A few feet away in the Tactical Operations Center, the net sprang to life.

Bushmaster Main, OP South, over. It was Ant radioing from Observation Post South, which was at the top of the Al Rasheed and the highest point in the Green Zone.

The radio squawked as Bravo Company's radio nerd keyed the handset. "Wooo, dude, I heard *that* one. OP South, Bushmaster Main, go ahead."

Main, South. Smoke plume observed in the vicinity of Palestine Way in Karada. Grid square to follow. Break. Golf Zulu 10498852. Probable VBIED. How copy, over?

Montauk was lacing up his boots and buttoning his uniform blouse in the controlled panic associated with waking up late on the morning of a final exam. He turned to Fields, who was in his cot a few feet away, doing the same. "Fields," he said, "tell the squad leaders to get their guys moving and report to me. Looks like we're rolling out."

"Yes, sir." Fields jolted out of his cot and moved down the row of bunks.

Montauk entered the TOC. The radio monitoring the battalion net came awake. Information was traveling up the chain of command. *OP South, Warhorse Main. Give us a BDA on that VBIED, over.*

Warhorse Main, OP South, Ant responded. *Looks like it's in one of the larger intersections on Palestine. Lots of black smoke. Too far away to see much other than that, but I would expect some casualties based on the location and size of blast, over.*

Sergeant Jackson found Montauk in the TOC, looking at the satellite map of downtown Baghdad. "Where is it?" he asked, tucking his laces into his boots.

Montauk jabbed a finger at the laminated map on the wall. "10498852, in Karada. VBIED in an intersection. Palestine Way and whatever that street is."

Staff Sergeant Nguyen strode into the TOC pop-eyed. "Well, that one was either small and close or big and far away."

"What's at that intersection?" said Jackson. "Some police station or something? Some Shi'ite mosque?"

"Not that I remember," Montauk said. "I think that's where the big department store is."

"Shit, AQI nuked the department store? Are we rolling out, sir?" Nguyen asked.

Bushmaster Main, this is Warhorse Six, put your QRF on the radio. Rad Rod Houston's voice was fat with Texan. Montauk imagined the battalion commander with an unlit cigar in his mouth. The company radio nerd raised his eyebrows and held the receiver toward Montauk.

Shit, here we go.

"Warhorse Six, Bushmaster QRF, over," Montauk said.

Listen up, QRF. I need you to get over there and secure that intersection. Wire it off in all directions, take up blocking positions, and facilitate traffic so we can start the medevacs. I've got an engineer platoon heading out there after you, so be prepared to pull your trucks to the east side of that intersection to let them in, over.

"Six, QRF, roger, over."

QRF, Six . . . have you done this kind of operation before?

"Six, QRF, negative, over."

QRF, Six, try not to fuck this up.

Montauk turned to Nguyen. "Go spin 'em up."

"Hooah, sir," Nguyen said, stomping out of the TOC just as Olaf and the other squad leaders were coming in. Montauk briefed them while Nguyen barked out orders to Rise and Shine and Get It On, and 2nd Platoon came alive like the inside of a shaken wasps' nest.

Montauk pulled the small map of Karada out of his thigh pocket and compared it to the laminated satellite map on the wall. He would lead the convoy in the Millennium Falcon, his preferred Humvee; it wasn't uparmored like the other Humvees—it had just a few scraps of welded-on sheet metal—but it was fast. Should they converge on the intersection from different directions? Or drive straight in as a platoon and disperse from there? Splitting up the platoon made it more vulnerable. But if the intersection was impassable, it might turn the platoon into a clusterfuck-ish parking lot. *Six, QRF, try not to fuck this up.*

Montauk looped his Kevlar over his head, gave his vest a quick pat-down, then ran out into the lobby of the Convention Center, his armor and full magazines rubbing rhythmically on his body like some cheap percussion instrument. He threw open the door and burst out into the dry morning heat. All six trucks were lined up and idling, their turret gunners working the bolt carriers back and forth. Montauk yelled for his squad leaders and platoon sergeant, and they fell in around him.

"Okay, listen up," he yelled at the huddle. "Everybody know where the bomb hit?" They all nodded. "The front three vehicles will follow me east down Palestine directly to the blast site. Nguyen and Arroyo will break off and hold at the traffic circle. It might be difficult to maneuver in the intersection, and I might need you to circle around and join us from the south. We're going to secure the area and block off all entrances with concertina wire. There's probably going to be a shit-ton of onlookers and wailing mothers and shit, and we need to clear them out and get standoff so we can make the intersection safe for EMTs, cops, and the engineer platoon—they're coming behind us to clean up the mess. The enemy's deal is to bomb someplace and then wait till everybody rushes in to help and then hit it again, so make sure your gunners are looking at the roofs and windows for snipers or anyone walking up with a bomb strapped to their chest. Platoon Sergeant, you got anything?"

Olaf shook his head.

"Okay, then, any questions?" A moment of silence. "We did a radio check and everything?"

"Yeah, we're up, sir," Nguyen said, breaking into a wide grin.

"What? What's so funny?" Montauk turned around to find that Aladdin had snuck up behind him and was standing there giving him a pair of bunny ears, statuesque, waiting to be discovered. Montauk laughed, shaking off his anxiety. It was just a mop-up operation. They'd be fine. "You're with me, Prince Ali. Get in the Falcon." Aladdin popped a goofy salute, then climbed into the Humvee. Montauk turned back to the huddle. "Okay. Mount up and roll out."

The traffic started to snarl up on Palestine Way about five blocks from the smoke plume, and the Millennium Falcon came to a stop. A Volvo in front of them was failing to do a three-point turn between the car in front of it and an abandoned shawarma cart to the right. Thomas was sweating under his Kevlar and laying on the horn. Montauk sat in the commander's seat; Aladdin sat directly behind him. Fields was up top on the fifty, screaming at the poor guy to get the Fuck Out Of The Way. Which seemed overly aggressive for Fields, but he was probably just feeling what Montauk was feeling. They were fucked. They shouldn't have taken Palestine Way.

"Thomas, Jesus. Give the guy some room," Montauk said.

"Trying to get him to move along, sir," Thomas said in the kind of overtly calm voice that meant his rage was already blowing gauges. Montauk tried to scan over his left shoulder, but his body armor made anything beyond a forty-five-degree turn impossible. He thought of Keaton's Batman. The heat was an airless blanket. He opened the door and stuck his head out to peer behind him. Debris everywhere. He keyed his hand mike but stopped himself before saying something pissy and nervous. There were probably wounded at site, and they couldn't fucking get there! Montauk took a deep breath. He had to sound collected, even if it was a lie.

"All trucks in my column, this is Two-Six. We're stuck in traffic here, and we need some room to maneuver. Everyone back up and keep enough space between you so we can turn around if we have to. Break. Two-Two, Two-Six."

Six, Two, answered Nguyen, who was standing outside of his Humvee back at the traffic circle, stretching out the hand set's cord as he strained to see the column.

"Two, Six. Come east on Kaditha and see if we can get to the intersection from the south. Don't get stuck in traffic and stop before you get to the intersection, over."

"Shit, man," Monkey muttered in English as he walked along the part of Palestine Way that could still pass as a sidewalk. He had been a block ahead of Montauk's column when it got stuck in traffic. Oily smoke was beginning to get into his lungs, and he coughed, but he did not stop walking or turn back, the enormous black smoke beckoning with what promised to be a display of awesome devastation; the unpleasantness of the smell itself was a novelty, like the reek of a carton of milk gone incredibly sour, passed around a group of school kids so no one would get out of making a disgusted face.

"Mohammed!" Monkey looked up and saw his uncle Omar holding open a door next to the large glass storefront that advertised Wali's Hair Cuts and Styles. The glass was complexly spidered from the blast. Inside, the jangle of a Khaled music video played on a small TV, a line of Algerian girls in head scarves and tight jeans, the singer lip-syncing straight into the camera with a prop microphone and a jazz hand. "What are you doing out here?" his uncle asked.

Monkey raised his dark eyebrows and shrugged.

Omar looked up the street toward the smoke plume, then back to the column of American military vehicles snaking slowly toward them though traffic. "Get in here."

Monkey was distracted by the sight of some American soldiers walking past the storefront; the leader looked like the new LT from the traffic circle checkpoint. Monkey began to holler at them but was almost immediately dragged inside by his uncle.

"You should stay away from the Americans, Mohammed. They don't care about you."

"Yes, Uncle."

"A carnival of problems," muttered the barber, reaching for the clippers.

Montauk had grabbed three soldiers from his column, plus Aladdin, then set out on foot after Fields had, from his gunner's perch, clued him in to what turned out to be the major source of their mobility problems: two black sedans, a BMW—they were curiously popular in Baghdad—and a cheaper version of a BMW known as an Opel, stopped in the middle of the intersection and blocking the cars behind them from taking a right off Palestine Way. The Opel driver stood next to his car, cell phone to his ear, studiously ignoring the BMW driver, who was yelling into his face. Montauk waved to get the Opel driver's attention, then walked in front of the guy and banged his palm on the Opel's hood. The guy held up his hand and said something that Montauk took to mean "Just a second."

"No, you gotta go. You have to move your car right now. Right now." The BMW driver had stopped yelling and had his hands on his hips, looking at Montauk to see if he would make the Opel driver move his car.

"Aladdin, can you talk to him?"

Aladdin spoke to the Opel driver. The guy shook his head, then went back to his phone. "He says he waits for police to fill out accident report," Aladdin said. "Maybe he thinks Saddam is still in charge. Hah!"

"Fuck this," Montauk said. He drew his sidearm and aimed it at the guy's head. "You need to move your car. Now." Apparently, what he'd heard was true: pistols scared Iraqis more than rifles; something about how, in the old regime, Ba'athist officers carried pistols and only officers had the authority to shoot people who pissed them off. The Opel driver hopped back in his car, took a right, and limped down the side street on a flat tire. The traffic started to unsnarl.

"Jesus Christ," Montauk said as he got back into the Falcon. "Nobody does anything around here unless you shove a gun in their face. Pretty soon I'll have to start shooting people."

"It's called *menacing,* sir," Thomas said as he started to move the Falcon forward again.

"What?"

"When you stick a gun in someone's face, that's menacing. It's a crime back in Cali."

"You ever been menaced, Thomas?"

"No, sir."

"Well, that's good."

They arrived at the intersection a minute later, fifteen minutes after the bomb detonated. Montauk had Thomas take the Falcon around the intersection clockwise so that everyone could follow and circle up the wagons, just like he was back in the woods at Fort Benning, emplacing a platoon in the defense. Nguyen's two trucks and the truck with the extra wire had linked up with the column, and the engineer platoon was a few minutes away. So far, so good. There was a big crater near the middle of the intersection, dug deep into the road as if God's fingernail had come down and scooped it out like pudding. There were a couple of flaming wrecks, but most of the cars had been pushed to the side by the force of the blast.

And then Montauk saw it, the mental souvenir of this particular bomb scene: a BMW sedan on the roof of a two-story department store, the edge of the car hanging a little bit off but otherwise looking almost as if someone had parked it there. Although missing a wheel and window-less, it looked more or less intact. Montauk did not see a driver, but that didn't prove anything, as he was looking at it from below. A blackish-red liquid was oozing out the car door. There was no activity on the roof or on any other roof in view, and the gunners looked like they were doing a good job covering them. Jackson and Urritia put on heavy gray leather gloves with metal studs and began unspooling the coils of concertina. The Falcon went 360 degrees around the tableau, and Montauk dismounted and began moving from truck to truck, making sure the wire got distributed evenly across each entrance to the intersection.

A man standing in front of the department store almost directly under the rooftop BMW was yelling in Arabic and kicking a signpost next to what appeared to be a body covered from head to toe with button-up shirts, which were starting to soak through.

"What's he saying?" Montauk asked Aladdin.

"He says God will make vengeance. I think he knows the person under the clothes."

Montauk began salivating, and he found himself getting weirdly hungry, but he became abruptly unhungry when he realized where the undercurrent of BBQ aroma was coming from. A bombed-out Volkswagen Rabbit near the crater. A charry-looking figure inside, posed as if stuck in traffic.

The figured moved, as if alive somehow. Should he call a medic? No, that was stupid. The guy was ash. His hand, his certainly dead hand, had just slipped from the wheel. Gravity.

A burst of rounds. Every soldier in the platoon turned toward Nguyen's truck. PFC Lo had just fired the fifty from his turret at the roofline of a building across the street. The bullets impacted with the wall, sending bits of plaster and brick down like confetti.

Pedestrians began fleeing the site, worried an attack was imminent. The other gunners were scanning the roofline, and even Jackson and Urritia had dropped their concertina wire and whipped out their rifles. Montauk swore he could smell the collective adrenaline. Everyone focused intently on the roofline. After thirty seconds of dead quiet, Montauk ran over to Nguyen's truck. "Lo, what did you see?"

"There was something, sir. Something up there."

"A person, someone with a gun?"

"I don't know, sir."

"Goddammit, Lo. What did you see?"

"There was a glint. Sir."

"A glint? You fired the fifty at a fucking glint?"

"Yes, sir."

"You think there might be civilians in that building, Lo? You think the fucking fifty-caliber M2 machine gun might shoot right through those shitty walls? *Positive identification* before you pull that trigger!"

"Yes, sir. Sorry, sir."

Montauk sighed. "Staff Sergeant Nguyen. Take Lo off the fifty. Put someone up there who understands the rules of engagement."

A bullet ricocheted off Nguyen's Humvee. Everyone took cover as a few more hit the dirt near the tires.

"Tall building five blocks south," Jackson yelled. He leaned out and fired a few rounds at it, shattering a window.

They waited. And waited.

No return fire.

Was Montauk supposed to send someone to go check in that building? His job was to secure the intersection. He looked at Olaf. "Think we hit him?"

"I doubt it, sir. Probably scared him off. He'll be long gone by the time we get there."

They waited another few minutes, scanning the rooftops, the windows, the alleys. Montauk could hear Aladdin on the ground next to him, chewing gum.

Eventually, tensions dropped and bystanders began trickling back toward the bomb site. The engineer platoon pulled into the intersection. Montauk went to confer with the engineer captain, who appeared nervous and distracted.

"Everything secure?" the captain said. "We heard gunfire."

"Someone took a plink at us a few minutes ago, sir," Montauk said. "No further contact."

"All right," the captain said, "we're going to start cleaning up the debris and haul what we need to haul. See if you can give us an outer perimeter so we can concentrate on doing what we can to make the intersection drivable again, and make sure the buildings aren't— Holy shit." He craned his neck to look up at the BMW on the department store roof. "How'd *that* get up there?"

"How indeed," Montauk said. The physical explanation for such a thing was within his grasp. Blast velocity. Inertia. Projectile motion. But the psychological explanation was beyond him.

"Who do you think that guy was?" he asked Aladdin as the captain left.

"I know this man, sih. He's a Sunni, from Baquba. His name is Fayed, or Amr. Maybe Amr is his friend. He works in his father's print office. He and Amr, they are both losers. Until Amr become a hero of Islam. Fighting the infidel. Now everyone is best friends with Amr. Who is dead. And Fayed become jealous. He thinks about watching at his own funeral, how sad everyone is, hearing them say they don't know him really, until now, until his glory. Hearing the pretty girls say that. And so Fayed parks his car on the roof. He wasn't even that serious, before. About Islam."

"Shit," Montauk said. "Was he your friend?"

"No," Aladdin said. "I do not know him. But I know many people like him. The story is always the same."

"Crazy," Montauk said.

"Yes, you think it's crazy. Because you are a good man, LT. But it is not so crazy. Next year, maybe, it is normal." Aladdin spit his gum into the dust. "Every day."

23

Opening the door to the port-o-john was like checking on how a piece of rancid pork was doing in the broiler. Montauk tore apart the Velcro flap of his armor and let it slide down to rest on the floor of the john as the door closed behind him. He propped Molly Millions in the corner and hastily began to loosen his rigger's belt. For a painful minute, he stood still, his hands frozen on the steel loops of the belt. Then, when a delicate equilibrium had been reached, he dropped his pants, opened the lid of the blue cauldron, and deflated as if someone had popped a water grenade stuffed up his ass—one that had been filled with a liquid that had the color, temperature, and consistency of Burger King coffee. Montauk made a weak *hoooaaahhhh* noise. He hadn't had a regular shit since the car bomb they'd responded to last week. The plastic latrine shook as a few armored vehicles rolled past it and out the exit lane. His entire body felt covered in a sheen of sweat and shit particulate. A kindred soul had written in Sharpie above the paper dispenser: "Saddam's Revenge says Fuck You."

Two-Six, this is Priority Search.

The plastic seat creaked as Montauk leaned over to reach the hand mike on his vest. "Priority Search, Two-Six," he responded.

Two-Six, we've got a body in the river.

The Priority Search lane was temporarily closed, and midlevel Iraqi contractors sat in their cars, annoyed, while Kyriacou, the Greek kid, stood behind the fifty. He looked overly alert, almost jumpy. The rest of the Priority Search crew, which today meant 3rd Squad, gathered twenty yards north of the road, at the edge of a gentle slope that ended in the muddy southern bank of the Tigris. Montauk could smell the corpse as soon as he left the road. Unless that was Bessie the Cow. She'd been there for months, apparently, stuck in the mud near one of the bridge's piers.

As he approached the riverbank, he saw Sergeant Fields struggling to drag the corpse ashore by the cuffs of its jeans; its hands were behind its back, digging into the mud. The body had swollen from the hot river water, and its clothes had shrunk until what had been a stylishly fitted look had become comical. Ant was standing a few paces away, staring at the ground near the corpse. Montauk propped Molly Millions against a rock and walked into the river. "Let's go, let's grab him," he said. "Ant. That means you." He bent down to grab a handful of soaked T-shirt, and the full evil of the reek made itself known to him. "Jesus, fuck." He paused to keep from retching on the corpse's bloated but strangely . . . familiar face. "Christ, it's Aladdin."

Ant took hold of the other shoulder, trying not to breathe as he waited for Montauk.

"Okay," Montauk said, looking back to Fields, who now had both knees tucked in his armpits. "One, two, three, up."

Aladdin was heavy, and the wet cotton threatened to slip from their hands as they stumbled up the muddy bank. They set him down among the reeds, then walked away from the body and bent over, trying to breathe. Montauk closed his eyes, tight-lipped. The death smell made him want to kill. Ant stood there shaking his head minutely back and forth, caught in a loop. Fields rolled Aladdin over onto his shoulder. His backside was covered in mud, but Montauk could see a strand of packing twine dangling wetly from his bound wrists. He took a breath and pulled out his Leatherman. It took a minute of careful sawing to avoid slashing Aladdin's wrists as he worked. There was an uneven line of small burns running up his swollen arm, maybe from a cigarette.

"Looks like he gained some weight since we last saw him," offered Fields.

"I was teaching him how to pack a can of dip," Montauk said. Aladdin's eyelids were cracked, as if he were half asleep. Montauk attempted to close them, but they wouldn't quite go down.

He breathed heavily on the walk back up to the CP, both to get the death out of his nostrils and to fuel the anger inside him that, if left untended, would subside into panic. The checkpoint felt quiet and focused. He saw Monkey standing at the base of the east gun tower like a kid lost at the mall. "What are you doing?" he yelled. The kid looked up to the tower.

"Just getting some shawarmas, sir!" yelled a voice from the tower. Urritia.

"You're gonna be pissing out your ass!" Montauk yelled.

"Speaking from experience, sir?" Urritia yelled back.

Montauk ignored him and turned to continue on to the CP, then stopped and called Monkey over. "You hear about Aladdin?"

"Yeah," Monkey said. "They kill him, man."

Montauk spat into the dust as an idea took shape in his head. Why the fuck not. "Listen," he said. "I'll give a reward to whoever can tell me who killed Aladdin. You understand?"

"Reward?" Monkey nodded doubtfully.

"Reward. Money. I want to know who killed Aladdin. You get it? Someone tells me who killed Aladdin, I'll give them—" He was going to say a thousand dollars. But that sounded absurdly high for Baghdad. "Five hundred dollars," he said. Monkey stared back and nodded. He didn't get it.

"Look, see this?" Montauk said, tearing open the Velcro pocket at his sleeve where he kept a few bills and a notepad. "Here's a dollar. I want to know who killed Aladdin. Whoever tells me who killed Aladdin, I'll give him five hundred dollars. That's this much," he said, writing and underlining "500" on the notepad. Monkey's eyes widened.

"It's got to be real. No lies, okay? Only real, true information. Who killed Aladdin."

"You gonna shoot him, LT?"

"That's right. And anybody who tells me who it was, they get five hundred dollars. My own money. Tell everyone you know."

"Yeah, man."

Urritia had descended the ladder from the machine-gun nest. "Damn, sir, you're putting a contract out on these fuckers?"

"That's right."

"Well, I got five on it. Hey, Monkey, I got five on that contract."

"You're gonna confuse him."

"Right, sorry, sir." Urritia handed a bill to Monkey. "Just the sha-warmas, then."

"Yeah, man," Monkey said.

"All right, scram," Montauk said to the kid. He turned to Urritia as Monkey ran off. "Keep it in the platoon, all right. Don't spread it around the company."

"Roger, sir."

Montauk walked back up to the CP to start filling out the report. Urritia went back to the tower. He was only a few rungs up when he heard Jackson, his squad leader, calling him from behind. "What's going on?" Jackson asked.

Urritia hopped down. "LT's offering a cash reward for the Al-Qaeda fuckheads who whacked the translator."

Jackson blinked willfully. "Serious?"

"Roger, Staff Sergeant."

"All he's gonna get is a line of stinky ragheads tellin' lies."

Urritia fished a tin of Copenhagen out of his cargo pocket.

"How much is he putting up?" Jackson asked.

"Five hundred bucks."

"Five hundred bucks?"

"Roger, Staff Sergeant. He said not to spread it around the company."

Jackson snorted and lit up a Gauloise. The sun had started on its way down, and traffic on Karada Dahil was picking back up after the midday siesta. "What a retard," he said.

"Yeah," said Urritia. "What a retard."

24

The pedestrian lane went up a concrete stairway and ended at the Ped Search bunker, which spat out the foot traffic onto the sidewalk on 14 July Bridge. PFC Lo had been taken off gun duty. He was scrutinizing an ID card at the bunker's entrance as Montauk arrived. It was a fibrous paper deal with a small photo affixed at the corner, laminated with sticky paper. It seemed to have been hidden alternately in the gearbox of some grinding machine and up the bearer's ass for the last few decades. The picture, scarcely visible behind the smudging and creasing of the plastic, looked to Lo like it had been taken in high school. It depicted a smooth-faced, olive-skinned youngster. Lo looked up at the face of the laborer—tough and creased, with a huge bushy mustache; his eyes seemed to express either confusion or docility. Lo returned the card and waved the guy inside to be patted down.

Montauk gave Lo an encouraging nod. At least he was trying. And hopefully on Ped Search, he wouldn't get anyone killed.

The bunker was a rectangular room with a doorway on either end, about twelve-by-thirty, and built of HESCO bastions, large wire-mesh, cloth-lined boxes filled with gravel. It had a plywood roof. Aside from Sodium Joh, who was doing the pat-downs, Olaf was in the bunker, standing next to a stodgy, plainly dressed Iraqi sitting on a plastic chair. "Afternoon, sir," Olaf grunted.

"Who's this guy?" Montauk asked, nodding toward the Iraqi.

"This is Ali Gorma. Our new translator. Hey, Gorma, come meet the LT."

Montauk got caught on the word *new*. Not new like a new car, undriven, but new to you, like a used car you bought to replace the one you'd totaled. A new girlfriend to replace the one you'd dumped. Montauk's litany of tasks and unexpected urgencies had been enough to keep him from obsessing about Aladdin for the last few days. But in confronting this "new" translator, he needed a concerted effort of will not to picture the waterlogged corpse like an overstuffed and rancid sausage, not to smell the rot, which was thick enough to taste in the back of his throat.

Ali Gorma stood up like it was a chore. He slouched under Montauk's blank gaze.

"Hey," Montauk said, extending his fist. "I'm Lieutenant Montauk. Good to have you on board."

Ali Gorma stared at Montauk's fist. It took Montauk an awkward half-second to realize that Gorma, unlike Aladdin, wasn't hip to contemporary American hand greetings. Aladdin had probably been the outlier. Gorma shook Montauk's hand the way you might shake hands with your friend's ugly sister at a party.

"I am Ali Gorma," he said, then he slouched back down onto the chair. Another pedestrian passed through the bunker.

"So, Ali G," Montauk said. "You a football fan?"

"Okay," Gorma said.

"I know everyone says Al-Shorta's the best team," Montauk said, "but I prefer Al-Zawra'a SC. They're leading Division B right now, aren't they?" The Iraqi Premier Football League had been suspended when the invasion began, and it had just resumed last week.

Ali Gorma shrugged, unimpressed.

"Well, let me know if you have any questions," Montauk said, hoping to create the impression that their lack of a conversation had come to an organic end. He fished out his tin of Kodiak and put in a plug of dip while looking out past the stairwell toward the pedestrians snaking up along the traffic circle. There was Monkey, rushing past the line and heading toward the stairs.

"He must have found someone," Montauk said. "That was fast."

"What was fast?" said Olaf.

"I told Monkey to ask around about Aladdin."

"What?"

He'd said it in a moment of emotional extremity. But now it was really happening. There was no choice but to own the decision. "I had him put the word out that if anyone had intel on it, I'd have a reward."

"How much?"

"Five hundred bucks."

"Your own money?"

Montauk nodded.

Olaf stepped closer and spoke quietly: "Sir, you sure that's a good idea? That kid could end up in the river."

"I don't know about that. He seems to get how things work around here. I don't think they'd go after the kid." Montauk felt stupid as soon as his mouth started moving with that last one.

Monkey tried leaping into the bunker, but Lo jumped in front of him, grabbed him by the shirt, and demanded ID.

"Hey, LT," Monkey said, out of breath. "C'mon, man."

"It's okay, Lo. Let him in," Montauk said.

Monkey shook off Lo's hands and strutted inside. "I got somebody who want to talk to you, man."

"Good work," Montauk said. He thought about telling Monkey to keep spreading the word, but he decided against it with Olaf standing behind him. "Here." He handed Monkey a five-dollar bill. "Finder's fee."

Monkey unfolded it, held it up to the light, and scrutinized it. Montauk felt a brief twinge of the kind of envy he and his other suburbanite friends had felt for black kids growing up in Compton after *The Chronic* came out. If only they'd had the fortune to be born into poverty, to have no choice but to hustle. If you succeeded in the world of the ghetto enough to leave it, you had undeniable respect. No one gave a shit if you made it out of the suburbs.

Monkey's whole body slumped, and he lolled his head to the side as if utterly disappointed. It was a good trick.

"What?" Montauk said. "You think you deserve more?"

"Yeah, man. I want a hundred."

Montauk laughed, looking around the bunker. Joh was smiling, but

Olaf looked like he was moderating the GRE test. "One hundred dollars? What would you even do with it?" Montauk said, forcing amusement into his voice. "You'd have to, I don't know, get me the head of Osama bin Laden if you want a hundred dollars." Monkey screwed up his mouth, as if contemplating how he might actually find bin Laden's head. "Okay, doesn't have to be bin Laden," Montauk said. "You want a hundred dollars? Get me a human skull, any skull. You know what a skull is?"

Monkey smirked.

"Now get out of here," Montauk said. "And tell whoever you found to come to the CP." He turned to Olaf as Monkey skipped out. "I wouldn't worry about him. That kid's a little hustler."

Olaf raised an eyebrow.

"And who knows," Montauk said. "Maybe we'll get some real intel out of this."

BRIEF INTERVIEWS
WITH IRAQI INFORMANTS

———

SWORN STATEMENT

For use of this form, see AR 190-45; the proponent agency is PMG.

LOCATION: CP 11	DATE: 20041026	TIME: 0930

Mehmet Soufan, ~35 YO Local National Male, states the following:

I know who kill the translator Aladdin. I am working down Karada Dahil at the Al-Sulimeneyeh intersection to sell food. I sell produce. People come up to my stall and talk about all the dead people in the Tigris River in Karada. That everyone sees dead people in the Tigris River. The man is named Ahmet. He says he sees groups of men in black cars by the Tigris a short distance from the food store. I think maybe they are putting people in the river. I think they are not from Baghdad. They are maybe from Fallujah. The man Ahmet says he sees them drive black cars and park near the river.

Q, 2LT Montauk.
A, Mehmet Soufan.
Q: How did Ahmet see the cars?

A: He lives in an apartment near the water. He can see cars from his apartment.

Q: How do you know Ahmet?

A: I see him at my food store.

Q: Did you yourself see the black cars?

A: No.

Q: Can you tell Ahmet to come here and tell us about the black cars near the river?

A: No.

Q: Why not?

A: Ahmet moved away to Hit.

Q: When was that?

A: Two weeks ago.

Q: Who do you think killed Aladdin?

A: I don't know, but I think maybe Al-Qaeda or Iranian. I am Shia.

Q: Why do you suspect Iranians?

A: Because they are enemies to Iraq.

Q: I see. Do you think it may have been the Israelis?

A: Yes, I think it was maybe the Israelis.

Q: Because they are enemies to Iraq?

A: Yes. Enemies to Iraq and to America.

NOTES:

Witness actually finds it plausible that IDF murdered Aladdin. Hate/fear of Israelis is probably normal among locals and may not be indicative of credibility one way or the other. Black cars by the river sounds about right, but not very useful. No real way to locate witness in Hit. Witness wore dark mustache, smelled like cologne and rotting vegetables. At one point, he withdrew a fig from his pocket, smelled it, and put it back in his pocket. Weird tic—Google symbolism of figs? Ali Gorma acted as translator for Mehmet Soufan. Nothing follows.

SWORN STATEMENT

For use of this form, see AR 190-45; the proponent agency is PMG.

PRIVACY ACT STATEMENT

AUTHORITY: Title 10, USC Section 301; Title 5, USC Section 2951

PRINCIPAL PURPOSE: To document potential criminal activity involving the US Army, and to allow Army officials to maintain discipline, law, and order through investigation of complaints and incidents.

ROUTINE USES: Information provided may be further disclosed to federal, state, local, and foreign government law enforcement agencies, prosecutors, courts, child protective services, victims, witnesses, the Department of Veterans Affairs, and the Office of Personnel Management. Information provided may be used for determinations regarding judicial or non-judicial punishment, other administrative disciplinary actions, security clearances, recruitment, retention, placement, and other personnel actions.

LOCATION: CP 11	DATE: 20041026	TIME: 1630

Walid Mahmoud Khazal, ~40 YO Local National Male, states the following:

I have information about the terrorist that killed the translator Aladdin. He is Ahmet Mohammed Ali from Sadr City. He lives in the Housseini apartment building on Palestine Way. Near the bus station in Sadr City. He is a terrorist in the Mahdi Army. He leaves letters for people who work for Americans saying he will kill them for Muqtada Al-Sadr. He left a letter for the translator Aladdin taped to his door. I know because Aladdin was a student at Baghdad University and I am a professor of Mathematics. Ahmet Mohammed Ali worked at the university as a cleaner but then was fired because he joined the Mahdi Army and was mujahideen. He was threatening university students and then was fired. He put letters on their lock boxes with tape saying mujahideen will kill their families. So he was fired. Everyone knows he is mujahideen and killed Aladdin, but they are afraid of Ahmet Mohammed. So they won't tell the Americans and the Iraqi Police won't go to Sadr City.

Q, 2LT Montauk

A, Walid Mahmoud Khazal

Q: Did Ahmet Mohammed Ali tell you he killed Aladdin?

A: My students told me that Aladdin found the letter on his door. Aladdin was kidnapped one week later.

Q: When did Aladdin find the letter?

A: September 20 about.

Q: Where is the letter?

A: I don't know.

Q: What apartment number is Ahmet Mohammed Ali's?

A: Apartment is 306 Housseini Apartments in Sadr City. His mobile number is 01285936618.

Q: Who else lives in the apartment?

A: I don't know.

Q: What does Ahmet Mohammed Ali look like?

A: Maybe 25, beard, big and tall.

Q: Do you have anything else to add?

A: I work in Algebraic number theory. I studied in the United Kingdom.

Q: How can we contact you?

A: My phone is broken. But you can call my neighbor Aziz. His number is 01285818663.

NOTES:

Witness was eager and well composed. A math professor at Baghdad U. Copied and forwarded statement to TF3/8 5-2 for processing/follow-up. Provided CP3 contact card. No translator was necessary, as witness spoke English. Nothing follows.

SWORN STATEMENT

For use of this form, see AR 190-45; the proponent agency is PMG.

PRIVACY ACT STATEMENT

LOCATION: CP 11	DATE: 20041028	TIME: 0815

Nadirah Ayad, ~45 YO Local National Female, states the following:

I am the mother of Aladdin. Aladdin was at home with me when men came in with masks and put their hands on me. Six or maybe eight American soldiers with masks on, and about half of them are black. I was trapped in my room with the black soldiers, who were putting their hands all over me. When it was over, Aladdin was gone. I am having trouble hearing after the attack.

Q, 2LT Montauk

A, Nadirah Ayad

Q: You are Aladdin's mother?

A: Yes.

Q: I'm very sorry for your loss. Aladdin was a good man.

A: Okay.

Q: Do you know who killed your son?

A: It was the American soldiers. The black ones.

Q: What was the American soldiers?

A: They were.

Q: What about them?

A: They are who killed my son, Aladdin.

Q: Why would they do this?

A: So that there would be no one can tell about how they put their hands all over me.

Q: You are Aladdin's mother?

A: Yes. I tell you this already.

Q: And what did Aladdin look like?

A: You ask a mother how her own son looks? Do not insult me.

Q: I'm sorry.

A: Will you punish the blacks who put their hands all over me?

Q: We'll look into it.

NOTES:

Ali Gorma acted as translator for Nadirah Ayad. Nothing follows.

SWORN STATEMENT

For use of this form, see AR 190-45; the proponent agency is PMG.

PRIVACY ACT STATEMENT

LOCATION: CP 11	DATE: 20041029	TIME: 1115

Ahmet Mohammed Ali, ~25 YO Local National Male, states the following:

I'm coming to tell you that a man is telling lies about me because he owes me money.

Q, 2LT Montauk

A, Ahmet Mohammed Ali

Q: What lies is he telling?

A: He says I am mujahideen and that I killed a translator. I did not kill anyone.

Q: Who is saying this?

A: Walid Mahmoud Khazal.

Q: Who is Walid Mahmoud Khazal?

A: He is a part-time worker at the university. He owed me money and then didn't pay me back, but I told him he needed to pay me back. He owed me money from before this war when you come and invade. Then he says he can't pay me on time so I give him more time. Then he says that he doesn't owe money from before the Americans came because there is new government now. But I say, it is the same, I gave you money, you give me back the money. But he says no, I will not give you the money. So I say okay I will take your truck. Then he says that I will tell the Americans that you are mujahideen and they will put me and my family in Abu Ghraib. But I say no, I am not mujahideen, soldier Americans know I am not mujahideen, you must give me the money or I take your truck.

Q: Do you know anything about Aladdin?

A: Who is Aladdin?

Q: Aladdin is my translator who was killed by mujahideen.

A: No.

NOTES:

Unlikely that witness would come to CP11 to clear his name if he were actually responsible for the death of Aladdin. Possible that this type of Judge Judy issue is responsible for some percentage of INTSUM VBIED warnings? Ali Gorma acted as translator for Ahmet Mohammed Ali. Nothing follows.

SWORN STATEMENT

For use of this form, see AR 190-45; the proponent agency is PMG.

PRIVACY ACT STATEMENT

LOCATION: CP 11	DATE: 20041029	TIME: 1805

Aliya Hussein, ~50 YO Local National Female, states the following:

My home is in the Green Zone. When the bombing started I drive from Baghdad to Hillah to escape the bombing. After the Americans come I come back to my home with my sons and sister, but there is a Shia family living in my house. I told the American soldiers and give them my ID card and they promised to give me the house back from the Shia. I told the police that it was my house, but the policeman officer is Shia and is giving Sunni house to Shia. I am Sunni. This is in 2003. I am living in Hillah now with my husband's sister. They told to me to not go back to Baghdad, but I believe that the Americans and Bush are good and friends to Iraq.

Q, 2LT Montauk

A, Aliya Hussein, wife of Mohammed Sayed Hussein

Q: Do you have information about the murder of the translator Aladdin?

A: Yes, I have information. I will give you information about Al-Qaeda. I only want my home back.

Q: Tell me what you know and I'll see about getting your home back.

A: I want my home back.

Q: We'll do our best, but first I need some information. What can you tell me about Aladdin?

A: I want my home back.

NOTES:

Unable to process this claim. Provided her with a claims form to present to the IAC at CP3. Ali Gorma acted as translator for Aliya Hussein. Nothing follows.

SWORN STATEMENT

For use of this form, see AR 190-45; the proponent agency is PMG.

PRIVACY ACT STATEMENT

LOCATION: CP 11	DATE: 20041030	TIME: 1010

Ali Mohammed, ~19 YO Local National Male, states the following:

I work at a DVD shop. I have information for you that you want.

Q, 2LT Montauk

A, Ali Mohammed

Q: You have information about Aladdin?

A: Yes.

Q: Did you know who Aladdin was?

A: Yes, he was translator who was killed.

Q: Did you know him before he was killed?

A: Yes.

Q: Do you know who killed him?

A: I heard.

Q: What did you hear?

A: I sell DVD.

Q: Okay.

A: Yes I have a shop down not too far.

Q: And did you hear at the shop?

A: Yes. I hear about Aladdin in the shop. We sell all kinds of DVD. Drama. Music Video. We have Freaky Freaky.

Q: Is that how you know Aladdin?

A: Yes, Aladdin loves DVD. He came to the shop. He like drama, he like Freaky Freaky. You like Freaky Freaky?

Q: No. Yes, but I don't care. I want information about Aladdin.

A: You want Freaky Freaky?

Q: No. I want information about Aladdin.

A: Okay. I don't know Aladdin too much. He liked the Freaky Freaky DVD. We have many for good price.

Q: Are you trying to sell me DVDs?

A: No.

NOTES:

Ali Gorma acted as translator for Ali Mohammed. Nothing follows.

SWORN STATEMENT

For use of this form, see AR 190-45; the proponent agency is PMG.

PRIVACY ACT STATEMENT

LOCATION: CP 11	DATE: 20041101	TIME: 1725

Farouk Allil, ~45 YO Local National Male, states the following:

I know everything that you are wanting to know. It is very fortunate for you to have someone like me.

Q, 2LT Montauk

A, Farouk Allil

Q: What do you know about Aladdin's murder?

A: I know a lot about Aladdin's murder.

Q: Do you know how he was murdered?

A: Yes.

Q: How was he murdered?

A: By mujahideen.

Q: How do you know this?

A: I have very good information. I will give you the information and you give me the reward.

Q: How did Aladdin die?

A: He was murdered by mujahideen.

Q: How specifically? How did they murder him?

A: They kidnapped him first, then they killed him.

Q: What weapons did they use?

A: The normal weapons.

Q: What are the normal weapons?

A: Maybe a gun, a pistol, knives.

Q: Did you know Aladdin before he was killed?

A: Sure, I know him.

Q: How did you know him?

A: We live nearby.

Q: How many mujahideen killed him?

A: The usual number, it's the same number what you're looking for.

Q: What number am I looking for?

A: The usual number.

Q: I'm looking for information about this murder. You say you have information.

A: Yes, I see. I have the information, I give you the information.

Q: Okay.

A: And you give me reward.

Q: How many mujahideen?

A: Five?

Q: Five?

A: Five? You want five mujahideen?

Q: I want the number that were actually involved in the killing. How many were actually involved?

A: Oh, many, many.

Q: Many?

A: How many do you want? I can give you names and addresses.

Q: I'm only giving you a reward if this is actual true information about Aladdin's murder. I want the actual murderers.

A: The actual murderers, yes. How many do you want?

NOTES:

Ali Gorma acted as translator for Farouk Allil. Nothing follows.

25

Like all men of Babylon, I have been proconsul; like all, a slave. Montauk sat in the shade of the CP with a cold Mr. Brown and a copy of Borges's *Labyrinths* that he'd received in the mail that morning. Corderoy had sent it—there was no return address, but it had to be him. Who else would have dog-eared "The Lottery in Babylon," a pretty academic joke about Montauk's current geographical circumstances. Corderoy had underlined several passages, including that first line. *For a lunar year, I was declared invisible—I would cry out and not be heeded.* Was he lonely in Boston? Why didn't he just write? Why didn't Montauk? He had read the story before, but not through Corderoy's eyes. *In many cases, the knowledge that certain happy turns were the simple result of chance would have lessened the force of those outcomes.* That sounded like Corderoy, all right, rejecting good fortune because he didn't deserve it. He had starred a longer passage:

> If the Lottery is an intensification of chance, a periodic infusion of chaos into the cosmos, then is it not appropriate that chance intervene in *every* aspect of the drawing, not just one? Is it not ludicrous that chance should dictate a person's death while the circumstances of that death—whether private or public, whether drawn out for an hour or a century—should *not* be subject to chance?

Poor Corderoy, trapped in his head, just like Borges. Montauk got the intended sentiment, the frustration and bafflement that life was subject to the dictates of chance, but it was such an intellectual, metaphysical framing of the idea. It could live only inside a library. It would fall apart as soon as some junky BMW raced toward the barricades with who knew what in its trunk, his men forced to shoot the dirt, then the tires, then, if the car kept coming, the driver. Center of mass.

Two-Six, Two-Three, can you come down to Routine Search? Got an issue down the line. It was Staff Sergeant Arroyo, 3rd Squad leader.

"Two-Three, Two-Six," Montauk said into his hand mike. "Moving."

At the head of the line, he found Sergeant Fields feeling up the upholstery of some old black Opel. Ant had finished patting down the driver, who presently fished a pair of cigarettes from his front pocket and handed one to Ant. Ant shrugged but accepted it. He gave Montauk a halfhearted *hooah* as he passed. The Iraqi gave Montauk a big smile and the motionless openhanded wave peculiar to Baghdadis. Montauk returned the *hooah* and the wave and strode by.

Behind that car, there was a long line of cars winding down Karada Dahil. Raggedy palms and a big pile of trash, complete with old hypodermic needles, made a natural barrier between the sidewalk and the vacant lot to the east of the checkpoint. Montauk didn't know what the needles signified other than medical waste. He didn't imagine Baghdadis did needle-type drugs. It occurred to him that he wouldn't know whom he could ask about it that he was confident would both know the answer and tell him the truth.

He found Staff Sergeant Arroyo a few cars down, standing next to the T-walls with Ali Gorma and another Iraqi. Gorma looked bored out of his skull; he was idly looking at a dusty BMW a few cars back from which some tinny Arabic-pop was emanating. Montauk had struggled for the last week to figure out what was going on in Ali Gorma's head, largely to no avail. The guy didn't seem to have any interests. He rode a motorcycle, and sometimes he'd sort of incline his head toward a car that wasn't a total piece of shit, but that was as close as he came to getting excited about anything. If only those terrorist fucks had killed Gorma instead of Aladdin. Of course, Gorma's perfect insipidness was probably why he'd never wind up in the river.

"We've got an abandoned car down the line," Arroyo said. "This guy says he saw the driver get out and run away. Says the driver's Al-Qaeda."

The Iraqi wore thin slacks and a button-up and the kind of thin-soled leather slip-on shoes that straddled the line between cheap and elegant.

"Why does he think he's Al-Qaeda?" Montauk looked at Staff Sergeant Arroyo, who looked at Ali Gorma. They all looked at the Iraqi as Ali Gorma repeated the question. In Arabic, Montauk noticed, it was pronounced more like "Al-Q'aye-duh." The man turned his hands up and said a few words to Gorma.

"He doesn't know," Gorma said.

"Well . . . did you mirror it?"

"No, sir," said Arroyo. He clicked on his walkie-talkie. "Ant. Bring the mirror up here."

Roger, came the reply. Montauk looked back down to the checkpoint and saw Ant and Fields moving toward them with the undercarriage mirror.

"Which car is it?" Montauk asked.

"Gray Toyota, ten cars down," Arroyo said.

"He says the man parked the car and ran away with a cell phone and hasn't been back," Gorma said. The Iraqi witness kept talking. "He says he thinks he is Al—"

"I know," Montauk said.

Ant and Fields arrived with the mirror.

"Okay, get some standoff, I'll go check it out myself. Ant, you post up twenty meters past the car while I have a look. Try to get some cover."

Ant gave a dubious look to Staff Sergeant Arroyo. "Hey, sir, should we call EOD?" Arroyo asked.

"We can't call the bomb squad for every parked fucking car," Montauk said. "They don't have time for that shit." A scent like a wood fire mixed with plastic and petrol drifted past Montauk's nostrils. Someone was burning trash nearby. Ant moved out past the gray Toyota, staying close to the T-walls.

"Look for a hajji with one of those Wile E. Coyote plungers," Fields called after him.

This was the second time Montauk had inspected a suspicious car, but the first time he'd done so after seeing the car bomb at the Iraqi T.J.Maxx. He knew now that the sound would be sharp, like the snapping of an enormous stick. It would happen fast, so fast that he would not see it coming. The Toyota was a junker. The driver's seat had a cover made of wooden beads, the kind that was supposed to massage your back. There was a large crack running the length of the windshield. He spotted an empty potato chip bag in the backseat. This made Montauk feel better, as it did not comport with the ritualized cleanliness he imagined suicide bombers adhered to. He slid the rolling mirror under the car and looked up at the dirty undercarriage. There were no bombs as far as he could see. But the obvious thing would be to just put it in the trunk and either try to remote-detonate it or wire it to blow when the trunk got opened. He thought of the driver observing him nearby.

He set the mirror down on the sidewalk and walked over to the trunk, sliding Molly Millions around his back to get her out of the way. Arroyo, Fields, Gorma, and the nervous Iraqi were watching him from down the street. Ant had tucked himself into a gap between two T-walls and was scanning the buildings across Karada Dahil. Montauk looked back at the trunk latch. *Labyrinths,* in his cargo pocket, rested damply against his thigh. The worst thought was that as fast as an explosion was, perhaps he would be aware of it for at least a split second, a sensation of dark impact and the taste of blood and teeth or metal as his face got blown in, like the way your eyes supposedly took mental still-frames every sixteenth of a second. *Is it not ludicrous that chance should dictate a person's death while the circumstances of that death—whether private or public, whether drawn out for an hour or a century—should not be subject to chance?*

He brought a gloved hand down to the latch and closed his eyes, hoping that if it did blow, he wouldn't live to regret it. It wasn't too late. He could call EOD. "Ahh, fuck it," Montauk muttered, and clicked open the trunk.

BOOM!

Montauk was lifted off the ground by his own fear. He turned to see Fields down the line, doubled over laughing. "Goddammit!" Montauk said. "What the fuck was that?"

"Sorry, sir," Fields shouted back. "Couldn't resist." He chuckled to himself.

The trunk was empty except for a small nylon gym bag and a stack of old newspapers. There was a tire iron poking up through the coarse carpet. Montauk slammed it shut, wincing at the sound. "Clear," he said to Ant, who was already on his way back, his face emotionless. Ever since they'd pulled Aladdin's body from the river, Ant had become more withdrawn. And Fields, who used to be so decent, had become a complete asshole.

Montauk handed over the mirror to Arroyo, told him to keep Fields in line, and fished his tin of Kodiak out of his jacket pocket. He checked his little black Casio as he walked back toward the CP. Another four hours until the shift was over.

"Hey, man," Monkey said.

Montauk turned and looked up to the edge of a T-wall. How Monkey had managed to scramble up there, Montauk couldn't tell.

"You find a bomb, man?"

"No."

"You know that old man say you shit, man."

Old man? Montauk looked down the street at the Iraqi standing next to Arroyo. "The driver said that? He wasn't that old. What did he say?"

"He said you shit American don't help anything, man."

"Did he."

Monkey nodded.

Fucking Gorma. Was he really leaving that out of his translation? Or was Monkey bullshitting him? Once again, as was so often the case, Montauk was confronted with the fact that in his position, certain things were not merely unknowable, they seemed to not even have definitive truth values. There simply was no answer; in asking the question, you couldn't help but affect the world you wanted to investigate. *Babylon is nothing but an infinite game of chance.*

26

It was the morning of November 3rd, 2004, and Montauk had whipped himself up about the elections. He came from a family of down-the-line Democrats and a social group that hated George W. Bush with a foaming intensity that made Montauk uncomfortable, especially as he had many acquaintances, if not friends, who assumed he'd volunteered for Iraq and therefore his presence here was proof of unscrupulousness, stupidity, or both. This line of thinking made Montauk angry. Which was unfortunate, as he'd been following the election coverage as a way to keep from dwelling on Aladdin's death and the futility of the interviews he'd conducted. "You're never gonna figure this out," Olaf had told him. "It's Iraq."

On arriving back at the Convention Center, Montauk took off his kit and hung it on the back of the black desk that served as his living partition. He loaded nytimes.com and cnn.com and foxnews.com to check the election results. Pennsylvania had just been called for Kerry—it was midnight back there—but results weren't in for Florida, Ohio, or Nevada. After a few minutes of fruitless refreshing, Montauk gathered up Molly and his cleaning kit and went upstairs to the Coalition Press Information Center. The CPIC was the medium-sized lecture hall with the big projection screen where CPA spokespeople gave their press briefings; on occasion it hosted movie nights or broadcast sporting events. Montauk guessed correctly that they'd have the election news on, though no one else was in there at 0715 except one woman who, as indicated by her press badge, worked for NPR. The big screen was tuned to MSNBC, where a commentator was blathering half-predictions between the actual results. The NPR lady glanced over briefly when Montauk spread out his grimy brown cloth and laid out Molly Millions in all her black, dusty glory. Molly hadn't yet fired a shot, so her bolt carrier was relatively clean, but everything exposed to the outside air wore a fine coat of dust, including the inside of the barrel. He swabbed it and held it up to the screen, and for an instant, John Kerry was framed by the bore, like in the opening credits of a Bond movie. Except for the flecks of Baghdad dust in the rifling. He threaded another swatch of cloth into the bore snake's slot and pulled it through. At 0827, Florida was called for Bush. The NPR lady looked over. "Did you vote?"

The bore snake made a metallic *thwoop* noise as it popped out of the barrel.

"I did," Montauk said. "I'm Bravo Company's voting officer, in fact."

"So you help other soldiers vote?"

"I make sure that everyone who wants to vote gets registered and gets an absentee ballot and knows how to send it in."

"Do most of them vote?"

"Most? Probably not. Maybe half. Probably less."

"Who do you think they voted for?"

Montauk shrugged. "Probably Bush. I don't ask."

He was back at his desk by 0850. He refreshed nytimes.com again and surveyed his surroundings. With his thoughts on civilian concerns, imagining his friends and their beer-fueled election parties, FOB Bushmaster felt alien. It was certainly unlike most of the other FOBs in the country and unlike most encampments in the history of warfare: a large office space with wall-to-wall carpeting, fluorescent lights, cubicles replaced with rows of identical bunk beds fitted with camouflage sheets and hung with rifles, helmets, and web gear. Sweat-stained body armor. Next to the bunks, automatic weapons on their bipods, ammunition belts hanging limply from ammo bags. Laptops everywhere. Energy drinks and bodybuilding supplements.

More than half of the company slept in a camouflage quilted poncho liner, nicknamed the "woobie" in the late sixties when troops tied
them into the grommets of their issued ponchos and rolled themselves
up against the night monsoons in the central lowlands of Vietnam.
The air-conditioning was running full blast, as usual. Ant's woobie was
draped over him like a sort of shawl or sorcerer's cape as the blue light
from his laptop illuminated his face from below.

On the laptop's screen, Ant's *Sims* avatar lived out his mostly quo-
tidian life. In some ways, it made sense that he had turned to the virtual domesticity of this "sandbox" game, so called because it lacked
any defined goals; it was both the furthest thing from and inescapably
similar to the sandbox of Iraq he was currently stuck in. The more Ant
withdrew from his own life as a private from 2nd Platoon doing security at Checkpoint 11, the more he invested in developing this virtual
person, giving him desires and sating those desires.

He had set up his *Sims* avatar in a two-bedroom, two-bath rambler,
the best he could afford with a service job's income. The avatar stood
by the window, eyeballing the neighbor lady as she got out of her mini-
van and walked to the front door of her house.

When she closed the door behind her, Ant's *Sims* avatar pulled himself away from the window and initiated a set of calisthenics. He was
a relentless self-improver, with Benjamin Franklin–level discipline,
who would work himself into wealth and physical hardness. Private
Ant's Sim would run through that neighbor lady like Drano, that was
the plan. Ant tracked the screen with the vapid intensity of a toddler
watching a *Baby Einstein* video. He wore a set of earbuds in deference
to those sleeping around him.

Gentle snoring noises came from Thomas's partitioned-off hooch.
He slept on his side in a modified fetal position, his hands pressed
together prayerlike under his ear. The orange tip of an earplug was visible next to the elastic band of his JetBlue sleep mask.

Not everyone was asleep. The clanking of weight plates and
Urritia-like exertion sounds came from the makeshift weight room
set up outside the far edge of the bay. And laughter escaped from the
office doors of the platoon room, where a dozen soldiers were watching *Team America: World Police*. Most of the troops were in some stage

of the Desert Camouflage Uniform, although a substantial minority wore interesting mash-ups of civilian and military dress. Lo was sporting his usual ensemble of UC Berkeley basketball shorts, brown issue T-shirt, and black PT watch cap.

Sodium Joh walked down the bay with a stack of mail, tossing letters, magazines, and package slips on bunks. "Sir."

"Thanks."

The letter slid into Montauk's hands. It was from Mani Saheli. He sniffed it for perfume, like he used to do in Officer Basic with letters from his ex-girlfriend. It smelled like a mail pallet. You pretty much had to be in the Army to get letters these days. Montauk tossed it beside his laptop. It was getting close. They would be calling it any time now. Unless there was a recount, a possibility *The New York Times* couldn't help but obsess about. Montauk refreshed the home page again, then checked *The Washington Post* and *Drudge Report*. Though everyone wanted to be the first to call it, no one wanted to be wrong. Montauk jammed a plug of Kodiak into his lip.

With his earbuds in, Ant didn't feel Olaf's presence behind him until the platoon sergeant's large hand had parked itself beside the laptop. Ant remained motionless in his hunched-over position. Olaf was more or less leaning on him.

"Ant, you lazy fuck," Olaf whispered, "you've got your Sim doing push-ups?"

Ant removed an earbud but didn't look up.

Montauk refreshed nytimes.com again and again. Pie charts and exit polling about national security and moral values. He spat into an empty Mr. Brown. The Kodiak wasn't just making him salivate; he felt his bowels loosen and the hot pressure of a large Class II download position itself in the straightaway. He instinctively looked around for some sort of book or magazine, then remembered the letter and tossed it into his cargo pocket. The bay was its usual somnolent self, except for the grunting from Private Antonin Ant. Olaf had shut Ant's laptop and was treating Ant like his own Sim, putting him through progressive stages of discomfort and muscle exhaustion in a quiet, almost respectful tone of voice, so as not to disturb the sleeping troops. Ant was on to slow-count push-ups as Montauk walked by.

The bathroom was in the middle of the bay and more or less first world, except for the foreign push-button flush system, the one-ply on the dispenser, and the constant thick reek. A live-in company of well-fed grunts was not the intended user group for this three-stall corporate restroom. Montauk spread his cheeks across the seat and reached for the letter.

Dear Mickey,

Rain is falling all over Boston right now. I'm in my new studio in Allston. After a week with my parents, I couldn't take it anymore. It's an old factory building. Nice ceiling-high windows. Lots of light. But the rain is so heavy I can barely see the cars on the other side of the street.

I bought rolls of canvas and tons of acrylic paint and brushes. And I've been dipping my brush in paint and swiping it around. It doesn't feel right to call it "painting" because it all sucks. I feel like a poseur. But at least I'm doing it.

It's a bit lonely here—I could look up some old high school friends, but it's too depressing to even think about that. I just know how awful it will be giving a rehearsed five-minute recap of the last few years, explaining about everything, about my hip. It's doing well, by the way, thanks to your tender ministrations. It's still kind of stiff, but pretty much when I've got jeans on, I can't tell the difference.

How are you doing, wartime husband? Are you keeping America safe for us innocents back home? I worry about you sometimes. It's weird having you come up in my thoughts. Like, I'll be walking around and see a newspaper, or someone will say something about Iraq, which is pretty much all the time now since everyone's talking about the election constantly, which is really annoying, or I'll be lying in bed and you'll pop into my thoughts for no reason, and I'll be like, "My husband's off at war," which is the weirdest thing ever because no one else I know is married or knows anyone in Iraq, and it's all so strange. But also romantic. I totally feel like some 40's girl from Wisconsin or something, hoping my husband will come back in one piece so I can have his babies. I'm not saying I think about it that way, but I do feel like I can all of a sudden empathize with those girls. What would blow that girl's mind is that we've kissed exactly once (I'd probably need to go back a few hundred years for knowing nods on that one). But also that it's this weirdly fake war. No one around here even thinks about it except to think how stupid it is, and how much they're embarrassed by it, and how much they hate Bush, of course.

Definitely, no one's worried about how battles are going, or whatever. Are there any? I guess there aren't, right? I don't even know how to talk about it. I think a lot of people want things to get even worse so we can leave and everyone will realize what a jackass Bush is. Which sentiment I certainly do not share, Mickey—I just want you to stay safe so you can come home and dump me with all your fingers and toes attached. Just kidding, I don't mind at all and I really appreciate how you've helped me. Because of you, I can spend time in my studio making shit, I mean art. Someday, soon, I'll make art. I'll have something to impress you with when you get back. Anyway, my hand is starting to hurt—you're giving my fingers a workout. Joke.
xoxo
mani

P.S. Sorry I was so awkward that time on the couch!

Montauk could feel his chest giving way to his heart as if it were a watermelon breaking through the bottom of a wet paper grocery bag. It made him angry, to be suddenly moved. "Are you fucking kidding me?" he mumbled, then self-consciously looked around, as if his platoon had been reading over his shoulder and making revolting jerk-off gestures. Just a few months ago, he'd been biking around Capitol Hill with a beer helmet on, trying to figure out which Encyclopad party theme would net the most babes with the least work. Now he was an officer in an occupation, reading letters from his wife back home. He wondered with dread whether the choices that had gotten him here had been subconscious attempts at the sort of hipster irony he'd claimed to be done with that time at Linda's, with Corderoy. The day after Mani's accident.

Montauk sighed and looked back at Mani's Millennial War-Bride letter. He couldn't decide whether he admired her or pitied her. She would probably hate him if she could peek inside his head at all the violent thoughts, the sourceless anger that made him even angrier with its sourcelessness.

"Fuck. Fuck fuck fuck fuck," he muttered, trying to put her out of his mind.

It was 0915. Past one a.m. back in the States. The results had to be in. Montauk stuffed the letter in his pocket. He stood up and flushed and was about to zip when he saw the small ragged stack of porno mags on the top of the throne in mute defiance of General Order Number One: the blanket prohibition of booze, sex, and porn in the entire Central Command area of operations. He flipped open a *Penthouse* issue to a photo essay of a waxed brunette riding a jacked Mexican guy. He imagined it was his own hands on her ass cheeks, the girl morphing into different girls he'd been with or wanted to. Then he pictured his own blushing bride, Mani Saheli, her hair down, shiny, black, and long like advertisement hair. He hadn't turned away from Mani that night on the couch out of noble concern, whatever he may have told himself at the time. He'd turned away from her for the same reason every other loser guy turns away from a beautiful girl—he was terrified of rejection, of admitting his painfully acute desire to a girl who, probably, like all girls he wanted to bang (which numbered in the tens of millions, worldwide, he'd worked out with Corderoy), didn't want to bang him back. And though he'd been able to sense a little heat coming from her, the higher chance of success with Mani had been offset by the greater price of failure. She'd seemed coquettish, even a bit nuts, when she was with Corderoy. She'd calmed down in that month since Corderoy left for Boston, and here in the bathroom stall, Montauk felt that perhaps she'd changed, or perhaps he'd been wrong about her all along.

Someone in flip-flops came in, panting, to splash water on his face and pat himself down with a paper towel. Montauk was ready to be done with this and went back to the photo essay. He imagined himself with Mani, flashing between flips of intense sex and scenes in a character drama that provided emotional context. Him visiting Boston after his return, her inviting him over, getting him to carry her around in coy reference to their days at the Encyclopad, feigning helplessness and asking him to help remove articles of her clothing, being shyly honest about her desire for him. Mani taking all the risks. His body released him. Montauk caught most of it in his hand but accidentally peppered the magazine's spread, along with his boots. He closed his eyes and exhaled slow and quiet. The usual twinge of sadness was, this time, deep and warm. His eyes watered. He stood for a moment in a darkness of his own making until the air-conditioning made him notice the cold liquid on his hands. He wiped it off with one-ply, the sperm probably dead already from the cold.

After washing his hands, he stepped out into the bay, almost colliding with Urritia, who was on his way in.

"Four more years, sir!"

"Oh . . . yeah?" Montauk was unsure whether Urritia was making an announcement or stating a preference. He barked out a *hooah* as he sauntered into the bathroom and slammed a stall door shut. Montauk walked down the hall and poked his head into the platoon room. *Team America* was still on. The Alec Baldwin puppet was making a speech to the F.A.G. war council.

"Did they call Ohio?"

Olaf looked up from a laptop. "For Bush."

Montauk went back to his makeshift cubicle and tossed the letter on his desk next to the pistol that he rarely carried. He took it out of its holster and broke it down. Dust on the outside, no surprise there, but the inside was clean. The reality was that she was probably sport-fucking some pretentious hipster in Boston right now. He wouldn't have had a problem with it if the pretentious hipster were Corderoy. Corderoy would have said something, though. Or maybe not. It probably wasn't Corderoy. Some dust in the barrel. He didn't bother. The only reason to schlep this thing around was the off chance that he'd get to empty it into someone's mouth, and who better than the guy who'd put the cigarette burns on Aladdin. He'd save one round for himself, maybe, as this was an army of laws, not men.

27

Montauk moved slowly through the buffet line, watching his Thanksgiving plate assemble itself as the Pakistani servers heaped the standard sides in designated quadrants. The DFAC was quieter than usual, the clattering of silverware barely audible above soft conversations, as if the cafeteria's patrons had temporarily developed manners. Suffused with the moist, fat smell of turkey, the atmosphere seemed to approximate "reverence" or "grace." But the DFAC was still the converted ballroom of the Al Rasheed Hotel—high ceilings and fluorescent lights. And it was decorated by the Pakistani staff, which meant papier-mâché pilgrims, eagles, and, for some reason, a tabletop display featuring Shrek and Donkey.

Montauk wandered past tables of Blackwater PSDs, contractors, CPA bureaucrats, embassy types, media, and Navy SEALs. He found some of his guys at a table in the corner. "Stuffing's good," Urritia said as Montauk sat down. He nodded and tucked into his meal. The stuffing was good.

He ate quickly, like he did every day, like most soldiers do, then sat back in his chair observing the room. It was an impressive feat of logistics, getting big turkeys out here, thousands of pounds of mashed potatoes, teaching the Pakistani kitchen staff how to put together a Thanksgiving meal. But to the servers, it was just any old Thursday. And outside these walls, the Iraqis probably had no idea it was

Thanksgiving. Ant was staring off into space. Sodium Joh was drawing infinity signs in the leftover gravy on his plate.

Montauk ate half of an unremarkable slice of pumpkin pie, then got up to leave.

"Some of us are going to Freedom Rest, sir," Urritia said.

"Oh, the place they got set up next to Warhorse?"

"Hooah. They got the pool open, and everybody gets two beers. It's only open today."

"Isn't that where they put all the PTSD cases?" Montauk asked.

"Roger, sir. They probably just hid them all in the closet or something for today. Two beers—you gotta sign up at the TOC, though, and roll down in a convoy."

"Two beers. That's two ounces of beer per month of deployment," said Joh.

"I'll pass," Montauk said. "Don't get pregnant."

He poked his head into the CPIC. About a third of his platoon was in there, along with other troops and civilian government types. The Colts-Lions game was about to start, but kickoff was still twenty minutes out, and the Armed Forces Network was showing the presidential turkey pardoning. Bush stepped up to the podium and said, "I'm pleased to welcome biscuits . . ." For a second, it seemed like he'd developed aphasia. ". . . the national Thanksgiving turkey," he continued. "Biscuits, welcome." Bush made a string of strange jokes about Biscuits' tough road to earning his White House pardon, saying that "Barnyard Animals for Truth" got involved, and that "a scurrilous film came out, Fahrenheit three-seventy-five degrees at ten minutes per pound." He carried on with some boilerplate praise of the armed forces, "many of whom are spending Thanksgiving far from home." Montauk always felt awkward when public figures glorified the military, like he was at a school assembly and the principal was saying, "You are our future."

Two aides brought the turkey forward, ass to the camera, trying to keep it from freaking out, and Bush said, "Not only will I grant the pardon to Biscuits, I will grant one to Gravy as well."

As Bush stroked the turkey's neck for a photo op, Montauk could not shake the feeling that he was experiencing some sort of CIA psychological torture designed to induce mental regression.

The Armed Forces Network logo swirled into frame and faded into a split screen showing a soldier on the left and a picturesque American family on the right. "We miss you, son," Mom said, turkey glistening on the table behind her. "We're grateful for your service, Daniel," Dad said. Younger Sister stood there timidly, looking not into the camera but presumably at some director behind it. "Mom, Dad, Jules. I love you guys," the soldier said.

The logo swirled, and another family reunion proceeded on script.

Montauk walked out and headed down the stairs to the phone bank. It was hard to be moved by the trite things strangers said to their families from afar. And yet he found himself wanting to hear and say those same trite things to his own family.

As in his college dorm, phone access at the FOB was provided in small closetlike rooms. Montauk had always wanted to bang a girl in one of them, but he'd never checked that off his list. He pulled out his calling card and dialed through to his parents' house in D.C.

The phone rang and rang and rang. And rang. And rang. Answering machines were already obsolete, yet his parents still hadn't acquired that technology.

"Oren Montauk."

"Hi, Dad," Montauk said.

"Son." He paused as if confused or searching for the right words. Montauk knew better. His father's silence was a statement. He spoke more with measured pauses than with words. "It's good to hear from you."

"Where's Mom?" Montauk asked. His mother usually answered and acted as mediator for anything his father wanted relayed, which wasn't much.

"Your mother is at the grocery store," his father said.

"Oh," Montauk said. "She start the turkey yet?"

"The McMinns are coming over," he said. "They're bringing a turkey breast." A pause. "Your mother's buying a pie."

"That's nice," Montauk said. "Well, tell her I called, okay?"

Montauk's father said nothing for so long that Montauk nearly said, "Hello?"

"Don't waste your dime," he said. "You called. Now tell me something."

Montauk leaned his head against the wall and flicked the safety of his rifle on and off. "What do you want to know?" he asked.

"How are your sergeants?"

"They're good," Montauk said. "Especially Olaufsson, my platoon sergeant. He's freakishly competent. Sergeant Nguyen's a little strong on the discipline, but he's smart, and he keeps PFC Lo from screwing up too much."

"Sergeant Nguyen?" Montauk's father offered his son a silence full of the timeless amazement that the Vietnamese were serving in the US Army. "Have you had any trouble with the blacks? Them getting along with the rest of the platoon, I mean."

"Dad . . . no. Look, I'm gonna get going," Montauk said.

"Have you been wearing your sidearm?" he asked.

"Sometimes," Montauk said.

"Sometimes? What if your rifle jams?"

"I've never even fired a shot."

"Just wear your sidearm."

"All right."

"I'm proud of you, son."

"Thanks, Dad. Tell Mom I love her. Okay?"

Silence. Montauk pictured his father's solemn nod.

28

A pair of Brads and a Humvee rolled across the bridge toward the Red Zone. Montauk gave a little wave. They waved back. Out in the middle of the bridge, some guys from 4th Squad were manning the BOB. One of them leaned out the top of the driver's hatch, flicking a pocketknife open and closed. The other sat in the turret, looking out across the water like a bored lifeguard. Down on Priority Search, Fields was standing in front of an Opel's open trunk, facing PFC Lo, who was holding a camera for a "thumbs-up next to the goat in the trunk" shot. The driver laughed as he closed his trunk full of goats and drove off into the Green Zone. There were no other cars in line at Priority, so Fields and Lo sauntered back to the bunker at the foot of the stairs.

As Montauk approached, he saw Olaf inside, leaning against the wall and dragging on a Gauloise. Ant was also inside, manning the machine gun, sort of. You couldn't spend eight hours a day white-knuckling the pistol grip of a 240, aiming down a street where nothing ever happened. A certain relaxation was normal, effective, even. Fields and Lo had just cracked open a few Mr. Browns. Montauk squeezed in and joined the party.

"LT, I heard you're next up for leave," Fields said.

"Yeah, I could use a beer," Montauk said.

"Where you going, sir, just home?"

"To D.C. to see my parents, then a stopover in Boston."

"Why Boston?"

"I've got a friend there."

"Ooh, I could use a 'friend' right about now," said Lo.

"Ant has a 'friend' in D.C., sir. Maybe you could look her up," Fields said.

"Oh yeah? Good friend?"

Ant gave a sad, lazy smile and looked down Priority Lane.

"Come on, Ant, let's hear the story," Fields said.

"Nah, I already told you."

"LT and Sergeant Olaf haven't heard it! C'mon, you gotta tell it."

Ant shook his head.

"Sir, order Ant to tell you his story about D.C."

Montauk looked to Olaf.

"Private Ant," said Olaf. "Tell us the story about D.C."

Ant sighed, and a little mirth crept into his smile. "All right. Gimme a cigarette."

Olaf handed him a Gauloise.

"*Shukran*," Ant said, peeling off a glove and getting the cherry going. Montauk tamped down his Kodiak can.

"All right, so. A few years ago, I'm out visiting my buddy in D.C. for spring break. He's doing pre-med at Georgetown."

Fields made the move-it-along motion with his hands.

"So we're driving around with his roommates and this car pulls up next to us at a light. It's full of cute girls, and one of them is leaning out of the car and starts talking to us. So we all start flirting, and when the light turns, we keep alongside of the car. There's one super hot brunette in the backseat that keeps talking to me. So, awesome. This goes on for like three or four stoplights, until we're at the last light before we basically have to get on the freeway, and the brunette writes down her number on a wadded piece of paper and throws it in my window before we drive away.

"So later in the evening, we're back at my friend's apartment, we start drinking and playing cards and stuff, and they start getting really fucked up and annoying to be around, and at some point I'm just like 'I'm gonna call this chick,' and they're like 'Cool, we're drunk, go for it.' So I call and she's like 'Yeah, my friends have gone home and I'm at home, but you should pick me up and take me out' or whatever."

"Yeeeah," said PFC Lo.

The Humvee carrying Staff Sergeant Jackson, Urritia, Sodium Joh, and Thomas pulled up to the Green Zone bazaar. It was a tourist trap, yes, but a pretty interesting one—only those with access to the Green Zone could patronize it, and who knew how long it would be around? Not for long, was the general sentiment, since the occupation would be over soon.

The bazaar was spread out in a vacant lot in the center of the Green Zone and was reminiscent of a small flea market in the American South. It was a city block long, and it boasted cheapo knives and nylon "tactical" holsters, T-shirts with slogans, a bunch of knockoff pro soccer jerseys. Sodium Joh was marveling at an electric lighter with Saddam's face on it. Pressing down on the thumb button ignited a gas flame that changed from white to green to red then back, along with a Casiotone sound system playing some kind of martial melody. Two plastic stars set into Saddam's eye sockets blinked on and off.

"Jesus," said Joh. He turned to the guy behind the table, a twenty-something in a fake Manchester United jersey. "How much for this?"

The guy held up five meaty fingers. "Fifteen."

"Fifteen?" Joh looked down the stalls for the other guys. Thomas and Jackson were across the aisle, picking through T-shirts that asked "Who's Your Baghdaddy?" Urritia had wandered down to Prince Faisal's Souvenir Shop, which offered photograph portraits of customers in Lawrence of Arabia getup, complete with scimitar and headdress.

"I'll give you ten," Joh said. The guy scrunched his lips as if deliberating. Joh turned his gaze to the sparse crowd of shoppers shuffling languidly down the dusty aisles like sun-drunk tourists at a seaside resort. One had stopped and was fiddling with something under his robe. Joh didn't notice.

"Okay," the vendor said. "I do for ten."

"Anyway," Ant continued, "my buddy lets me borrow his car, and I drive out to this swanky suburb in Virginia or Maryland—columns on the porch and shit—and I roll up the driveway and ring the doorbell, and her dad opens the door. And I'm like 'Uhh, nice to meet you, sir, I'm here to pick up your daughter' or whatever."

"Right."

"And then behind him, I see the girl coming down the stairs on one of those power-lift things in a wheelchair."

"Yeeeeah!" Fields said.

"You're right, Fields," Montauk said. "We do need to hear this story."

"So I played it totally cool," Ant continued. "Didn't even blink."

"Nice."

"And he's like 'Okay, well, you have to be back by midnight, absolute latest,' and I'm like 'Yes, sir,' totally polite and unfazed. Turns out this girl's a paraplegic, but she's a fucking paraplegic ten."

"Yeeah, baby," Lo said.

"So she's like 'Take me out to my favorite bar, they never card me there,' and I'm like 'Okay, cool.' And we go to this bar, and I carry her in and sit her on one of the barstools. And we're flirting, she's getting drunk, whatever. We stay for a while. Then she wants to go to this other bar down the street, so, okay, I stick her in the chair and roll her over. So we're carrying on, it's going well, she's super hot, but we're not making out in the bar or anything, I mean, I'm not going to drive her to my buddy's gross house and try to fuck her on his bed."

"Why, because she doesn't have any legs?" Lo asked.

"She has legs, idiot," Fields said. "She's paralyzed, she doesn't just not have legs."

"Yeah, look, she has legs. I just . . . Whatever, my plan was to be a good guy and take her out and then bring her back to her dad. I mean, she was super hot; if I was actually living in D.C. and had a place to take her that wasn't my drunk friends' crash pad—"

Fields made the move-it-along hand motion again.

"Whatever. I'm supposed to have her back by midnight, and I've got to drag her out of the bar because she wants to stay longer. So we're in the car, and I'm trying to get back to her neighborhood. I'm already late. But then we're passing this big park and she tells me to pull over 'cause she really has to piss. And I'm like 'Shit, I told your dad you'd be back by now,' but she insists. So I get her out of the car and she tells me to get her swing out. She's got this kind of hammock thing under her wheelchair that has Velcro loops that attach to a tree or poles. So I'm like 'Uhh?' But okay, I roll her into a group of trees and get the Velcro attached between two of them and lift her into the swing. Then I start to walk away to give her a little privacy, and she shouts, 'Just kidding!' I'm like 'What?' and she's like 'Just kidding, I don't actually have to pee. This is where you get to do whatever you want to me.' "

Urritia stood in front of Prince Faisal's Souvenir Shop, weighing the pros and cons of getting a Lawrence of Arabia picture taken. The cons were that it was extremely lame, that the rest of the squad would give him hell for it, and that it would cost money. The pro was that he'd have something to give Mom for her birthday, and there was nothing Mrs. Urritia loved more than photos of Urritia, preferably cheesy posed photos. Urritia in a baseball uniform, holding a bat; Urritia with a prom date in front of a stylized backdrop of moon and stars. He turned around to look for Jackson and found himself looking at a sweating, wide-eyed Arab who stood about ten feet away. The Arab was looking straight at him and saying something, his head cocked to the side, his dark hair slicked to his forehead, his lips moving and then ceasing to move. Urritia thought: *Oh.*

The Arab expanded, faster than the eye could see or the ear could hear, pushing out before him a wave of pressurized air filled with carpentry nails and washers, some of which flew straight into Urritia's body as he was lifted off the ground and pushed onto the table with the loosely folded robes, keffiyeh, and ersatz scimitar of Lawrence of Arabia.

The dull crack of the distant explosion reached the Priority Search bunker.

Two-Six, BOB.

"BOB, Two-Six," Montauk said into the mike.

Two-Six, BOB. White smoke plume, looks to be somewhere in the Green Zone.

They stepped outside to look at the tall off-white puff rising over the GZ, about a klick and a half away.

"BOB, Two-Six, roger, keep me posted."

They filed back into the bunker.

"A paraplegic ten on a sex swing in a park? Oh, man, you're such an idiot," moaned Fields.

"Yeah," Ant said. "I know, but I just couldn't do it. It just felt so wrong, dude. I just said, 'Look, no, I've got to get you home,' and she gave up and went with me. We rolled back into her driveway and made out for a minute, but I was like 'Okay, it's like one-thirty, I've got to get you back inside,' so I roll her to the front door and I'm about to ask her for the key or something, then the door just opens and her dad is standing there in a sweatsuit."

Jackson reached Urritia first. A chunk of Urritia's cheek had peeled off, and there were small patches of blood seeping through his DCUs. Urritia was making a *hmmmmm* sound that was gradually rising in volume and pitch. Jackson thrust the radio at Joh, who had just arrived, and told him to get a medevac there with a neck brace. Joh called the company, and Thomas ran off to find a medic. Jackson felt around for entrance and exit wounds. Urritia started blubbering something unintelligible, and Jackson told him that he would be okay, then started cutting off his shirt. There was a small hole in his chest that didn't look very deep and a larger, more concerning one below his navel. No exit, so something was in there, maybe deep. Urritia starting crying and squirming. Jackson yelled at him to stop moving his head, then realized that Urritia was saying, "My dick! Where's my dick?" Jackson put down the knife and started undoing Urritia's belt and trouser buttons.

"Well?"

"So she rolls past him down the hall," Ant said. "And he's like 'So, what happened to midnight?' And I'm like, 'Sir, I'm really sorry, it just got late, we were having a good time, and I miscalculated how long it would take me to get her back here. But it's my fault, I should have had her, you know, back a while ago.'"

Sergeant Jackson told Urritia to shut up, then slid a hand down his boxer briefs to feel for damage. Urritia's junk was sweaty and hot to the touch, and Jackson felt wetness. He craned his head around to try to get a better angle and gently pushed the elastic band of the underwear back as far as he safely could. Urritia was one of those guys who trimmed his pubic hair. His penis was covered in blood. "Uhh," Jackson whispered to himself. Urritia said, "Oh, no," and Jackson told him to shut up again, a bit softer this time.

He gently manipulated Urritia's penis to check for some kind of pinhole entrance wound. There was nothing obvious. He went over it inch by inch as fast as possible, but Urritia's scrotum was covered in hot sweat and blood, and the skin was difficult to hold on to. And then Jackson realized: all the blood down there was from his own hands, from touching Urritia's belly wound. He'd been feeling up Urritia's dick for nothing.

"It's fine. Hey, look at me. Your junk's fine."

Urritia looked back at him and said, "Really?" And Jackson said, "Really," and Urritia started to smile and giggle.

"Yeah, well, don't laugh at it, we got to get you on a backboard and back to the Cash. Stay awake and stop moving your head." Jackson cut through the thighs of Urritia's trousers—no punctures near any of the arteries. Just the shallow one in the chest and the deeper one in the lower gut. Urritia's breathing had stabilized.

Jackson looked back for the medevac, but it was still a minute away. All that remained of the bomber were his legs and pelvis, which had fallen into a kneeling pose over a dark pool in the dirt.

"And what he does is, he gives me this long look and puts his hand on my shoulder and says, 'Don't worry about it, son. Most guys just leave her in the swing.'"

29

The platoon slowly rotated over to the night shift. In the beginning of December, they pulled their thermal underclothes from the bottoms of their duffels. The seasons were turning.

The e-mail from Urritia in Landstuhl suggested that he was healing up nicely. But the rest of the platoon was losing it around the edges as the constant trickling of stress carved new and aberrant patterns into their personalities like underground streams in a limestone cave.

Thomas had purchased a Maglite flashlight with which he nearly caved in the head of a drunk local who had staggered up the exit lane after midnight. Montauk let Thomas keep it after he promised to use it only when legitimately necessary.

Not long after, Olaf told Montauk the disturbing news that Staff Sergeant Arroyo, the 3rd Squad leader, was hiding in the bunker the entire time that 3rd Squad was on Routine Search; he wanted Montauk to consider replacing Arroyo as squad leader unless he turned over a new leaf quickly.

The one good change was that Jackson seemed to have gained more respect for Montauk, especially when he saw him disciplining Fields for unnecessarily roughing up a driver at Priority Search. It meant that Jackson's attitude toward Montauk had climbed from negative up to about zero.

The Intelligence Summary that came every morning at 0700 via Humvee from Warhorse had become increasingly shrill and alarmist: *Possible VBIED at CP11 between 1300–1700 02DEC04. LN sources indicate coordinated attack mixing VBIED with SAF. BOLO for a silver BMW sedan.* A note that translated to mean Montauk's checkpoint might be targeted by a suicide car bomber between one p.m. and five p.m. on December 2nd, and that there might be some kind of coordinated small arms (AK-47) assault, and to Be On the Look-Out for a silver BMW sedan, which they'd have to add to the BOLO list of more than fifteen specific vehicles, most of which were common Baghdadi cars. Montauk gained new insight into why the warnings of a possible Al-Qaeda hijacking were ignored before September 11—it was just one warning in a daily mail call of dire warnings, the defense against which would consume the daily affairs of federal and state governments to the exclusion of almost anything else. The vast majority of possible CP11 attacks never materialized, and the attacks that did were never predicted accurately enough to make the intel useful, or to convincingly tie the attack to the intel warning. Even when scary intel was right, it was right only accidentally.

The daily INTSUM farce jaded Montauk on the entire idea of Army Intelligence cracking the code of the insurgency, if there was such a thing as the insurgency apart from disparate, raggy groups of pissed-off, nihilistic locals and imported religious freaks. The insurgency in Baghdad consisted of random, ineffectual violence directed against everyone or no one. Montauk just didn't get it, and the constant false alarms dropped off by other baby-faced lieutenants at 0700, which referred to Anti-Iraqi Forces (AIF) and Al-Qaeda in Iraq (AQI), convinced him that the folks at Intel didn't get it, either, and perhaps didn't get that they didn't get it, a far more disturbing possibility. Some version of Rumsfeld's "unknown unknowns."

So when the daily INTSUM predicting SAF attacks against CP11 turned out to be onto something, Montauk thought of it as a lucky shot in the dark rather than confirmation that Army Intel knew what they were doing. The first potshots came from an apartment building across Karada Dahil and smacked into a T-wall right next to an Iraqi National Guardsman who opened up with a burst of his own before Sergeant Jackson ran over and screamed in his ear to knock it off. They didn't have enough troops to make a recon by fire worth it, so Montauk had CP11 halt search ops and hunker down until the QRF from Warhorse rolled into the neighborhood to poke around. That often felt like the most useful thing they could do: sit and wait, call in the distance and direction of random gunfire, fish bodies out of the Tigris, and cajole the Baghdad cops into hauling them off.

The last body that had washed up on the riverbank stank so bad that Montauk's vest seemed contaminated after the checkpoint shift, as if an aerosol particulate of putrid torture victim had somehow wafted up from the paunchy gas station clerk's corpse and embedded itself into the Kevlar weave, which then seemed to exude a subtle miasma of death. He didn't realize what a foul and angry mood he was in until getting on the phone with Mani and hearing her talk about joining a War Is Terrorism art event run by some thirtysomething Ralph Nadery douchebag whom she seemed to want to fuck.

"It's just anti-war, Mickey. I mean, I'm anti-war, too, especially with you over there."

"It's not 'just anti-war,' it's a stupid fallacy. War is not terrorism. Terrorism does not equal war. They are two distinct, like, things in a broader category of types of violence. But they're not the same, that's fucking stupid, and people should read a goddamn book."

"Okay, fine, do you want me to not do it, then?"

"What's wrong with 'War Is Bad'? Wouldn't that get across the— whatever passes for ideas for these people? It would even be pretty much correct: war is bad. But if it's referring to what I'm doing over here, which it probably is, they're wrong again. There's no war here, we're just peacekeepers in a really shitty neighborhood. We're like the Detroit PD in *RoboCop* or something."

"Mickey—"

"This guy probably thinks in some vague way that we're actually fighting a war, which is equal to terrorism, and so if we just stop the quote-unquote war, which I guess means sending me and my guys home, that everyone here will realize what they knew all along but were blinded to by the hegemony or the false-consciousness narratives that racialized and quote-unquote othered them or something, and that if we would just go home and use our upper receivers as one-hitters or daffodil holders and *give peace a chance,* well then, the violence would stop and there could be a happy independent Iraqi republic. You know, we dragged a guy out of the river today with his fucking *eyes* poked out. He had his *eyes poked out*. Fuck this War Is Terrorism guy. He just wants to sleep with you."

Montauk took a breath. No response. "Hey. Mani?"

She wasn't there. He hoped she'd hung up long ago.

A week later, he was rattling around the troop compartment of a Bradley on the IED-rich road to the airport, on the lip of a fourteen-day midtour leave. Some platoons got leave early in their deployments. Some late. He'd be home for Christmas. He should have felt lucky. He pictured himself showering with fancy soaps in his parents' guest bathroom, walking the streets of Boston without a rifle slung across his chest, Mani at his side. It didn't seem right. There was something off about it, like a house made of candy in the middle of a dark forest.

article | discussion | edit this page | history

♟ Log in

WIKIPEDIA
The Free Encyclopedia

navigation
- Main Page
- Community portal
- Current events
- Recent changes
- Random page
- Help
- Donations

search

[Go] [Search]

toolbox
- What links here
- Related changes
- Special pages

The Encyclopaedists [edit]

The Encyclopaedists . . . fucking A. Those were the days. A sentiment with a shelf life: all reminiscence eventually becomes pathetic. The Encyclopaedists would do well to have no opinions about the Encyclopaedists. Which means to disbelieve the Encyclopaedists. You must believe in something to be for or against it. Those in the University believe in the War. Those in the War believe in nothing.

Contents [hide]
1 Precursors of the Encyclopaedists
2 Motivations of the Encyclopaedists
3 Ice
4 Used goods
5 Things that don't exist
6 War

Precursors of the Encyclopaedists [edit]

Aristotle, Alexander the Great, Saddam Hussein, Jeffrey Dahmer. The list of one's antecedents may be less meaningful than the list of one's descendants.

Motivations of the Encyclopaedists [edit]

You gotta do something with your life.

Ice [edit]

A curious result of the structure of the human nervous system is that extreme cold sometimes feels hot, and extreme hot sometimes feels cold, both extremes of thermoception becoming indistinguishable when registered as pain. This is why a walk through the cool evening air or a warm bath with an intimate are such prized moments: not being extremes, they cannot be thermically confused or re-created on the cheap through self-induced pain.

Used goods [edit]

The used has an affinity for the used. How else to explain the spread of STDs in nursing homes, the way garbage congeals in oceanic gyres. Someone else invents you. You can only reinvent yourself, sifting through the cast off with castoffs in a thrift shop. When you pass the point where fucking a virgin no longer appeals, you must admit to yourself that you want something used but not too used; broken in, not broken down.

Things that don't exist [edit]

Things that don't exist are not necessarily a waste of time. Products of fancy, such as the *Transformers* or *G.I. Joe*, may introduce a young child to important concepts, such as the value of knowledge ("half the battle") or good and evil. Which do exist in some forms. Pure good and pure evil don't exist, which is fine. Though when things that don't exist become sources of anxiety, they are generally a waste of one's time. Nothing doesn't exist: true. So why worry about nothing? There are so many things that do exist, especially the world. Your life in the world, aka what you should be worrying about. Retard.

War [edit]

Generally, the definition of "war" is achieved when several factors are met:

1. There must be a violent conflict.
2. The conflict must be between two or more states or organized armed groups. Although the belligerents need not wear uniforms, they must have some level of organization, command, and common purpose.
3. War is necessarily finite—chronic unrest and violence do not equal a war.

War can be distinguished from disorganized, nihilistic violence, which may result from individual manifestations of a wider social pathology. The occupation of Iraq by the US-led coalition seems to be a hybrid of these two kinds of violent conflict (the nihilistic and the organized), as a military expeditionary force is used and all of the appropriate wartime medals are offered to troops, and yet the enemy is not a state or an armed group or even, arguably, a nebulous network of armed groups, but possibly more of a social malaise exacerbated by the appearance of small armed factions, some domestic, as in the Mahdi Army, some international, as in Al-Qaeda.

It is thus not clear to what extent the Occupation of Iraq is an armed conflict under the Geneva Conventions, because it is neither an International Armed Conflict nor, arguably, a Non-International Armed Conflict given the participation of Transnational Terrorist Groups. Which makes its status as a "war" doubtful.

The word "war" is sometimes used to describe a concerted effort on the part of an organized group to destroy an inchoate thing or idea, such as the "war on drugs," the "war on poverty," the "war on rape culture," the "war on terror," the "war on apostrophe misuse," etc. "This is war," another example of the word's mission creep into wider meaning, which one day might be wide enough to be all-encompassing: the war of all on all. The war of who can say less. The war of drifting apart.

External links [edit]

1. ^ "The Encyclopaedists of Capitol Hill."
www.thestranger.com/apr04/encyclopaedists.htm

2. ^ "C. PLINII NATVRALIS HISTORIAE PRAEFATIO."
www.thelatinlibrary.com/pliny.nhpr.html

3. ^ "Stanford Encyclopedia of Philosophy entry on 'War.' "
plato.stanford.edu/entries/war/

FESTIVUS

30

Hal's grandfather Francis had purchased the *White Center Weekly* from his wife's ailing father in 1959. He and his partner, Charles Halifax, then acquired the *West Seattle Star* three years later. The following year they founded the *Queen Anne Chronicle,* the third paper of their growing company. Over the next few decades, Puget News & Publishing expanded, founding *The Ballard Review, The Bainbridge Tribune, The Des Moines Reporter,* and *The Federal Way Herald,* all community papers in tabloid format with circulations between five and nine thousand. Francis and Charles became moderately wealthy.

The whole family grew up working for the papers. Hal's father, Henry, and his uncle Theodore got jobs mopping and melting slugs from the day's Linotype, ladling impurities to the slag pile, letting the molten lead harden into ingots that would be set the next morning in the Linotype machine, where the typesetter would stamp out the columns, lock them in the galley, ink them in the proof press. Their sister, Carol, was a prodigy photographer—by the age of twelve, she was taking excellent shots for the papers.

Puget News & Publishing became a local empire, but by the year 2000, they were competing with Craigslist and community blogs. By 2004, after extensive downscaling and staff cuts, the company was on its last legs, but Francis Corderoy refused to let it die. And though Henry was running things now, Francis still drove to the office a few times a week and interrupted the course of business with superfluous questions.

Henry was already under a lot of stress, but the holidays were more difficult because he and his siblings—who disagreed about how and if to keep the papers running—could not avoid each other so easily as they did the rest of the year. On top of that, their mother, Mary-anne, had emphysema and probably wouldn't make it through another Christmas. And last month Francis had fallen and fractured his hip—he had gotten out of the hospital just last week. Thus, the family Christ-mas party at Grandpa Frank's was more tense than usual.

But for Hal, it was especially bad. The flight back to Seattle had jet-lagged him, but worse, he was stone-sober. After that lonely Thanks-giving, he'd made a resolution: no more booze until he felt happy, a real organic happy. It was a temporary fix, but a necessary one—a tourniquet. And so he plodded through his final classes, blew off his final papers, and didn't do much of anything in wintry Boston. He thought he saw Mani once, walking into an art-supply store, but he had done dozens of double takes at skinny, black-haired girls in the last few months, as if a part of his brain were permanently on the lookout for those indicators, a process that would necessarily yield a staggering number of false positives. Without alcohol, he came to view himself more and more as a computer, his habits as background programs he had difficulty uninstalling. By the time he was in Seattle, after nearly three weeks without booze, his body had adjusted—he no longer felt those cravings set in at about six o'clock—but that didn't mean his adult social skills, which he'd developed through alcoholic consump-tion, were up to the task of navigating the family Christmas party.

They arrived at five-thirty, an hour late. Aside from Grandpa Frank and Grandma Maryanne, there was Frank's sister, Corderoy's great-aunt Jane (Crazy Jane, who'd been in the sanitarium), Uncle Ted and his wife, and their two daughters, Emma and Samantha, who were a few years older than Corderoy. Emma was married, with a three-year-old and another on the way. Samantha had brought her boyfriend, a guy with dreadlocks whose arms were sleeved in tattoos. With Cor-deroy, his brother, and his parents, that made more than a dozen peo-ple, and his aunt Carol and her husband had yet to arrive.

After a quick battery of hugs and hellos, Corderoy's father asked him to open up a few bottles of wine.

Crazy Jane approached Corderoy as he uncorked a zinfandel. Her frizzled white hair was pulled back by a headband. Thin wire-frame glasses sat crooked on her nose. As he poured her a plastic cup of wine, she said, "How are you, big guy? You been enjoying your time, all this freedom you have now, spoiling yourself?"

"I'm in school," Corderoy said, baffled. "I have to read a book a week."

"Sounds like retirement. Think they'll give me a degree?" She made the motion of elbowing him in the ribs but didn't actually touch him. "So, you read books for a few years. Then what?"

"I don't know. Be a professor?"

"Hah. My husband was a history professor. Not a career I'd wish on anybody. I feel sorry for your future wife." Crazy Jane laughed. Corderoy tried to laugh with her, but she stopped as soon as he joined in. "Where's your girlfriend, then?"

"Between girlfriends at the moment."

"And I'm between husbands."

Corderoy glanced around the room and realized that he and Crazy Jane, who was at least eighty years old, were the only single people here.

"No harm in not having a lady on your arm."

"You should have been a poet," Corderoy said.

"You should try this wine," Crazy Jane said. "You'll like it. It's fruity—intensely fruity."

What the fuck. How had he ever gotten through a conversation with this woman? Alcohol. He'd either been young enough to simply run off and play, or he'd blurred out her crazy with a strong buzz. "No thanks," he said.

Just as she was about to continue, Corderoy saw his cousin approach. As she gave Aunt Jane a hug, Corderoy sidled away. He saw his brother and his brother's girlfriend sitting alone near the Christmas tree. Katie always looked so chipper, and not in a false way; she seemed to have a genuine faith in the goodness of the world. Right now Corderoy resented her for it. He could feel his own willed smile sloughing off his face as he approached.

"You doing all right, bro?" Max asked. He was wearing a tight V-neck T-shirt that showed off his pecs and biceps. While Hal had been reading comic books and playing video games, Max had taken to athletics, following in their mother's footsteps. She had played fast-pitch softball at the University of Puget Sound, where she'd earned a degree in physical therapy. According to his father, who'd profiled her for the papers early on, her windmill pitch whipped that softball through the strike zone faster than he could throw overhand. She was lithe and tall, more Artemis than Aphrodite, and Corderoy had always felt that she was more proud of Max, who had become the athlete she wished Hal had been.

Though Max would never outstrip Hal in height, by the age of twelve, he was already stronger than his older brother. He spent his high school years on the mat, in the gym, and at the sort of parties Hal had never been invited to, with beer, girls, marijuana. He'd gone off to Oklahoma State on a wrestling scholarship.

"I could use a drink," Corderoy said.

"What are you having?" Max said, standing up.

"Nah, I'm trying to cut back."

"Wrong night."

"Tell me about it."

"We could leave and go see *Blade: Trinity*," Max said.

"No, we can't, actually. Besides, *Blade II* was worse than *Blade*. How could *Blade III* be anything but worse than *Blade II*?"

"Shut up," Max said. "*Blade II* was awesome."

"It had a shitty plot and even worse dialogue," Corderoy said.

"You're doing it wrong," said Katie. "*Blade* movies aren't meant to be analyzed."

"I'm critical," Corderoy said. "Can't help that."

"You can be critical," Katie said. "You just have to take things for what they are. If you have high-art expectations for everything, you'll be disappointed all the time."

"Great. I should just expect life to be shitty. Then when it is shitty, I'll be happy!"

"Damn, bro. Grad school's making you a pessimist." Max was holding a half-empty beer that he hadn't sipped since they'd been talking. "I'm gonna get some food," he said, and he and Katie walked off.

Corderoy turned to find Aunt Carol and her husband, Darren.

They'd just arrived. Aunt Carol leaned in and gave him a big, overly long hug. This was one of her good nights. She was always slightly manic.

"Have you missed your favorite aunt?" she said on a rising note. After the usual pleasantries and life-update questions, Carol leaned back and Uncle Darren took over. Corderoy liked Darren. His father said he had "a twelve-cylinder mind"—but Darren was depressive. He'd gone to Yale Law, but he didn't practice. Together, he and Aunt Carol made one bipolar person.

"How are you doing," Darren said. "You look a little down."

God. Was it that obvious? "Jet lag," Corderoy said.

"We got something for you," he said. Aunt Carol withdrew a holiday-wrapped book-shaped object from her bag and handed it to him.

Corderoy unwrapped it. It was Alfred Lansing's *Endurance,* the true story of Ernest Shackleton's doomed expedition to cross Antarctica.

"One of my favorite books," Uncle Darren said. "Inspiring stuff."

Corderoy thanked Aunt Carol and Uncle Darren and made his way over to the red leather easy chair where Grandpa Frank sat.

"This place is jumping," Grandpa Frank said in his shaky voice as Corderoy bent down. His eyes could never keep still; they darted around the vicinity of Corderoy's face.

"Heard you had a big storm out here," Corderoy said.

"Poke your head outside," Grandpa Frank said.

Corderoy got up and went to the back door. His grandpa's house was on Puget Sound, and there had been a large deck with a glass-walled windbreak sitting on short pilings above the rocky beach. It wasn't there. Corderoy returned and knelt again. "The deck's gone," he said.

His grandpa didn't say anything.

"I can't believe it," Corderoy said.

Grandpa Frank nodded slowly. "Fifteen-foot waves. Twenty-five-foot logs. Pounded the piss out of it."

"You gonna rebuild it?"

"The state has a law now. Trying to eliminate bulkheads. Because of the sand lance. Looks like a small eel, but it's really a kind of fish. It needs waterfront vegetation to nest."

Corderoy watched Grandpa Frank's eyes roam about the room. They were so wet.

"The salmon eat the little suckers. That's what drives everything. It's all a charity for the Indians."

"The Indians?"

"I don't know how long we're going to live here anyway. I'm ninety and she's eighty-six." Corderoy looked over at his grandmother, sitting in the easy chair to the left. His cousin Samantha was talking to her. And she was stepping on the oxygen tube that ran back into the bedroom where the tank was. Corderoy was about to say something, but Samantha moved her foot. "I'm fine except for the lack of balance," Grandpa Frank said. "Lucky at my age not to have any aches or pains to speak of. I love this house. Such a good spot."

"It is a great house," Corderoy said. He stood up, but Grandpa Frank wasn't done with him.

"Are you satisfied with the progress you're making?" As he'd gotten older, Grandpa Frank had become increasingly sentimental and direct; talking to him was like being interrogated by a Hallmark card.

"Guess so," Corderoy said.

"What's your ultimate goal?"

Fear, murder, respect, beer, honies, and sex. Grandpa Frank wouldn't get a *Big Pun* reference. "Happiness?"

Grandpa Frank laughed. "You already got that. Has there ever been a time you weren't?"

"Guess not," Corderoy lied. He tried to smile. "Can I get you anything, Grandpa?"

"I'll have what you're having."

"Just soda tonight."

"Not drinking, aye. That's good. My older brother, Will Jr., died of drink. So did my best friend, Charlie. Your namesake."

By the time Corderoy returned with a soda for his grandfather, his mom had taken center stage. Her softball days were over, but she'd never lost her competitive spirit, and at family gatherings, she could be counted on, without fail, to initiate party games. In her fierce attempt at victory, she would often leave the room in a sour mood. It even happened with the annual white-elephant gift exchange. This year only one person had brought a gift. So in lieu of the exchange, she instigated a round of singing. Susan's singing voice was quite good: years in the church choir. She began with "Silent Night," and Grandma Maryanne was delighted. She joined in, wheezing out the words. Corderoy wasn't much for singing, so he mouthed the words under his breath, letting his mother and his aunts and uncles carry the song. Afterward, his mother struck up "It's Beginning to Look a Lot Like Christmas" and then "Frosty the Snowman."

Aunt Carol began circulating, whispering manically to everyone that Grandma was fading, that the party had to be over. In five minutes. Corderoy looked at his grandmother. She did look tired, but that didn't mean Aunt Carol wasn't overreacting. No one seemed willing to pay the drama cost of disagreeing with her.

The car ride home was awkward and silent; Corderoy was crammed in the backseat with Max and Katie. But as soon as they dropped Katie off at her house, Henry and Susan broke the tension.

"Why'd you have to do that?" Henry asked her.

"What?"

"The singing. It wore Mom out."

"She loved it. I've never seen her happier."

"For the first song. But you had to keep going. You had to outdo everyone."

"That is just, just—"

"Mom, Dad," Corderoy said. "Chill out."

"We're fine, honey," his mother said. Corderoy looked to Max. He was stoic. A defense mechanism for these quarrels. "Are you okay, Hal?" his dad asked. They were nearing home.

"Why does everyone keep asking me that? I'm fine."

"You just seem a little down."

"He said he's fine," his mother said.

"I know that, I heard him."

"Then why are you pestering him?"

"I'm not."

"No wonder he's down."

"I'm not down," Corderoy said.

"For God's sake, it's Christmas Eve," his father said, turning sharply onto their street—the car hit a patch of ice, Henry swerved, and they plowed into the mailbox stand on the corner, knocking it flat and sending the cedar shingles of its small roof tumbling into the darkness. The bumper and the hood of Henry's pristine mid-nineties Lexus were bent out of shape.

"Just great!" his mother said. "Wait till the neighbors check the mail."

"There's no mail on Christmas," his father said.

"It doesn't matter. They'll see it. How much is that going to cost us? Two, three thousand? Not to mention the mailboxes."

"Will you just shut up a second." No one said anything for a moment. Henry slowly backed up, then drove down the street and parked in the driveway. He turned the car off, but he didn't get out. Neither did his mother. The four of them sat there, steam from the car rising up to the icicle lights on the gutter. Corderoy needed a drink. Fuck the resolution. Fuck organic happiness. It wasn't worth this.

Without looking back, his father said, "Boys, finances aren't so good right now. The papers haven't been making any money—it's a dying business, as you know, and Grandpa's been using up what money there was to keep the papers alive. And to keep himself alive."

"What?" Corderoy said.

"I'm trying to explain something."

"Why now? What does—"

"Just listen, it's important. When Grandpa's gone," his father continued, "which won't be that long, there won't be much of an inheritance. And I'll be out of a job. Without a pension. So we have to be careful. We won't be able to help you out much. With tuition, or rent, or anything else. You understand? Hal? Max has a scholarship, so this is mainly for you. We have to watch—"

Corderoy got out of the car and walked up to the front door alone. He knew his mother kept a bottle of Christian Brothers brandy, for eggnog, in the top cupboard, near the salad spinner. But fuck eggnog. As soon as he got inside, he was taking a swig right from the bottle. But the door was locked. So he stood there under the green glow of the holiday porch light, like a child or a dog, waiting for someone in charge to let him in.

31

Montauk's parents had met him at the airport in their blue Volvo, and his mother, Veronica, after a long hug, insisted on heaving his heavy green duffel into the trunk herself, boasting about the boot camp class she attended every Monday, Wednesday, and Friday.

During the ride home, his father had barely spoken. His mother, who worked as a collections manager at the Smithsonian, had given him a rundown of everything he'd missed in their personal lives. In chronological order. She'd told him how they remodeled the upstairs bathroom, how a tree fell on the neighbors' car during a windstorm in October, how his father got a cortisone shot in his knee. She told him about the latest acquisition at the museum of some intricately carved Chinook dugout canoes. She told him that she'd been looking at travel packages to Peru, that she'd always wanted to see Machu Picchu, that they were going to go, once she convinced his father that it wouldn't kill him to leave the country—which first meant convincing him to leave the house and his easy chair. She also wanted to take a trip to Greece. She was half Greek, named after her grandmother, Berenike Stavropoulos, and she'd never been. Oren, who'd been at port in Athens for a few days during his time in the Navy, had no interest in going back.

What she did not tell Montauk, and what he found out over the next two days, was that his father, now retired and dealing with a variety of joint pains, had retreated so far into the comfort of his easy chair and his fifty-inch LCD TV that he rarely left it except to grab another beer. He was also getting fairly drunk each night. He had only three or so bottles, but he was drinking high-percentage Belgian beers. Montauk's mother, not a beer drinker herself, hadn't caught on that different beers varied in alcohol content. She would call to Oren from the kitchen, telling him about an article she was reading in *Newsweek,* and he would sit in his chair, bristling like an artichoke, giving her curt responses or grunts or sometimes just ignoring her.

It wasn't all that surprising to Montauk; it seemed like a natural outgrowth of what had characterized their relationship for decades. Perhaps personality traits, like ears and noses, became exaggerated as one got on in years. He sensed something deeper, though, and it wasn't until Christmas dinner that it surfaced.

His mother disliked cooking, but she made it a point to put together a meal on special occasions. And what could be more special than having your son home from war on Christmas?

This year's tragedy was the roast. It was like eating beef jerky soaked in water. Montauk choked down a slice and a half as a kindness to his mother, who spent most of the dinner bemoaning the unbelievable fact that George W. Bush had been reelected. "After all the lies about 9/11 and everything else," she said. "You know people talk about moving to Canada. Maybe it's not such a bad idea, where this country is headed."

"You can move if you want to," his father said. "I'm staying right here."

"Who's going to pay the bills?" his mother said. "Who's going to buy your fancy beer?"

His father refilled his glass from a bottle of Delirium Tremens and took a swig.

"Who's going to wash your underwear?" Veronica laughed awkwardly, then poured an excessive amount of gravy on her slice of dry roast.

Montauk had always thought of his parents as left-leaning political moderates. His father, presumably, still was. But his mother had become increasingly liberal since her son's deployment. She set her silverware down and looked at Montauk with her you're-not-going-to-believe-what-I'm-about-to-tell-you face. "I went canvassing for Kerry," she said. "In Virginia. On the weekends. Everyone I talked to, everyone, was against this ridiculous war."

"It couldn't be everyone, Mom," Montauk said.

"Everyone. And Virginia went to Bush by more than eight percent. It's disgusting."

After they'd all had a piece of pie, Montauk's father brought his plate to the kitchen, came back and patted Montauk on the shoulder, then said, "I'm turning in."

"It's only ten, dear," his mother said.

"I have to fall asleep before she gets in bed," he said to Montauk. "She moves around so much it's impossible to fall asleep."

His mother scoffed, then turned to her son and said, "I don't move that much. He just doesn't move at all. He's like a stone. With gas."

He helped his mother with the dishes, told her a few sanitized stories about things he'd done and seen in Baghdad, and by eleven, his mother was ready for bed as well. Montauk went into the den to check his e-mail, there being no Wi-Fi in his parents' house. He deleted a fair amount of spam and newsletters he'd subscribed to, willingly or accidentally, then sat there staring at his lonely inbox. The inbox of a man whose friends had forgotten him. He scoffed at his burst of self-pity and navigated to the Encyclopaedists Wikipedia article. He clicked edit. But he couldn't figure out what to write. He swiveled around in the desk chair, observing the room, which felt oddly lived in. There was a pillow on the couch, along with a blanket. There was a Patrick O'Brian novel and a glass of water on the small table near the couch. And there were his father's slippers behind the door.

REUNION

32

Mani's father, Nasir Saheli, was born in Tehran in 1949 to an upper-class family of doctors, lawyers, and academics. When the United States helped overthrow Iran's prime minister, Mohammed Mossadegh, in 1953, the Saheli family cheered the shah, friend of the West, for bringing Iran onto the world stage. When the shah declared his autocratic rule in 1961, young Nasir had been thrilled that his emperor was the foremost leader of the Middle East. How proud they were when the shah extended suffrage to women. And with the oil boom of the seventies, when the shah and his family earned billions of dollars, the Sahelis were happy to overlook the growing wealth gap, of which they were on the better side. In 1973, at the age of twenty-four, Nasir graduated from medical school at Tehran University and began practicing pediatrics. In 1977, as Khomeini's militant anti-shah protestors took to the streets by the thousands, Nasir treated a young girl with an ear infection and fell in love with her beautiful older sister, Shaady Binazian.

Shaady was twenty-two at the time. Her father had owned a fabric store and labored to get the best education possible for his oldest daughter. Shaady was fluent in Farsi, Arabic, English, and French, and she had just secured a teaching position in the Foreign Languages department at Tehran University. Though she was not as pro-shah as Nasir, she was a vehement supporter of women's rights, and she longed for an Iran with the freedoms of the West. They married in '78 and had one happy and carefree year until the shah was deposed in the Islamic revolution and Shaady was removed from her teaching position and forced to obey Islamic dress code. What upset her more was that her younger sister was barred from attending regular schools, and though she was only thirteen, she was now of legal age to marry.

When Saddam invaded the following year in the midst of revolutionary crisis, their hope for a secular and socially progressive Iran dwindled. By late '81, the Islamic revolutionary sentiment had swelled enormously with the war effort, and Nasir and Shaady had begun talking about leaving Iran and moving to America. And then Shaady discovered she was pregnant. As they sat in a café sipping tea, only the small oval of her face revealed by the mandatory hijab, smoke rising from a building down the street, and soldiers with automatic weapons standing on the corner, she told Nasir that she would not raise a child in this repressive and hostile environment.

Nasir had enough family money to get them to Boston, where a distant cousin helped set them up in a small Brighton apartment to start over in the American middle class in the winter of '82. Shaady was lucky enough to get an adjunct position at Boston College, teaching beginning Farsi and Arabic. When Mani Saheli was born in September, Shaady took only two weeks off before returning to teaching, depending on Nasir and a friendly Irish family who lived below them to watch over Mani.

Nasir's medical license would not be accepted in Massachusetts until he redid at least three years of residency with fresh graduates five years his junior. He drove a taxi to keep the family afloat. Those first years were difficult, but by the time Mani was ten years old, they had moved to a large house in Newton. Nasir was running his own pediatric practice, and Shaady had been promoted to associate professor, teaching Middle Eastern literature.

For a couple who had left Iran to escape the social regression of the Islamic revolution, they were very strict with Mani's upbringing. She was an attractive young girl, and there were several boys in her seventh-grade class clamoring for her attention, but her mother forbade her to date until she was fifteen. Like any teen girl, Mani secretly broke this prohibition. She began dating Jeremy at fourteen, which brought her into the entirely new social world of Goth. When she came home with her nose pierced, her parents confined her to her room. She spent the next week lying on her bed, staring up at her poster of Marilyn Manson, playing *Smells Like Children* on repeat, and slapping her wrist with a slap bracelet until the thin fabric wore through and the sharp metal edge began cutting into her skin. As soon as she had her freedom, she dyed her hair bloodred. She traipsed around that summer with Jeremy and his Goth friends until she found a new boy, Michael, who was the bassist in an "amazing" rock band called Bonehenge. When Michael introduced her to alcohol and cigarettes, her hairstyle and accumulating number of piercings officially became a minor issue for her parents. When they caught her smoking weed a year later with Drew, her then-boyfriend, they tried to ground her for a month and revoke all telephone and computer privileges, but Mani replied by showing them her grades—straight A's—and asking with complete nonchalance what the fuss was. Aside from introducing her to pot and taking her virginity, Drew also got her interested in the erotic sci-fi/alien art of H. R. Giger, and when Mani took an art class her sophomore year, she realized that she had a talent for drawing.

She continued this way, changing social groups as she moved from boyfriend to boyfriend. At seventeen, she tattooed her back with cello f-holes to express her devotion to Eric, her nerdiest boyfriend to date, who played in the school symphony. And through the binge drinking on weekends and the after-school joints, Mani managed to keep up her grades; to her parents' relief, she was accepted to UMass Amherst.

When it came time to choose her major, Mani decided that she wanted to be a painter and chose visual art. Though her parents had backed down in these contests for years, they finally stood firm: unless she switched to pre-med or business or some major that would provide real career opportunities, she'd have to finance her own education. Mani had her first bout with depression that semester, and after seeing several therapists, she was given a prescription for Paxil. When her boyfriend Chad graduated that summer, she dropped out of Amherst and moved with him to Santa Cruz. She lived with him for nearly a year, spending her days painting portraits of the homeless and the junkies who wandered the beach. She eventually left him and made her way to Seattle, refusing to ask her parents for help. Her plan had been to wait until she qualified for in-state tuition, then apply to the University of Washington for art. But she never quite got around to putting a portfolio together. She found a job selling produce at a farmer's market in Ravenna but was soon fired for showing up hungover and stoned. She might have been on the street again if it hadn't been for Steph, though that situation had ended poorly.

When Mickey Montauk shipped out at the beginning of October, Mani took his advice and moved back to her parents' house in Newton, Massachusetts. For the first week, they asked no questions, and Mani lived in an alternate reality in which she'd never disappointed them, never left home, never fallen in love with a nerdy boy named Halifax who'd abandoned her (leaving a void that she filled with the generosity of his best friend), an alternate reality where she'd never married Mickey in the county court for his military benefits, where she'd been a hardworking student, making her way through pre-med, showing her parents that their struggles to leave Iran and start a new life had been worth it.

But after a week of her mother's cooking, of her father's reminiscing about his youth, the questions began.

"So, dear, what's your plan?"

Mani put her fork down.

"Your mother is asking if you're going back to school."

"I am, in spring semester." Mani had not decided on this, but she didn't know what else to say to end this line of questioning as soon as possible.

"Will you be getting a job?" her mother asked. "You can't simply sit around the house for the next three months."

Mani did her best to delay answering such questions, but when her mother found her bank statement, she had to lie. Montauk's Basic Allowance for Housing had increased when he and Mani got married, and he'd set up a monthly automatic transfer of a thousand dollars to Mani's account. Mani wasn't about to tell her mother that she'd married her friend Mickey—just her friend, not even her boyfriend. So she lied and said she'd gotten a job sitting for a gallery downtown. Shortly thereafter, she moved into a studio in Allston.

It was fairly spacious and lit by large factory windows on the eastern wall. The floorboards had been coated and recoated with thick white paint over the years as they collected uncleanable grime. With all the new art supplies she bought, with the rolls of canvas, the frames in various states of construction, the stretched and half-painted canvases on easels, the tarps and sheets and oil paints, the stacks of sketchbooks and charcoals and brushes, there was not much room for actual living. She spent most of her days painting, smoking joints, and flipping through art books for inspiration. She trashed most things she began until mid-October, when, after writing a letter to Mickey, she began a painting that felt real, that felt important.

When the subject came to her, it was not at all surprising, and she knew exactly why she had chosen it: her nominal husband was an American soldier in a war zone, and the number one cause of death for American soldiers was the Improvised Explosive Device. After looking at images on the Internet and reading some firsthand accounts, she began painting a Humvee tilted onto its right wheels, the explosion from an IED lifting it off the ground, the terrified face of the driver who knew they would flip and burn and die.

What she couldn't explain, what she began doing without realizing it, was painting this scene of extreme and sober violence in the cartoonish style of Dr. Seuss, a surreal and childish distortion of bright primary colors and silly elongated shapes: striped and bendy palm trees, fantastic dunes in the background, the Humvee disproportionate and bright green, sporting oddly placed knobs and gears, the explosion bulging like an image under a magnifying lens propelling the truck right out of the canvas and toward the viewer, the driver's face squashed and birdlike, six eyelashes on his wide right eye, a small pimple on his nose, the mouth a black hole with the barest hint of a tongue, a dark red mass being sucked back into the throat, a few wisps of candy-blue hair curling out whimsically from his helmet.

She was drawing from a sense of loss; it was not an overwhelming condition but a subtle one that resided in the nethermost regions of her consciousness. The morning after she'd been hit by that dark sedan, when she'd been caught between her crushing need for morphine and the thought that perhaps she was pregnant, an entire future had come into being, a settled future with Hal. Or perhaps without him, but with an inescapable lodestone to guide her through the rest of an otherwise messy life: a child had been born in her mind. And it had been lost.

As she perfected the last details of the driver's face, an incredible anxiety overcame her, as if she'd turned the curve of a highway, going thirty miles over the speed limit, only to see a cop car screeching off the shoulder, its manic sirens and lights propelling her heart rate and breath to unmanageable levels. And then she was done and the police shot past her in pursuit of some unknown, and as she stepped back and looked at her work, her body fell into a peaceful and unsettling darkness. She rolled and lit a joint, a small comforting light, and smoked her way to equanimity.

The next day she began work on a second painting in the same Seussian style, this time of a few bodies on the street, soldiers, clods of dirt scattered like popcorn from the small crater left by a home-made bomb. Small Iraqi children with gigantic eyes looking on from the periphery, peering out the curved windows of wobbly buildings, smiling. One of the soldiers was clearly dead, his eyes squinched into outsized X's; the other with his legs blown off, was still alive, pleading with an outstretched hand toward the foreground, the plump four-fingered hand of a cartoon, the pool of blood and oil and dirt behind him swirling like a rainbow of melted Starburst.

It took her a week to finish, and when it was done, she felt an after-shock of what she'd felt for the first painting, but it came with a greater sense of fulfillment, that she'd brought forth value out of nothing, created something alive; she realized that she was not finished, that these were the first two paintings in a series. Over the next month, she confined herself to her studio and worked simultaneously on three new paintings. These proved more difficult, and she progressed slowly, limning the outlines of a dreamlike Bradley flipped on its back, a twist-ing convoy of supply trucks and Humvees, a rusty late-eighties BMW bounding through the chain-link at a checkpoint. In a month's time, though these three were still unfinished, her confidence, her feeling of impending accomplishment, had grown significantly, enough that she took high-resolution photos of her first two and submitted them to the curators of a few Boston galleries. From then on, she worked methodically, the precision of her surreal lines and colors increasing while the rate of her progress diminished. On December 31st, she got a phone call from Mickey, on leave from his tour of duty. The last time they'd spoken, he'd flipped out and she'd hung up. She was a little wary of seeing him, but how could she not? That night, just after ten p.m., she buzzed him in and began rolling a joint while he trudged up the three flights to her studio loft. When she heard his footsteps on the landing, she panicked and quickly threw a few sheets over her new paintings, uncertain what he would think of them.

Montauk flung open the metal door and let his duffel bag thud on the floor: there was his wife, standing before him in all her pajamaed glory. They fell into each other and hugged long and close, but they parted with some minor awkwardness, neither wanting to be the first to release nor the one to hold on.

Montauk wanted to say something grand about how great it felt to see her, but all he could manage was a long pause, punctuated with "Hi."

Mani laughed, lit a joint, took a drag, and said, "Welcome home." She offered it to Montauk.

"Can't. Routine drug tests."

She took another few puffs, then stubbed out the joint and left it in an ashtray. "You can have liquor, though, right? Let me make you a drink."

"What can you make?"

"Hot toddys. That's about it."

"A hot toddy, then."

Mani clicked on an electric kettle, then poured whiskey into two mugs, added a cinnamon stick, a dash of lemon juice to each. While the kettle boiled, Montauk looked around her studio, examining a few scattered sketches, some small half-finished self-portraits. He noted that all the large canvases were draped with sheets.

"Cheers," Mani said after handing him his steaming mug.

"Hooah," Montauk said. The hot toddy was strong. Really strong. If his alcohol tolerance had weakened over the last few months of sobriety, Mani's had increased. Either that or she was trying to get him drunk. "You feeling good about the work?" he asked.

Mani shrugged. "It still feels . . . not fully formed."

Montauk nodded toward the covered canvases, but before he could ask about them, Mani said, "You're alive. You're still alive."

Montauk smiled.

"Not that I thought—but—just tell me everything."

"There's not that much to tell," Montauk said.

Mani tilted her head to the side like an unconvinced mother.

And so Montauk told her everything, or nearly everything, with enough flavor to get the idea but without getting too specific. He didn't want to lose control like he had on the phone. Mani was particularly intrigued by the little ruffian Monkey—she asked more questions about him than about the various car bombs or about Aladdin's death. She sketched what she imagined his face to look like, based on Montauk's descriptions, and as Montauk watched the shape of the skull take form on her sketchpad, he thought of the last time he'd seen Monkey and of the morbid request he'd put in. Mani didn't need to know about that.

"And how's Boston been?" Montauk asked. "Have you hung out with . . ."

Mani stopped sketching and reached for her joint.

". . . any high school friends?" Montauk said.

She lit it, inhaled, and stared at him while the smoke filled her lungs, considering whether she should answer the question he'd obviously meant to ask. She exhaled, then told him about her time in Boston.

And after a while, Montauk let his posture slip; he relaxed as the whiskey heated him from inside out. He began to see Mani, his wife, not as a sexual figure but more as a sister for whom he could wish only the greatest happiness and love. Whatever awkwardness had been nosing at the surface of their conversation sank into a deep black place.

"So are you going to show me these paintings or what?"

"You'll see them, you'll be the first. Trust me. I want you to see them. Just—not now."

"What are you worried about?" Montauk asked.

"That . . ." That he would be offended? At her appropriation of the violence he'd lived with for the last few months? That he'd see through them? That they were false and he would know it and so would she? Mani sighed. "That you won't like them," she said.

Montauk laughed. He stood and walked over to one of the large canvases. Mani made no motion to stop him. He whipped the sheet off the first painting and then stood back, taking it in—the bright primary, wobbly Humvee in mid-explosion. Mani tucked her legs up into her arms and stopped breathing as Montauk drew the sheet off the second painting.

He let the slippery lines lead him around the painting's plangent colors, pausing on the face of a small Iraqi boy, the stump of a dead soldier's leg, and he did so with amusement and horror. He turned to her as if she'd just popped into the room.

"These are good," he said. "Really fucking good."

"Really? Really fucking?"

"I mean it. These are something."

Mani had been holding her breath for fear that the air in the room had grown acrid, but when she exhaled and filled herself up again, it was sweet and so crisp that it belonged with a view after a long strenuous hike.

"Not that I'm not worried about you," Montauk said.

Panic flashed back into her eyes.

"I mean, you've set the bar so high, you're going to need to work your ass off."

Mani laughed.

"Are you going out tonight?" he asked. "It is New Year's Eve."

"I don't really dig on crowds."

"No parties or nothing? Don't you have any friends in Boston?" He'd said it jokingly, but she glared at him.

"We both know why you came back to Massachusetts. It's not for your parents."

"Are you staying with him tonight?"

"Don't know yet," Montauk said.

"You kinda suck at planning ahead."

"Not planning is a luxury. I'm indulging."

"Stay here tonight."

"Sure?"

She nodded.

This time he climbed into her bed, overpowered by the smell of her, wondering if that was what she'd felt that last night in Seattle, aware of his scent in a way he never could be. They did not touch, but they were close enough to feel the heat transfer between them. How unlike his cot in the Iraqi Convention Center. As he stared up at the dark ceiling, he said, "I'm gonna go see him tomorrow."

Mani didn't respond. But he knew she was awake. "I could tell him to call you," he said. "But I think you should contact him."

"Don't tell me what to do," she said.

"I'm not. Just a suggestion."

"Well, it's been suggested. And don't you dare tell him I'm in Boston."

"I won't," he said.

They shared a minute of silence, hearing only their mutual breathing, the small sounds of blankets moving against skin.

"It's good to see you," he said.

"Really fucking good?"

There was no radio noise from down the hall. Outside the loft windows, wind, just wind. Montauk waited for the chattering sound of small arms fire. Nothing. "Really fucking," he said. He had never felt so safe.

33

At 15:36 Eastern Standard Time on New Year's Day, Second Lieutenant Mickey Montauk walked up to the olive-green duplex at 52 Fairmont Street and, as if drawing back to throw a javelin, balled his fist and pounded on the door. The January sun was bright over the snowed-in city of Cambridge, Massachusetts. A hand holding a lit cigarette protruded from a paneled bay window on the second floor. The hand withdrew, and a few moments later, Tricia Burnham opened the door. She was wearing knee-high boots, a black skirt, and a white button-up blouse with frilly shoulders. Her hair was held in a bun with a chopstick. Her lips were bright red and her cheeks were powdered. One eye was deeply shadowed a midnight blue, the other was bare. She held an eye shadow palette in one hand and her cigarette in the other. "Can I help you?"

Behold: a young woman. American, civilian, not off-limits to Montauk (as far as he knew). Seeing Mani in her pajamas had put him in a place of comfort. But here, seeing this girl in the act of beautification, the world of female display and male posturing came rushing back to him. He inhaled like a parolee stepping out of the pen on a fine autumn day. "Sorry to trouble you. My name's Mickey. I'm looking for Halifax Corderoy. Does he live here?"

"Yeah, come on in."

Montauk followed Tricia up the stairs, his head level with the shifting hemispheres of her ass. He was wearing a large black backpack, and in his left hand he carried an eighteen-pack of Miller High Life: the Champagne of Beers. Tricia slipped back into her room to finish her eyes. Her nerdy housemate had friends after all.

Corderoy, having woken from a nap several minutes ago, was lying on his bed with his laptop open, looking at the recent changes to the Encyclopaedists article.

There was a pounding at his door. "Hey, asshole, open up."

Corderoy opened his bedroom door to see Montauk wearing a coprophagous grin. "Holy what! What're you doing here?"

"I'm on leave. Back to Baghdad tomorrow."

"Well, where the hell you been?"

"Visiting my parents, fuckhead."

"Right. How are they? I hope my affair with your mom hasn't been causing any marital problems."

Montauk's grin slipped a notch. "They're fine. Though my dad's getting suspicious. Apparently, after your visits, he keeps asking what smells like fag."

Corderoy laughed. "Hey, chill on the faggot stuff, my roommate is super . . ."

"See you boys later," Tricia yelled from the stairwell.

The front door shut and Montauk looked back to see the living room empty. "She's a lesbo? Too bad. She's fucking hot, man."

"No, not gay. PC. And she's not hot."

"Oh, please, dude."

"Her face is too sharp. She smells like cancer. And I hate the way she dresses."

"You must not have spent the last few months in Iraq."

"Don't you fucking sleep with her. I mean it. The very thought . . ." Which was what, exactly? That Montauk and Tricia might have fun together? Why did it bother him to imagine her happy?

"Fine, fine."

"Also, don't tell her you're in the Army."

"Why not?"

"It would be, I don't know, awkward."

"What if she asks?"

"Tell her you're a blimp pilot?"

"You idiot. Good to see you. Beer o'clock yet?" Montauk held up the eighteen-pack.

Corderoy's no-alcohol policy had shattered on Christmas Eve, and he wasn't exactly happy about it. He wanted to live in moderation, to be able to have a few beers and call it quits. "It is now," he said.

They cracked a couple and sat down on the couch.

"You look homeless, dude," Montauk said. "When's the last time you got a haircut?"

"Seattle." His reddish-blond beard had grown out considerably.

"So. Tell me about Boston."

"Not much to tell. Been kind of depressed."

"Gotten laid?"

"Nah."

"C'mon, man. It's your job to be fucking chicks while I'm out defending democracy. You must have got some action. A date, at least?"

Corderoy thought about bringing up ♥Sylvie♥. It was the kind of story that would be funny to others if he could laugh along with them, but pathetic if he couldn't. He pictured himself telling the story, willing himself to laugh, and Montauk seeing right through it and awkwardly changing the subject. "Fuck Boston," he said. "Tell me about Iraq."

For the second time in as many days, Montauk related his life thus far in Baghdad: the havoc of car bombs, bodies in the Tigris, waking up to the sound of mortars, shooting up a car as it rushed toward the checkpoint and killing the family inside. Or imagining that happening anyway—a hundred horrific possibilities every single day. The tone had gotten serious, and Corderoy said, "Sounds rough, man."

"It's not so bad. We got plenty of time to watch movies, read, and fuck around. Some of the guys in my platoon are pretty cool. Actually, you won't believe this, but one of my guys, Private Ant, was at the fourth Encyclopaedists party."

"That seems so long ago."

Montauk pictured the small journal Mani had sewn together, its collaged cover with the snipped-out image of a bicycle carefully overlaying an old lithograph of the Trojan horse, Greek hoplites rappelling, each with a double-edged xiphos and round hoplon shield. The journal was in his duffel bag, only a few feet away, underneath an end table. "You want another beer?" Montauk asked.

When he returned from the kitchen, he found Corderoy loading up his Xbox.

"I'm not really feeling Xbox games," Montauk said.

"Nah, son. I like to start off the New Year with an old-school Nintendo game."

Montauk looked at him quizzically.

"It's modded," Corderoy said. "I bought a chip and soldered it onto the Xbox motherboard. Now it can run emulators and shit. I downloaded every Nintendo game."

"Do you have *Kid Icarus*?"

"I have every game."

"Like, every game ever?"

"Yes, every game ever. Including the Japanese ones. But *Kid Icarus* . . . I don't know. He's not exactly an uplifting mythological figure. Let's play *Blaster Master*." Corderoy loaded the game, and after he pressed Start, a perfectly ominous four-toned MIDI progression played over a black screen. "Watch the intro," he said.

The backstory of the game unfolded in a short sequence of still frames: a boy's pet frog escaping, bounding toward a radioactive crate; the frog growing by a factor of ten, diving down a hole in the earth; the boy leaping after it, finding a futuristic tank at the bottom of a cavern; fanfare and a revving engine and the boy driving the tank into a vast under-the-crust world to reclaim his pet frog.

"Simple," Corderoy said. "Ours is but to do or die." He maneuvered the tank, jumping over chasms from platform to platform and firing missiles at slow-moving mutant enemies.

"I can see why you like this," Montauk said.

"It really does cheer me up to play through the first half of this game. Then it gets too hard."

"Isn't that your problem with life in general?"

"Shut up."

"New Year's, you know. Fresh start. Maybe you should make a resolution."

"Resolutions are just predictions of what you're going to fail at."

"Maybe you should make a resolution to fail, then," Montauk said.

"Very clever."

As Corderoy approached the first-level boss, the music taking on an adrenal intensity, his cell rang.

Montauk picked the phone up from the table. "It says *unknown*," he said.

"Answer it."

Montauk said, "Hello," then after some mumbling on the other side, he cupped his hand over the phone and said, "It's some professor from BU. Flannigan or something. Says you owe him a paper, that you still haven't registered for classes for next semester, and that you haven't been responding to e-mails."

"That's nice," Corderoy said. "Take a message."

As the day wore on, Montauk tried probing into Corderoy's grad school woes, but Corderoy steadfastly refused to discuss—because he refused to think about—the fact that he still had several papers to turn in if he wanted credit for his first semester, that he had no money to pay for tuition next semester, that he'd lied to his parents about receiving a fellowship from the English department to cover his expenses. They polished off the rack of High Life just as Tricia returned.

Since the Kerry loss, she'd become annoyed with Jenny Yi, Jeff Alessi, and all her other friends who were so quick to say, "It's only four more years. America will hate the Republicans even more by then. This could be a good thing." It most definitely was not a good thing. And this made the cloying optimism of her social group all the more unbearable. She became frustrated with school as well, with writing papers and having class discussions. It had all begun to seem like superfluous preparation, research for a project that would never commence, work whose sole purpose was to create the illusion of accomplishment without setting foot outside and confronting the real problems of the world. To make matters worse, several of her professors at the Kennedy School were angling for positions in the White House, repeatedly missing office hours because of trips to Washington.

Over Thanksgiving, her mother had tried to console her about the election, but Tricia wasn't just upset about Kerry. The idea of Baghdad had bloomed in her mind over weeks and shriveled in the course of a night. Her mother would never understand. Her world was one of local politics and petitions and fund-raisers, and she would have been horrified at the prospect of her precious daughter traveling to a war zone.

As such, Tricia had been drinking steadily through the month of December, going out to dance clubs, hitting on boys—and girls—and generally keeping herself distracted from her own futility. She was a little tipsy when she arrived home, having drunk her way through a rather boring party that she'd gone to out of a sense of social obligation. She found Hal and his friend sitting on the couch listening to classical music. She brought out her bottle of Johnnie and poured them all glasses.

"I thought you only listened to music with rapping in it," she said to Hal.

"I pretend I'm cultured when he's around," Corderoy said.

"Dvořák's New World Symphony," Montauk said.

Tricia lit a cigarette and offered the pack to Montauk.

"No, thanks, I got the Grizz." Montauk pulled out a can of Grizzly long-cut wintergreen chewing tobacco, slapped it against his finger, then took a dip.

"Give me that," Corderoy said.

Montauk did. Then he watched as Corderoy attempted, awkwardly, to flick his wrist in imitation of Montauk's own fluid tobacco-packing snap. He looked just like Aladdin. Tricia watched the scene with interest. After a few seconds, Corderoy gave up, took a clumsy pinch, and shoved it into his mouth, getting a fair amount on his tongue. He spent the next minute trying to maneuver the tobacco into the pocket of his lip.

"How was your New Year's?" Montauk asked Tricia.

"Kinda boring," Tricia said. "Though New Year's Eve was fun." She began telling Montauk about a cute girl named Autumn whom she'd met at a house party the previous night.

Montauk wondered if this was some kind of ploy. Corderoy hadn't said anything about Tricia being bi. Perhaps she was testing Montauk. "You can't be serious," Montauk said. "Autumn? No one is named Autumn."

"Maybe she had hippie parents?" Tricia suggested.

"What happened?"

Corderoy looked down at his feet to steady himself. He was feeling nauseated.

"You all right, man?" Montauk asked.

Corderoy nodded. He looked up to see Tricia take a long, slow, and disgusting drag on her cigarette.

"We'd been making out in the back of the house," Tricia said, "but then that Snoop Dogg song came on."

"Which one?"

"You know, that one where the guy is singing at the beginning."

"Nate Dogg," Corderoy said, under his breath.

"Ah," Montauk said. " 'It Ain't No Fun (If the Homies Can't Have None).' "

"Right, so I wanted to go dance, and Autumn says, 'That song is one of the most disgusting, sexist songs ever made.' "

"That's what makes it so great," Montauk said.

Tricia hit him on the shoulder playfully. "I mean, time and place, right? You wouldn't be able to dance at all if you subjected every song to some musical version of the Bechdel test."

"But I thought," Corderoy said, "you said the subtle sexism, it's the most insidious, or whatever. About *Star Wars*."

She shook her head, smiling. "You leave your goat untethered so often. How am I not supposed to get that sucker when I see the chance?"

Montauk laughed.

Corderoy puked into his mouth. "Blee light black," he said. He rushed to the bathroom, flung open the door, dropped to his knees, and dumped his mouthful of minty-brown vomit into the toilet.

He spent the next five minutes on the floor, breathing heavily between the occasional heave. He could hear muted laughter coming from the living room. He wondered if they could hear his retching.

Once he'd gotten it all up, he washed his face and gargled mouthwash. He stared at himself in the mirror. His nose was covered in blackheads. His eyes seemed to be open wider than usual—nicotine? Maybe he was just tired.

"That's so cool," Montauk was saying as Corderoy returned.

"It's not *cool*," Tricia said. "It's tragic. And in our own country."

"I didn't mean *it* was cool, but you know, it's cool that you helped with that documentary."

"*Everyone* should live on an Indian reservation for at least a few months."

"What if you're from Sudan?" Corderoy asked. "Should you live on the rez then?" He stood up, stretched his arms above his head, and made a face as if about to yawn, found that he didn't have enough sleep in him to get past that critical point, and then faked it, opening his mouth wide and long. "I'm going to bed."

"You feeling okay?" Montauk said. "Dip hit you pretty hard, huh?"

"I'm fine. What time you gotta wake up?"

"My plane leaves at eight-fifteen, so I guess be there by seven, leave here by six?"

"Sounds good. See you shortly." Corderoy gave him a stony look that said, *Don't, don't you do it,* then shut himself in his room and went to sleep.

"What do you do, really?" Tricia asked.

"I told you," Montauk said. "I fly blimps."

"You do not!" She hit him on the shoulder again. "For who?"

"UAI. United Airships Incorporated. You think Goodyear owns their own blimps? They contract out to us, and we slap on their logo."

"But aren't you a little young to be a blimp pilot?"

"An aeronaut. And no, actually, most of us are young. The more experienced you get, the more likely you are to work ground control. Pays more."

"Shut up." Tricia was grinning despite herself, and Montauk could see exactly where this was leading.

"I didn't create the industry," he said.

"How long's the training? You go to school for it?"

"Blimpsmanship is still on the apprentice system. I was going to go to grad school for literature. Got into Harvard, even, but UAI promoted me to Senior Aeronaut. Couldn't turn that down."

"You got into Harvard?"

"Yeah. Ask Hal. He's still a bit sore about that." Montauk smiled, leaned forward, and kissed Tricia. Within a minute, she was straddling him on the couch, pressing her mouth on his so fiercely that Montauk could feel her teeth and jaw and the entire weight of her head bearing down on him.

Somehow, through his joking deceit, Tricia saw Mickey Montauk as an honest and thoughtful person, someone willing to consider anything, and in that, she envied him—it seemed a hallmark of wisdom, of experience—and it made her wet.

Tricia pulled Montauk into her room, her mouth on his neck as they both stripped off articles of clothing. Montauk went down on her for several minutes, until Tricia lifted his head and said, "Do you have a condom?"

"Hold on," Montauk said, and he ran out into the living room in his boxers. He knocked on Corderoy's door and said in a loudish whisper, "Hey, man, I need a jimmy hat."

Corderoy's muffled voice said, "What?"

"I need a condom. Do you have any?"

"I'll give you one in the morning," Corderoy said.

"No, idiot! I need it now." Montauk tried the door. It was locked.

"I'm sleeping," the voice came back, then something unintelligible.

Montauk sighed and went back into Tricia's room. "Sorry," he said.

Tricia was lying naked under her comforter. "We probably shouldn't, then," she said.

"Okay," Montauk said, climbing into bed with her.

That resolution lasted all of ten minutes. They moved through several positions until Tricia was on top. The lights were off. Montauk's left hand was clenched on her right hip, where a small mole moved back and forth under his palm. His right kept awkwardly groping for her breast, but with the bouncing and the darkness, this was difficult, and he gave up after a short time and settled on slapping her ass. She wasn't loud, but she was vigorous.

She leaned down and placed her open mouth on his, taking in his tongue as the bouncing settled into a slow circular grinding. They breathed into each other. Then Montauk dug his nails into her back and brought them down toward her ass in a slow, deep scratch—and as if he were pulling a drawstring, she arched upright again, placed her hands on his chest, and began slamming her hips into him with more force. Montauk could feel his cock swelling and hardening beyond his control.

His chest was suddenly wet. And then his face. Tricia must have been sweating hard. And then he felt drips land near his mouth and on his neck.

"Oh my God," Tricia said, jerking to a halt. "My nose is bleeding."

Montauk licked his lower lip and tasted iron. Tricia reached over and flicked on her desk lamp. There were bright red spatters of blood on Montauk's chest, his neck, Tricia's bedsheets, and, though Montauk couldn't see them, his face. Tricia had a line running down from her nose and off her chin. A few drops had dribbled across her pale and perky breasts. She looked mortified. But then Montauk started laughing. He could feel his penis, which had gone soft, get slightly hard again inside her, and they laughed and laughed until their abs hurt.

Tricia climbed off, plugged her nose with tissues, grabbed a towel from the back of her door, then straddled Montauk and gently wiped the blood off his chest and face.

It was 6:40 a.m. when Corderoy stumbled to the bathroom to empty his bladder; Montauk was half-naked on the couch. Corderoy nudged him awake. "Hey. Isn't it—shouldn't you . . ."

Montauk's eyes flashed open. "Oh, shit. What time is it!"

"It's . . ."

Montauk looked at his watch. "Fuck." Then at his bare legs. "My pants."

"What about your pants?"

"They're in Tricia's room."

"Shut up. No."

"Yeah."

"Goddammit. Go get them." Corderoy got dressed as Montauk crept into Tricia's room.

He came out a moment later buttoning his jeans. They threw Mon-

tauk's shit into his backpack and ran down to Central Square to catch
the T. As the train pulled into the tunnel, they caught their breath and
Corderoy turned to Montauk and said, "All right. Tell me."

"What?"

"How did that happen?"

"I just kissed her. We made out for a while on the couch, and then
she took me into her room."

"You idiot."

"Sorry about waking you up."

"What?"

"I knocked on your door at two."

"You did?"

"Yeah. I said, 'Hey, man, I need a condom.' And you said, 'I'm sleeping. I'll give you one in the morning.' "

"Hah. So . . ."

"So we decided not to."

"Oh?" Corderoy raised his eyebrows with affected surprise.

"But then after making out for a while more, I got her too wet, I
guess."

"Aww. No, don't tell me that."

"She was a fucking tiger, man."

"Whatever."

"The weird thing was," Montauk said, "well, she got a nose bleed.
It got all over me."

Corderoy looked at him, shocked. "That's disgusting."

"Yeah. Except it wasn't, really." He could see that he was only feeding
Corderoy's loathing of Tricia, a girl who, in Montauk's eyes, was completely undeserving of such contempt. "It was intimate," he said.

"You know what bothers me the most is just knowing that she felt
pleasure and comfort, that she was happy even for a minute." Corderoy
clenched his fist in mock rage.

"Dude, you're becoming a supervillain or something. Like you
don't just have a twisted perspective, you actively want evil to win,
knowing it's evil."

"You're saying it's evil of me to loathe the thought of someone else
being happy in any respect?"

"I'm sure there are exceptions, but yeah, that's the general idea."

When they arrived at Logan Airport, they discovered that the line to get through security was ridiculously long.

"Fuck, I'm gonna miss my plane. I can't miss my plane."

"You won't," Corderoy said. He left and found one of the airport security people, then explained that his friend, his active-duty friend, was in a rush. The lady escorted Montauk to the front of the security line. There wasn't really time for a proper bro-hug good-bye. Montauk saluted to Corderoy just before walking through the metal detector. Corderoy smiled and flipped him off.

As he walked out of the airport, he wondered if he really was evil. He'd never done anything too immoral. There was the night of the last Encyclopaedists party, of course, but that moment had been blocked from mental search queries. He'd never cheated on a girlfriend, but maybe the opportunity had simply never presented itself. It was entirely possible that he'd lived a moral life thus far out of nothing other than circumstance.

34

After Mickey's encouragement, Mani felt less like she was appropriating the imagery of war and more like she was entering a conversation about war; she quickly finished two of the three new paintings she'd begun: the flipped-over Bradley and the BMW crashing through a checkpoint. She'd discarded the third. She now had four completed paintings, and in the last week, she had started two final ones. These two proved the most difficult yet, for they were focused on people rather than vehicles. The first was of a woman dressed in a black abaya, cradling an infant with a single cartoonish curlicue of hair and an expression of blissful idiocy. The woman stood in a line of Iraqis waiting to be processed through a checkpoint into the Green Zone. A boxy soldier was patting down a spindly man in front of her whose head was out of the frame. And the woman herself: her midsection burgeoned as if she were horrendously pregnant—flames slipped through fissures in her garment, out her sleeves, indicating her imminent explosion. In the corner, inset in a circle, a close-up of her fist clenched around a detonation plunger. The earlier paintings had been all aftermath and explosion. This was detonation. It was not a painting of violence proper but of the birth of violence.

The second painting was of a boy no older than ten with his back to the frame, walking through concrete corridors lined with Gordian spools of razor wire. In the distance, up in a tower bent like a palm tree, a bored soldier manned a fantastical overbarreled machine gun.

Below him, near the iron pedestrian gate of the checkpoint, two soldiers rested their hands lazily on the bright orange M4s slung around
their necks. And the boy: fuzzy green hair, loose-fitting blue shirt, his
hands behind his back holding a grenade the size of a pineapple. It was
not even the birth of violence, it was violence in utero, which made it
all the more horrifying.

At the rate Mani was going, scraping paint off and redoing the grenade, fixing the woman's face, it would take her another month to finish these two paintings. But she would finish them, and they would be
a part of the world.

It was the 4th of January, and after a long day of painting, she made
herself a drink and sat near her space heater, giving her back, her
shoulders, her arms, but mostly her mind a rest. And then her phone
rang with an unknown number. And she was terrified that it was Hal.
That Mickey had told him to call her. Though she hadn't spoken to
Hal since last July, he had been an intermittent but persistent presence
in her head. He mattered, for some annoying reason. Perhaps it was
because he had betrayed her in a way that lacked finality or resolution.
She felt an illogical and visceral fear that he was calling to take credit
for inspiring her work, as if it wouldn't have been possible without his
emotional immaturity and general shittiness. Worse was the possibility that he was calling to apologize, which seemed like something she
should want but also something that might somehow sap her creative
drive.

It was not Hal. It was Nikolai Andropov from the Lewis Gallery in
SoWa. He loved the slides she'd submitted and was offering to display
her work in the gallery. She absorbed the details numbly: she would
have room for all six paintings, and the opening would be in late April.
Her work would remain up for a month—anything she sold would be
split between her and the gallery fifty-fifty.

After she accepted and hung up the phone, she walked over to the
windowsill. She lit a half-smoked joint from earlier, and as she inhaled,
she realized that her period had begun. But instead of going to the
bathroom to get a tampon, she lay down on her bed, a twin mattress in
the corner, half covered in sketches and books. She finished the joint,
letting her underwear stain. She felt like crying, and tried to briefly, but

her eyes were dry, almost to the point of irritation. She felt like dancing, but she was exhausted. She didn't know what she felt—she only dimly understood some urgent need to be understood.

The next day Mani tried to throw herself back into the work. But it wasn't happening. She kept looking at her phone, cleaning, preparing meals she didn't eat. Two things had happened: Mickey's visit and his prompting had brought Hal squarely into the center of her consciousness, and Nikolai Andropov's phone call had more than doubled the significant pressure she already placed on herself to make each line perfect, to make each moment of the painting own itself and inform the time-scape of all six. She was no longer working for herself.

She left the house and wandered through the aisles at the Blick art store near Fenway. She was running low on violet pastel and cadmium yellow, and why not buy a book of Caravaggio prints? If Mickey was sending her money, she might as well spend it. She was examining a palette knife when her cell rang. "Hi, Mom."

"Hello, dear. I was shopping down on Newbury and thought I'd see if you wanted to go out to lunch."

Mani dropped the knife on the floor. She'd told her parents that she'd gotten a job sitting at the Alpha Gallery on Newbury. And now her mother was there!

"I asked at the desk, but the girl, Amanda, she'd never heard of you."

Mani's hairline began itching with perspiration. "I . . . took the day off, Mom. Amanda must be new. I had to run down to drop off applications. For school." Why was she lying?

"Tomorrow, then? I'm free after my morning lecture."

"Sorry, I won't get much of a break tomorrow—new work being installed." So what, so she had lied to her parents about getting a job, but she was painting, and it was finally paying off. Her work, featured in a gallery. Why couldn't she tell her mother? She would be proud. All sins would be forgiven.

"Are you okay, dear?"

"Yes. I'm fine. I'll call you soon, okay?"

When she got home that afternoon, she crawled into bed and plummeted into sleep. Then slept all through the night and into the next day. She got up to make a drink, to roll a joint. She flipped through a book of John Singer Sargent's portraiture—searching for an aesthetic distant from her current work—then went back to sleep.

She woke up at some indeterminate hour, the light outside that gray half-light of early morning or early evening in winter, and she knew she had to call Hal. She had yet to process the turbulent emotions surrounding his disappearance last summer, her ensuing accident; she had bookmarked that indefinitely, when things got complicated with Mickey. But now that Hal was back in the foreground of her thoughts, that unresolved cluster of resentment and curiosity and anger and lingering love, it had become a block that she urgently needed to dissolve. She didn't know what she would say to Hal. But she knew how to figure it out. She had to paint him.

She stretched a canvas and began sketching the outline of a figure seated on a metal folding chair, legs crossed. She put a book in his hand, open and held aloft as if to suggest the figure cared deeply that whoever might be looking should know what a great book he was reading. She spent hours getting the posture right, then worked in a few details: the Converse, the skinny jeans, the plaid shirt. She worked through the night. Around dawn, she finished a rough version of his face. It was Hal, but she'd made him more clean-shaven than she'd ever seen him, his chin polished and reflective, and she'd given him long, wavy hair, though she couldn't say why. The cover of the book remained blank for the time being. She stood back to take in her work. Hal had a smug aloofness about him. But it was still missing something. Two somethings. She painted on a trim and ironic mustache and repainted his crotch with an open fly.

Compared to the Seussian war paintings, this seemed pointedly antiquated. Mani was a great admirer of Sargent, and in this piece she'd taken after him, just as he had taken after Velázquez and Van Dyck. But where Sargent had operated within the Grand Manner of portraiture to depict Edwardian luxury, she had put Hal on a folding chair. She'd mixed a hint of blue into everything, making his skin pale and lighting the scene with a sterile fluorescent quality, as if he were sitting in a church-basement A.A. meeting. Though she hadn't touched the background, she knew it would have to be an amorphous gray swirling, like the backdrops for school portraits. It was a picture of someone who desperately wanted to be seen looking maximally indifferent to the opinions of others. It was a portrait commissioned to look accidental.

Of course, Hal hadn't commissioned anything. And Mani wasn't about to imagine him with any sort of power in this situation. But the painting needed power. It needed Mickey. Over the next three days, she tried a dozen ways to work him into the background of the painting, and each became more violent than the last. Mickey changed as well, in both clothing and facial hair. What had started as a clean-cut Mickey hovering authoritatively behind Hal, wearing his DCUs with crossed arms, eventually became an enraged Mickey screaming through a ragged beard, wearing Civil War Union blues, his rifle drawn back, bayonet affixed and ready to plunge into the unwitting skull of Halifax Corderoy.

Poor Hal. Somehow pity had crept into the painting, pity for the villain.

———

It was snowing outside in thick, cumbersome flakes. Corderoy stared out the window, content to be alone, doing nothing. But the universe wouldn't allow that to continue for long. He heard the front door open and the sound of heels clicking up the stairs.

Since Mickey's visit, Corderoy's relationship with Tricia had petrified. They hardly talked at all, the necessary communication—*Any mail? It's your turn to buy garbage bags*—happening through passive-aggressive notes. Corderoy had passed his classes, barely, but hadn't registered for second semester, which began in two days. The Jennings Fellowship for Promising Scholars, which his parents believed he was the proud recipient of, was a fiction. He didn't have much of a plan aside from playing video games and trying not to drink before six p.m.

"Guess what?" Tricia said, walking into the kitchen.

Corderoy turned reluctantly from the window. Tricia was wearing a slim black dress, and her hair was mussed. She looked like she'd been partying all through the previous night. Corderoy did not want to guess. He hated it when people asked him to guess what. Tricia smelled like booze. Her smile was pleasant enough, but Corderoy nonetheless had to fight the urge to recoil, as if her face were the crooked arm of a leper extending toward him.

"All right," he said. "What?"

"You remember that guy Luc Dubois? The photographer?"

"Okay."

"He's going to Baghdad as an unembedded journalist to document human rights violations."

"And . . ."

"Well, he was going to go with this guy Will he knew from *Truthout,* who had lots of journalism experience—which is important."

"But . . ."

"But Will's wife got pregnant! He had to back out. And Luc called me yesterday, and I'm going! I'm going to Baghdad. I mean, it's too bad that Will can't go." Which Tricia truly believed, if only because she hated the fact that a fluke like this, and not her talent, was landing her this opportunity. "But Luc needs me," she said. "I'll be in Baghdad by the end of January! I'll be writing articles for *Truthout* and *Counterpunch.*"

"That's crazy. How can you be qualified for that?"

"Hal, no one's qualified to be there!" She was too excited to take his comment as an insult. "They're all making it up as they go. Anyone can buy a plane ticket to Baghdad. The hard part is choosing to go there when it's so dangerous."

"Wait, what about the apartment?" Corderoy asked.

"I'm giving it up. I know it's short notice, sorry. We have to be out by the end of January." Tricia tried to cringe, but her glee just made it look comical.

"What? Where am I going to go?"

"You'll find a place. I'll ask around for you. But isn't it exciting!"

Corderoy's check-engine light came on. He glared at Tricia. "Yeah," he said. "It's great. Maybe you'll see Mickey there."

"What?"

"He didn't tell you?"

"Tell me what?"

"He's not a blimp pilot," Corderoy said with a mischievous smile. "He's a lieutenant. In the Army."

"That's not funny," Tricia said.

"I know. He's probably committing some human rights violations right now."

"Shut up."

"If you get horny, just look for the guy standing over a pile of corpses like Galactus."

"Asshole," she said, and stalked into her room.

"You don't even know who Galactus is," Corderoy muttered. He wasn't sure why he was being an asshole. He was still angry with Montauk for sleeping with Tricia, and he was angry that Tricia might see Montauk in Iraq, and he was angry that she was happy and that everything seemed to be working out for her. He was an asshole because why not? If he failed at everything else in life, there was always that one thing he was great at: being an asshole.

35

In attempting to figure out what book her fictive Hal was reading in the portrait, Mani had turned to *The Thousand and One Nights*. Her mother had read her the stories as a child, and over the years they had become, for Mani, a sort of whimsical encyclopedia of the imagination.

The tales within the book were framed with the story of a king, who, fearful of marital betrayal, murders his virgin wife each night, then takes a new wife the following day. When the kingdom runs out of virgins, the vizier's daughter, Scheherazade, volunteers herself. Each night she tells the king a tale, stopping short at a cliffhanger, prolonging her life a further night. When she tells the king the tale of *The Thousand and One Nights* itself, the king has lost, for he can never escape the loop. It is an infinite prison. Such a metaphysical solution made perfect sense for someone like Hal. Of course he'd be reading a book about himself.

Mani carefully replicated the painting in miniature on the cover of Hal's book, then did so again within that replica, and again, the image becoming abstract dabs of color as it receded within itself, drawing the viewer's eye into the black hole of the book—but somehow also casting the viewer out beyond the frame, for the painting itself was the cover of an enormous book that the viewer would never be able to read. No, only that smug-looking hipster in the painting could read it, the corner of his mouth curled up—in amusement at the book or merely as a pose, even Mani couldn't tell. It was dizzying, in her head and in her heart, and that was how she knew she'd done good work. She texted Hal.

———

The text had been an address. And a time: eight p.m. It did not say *come see me* or *let's talk*. It did not attempt to explain or palliate the six months of rough silence that had festered between them. It didn't cast blame and it did not invite apology. It presented itself as a fact, as part of the natural order of things. And so Corderoy, who was otherwise too cowardly to reestablish contact, too guilty to reply, obeyed, for what else could he do? The universe happened, and this meeting at Mani's studio was a thing that happened within it.

As he walked up the stairs, he pictured Mani not in a wheelchair or covered with bandages but spry and vigorous. He paused in the hallway. The door to her loft was cracked. Years later, he would remember this as the moment he turned and walked away.

No. He would remember this as the moment he knocked.

He knocked timidly as he pushed the door open. Mani was standing at the window with a cigarette, wearing sweatpants, her hair oily and pulled back in a ponytail.

She turned and smiled and it killed him. He felt something emanating from that smile and it was not love. It was power. A form of power that was not rigid or controlling, that was not concerned with dominion. It was power that derived from an essential goodness. The smile he offered back said, *Please don't hurt me, I know I deserve it.*

"I have something to tell you," Mani said, putting out her cigarette. "But first I need to show you something."

Corderoy walked farther into the room. "You look good," he said. "How long have you been here?"

"We can talk about that stuff later," Mani said. "This is important." She walked up to a large canvas in the middle of the room and pulled the sheet off it.

Corderoy took in the painting. A hipster about to get his head ventilated by a Civil War soldier. And the soldier, he looked a lot like Montauk. But who was the hipster kid? Corderoy tilted his head to the side. "That's not . . . is that?" he said without looking away from the painting. It was. It was him. It was so obviously him.

Mani observed Corderoy's face, how it moved from confusion to recognition and then into an even deeper confusion. "What do you think?" she asked.

There he was, reading a book whose cover depicted the death he was about to experience at the hands of his best friend, and yet he looked so self-satisfied, so smug. As if he could keep death at bay through infinite recursion. The painting had contempt for its central figure. And yet such care had been taken to perfect the lilt in the brow, the sheen of oil on the forehead under the fluorescent light. In contrast, the image of Montauk leaping from behind was almost blurry with rage. A rage that seemed neutered by the frozen moment of the painting. "I . . . don't know," Corderoy said. He finally turned to look at Mani. "I'm stupid," he said. "I'm so, so stupid and sorry."

"Don't be sorry yet," she said. She took a breath. "After you left, when I got out of the hospital, I didn't have anywhere to go. So, I moved in with Mickey for a while."

Corderoy blinked.

"I told him not to tell you. I thought it would be weird."

"It is weird," he said. He willed his face to relax. "But. I get it."

"Also, we kinda, sorta. Got married."

Corderoy steadied himself on the edge of a chair.

"Just at the courthouse. It was Mickey's idea. To give me health insurance and a thousand bucks a month from the Army. That's how I paid for physical therapy, and this place."

Corderoy looked back to the painting. He tried to bury his consciousness inside of it. "I. I." *I don't deserve this? I have no reason to be angry?*

"Cards on the table," Mani said. "I had to."

Corderoy stared at her feet. He couldn't say another word. He turned and walked out, leaving the door open behind him.

It was dark and chilly on the street, and Corderoy strode with purpose toward anywhere. He wanted to bang on parking meters and signposts as he walked, to kick garbage cans, but he didn't. He held his breath. Montauk had taken Mani in and helped her with her medical bills, asking nothing in return, and that made Corderoy, in comparison, even more of a jerk. He closed his eyes and walked blindly. Montauk had given him an escape route when he needed it, and Montauk had stuck around to clean up the resulting mess. He stumbled, he ran into someone. He kept walking. No, he had no right to be angry. But he was. And realizing he was wrong to feel angry made it worse. The flames were nearing his gas tank, and knowing it wouldn't blow on its own, he saw himself rigging it for detonation.

He heard the sound of water, a washing, a spraying. He stopped abruptly. He breathed in. He opened his eyes. He was standing in front of the Allston Car Wash. A sedan had just pulled in and was being slapped around by the massive felt arms and rollers. He walked in behind it. An attendant saw him but was too late to stop him from entering.

The jets of water soaked him through in a second, and the large slapping brushes nearly knocked him over. Soap got in his mouth, and he started choking before another brush, stiffer and more painful, came from his right and sent him to the floor. The conveyor belt was moving him forward along with the car, but he could hardly breathe. The constant attack of the water and the soaped-up brushes didn't give him time or space to inhale. As he reached for the car's rear bumper to pull himself up, he realized that this was what the car always went through, though you couldn't possibly know from inside. He felt as if he were outside his own body, shocked at what the exterior must put up with on a daily basis, the rigors of gravity and light and water, and outside of his life, as if the thing that was really him were so tiny and small and protected that it couldn't possibly be exposed to the traumas that defined his life.

He plunged through one last curtain of water and was hit by gusts of heated air that invaded his crevices. He struggled to stand under the force of the fans.

The manager of the car wash was waiting for him as he emerged. "What are you fucking nuts? I oughta call the police."

"Can I have a towel?" Corderoy asked.

"Get the fuck out of here."

He walked into the first bar he could find, leaving sodden footprints behind him. He ordered a glass of whiskey, paid with sopping cash, downed it, then ordered another. Twenty minutes later, he stumbled out, drier, warmer, and drunk. When he got home, he checked his pockets. His phone was a wet, functionless brick. His keys were missing. He banged on the door until Tricia let him in. He said nothing to her. Inside his cave, he opened his laptop and navigated to the Encyclopaedists article. He created a new subsection: "Betrayal."

36

That night Corderoy dreamed of the painting, saw it move forward and backward in time, Montauk's bayonet piercing his skull and protruding from his eye socket. Then it sliding out and Montauk receding into the background. When he awoke the next morning, a strange calm had come over him. His fever had broken. He did not reflect on what he'd added to the Wiki article the previous night or whether he still believed it. It belonged to its moment in time as he belonged to this moment. And this moment felt good, but more important, it felt momentous—like the end of *Ulysses*—it was carrying him somewhere, and he was content to give himself to its design.

And so he arrived at Mani's apartment without warning and pushed the buzzer. Up until the moment itself, he wasn't sure what he was going to say, and it surprised him as much as it did her when he walked in and said, "I love it. I love the painting. It's weird and it's true and I absolutely love it."

Mani was speechless. She sat down on her bed and began rolling a joint. She held it up when she was done, and Corderoy sat down next to her. She lit it and they smoked it and they said nothing until it was finished. Then Mani said, "I didn't need you to like it. It's not for you."

Corderoy stiffened.

"You know how sometimes you have to say something out loud to see if you believe it?" Mani asked.

"Do you believe it?"

"This is me extracting myself. I'm trying to see who I am—not in relation to these other things."

"Things? You mean me and Mickey."

"Not you, but what I feel about you and Mickey. I had to take all of that out of my head and put it in the painting." She paused and looked up as if examining whether she believed that last statement. "I'm glad you like it," she said.

"I don't like it," Corderoy said. "I love it."

"Thank you."

Corderoy looked through her eyes into the well of her being. What a lucky fool he was to be sitting so close to a human so perfect. "This is going to sound weird," he said, "but can I ask you a favor?"

Mani stared at him. What favor could he possibly think he had the right to ask of her?

"My." His voice evaporated. Was he really going to ask her this? It was ridiculous, given the history. It was insane. It would demolish whatever new foundation he was building with Mani, leaving a crater in its place. "My roommate's leaving for Baghdad," he said. "I need to find a new apartment. I don't expect you to say yes, but . . . do you think, maybe, starting in February, I could crash here, on the floor or something, until I find a place? I got nowhere else to go."

Seriously? *Fuck off.* She tried out the words in her head. But she couldn't get the right emotion behind them. She'd given her rage to Civil War Mickey and his bayonet. "You're right," she said. "That is weird."

"Is that a no?"

The absurdity of Hal's request welled up and Mani nearly laughed. The idiot was audacious. That was something. "I need to think about it," she said. "I'll call you, okay?"

"I don't have a phone," Corderoy said. "I— It broke."

"I'll write you an e-mail, then."

"Okay."

"You should go now."

"Yeah," he said. "Of course."

"It's good to see you," she said.

Corderoy nodded and left.

That weekend passed in a fugue. Tricia was busy preparing to leave the country. Corderoy shut himself in his room and watched *Twin Peaks* to keep from obsessing about when Mani would write, what she would say. When the e-mail finally popped into his inbox on Monday, his heart began racing. She had written: *I'm having dinner with my parents in Newton tomorrow. Come.*

———

"So, Hal, Mani tells us you're studying literature?"

"Yeah," Corderoy said, taking a bite of Persian-spiced meat loaf. "I mean, yes, Mr. Saheli," he said through his mouthful. He'd taken the bus to Newton and walked a mile to Mani's house, and as soon as he'd crossed the threshold, Mani had pulled him aside and told him that her parents insisted on social formality. It reminded him of Professor Flannigan's class.

"That's wonderful," Mani's mother said.

"And how do you plan to make a living?" her father asked.

Corderoy looked over at Mani. She looked as indignant as he was bewildered. She said, "Hal plays the market. He invested in Google early on. He doesn't have to worry about money at all."

Corderoy almost choked.

"Good for you, Hal," Mani's mother said. She refilled her wineglass, which didn't need refilling.

"Got lucky," Corderoy said. He glared at Mani.

"He's being modest," Mani said. "He knows more about the futures of tech companies than most Harvard MBAs. He even published a paper in the *Harvard Business Review* about the dot-com bubble."

"You're a multitalented man, Hal," Mr. Saheli said, wiping his mouth, which didn't need wiping.

"Thank you, sir." Corderoy kept his eyes on his plate. He wondered if his face was red. Why couldn't she just tell small lies, like a normal person?

"How is your job going, dear?" Mani's mother asked her. And Mani dove into an imaginary world where everything was working out great

but for one annoying coworker, Amanda, who wore too much perfume and spoke with an affected British accent. Corderoy hadn't had
a chance to catch up with Mani and had no idea whether any of this
was true, but after hearing her tale about his investment wealth, he
suspected it was pure bullshit.

They had coffee after dinner, and Mani's father told Corderoy a few
stories from his years driving a taxi. Corderoy listened politely, occasionally asking a question to keep the conversation focused on Mani's
parents and off him. Around eleven, they retired, and Mani's mother
set Corderoy up in the guest room.

Mani gave him a knowing look as she shut his bedroom door. Sure
enough, about an hour later, she crept down the hall, silently opened
the door, and finding him wide-awake, motioned for him to come
back to her room.

Mani crawled under her comforter and lay back in the center of
her double bed. That seemed to be a sign that the bed was meant for
one person. But the comforter was pulled back on the near side, which
seemed like an invitation. Do not fuck this up. Corderoy decided to sit
on the edge of the bed, facing away from her.

"My parents can be intense," Mani said.

Corderoy surveyed the room. It was a time capsule from an
eighteen-year-old girl circa 2000. Which meant that the most recent cultural artifacts were a Rage Against the Machine *The Battle of Los Angeles*
poster and a pair of Etnies skate shoes in the corner that looked like
they'd actually been skated in—the telltale scuffs along the outside toe of
the left foot, where the shoe would have scraped against the grit of the
board to ollie. There were also curious remnants from the late eighties.
Garbage Pail Kids stickers on the back of the door. A small porcelain
pony sat on a bookshelf, no doubt some childhood gift that had become
a sentimental burden, just like the bejeweled music box next to it.

"Why did you lie to them?"

"I hate it when they pressure me about that shit. I didn't want them
to grill you."

"I mean about you. Are you applying to schools? You don't really
work at that gallery."

"How do you know?"

"When I saw you in your studio. You seemed content. Like that's where you belonged. Why would you be reaching anywhere else?"

"That's why."

Corderoy furrowed his brow. He rotated so that he was facing her.

"Because if they came to visit me at my studio," she said, "they wouldn't see that. They wouldn't see that I am. I'm happy there."

"Why did you want me to come here?"

"I guess I thought that seeing you here, with my parents, would help me make this decision."

"What decision?"

"To let you stay with me. For a while."

"I shouldn't have asked you to—"

She put her hand on his, and it short-circuited his nervous system midsentence. Corderoy looked into her eyes, then closed his own and gave himself to this moment of intimacy. A second later, he felt Mani's lips on his. She pulled back and he opened his eyes. What was he doing here? Helping Mani to make a mistake. "Why?" he said.

Because this decision was big, because letting him back into her life was difficult, because it would force her to grow? "To see how it felt," she said.

He leaned in and kissed her. "How did that one feel?"

She studied his face. He was tied to her by guilt, she to him by injury. Those weren't good reasons to be doing this. But this wasn't about reasons. "It didn't feel wrong," she said.

"I love you," Corderoy said. He wasn't sure if he meant it. It could be a lie.

"I know," Mani said.

A smile spread across his face. Did she know she was quoting Han Solo? Even if she didn't, those words made him realize that he did mean it. He loved Mani in a way that was so much more messy and uncertain than all the portrayals of love he'd assimilated as a child. It was precarious. It was unlikely to last. But that's how he knew it wasn't bullshit. "Is that okay?" he asked.

"You can stay with me," she said. "Until you find a place."

article | discussion | edit this page | history

👤 Log in

The Encyclopaedists [edit]

The Encyclopaedists pop in and out of being like particles on the edge of a black hole. That black hole is war.

Contents [hide]
1 Precursors of the Encyclopaedists
2 Motivations of the Encyclopaedists
3 Ice
4 Used goods
5 Things that don't exist
6 War
7 Betrayal

Precursors of the Encyclopaedists [edit]

Oren and Veronica Montauk, Henry and Susan Corderoy. In the most literal sense. These are the people who teach you how to be them while you teach yourself how not to be them and how to be who you are, which is inescapably very much like them, a fact you must learn to digest.

Motivations of the Encyclopaedists [edit]

There are two modes of thinking about this topic: to achieve happiness for oneself, or to destroy it in others. There is as yet insufficient data to meaningfully resolve this dispute.

Ice [edit]

Ice reduces friction, which allows us to move massive things, which is awesome, but it also allows massive things to move outside our control, which is dangerous.

Used goods [edit]

Rather have a used good than a brand-new bad. That's the tricky part, for all brand-new things are like magic rings found in dungeons. They may be goods (ring of invisibility!) or they may be bads (ring of clumsiness…). Safer to prefer the used, things slipped on someone else first.

Things that don't exist [edit]

It is tempting to think of the Encyclopaedists as a relationship that doesn't exist except when it's happening. But the Encyclopaedists are not special. That is the truth of all relationships: they only exist when they are happening, which sounds like a trivial tautology but is not. Consider the development of object permanence in infants and the ways in which computers create the illusion of multitasking, though all data operations proceed in single file through the CPU chokepoint. Only one operation can happen at a time. The idea that things persist when they are not happening is a convenient fiction.

War [edit]

From an Orwellian perspective, the Global War on Terror approaches the ultimate and purest expression of war, which is designed to consume human labor and commodities, to justify and even create support for inequality and the panopticon, the former of which follows from oligarchy, the latter of which is necessary to sustain it.

A war between individuals may function in the same way. The goal is not to win but to consume mental resources as a grand distraction from the actual source of one's existential woes: the insufficient self.

Betrayal [edit]

Betrayal (or backstabbing) is the violation of a trust that produces, in the victim, a signature constellation of moral and psychological mind-breaking, earth-warping, fuck-everything rage! And confusion. Something in the victim's understanding of the world breaks: the value of truth, the importance of respect, etc. A return to sanity requires that the victim redefine one or more of these terms: respect is when you lie to your best friend for six months, truth is one flavor out of many worthy options.

Men reinterpret past villainies. When he was a boy, in third grade, he played with sticks at recess, hacking leaves, having sword fights. His stick was called "Slicer." His friend's was called "Shoulder Blade." They'd hide the sticks in birch trees so they'd blend in with the living limbs, then retrieve them the next recess. One day he arrived early, found his friend's stick, and broke it in half for no reason but to experience cruelty and to flood himself with guilt.

Here is a list of famous traitors: Guy Fawkes (tried to shove gun powder up the asses of the English aristocracy), Benedict Arnold (tried to hand over West Point to the British in exchange for a plate of eggs, specially prepared), Jane Fonda ("Hanoi Jane" had sexy-time with North Vietnamese anti-aircraft guns), the Rosenbergs (Julius and Ethel, got their rocks off by giving atomic secrets to the Soviets), Marcus Junius Brutus (shanked his patron, pal, and king, Julius Caesar; erased his own map two years later), Judas Iscariot (for thirty pieces of silver, he kissed big JC into crucifixion, then he hanged himself).

Of all these traitors, Judas is the purest. He even gave us the word "traitor": from the Latin *tradere*, to hand over. He is also the most complex. Borges suggests that God came to earth not as Jesus but as Judas, to take on the ultimate sin in order to save humanity. It is tempting, as a traitor, to see oneself as a savior. But the traitors have nothing to trust, nothing to prove to themselves that they are saviors. Perhaps this is why so many of them suck exhaust.

External links [edit]

1. ^ "The Encyclopaedists of Capitol Hill."
www.thestranger.com/apr04/encyclopaedists.htm

2. ^ "C. PLINII NATVRALIS HISTORIAE PRAEFATIO."
www.thelatinlibrary.com/pliny.nhpr.html

3. ^ "Stanford Encyclopedia of Philosophy entry on 'War.' "
plato.stanford.edu/entries/war/

4. ^ "Project Gutenberg Bible, King James, Book 42: Luke."
www.gutenberg.org/dirs/etext05/bib4210h.htm

INK
AND SKULL

37

This iiiiisssss 107.7, Freedom Radio. Rock On!

The waterproof stereo floating in the kidney-shaped pool blared 50 Cent's "Candy Shop." Big pink human beans splashed around, not having too much fun without female company. And the sunburns, my God, the sunburns. The scorching air—elsewhere bone-dry and flecked with gasoline and gunpowder—was a steaming aerosol of chlorine, suntan lotion, sweat, and grilled hot dogs. Big Costco Polishes. The kind served up at backyard barbecues in Fayetteville, NC. But this wasn't Fayetteville. Luc had brought Tricia to the American embassy in Baghdad, which was housed in the old Republican palace. And what would anyone do with a palace but have pool parties.

"You're right," Tricia said. "It *is* like a frat house."

Three young men were looking at her from the other side of the pool, posed like a movie poster for the Three Musketeers. Two wore wraparound Oakleys. One took a swig out of a giant water bottle filled with fluorescent blue liquid. Tricia felt the compulsion to look busy but had no cell phone to fiddle with.

Luc pulled his shirt off and said, "Go on, *allez-y*." Tricia glanced at the sparse black hair on his chest—it was economical and subtle, like a miniature Chinese garden. She peeled off her dress, revealing her green bikini, pleasantly aware of the Musketeers' gaze. She wondered if Luc saw them looking at her.

"And what big story are we looking for here," Tricia said, feeling awkward in the ensuing silence.

"Due time, due time," Luc said. "It is necessary to arrange security."

"Are you talking about Blackwater? We can't be running around with—"

"No, not Blackwater. I'm looking to get some locals. But not just some kid off the street, you know? Ah, hallo, he's here already." Luc waved across the pool at a row of occupied lawn chairs with plastic parasols. "Give me a minute, okay? I need to catch up with this guy, and then I'll make your acquaintance. Have a dip." Luc headed off around the side of the pool without waiting for an answer, making a beeline to a sunburned, slightly chubby, middle-aged white guy. Tricia fished some sunscreen out of her bag and began rubbing it on. The radio was now playing Destiny's Child.

Everything here was so different from her expectations that she had to remind herself she was in Baghdad. The city she'd come for lay outside the embassy, among crumbling tenements and piles of garbage, where a traumatized populace struggled to survive the fallout of their liberation. She felt ready to engage them; she'd been memorizing her Arabic phrasebook, studying maps of the Green Zone, researching Iraqi cultural norms. She hadn't been working on her crawl stroke.

They had come in from Amman yesterday on a small Royal Jordanian flight full of Filipinos, Europeans, and the odd non-government-affiliated American aid worker. The only other way in was through US military air from Kuwait. Baghdad International itself was a US government operation full of military traffic, with lines of troops marching on and off big propeller-driven Air Force planes. They looked like lines of worker ants, shuffling across the tarmac under the almost comical weight of bags and guns and assorted Army stuff. Luc and Tricia had sat in a plywood waiting area until their driver came to take them on the hair-raising ten-mile trip to downtown, keeping prudent distance at all times from the Army convoys barreling through with guns pointed everywhere. They'd reached the Palestine Hotel at dusk, and Tricia barely had the energy to carry her bags up to her room before falling asleep.

Luc was still ignoring her in favor of the pudgy guy. Several older men padded by, speaking in Army-type jargon complete with code names that Tricia guessed stood for people or bases or groups of soldiers. She slid into Saddam's pool, which was so highly chlorinated that it fizzed slightly when she disturbed the surface. What the hell was she doing in Baghdad, swimming? She had told herself that she wasn't going to be a passive little puppy at Luc's heel. She was going to define the terms of their working relationship. And so far all she'd done was follow his suggestion to have a dip. Great. She watched out of the corner of her eye for the Three Musketeers, watching her out of the corners of their eyes. Then felt stupid for caring about poolside flirtations. Especially with these guys. She thought back to her freshman year, when she had been persuaded to attend one of the Columbia Rugby Club's spring parties. After many months of collegiate life in the Big City, she'd finally been Hit On, Neanderthal-style, by a drunken rugger who'd told her that her tank top had "a good fit," just the way she had it on, "like that, all [unintelligible] like that." She shut him down and went to sleep happy that night but had to keep the crowing about it to a minimum, as he had more luck with one of her friends.

She spotted Luc waving for her to come over. She swam straight there in accordance with his impatient hand gestures and regretted it as soon as she hauled herself out of the water and walked in her soaking-wet bikini toward the two men.

"Tricia from Harvard, yes? Luc tells me you're a first-rate scribe. Pleasure to meet you. Barney."

Barney's accent came through big English lips and a face that sported the hot blush of a Liverpudlian drinking beer in the desert. He smiled drunkenly as he took her wet hand in his, which was hot, meaty, and sunscreened.

"Likewise," Tricia said.

"Lovely, lovely to have you. Anyone fancy a lager?" He held up his bottle and pointed to both of them in turn. Before they could answer, he said, "Brilliant. This way," and led them to a small plastic table.

From a distance, the Musketeers way outclassed Barney, but she suspected they would turn into Blackwater assholes up close. Barney was on the downslope, the way he was day-drinking. Luc was explaining that it would be difficult to follow up on rumors and interview locals in the city now that the insurgency seemed to be picking up the pace. He seemed to be asking about hiring mercenaries.

"We specifically don't take on locals, though," Barney said. "Because of the security risk." He was looking at Tricia, as if undermining Luc were a method of hitting on her.

"How are locals less secure?" Tricia asked.

"Because they know the people you'll be interviewing, so they'll be in a spot to wheel and deal for some blond American hostage, you see? But if you hire security from Kurdistan, right, their loyalty is to you alone, and they've got no love for the locals."

"And the locals don't trust them."

"Precisely. So they won't make an offer. It's far less hazardous. You don't fancy yourself Nick Berg, right? You know, some of these jokers will take your head off even if you're not Jewish, won't they?"

Luc was about to speak, but Tricia drowned him out. "Of course there's risk," she said. "But our purpose here should mitigate that risk, especially if we have locals to explain what we're doing." Luc seemed annoyed and stared at the pool. Tricia's projected confidence wasn't having the desired effect. She glanced at Luc's navel and the wispy happy trail dipping into his shorts.

"Doubt Zarqawi will look twice at your press badge, love," Barney said. "No offense."

Tricia rolled her eyes behind her Ray-Bans. A cannonball impacted the deep end of the kidney-shaped pool. The dark, lean Musketeer laughed, arms crossed on the pool's ledge as his compatriot came up for air. He looked over at her as she looked at him.

"I'll bet *you* could get one of them to do it for free," Barney said, following her gaze.

"Funny," Luc said.

"Yeah, I'll go ask," Tricia said with a snide smile. Luc touched her arm softly to stop her.

"That a problem?" she asked. Luc backed off, and Tricia strutted over to the pool, feeling powerful in the aura of his unease.

But the feeling evaporated as soon as she slid into the water. She pulled herself forward and under, wetting her hair, trying her best to feel relaxed amid the chaos. She swam a few lazy half-laps, then parked herself in the corner not far from the Musketeers.

"Not from around these parts, are ya," the lean one said.

Tricia acted vaguely annoyed. "You don't look very Iraqi yourself."

"I am from Adhamiyah, only half-kilometer away!" he replied with a forced accent. "Why you come to my country?"

Tricia glanced back at Luc, who was not looking in her direction, though Barney was.

"I'm an unembedded journalist," she said. "We're looking to hire some personal security."

The Musketeer smiled awkwardly. "You're already talking to the right man," he said, nodding back toward Barney. "But if you're looking for a personal masseuse—I might be convinced—"

"Seriously?" Tricia climbed out and walked back to Luc and Barney.

"It's not simply whether they can hit a target, right?" Barney had gone so far as to set down his lager on the white plastic umbrella table. "If you hire some tosser off the street who doesn't know how to handle a weapon, you'll end up with him emptying a magazine when he gets nervy. They're dangerous. You need someone with a bit of professionalism or you're better off on your own."

"Well?" Luc said, finally turning to Tricia.

"He said to talk to Barney," she muttered.

"Everyone loves Barney," Barney said.

Tricia gulped her beer.

"You've got some Kurds?" Luc said reluctantly.

38

The Volkswagen Rabbit pulled out of the Palestine Hotel's barricaded lot and swung east down Karada Dahil. Tricia sat in the backseat with Yasmin, the translator Luc had hired, and looked out the window at the machine-gun towers looming over the traffic circle outside the American checkpoint. She was embarrassed by the sight. Yasmin was carefully applying lipstick with a tiny travel mirror as the car rattled south to the edge of the peninsula. She puckered her lips and turned to Tricia. "Do I look good for kissing?"

"Do you look good for kissing?" Tricia repeated, smiling awkwardly. "Hah. Okay."

"Okay, what?"

"Yes, you look kissable."

Luc's head did a quarter-turn of annoyance from the front passenger seat. "How far?" he asked their driver, Adan.

"Not far," he replied. Adan was also the "security" arranged for them by Barney the Brit. He had taken to them immediately, which was reassuring, although Tricia suspected it was because he was an outsider here and had no one else to befriend. He was a Kurd from Sulaymaniyah, in the north. He looked like he could have been a graduate student at MIT except for the boxy cut of his black suit, which he wore with an open collar.

After a few blocks, Adan slowed down to check the houses against the description he had written down in a notepad. They were looking for a house that had been hit by a mortar last week. The election was just around the corner, but there was plenty of random violence in Baghdad and Luc wanted to get a local, nonmilitary perspective on the stability and security of the city. The house in front of them was a blocky sandstone affair. Tricia found it weirdly reminiscent of bad L.A. suburban architecture, made ramshackle by bundles of hanging wires.

Adan parked the Rabbit, retrieved his pistol from the armrest, and jiggled it into the holster under his jacket. They walked up to the steel front door of the house, which had a cheap decorative inlay, painted green. Yasmin stood by Luc. Tricia was behind them both, trying to look vaguely Iraqi with the scarf Yasmin had helped her tie on earlier. Adan stood a few feet behind her.

The door opened on a boy who looked to be around thirteen. Yasmin asked him a few questions. The boy answered and then called into the house. An older woman appeared with a head scarf and a gray dress. Grandma? She and the boy pointed out into the street.

"She says the boy's father was hit by a bomb in the street."

Tricia flipped open her notepad and jotted that down as they walked out toward a small gouge in the concrete with some scorch marks around it.

"She says it flies in here and hit her son when he is standing next to his car." Grandma raised her voice, jabbing a finger at the gouge.

Yasmin translated as Luc snapped some photos of the scorched hole. The heat of the late morning had just broken some strange threshold, and a small volume of sweat trickled down Tricia's back. She had the feeling that she was writing way too much, but she'd figure out how to pare it down for the actual article. Her first. Luc said he'd find her the right photo and the article would write itself. Yasmin was telling them that the man was at the hospital, but they didn't know when he would be back. They didn't seem to think he was in danger of dying. "She says there is another bomb in the back of the house."

"What, inside the house?"

"No, behind the house. It is still there."

Luc glanced at Tricia excitedly.

They followed the woman behind the house. Her long, gray dress swished as it trailed over the rough-brushed concrete. She stopped at the edge of the patio and pointed at a small greenish metal object half-buried in the brown grass.

"Whoa," Tricia said.

"Let's not get too close," Luc said, holding a hand out to keep her back. "That is definitely a mortar."

A door opened and another young boy came out of the house, carrying a plate with cans of iced tea on it.

"*Shukran,*" Luc said.

"*Shukran,*" Tricia repeated.

The cans were cool to the touch but nowhere near cold. Tricia smiled and popped hers open. She sipped its cloying sweetness and stared calmly at the mortar as Yasmin continued talking to Grandma.

"I'm telling her that it is dangerous, but she says it is been here for almost two days."

"Have you called the police about it?" Luc asked, fishing through his camera bag for another lens.

"She says the police want too much money," Yasmin said.

"Maybe I can find some soldiers at the embassy who could come over and take a look at it," he said to Tricia. "I know some of the Brits and Australians."

"You don't want to ask the Americans?" Tricia said.

"I'd be concerned about that, as they often don't treat civilians very well."

"The Brits do? There's an unexploded bomb in her yard. Seems like a risk she should take, maybe."

"I'll ask someone at the embassy. Yasmin, tell her I'll try to get someone to take that bomb away."

"She wants to know if you can just take it," Yasmin said.

"No, we can't handle explosives. It could go off."

Yasmin translated, and the woman raised her eyebrows and looked to the sky, nodding in a way that seemed oddly sarcastic to Tricia. Though how could you ever really tell when your mannerisms and cultural cues were worlds apart?

Luc walked off with his phone to his ear, looking as important as he could. Grandma began talking to Yasmin and gesticulating. After a few exchanges, Yasmin turned to Tricia. "She says that she will tell her son to take it when he gets back from the hospital."

"That's ridiculous." Tricia glanced back at Luc, then lowered her voice. "Why can't we just ask the American troops?"

"I think here, in Baghdad," Yasmin said, "you must call who you know. You help to someone and later they help to you."

Of course Yasmin was right. Luc was making use of his contacts. But in a broader sense, shouldn't they be currying favor with the most powerful force in the region, the group that could help them—and impede them—the most? Luc would never. But that wouldn't stop her from making a few inquiries.

Luc returned with a satisfied grin. "Yasmin, tell her that I left a message for some Australians at the embassy who may have bomb disposal teams that can help her with this."

"How long will that take?" Tricia asked. "There's an American checkpoint around the corner."

Luc glared at her.

"Fine. Then can you ask her what she thinks about the election?" Tricia added.

As Yasmin spoke, the woman put a hand to her heart; she avoided looking at Luc. Tricia wondered if this was because older women were not supposed to look at men. Yasmin jotted down notes as Grandma answered her questions. The suggestion of a breeze crept through the alley from the sluggish Tigris, putting pressure on the heavy air without quite being able to move it. Adan kept looking back toward the street. He seemed nervous. There was a smell in the air of tar or trash mixed with dirt. It was a little like Mexico, Tricia decided.

"She is doubtful," Yasmin said. "She does not think the election will change anything. Still there will be bombs and guns shooting in her neighborhood. And there is not enough gasoline, she says, for cooking and heating."

Tricia nodded while transcribing. Luc took a few photos of the mortar. They thanked the woman and headed back to the Rabbit.

"This is perfect," Luc said as they climbed in. "If you can get this written up tonight, we'll send the piece off to Matthias at *Truthout*."

That was it? Time to write the article? Was this supposed to be breaking news? An unexploded mortar in Baghdad. "Maybe we should talk to some people who haven't been mortared," Tricia said.

"That's not a story," Luc said.

"I thought we wanted to get a local picture of the stability of the city."

"I just did. It's a picture of a live mortar in that woman's backyard."

"I'm not trying to be difficult," Tricia said.

Luc turned to look back at her as Adan weaved through traffic. "Tricia. Think about the size of the embedded media machine, sitting behind the fence, pumping out stories vetted by the military. It will take all our efforts in collecting stories like this to counter that even a little. Okay?"

Tricia sighed.

"Your first publication from Baghdad," Luc said. "You should be excited." He smiled. She forced a smile and a nod until he sat back in his seat.

The Rabbit turned onto the arterial, and the checkpoint's gun towers reappeared in the distance. Yasmin reached across and held Tricia's hand, like she was some college friend in a taxi after a breakup. Tricia swallowed hard and looked out the window at a small clutch of boys bouncing a soccer ball between them in an alleyway. The Rabbit began the slow curve around the traffic circle, a black barrel from a gun tower lazily tracking their progress.

―――

". . . We are shutting down all traffic in central Baghdad while the polls are open. Details on further precautionary measures will be kept secret for security reasons until the day of the elections. Yes, Jim." The press colonel nodded toward a reporter in the front row. Tricia had seen his press badge when they'd walked in. *Washington Post*.

"I understand that over seven thousand candidates on the electoral lists are choosing to remain anonymous for fear of being assassinated. Understandable, given that at least eight political leaders, including Baghdad's provincial governor, have been killed in the last month. Why not postpone the election until voter and candidate safety can be guaranteed?"

It was a good question. How were voters supposed to make informed decisions if they didn't know who the candidates were until they reached the ballot box? Luc had told her that going to the press conference would be a waste of time, that she'd get nothing but propaganda. But she'd insisted. It was insane that he thought she could write a decent article about the Stability of Baghdad on the Eve of Elections after visiting a single house. She at least had to hear the official Coalition story.

"A delay will only prolong the increased violence we've seen this month," the press colonel said. "It will also likely bolster the insurgency, whose campaign of violence has been aimed at derailing the vote."

Tricia was trying to come up with questions to ask (although she didn't quite have the guts to raise her hand, sitting as she was in the cheap seats behind the "actual" reporters—the ones paid by official news outlets). She was also listening to the press colonel's answers, comparing them to everything she knew, and trying to divine what they were intended to convey or hide. She looked around at the reporters in front of her and was a little chagrined, but not surprised, that she didn't recognize anyone. Of course she didn't—these were journalists, not anchors or talking heads. Luc had pointed out to her some people he knew from *The Chicago Tribune* and *The New York Times*. And she'd been furtively glancing at people's press badges, noting multiple APers and a woman from *Bloomberg*.

"Bullshit," whispered the guy to her left. Tricia looked at him and he leaned closer. "They know the violence won't decrease post-election. The major Sunni parties are boycotting it. The Shiites will vote themselves into power, and then we'll probably have civil war."

The press colonel was wrapping up. "We ask all journalists to use extreme caution tomorrow," she said. "To abide by the prohibition on automobiles and to be very careful to avoid any behavior that could be construed as attempting to influence the elections."

The press conference began to break up. "I'll introduce you to some people," Luc said to Tricia. "Just give me a minute." He walked off toward the front of the room.

Tricia turned to the guy who'd whispered to her. "Who do you work for?" she asked him.

"I'm with AP. Ivan Volokh."

"Tricia Burnham, nice to meet you. I'm with IPS."

"IPS?"

"Interpress—"

"Oh yeah, yeah. Unembedded, right? You a reporter back home, too?"

"Well, no. I'm at the Kennedy School."

"You're a grad student? Hell of a study abroad!"

Tricia laughed, trying to cover her sudden annoyance.

"You having fun with it? Hitting the journo parties and all that?"

"Journo parties?"

"Oh, God. It's like Sarajevo, basically. I suppose you're a bit young, but in Sarajevo there was the same deal—danger, uncertainty, stress. It's inevitable. You end up having terror sex."

"Terror sex?"

"Oh, yeah. You've never had an affair until you've had one in conditions where you could get kidnapped or killed pretty much every day. It's intense."

"I'll look forward to it," Tricia said. She was realizing that this Ivan character was some kind of conflict-journo slacker who studiously affected a deep cynicism and aloofness from the profession. Either that or he was trying to hit on her. She didn't like him.

She ducked away from Ivan when she saw Luc walking up with a tall woman in a blue suit. "They could easily be lying," Luc was saying. "Ah, Tricia. This is Kate. Kate's with the *Tribune*."

Kate shook Tricia's hand, then ignored her. "No. Actually," she said. "Because if the Coalition lies and we catch them, they have egg on their face. They'd much rather mislead or misdirect, leave things out. It's no less deceptive, but the public doesn't have the context, so they'll never get called on it. We can pretty safely assume that nothing they're saying is a straight-up lie, which means we can probe the edges of what they don't say. If it were all bullshit, coming here would be a waste of time. Why do you think we show up?"

"Well, yeah . . ." Luc said.

Tricia raised an eyebrow in his direction. He looked away.

"I gotta run," Kate said. "See ya 'round." She nodded toward Luc, glanced at Tricia—probably didn't even remember her name—and left.

It was becoming clear to Tricia that Luc wasn't as respected or connected as he'd made out back in Boston. Worse, it seemed like all the mainstream journalists regarded the unembedded Inter Press Service types as backwoods ideological hacks, like evangelical Christians at a Cato Institute soiree. Tricia found it hard to blame them. They were professionals. They actually knew what they were doing.

39

Iraqis all had the same three or four names, just arranged in different orders. They adhered to a bizarre, dogmatic, almost theological conspiracy theory in which the invisible strings that moved almost every event in the world were clutched by Saddam, who was an agent of the Americans, who were secretly controlled by the Jews. They lied like a gaggle of third-graders waiting at a bus stop on Opposite Day. They wiped their asses with their hands, probably, with the help of cut-up water bottles they left lying around in the port-a-johns. These were a few of the perceptions that US Soldiers of the occupation had of their refractory charges.

There were as many stereotypes on the Iraqi side: American men walked around sucking on candy like teething infants. They became confused and agitated when no one spoke their language. They sent boys barely out of school to parlay with sheiks. They gave their women rifles and let them strut around like whores. But one of the most damnable things about the Americans was that it was difficult to tell who was in charge—none of them had beards—and their most senior commanders trooped around in the same combat gear as everyone else; they rolled around in the same dusty Humvees.

Even the Americans themselves had trouble recognizing senior officials—Americans like Private Ant, who could sometimes tell by the size of an entourage that one of the Humvees had someone important in it. Today, manning Priority Search for the special election-day traffic checkpoint, he could have craned his head into the window of the first of ten Humvees.

But Ant was lazy and withdrawn, thinking about the lives of his *Sims* characters he would manipulate after his shift. Not having leaned into the window, he did not see the embroidered black eagle sewn onto the passenger's armor and thus did not realize he was waving through none other than Greywolf Six, the commander of the entire 3rd Brigade Combat Team, the couple thousand troops tasked with securing the center of the capital.

Greywolf Six, otherwise known as Colonel Moretto, had been running a sleep deficit since before the brigade left Texas, and the lead-up to the election had put him further in the hole. At this point, the next best thing to his cot was the canvas passenger seat of his Humvee, which was also known as Greywolf Six. The constant beeping and muttering of two radio nets, the stiff suspension on the rutted streets, the shuffling of the turret gunner's feet against the turret sling: these had become a lullaby signaling precious moments of nap time between meetings and the million other things on his view screen. He slouched in the seat and let his Kevlar collar hold his head still as he relaxed his neck muscles in a meditative sequence.

When Greywolf Six the Humvee was stopped at the checkpoint, Greywolf Six the person almost failed to open his eyes. But when he did, this was what he saw behind Private Ant's expressionless face and apathetic thumbs-up: strung between the whip antennae of two parked Humvees, a banner made from cut bedsheets with green duct-tape letters exhorting the reader to VOTE FOR PEDRO.

One day far in the future, Greywolf Six would find himself watching *Napoleon Dynamite* with his grandson and would finally understand this moment. In the present, however, the reference was lost on him. Finding it inexplicable, he found it inexcusable. Rage began to percolate behind his eyes.

———

The morning of the elections was pleasantly cool—about fifty Fahrenheit when the sun came up. Tricia had slipped out early to avoid Luc. He'd shut her down the previous day when she'd asked about observing

306 ROBINSON | KOVITE

the elections. He'd said that foreigners weren't allowed anywhere near the polls. Besides, it was far too dangerous. They were expecting many polling locations to be targeted by suicide bombers.

But they were in Baghdad. Everything was dangerous. And this was an historic moment. The big-time embedded journalists were covering it. Maybe Luc didn't have enough sway to get them an official pass from the Iraqi Interim Government. But did they really need an official pass? They were doing this DIY. Unembedded. Didn't that mean bending the rules where they could? Rather than try to convince him, Tricia resolved to go anyway, without telling Luc or Adan. Maybe Luc was a great photographer, but he had an underdeveloped sense of journalistic ethics and obligation, of proper research methods—he didn't know when it was worth taking a risk. With Yasmin along, she'd be fine.

Inside the Green Zone, life carried on as usual. They rode in Yasmin's Opel down the main drag, past rows of T-walls topped with razor wire, past a column of Humvees and a few Bongo trucks, past the newly opened pizza café and the bronze statue of a soldier from the Iranian war.

Outside the Green Zone, Baghdad's streets were closed to civilian auto traffic in an effort to protect voting stations from car bombs. They parked the car at the Green Zone side of the 14 July Bridge and got out to walk across. Yasmin would have taken them a different route, but Tricia had insisted on Checkpoint 11. She'd e-mailed Hal, and he'd provided the crucial information: 2nd Platoon of Bravo Company. Once she knew that, it had been easy enough to find out where Mickey was stationed.

Tricia kept her head down as they passed through the checkpoint, discreetly looking at the soldiers to see if there was a blimp pilot among them. She swam in the folds of the long black jilbaab that Yasmin had loaned her. She pulled the fabric to her body to show a hint of her figure. Still no sign of Mickey. Her face was shadowed under a hijab. She'd accepted the fact that it would be much easier for her to maneuver in Baghdad if she covered up like this, but she still felt a deep hostility toward the practice and the cultural coercion behind it. Yasmin wore a puffy coat and had a lavender hijab over her knit Puma hat. She seemed to wear the hijab with pride, like a new pair of earrings, which made Tricia feel ignorant and sheltered.

She met the eyes of the American soldier who checked her ID.

"Tricia, huh?" he said. "Looks like you've gone native."

"Are you in Second Platoon?" she asked.

He sized her up as if she'd offered to buy him a drink. "Third," he said. "Second has the next shift."

She and Yasmin descended the stairs in silence and stopped for a moment to take in the eerie emptiness of Karada Dahil. They could hear the Tigris moving languidly behind them, punctuated by the sound of mortars exploding in the distance.

The polling location was in a nearby school gymnasium. As they approached, they saw men in suits ushering a line of prospective voters through sandbags, concrete blocks, and razor wire. The Iraqi police at the door were searching people. Yasmin stopped Tricia before they were within earshot. "Everyone is very nervous," she said. "They do not trust people from outside. They are told that it is only Iraqis here. You must act Iraqi, okay?" Tricia nodded, swaddling herself further under her hijab.

They waved Yasmin and Tricia through just as an old woman with a satisfied mug walked out, her right index finger freshly stained with purple ink. Tricia didn't think the elections would change much of anything. But seeing that old woman, she felt a swelling sense of admiration for the Iraqi people. Even if the violence continued to worsen, they were turning out. They were voting, despite threats from the insurgency, despite the fact that their country would fall apart without the sloppy care of the United States Armed Forces, which had caused the chaos to begin with, shattering the old stability (yes, Saddam's stability, but stability nonetheless). Tricia took a mental snapshot of that creviced old woman and her purple finger and imagined seeing the photo grace the cover of *Time* magazine, and inside: *Cover photo by Tricia Burnham.* She shook her head instinctively, reminding herself what an honor it was to witness this moment of social evolution, the Iraqi people like curious fish crawling out of the seas of dictatorship up onto the shores of democracy. No. She clenched her jaw, annoyed at herself for thinking like such an asshole, looking down on them. It was an honor to be here precisely because they were confronting risks she would never have to face, in order to have their voices heard. She was in awe of them. Tricia had convinced herself that as a white American, her default attitude was to be an asshole, that it took constant vigilance to see through the lens of her privilege. She could sometimes see herself overcorrecting, but wasn't it better to err on the side of humanism and generosity?

They reached a small table where a poll worker checked Yasmin's ID and had her sign her name on a clipboard. Another poll worker held out the inkwell for people exiting the booths.

Yasmin was speaking with the first poll worker in Arabic. He seemed displeased. Tricia tried to wear a face of stoic comprehension, though she understood nothing.

"And who is this?" the poll worker said.

"She is not voting today," Yasmin said.

"Is she eligible to vote? Who is she?"

"She's not eligible to vote . . . she has a mental problem and can't understand things. Can she please wait in the hall for me?"

Tricia gave a small dignified nod in response to whatever had just been said.

"No, she cannot wait in the hall, she must go outside."

"But please, she is my cousin and cannot take care of herself, that's why I had to bring her."

The poll worker shook his head. Yasmin turned to Tricia and said, *"Tania, you must wait outside . . . will you wait outside for me and then I will come back?"*

Tricia saw Yasmin pointing to the door; she nodded and walked back down the hallway to the entrance. She had hoped this would not happen. She felt very American as she slipped out into the heat. Nearby, some kids were kicking around a soccer ball.

"It's good to see them playing in the street again."

Tricia turned toward the woman who was saying something to her in Arabic. She tightened the hijab over her face and nodded stiffly.

"Why don't you vote, are you from Al-Karada?"

Tricia nodded and tried to turn away a little. *"La, la,"* she ventured, but the way she said it was wrong.

"Then why don't you vote?" The woman's voice was changing. *"Who are you, are you Iraqi? Speak to me, what are you doing here?"*

———

Montauk was in good spirits. There had been only a few minor bombings so far, a few dud mortars launched at checkpoints, and though it was still midmorning, it seemed like the doom-and-gloom intelligence reports—indicating massive attacks throughout the city and general hell from the AIF—were overblown. His mood quickly soured when he saw Captain Byrd storming into the CP. Intelligence had been silent regarding Anti-Montauk Forces.

"Vote for Pedro? Jesus, Montauk. If it even looks like we're interfering with the elections. What the hell kind of platoon are you running here?"

Montauk almost said *I don't know,* a reversion to elementary school if there ever was one, but he held it in. "I'm assuming it's down now, sir," he said.

"Don't assume. Check on it."

"Yes, sir."

"I just got a good twenty-minute ass-chew from Warhorse Six."

Montauk imagined the veins in Rad Rod Houston's forehead as he stared down Byrd, his eyes bulging with some kind of Viking blood rage.

"Just so I get it straight, someone drove by it and told Lieutenant Colonel Houston?"

"Yeah, Montauk, and the guy who told him gave Houston his own twenty-minute ass-chew."

"Then—"

"That's right, LT. Your idiot soldiers flashed their banner to Greywolf Six."

Montauk imagined the veins in Colonel Moretto's forehead as he stared down Rad Rod Houston, his eyes nearly popping out of his face with some kind of Mongolian blood rage. And now that Byrd was chewing him out, he'd have to chew out Staff Sergeant Arroyo with his own blood rage and bulging Klingon eyes; Arroyo would in turn chew out Sergeant Fields, who would chew out Private Antonin Ant, who probably hadn't made the banner—didn't seem his style—but who wouldn't mind taking the blame for it. Maybe Ant would chew out Monkey. Even Monkey probably had someone to rage on. It was turtles all the way down.

————

"Ameriki? Ameriki? Israeli?" The old woman and a few of her friends were crowding around Tricia.

"France," Tricia said. *"Je suis Francaise."*

The old woman grabbed at Tricia's hijab to tug it off her face. A man had come out of the school and the old woman yelled to him, jabbing her finger at Tricia. When Tricia failed to respond to his question, he stood in front of her, next to the old woman, and pointed at her hijab, motioning for her to pull it off.

The old woman grabbed at her again and yanked at her scarf. When Tricia grabbed the woman's wrist, the man grabbed Tricia's and yelled at her. His breath smelled like pastry. A second later, the scarf had come off and most of her field of view was filled by the woman's fingers, jabbing toward her face. Tricia couldn't get enough oxygen.

She was grabbed from behind and pushed forward. It was Yasmin, who yelled back at the old woman and the pastry-breath man as she pushed a shocked Tricia back up 14 July Street toward the checkpoint. Tricia thought she heard one of the boys in the crowd use the word *faggot*. The yelling ceased when they had walked half a block up the street. Tricia began to cry.

"It is okay, you are safe now," Yasmin said.

"I'm sorry, I'm so sorry."

"They don't know you. That's all. They are frightened at a strange person being there today."

"I shouldn't have come."

"Oh no, I have gotten ink on you."

Tricia looked down to see the purple smudges on her sleeve and laughed a little. "It's your jilbaab," she said.

"Yes, it is," Yasmin said. She laughed and gave Tricia a quick tight hug. A weight lifted from Tricia's forehead. She was fine. She had been quietly imagining crawling back to Luc, apologizing, saying how right he'd been. But she was fine. He wasn't right. She had taken a risk, and she'd witnessed something important. That was the whole point of being here.

They reached the checkpoint and were waved into the Pedestrian Search lane. Tricia wrapped her hijab back around her face.

Then she heard his voice. With all the exhilaration, she had nearly forgotten why she'd insisted on Checkpoint 11.

She wasn't sure what she would say to him or even how she would feel around him. Their night together, apart from the bloody nose, had fit the standard hookup routine. It began with the man circling, testing the waters, her hunger for sexual attention, which itself was almost sexual. Then the climactic act in which she left her mind and inhabited her body, giving herself to unadulterated pleasure, like licking a sugar cube. Then there was the afterglow, pleasing for a brief moment, until she began to reenter her mind, to analyze her performance, his performance, the quality of their intimacy—would he want to do it again, would she want to? And then to crush these anxieties: abrupt separation. Time to leave. Nice knowing you. Where are my socks? Let's hope we don't run into each other on campus. Hal's blimp-pilot friend had been a good hookup because he was from out of town, a one-night stand from the get-go, and no lack of phone calls or contact could be attributed to his interest or lack thereof. She had been able to enjoy the afterglow without falling into anxious analysis. They were airships passing in the night. Seeing him now, a stranger who had seen her naked, she expected the usual anxieties to well up— but instead of falling into the nerve-racking and involuntary mental review of the entire history of their contact, she found herself fixated on a still frame: the two of them laughing, blood dripping off her chin onto his chest.

"Mickey!" she said.

Montauk cocked his head like a threatened animal. Tricia revealed her face and he blinked several times, unable to recognize her out of context.

"Tricia, remember me?" she said, giving a little wave.

"Holy shit, Tricia! What? How are you . . ."

"I'm on a grant from the Investigative Fund with— Well, I'm

reporting for the Inter Press Service and *Truthout,* which— Hal told me Second Platoon, so . . ."

"Crazy." Montauk became self-conscious of the fat plug of dip in his lower lip. And of the fact that their conversation had caught the attention of Sodium Joh and Sergeant Jackson, who were looking on with interest.

"You weren't . . ." He noticed that the Iraqi woman with Tricia had a purple index finger, and that Tricia herself had purple ink smudged on her clothing. "Did you go to the polls?"

"Yasmin voted. I went with her to watch the election process."

"Americans are barred from getting even close to the polls today."

"You mean American military are. I'm not military."

At once, Montauk's rage almost boiled over. It was that attitude of civilian privilege, her careless violation of, if not the letter, at least the spirit of a very sensible prohibition. But he liked Tricia. He admired her audacity. Which meant he couldn't be unequivocally angry, though he wanted to be. He wanted to break something. The desert had taken hold of him and he knew it. In the past weeks, he had witnessed this tendency toward anger taking residence in his skull like some kind of deadbeat relative he couldn't turn away. He bit his lip, thrummed his fingers against Molly Millions, and stared upward for a moment, trying to rein it in. You like this girl. Be nice to her.

"Let's see your badges," Montauk said.

Tricia stepped forward and pulled out the plastic access badge from a lanyard around her neck. Montauk took it in his gloved hand. It was probably warm, the same temperature as her breasts. He regretted wearing his gloves.

40

"Heard you got chewed out by the CO, sir," Thomas said.

"Sorry, sir," Joh said.

Montauk held a stoic face, basking in their apprehension. Dinner was almost over as the three of them entered the DFAC. "Vote for Pedro . . . I took it in the ass for that," he said. "And I would have recommended you two for an Article Fifteen." His face broke into a smile. "If it wasn't so goddamn funny."

They laughed, relieved.

"Why did the brass freak out so much?" Joh asked as they stepped into the chow line.

"Yeah, it's not like the Iraqis would even know enough to be offended," Thomas said.

"You know how everything bad that happens in Iraq is our fault?" Montauk said. "No matter how fair the elections are, people will say the US rigged it." He could feel her eyes on him. She was seated at a table right there in the DFAC. A part of his other life, the college-kid one, the one he shared with Corderoy. "They'll point to any evidence," he continued, "no matter how stupid." Right there across the dining hall. He met her eyes. "That's why the brass is pissed at the Pedro banner. That's my take, anyway."

Montauk took a tray and went to the entrée section. The Paki servers were dishing up "tacos," which turned out to be burritos, the same ones you would find at an upscale buffet in the outskirts of

Atlanta. Get ahold of yourself. You banged this chick. Montauk stood a little straighter and looked back at her table. She was still looking. He gave her a small smile, then turned to the server to accept his tongful of *carne asada*. After several ingredients, Montauk realized that the tortilla would not be large enough to wrap it all into a clean bundle. He considered skipping the *crema* to avoid messiness while eating next to Tricia and whatever dude was next to her. Calm the fuck down. Sit over there like you own the place and eat a giant messy burrito.

"Tricia Burnham, I presume."

"Lieutenant. Montauk."

"Hi there," he said to Luc. "Mickey. Nice to meet you."

The guy nodded curtly, chewing slowly as if that were a sufficient placeholder for his name. Montauk set his tray down and went to the drink machine.

"You know this guy?" Luc asked Tricia as soon as Montauk was out of earshot.

"Kind of. He was my roommate's best friend in Boston. Only met him once."

"Strange."

"Yep. Small world."

Montauk returned, slurping an icy soda.

"So we visited this local family the other day," Tricia said. "There was an unexploded mortar in their backyard. I wrote up an article about it for *Truthout*. We contacted the Aussies but haven't heard back . . . think your platoon can get rid of it?"

Luc glared at her. "Maybe they put it there," he said with a hint of self-satisfaction.

This particular brand of bullshit was almost too stupid for Montauk to take offense at. Almost. "Unlikely," Montauk said. "We haven't fired a mortar into central Baghdad since 2003. Plus, if it was American ordnance, it would have exploded. Also, if my guys are aiming for a civilian house, we hit the house, not the backyard. But anything's possible. Give me the address and I'll contact EOD."

Montauk took a huge, sloppy bite of his burrito, *carne asada* falling back onto the plate, an oozing thread of cheddar cheese hanging from his lip. He chewed slowly with his mouth slightly ajar while looking at Luc, letting the sounds of mastication slursh out in an alpha-male display of territorial dominance. Montauk felt powerful as Luc glanced down at his own plate, until he noticed that Tricia, unlike Luc, looked disgusted. Montauk swallowed and wiped his mouth.

He half participated in small talk for the rest of the meal, trying to eat through his mild embarrassment at his own aggro behavior. When they'd all finished, he stood first and reached for their plates, saying, "Let me get those for you." This offer of generosity surprised him as much as it did Luc and Tricia. Montauk knew he was acting weird, but in seeing Luc's bewildered expression, he quickly came to accept his own confusing behavior. Kill them with kindness. As he carried their plates to the dish bin, he imagined both of them thinking: Lieutenant Mickey Montauk . . . who the fuck is this guy? He was under the impression that this sort of exasperating mystery made dudes angry and got chicks wet.

———

Montauk found Tricia's e-mail address on the Truthout.org website. Her article wasn't half-bad—more balanced than a lot of the lefty swill on the Internet. Even the accompanying photo by Luc Dubois, he had to admit, was well composed. The article began as a human-interest piece about a family with a mortar in their backyard, but expanded to address the violence surrounding the elections. A suicide bomber had detonated himself in a queue of voters in Sadr City, killing four. At least twenty-five more people had been killed in attacks on other polling stations—that number seemed to have made an impression on Tricia, though it didn't seem terribly high to Montauk for a day's worth of violence in Baghdad. He wanted to write to her immediately, but he held back for several days. "Hey, nice article, let's fuck again" didn't seem like the appropriate thing to say. "Want to grab dinner" seemed too transparent. What he needed was a plausible work-related excuse to spend enough time with her to make a further sexual encounter all but inevitable. It was hard to plan this out, though, with the headache Ali Gorma was giving him.

For weeks, Gorma had been showing up late to his shifts. And just recently, he'd no-call/no-showed. That alone might have been reason enough to fire him. But Montauk had also repeatedly found himself in situations where Gorma's translations didn't match the facial expressions of the distraught Iraqis whom Montauk was attempting to communicate with. This suspicion—that Gorma was leaving out information, due to either apathy or a misdirected sense of propriety—had been gnawing at him for weeks. He had even begun to worry that Gorma was actively sabotaging day-to-day operations. The most infuriating part was that when Montauk got up the courage to send Gorma packing, he stood there looking bored as ever. "Do you get what I'm saying?" Montauk had said. "You're fired. Don't come back." Gorma had said, "Okay," shrugging with the least amount of exertion possible to convey his indifference.

But with Gorma gone and Olaf looking for a replacement, Montauk could focus on the more important question of how to get Tricia alone in a dark room. He'd begun the e-mail by complimenting her article and telling her that EOD had gone out to remove that mortar. This put him in a good light. But Tricia didn't seem like the kind of girl who would come running to him because he was big and strong and could solve all her problems. She had a very developed sense of her own agency. He'd grinned at his cleverness when the idea came to him. Just a little afterthought at the end of the e-mail: *P.S. Maybe we can trade information. Let's talk.* How could she resist that? He'd offer her some leads about civilian casualties from the daily INTSUM—stuff that would make great human-interest material for lefty publications. And in exchange, maybe she could . . . keep an ear to the street—that was a good phrase—for rumors of insurgent activity. It wasn't entirely bullshit. Maybe Tricia and her journalist cronies could turn up information that Montauk, as a US soldier, would never get from the locals. And though sharing bits of intel with an unembedded journalist wouldn't endanger anyone, he could get in serious shit if Captain Byrd found out. There was real risk, which made the elaborate attempt at a liaison even more erotic.

They had arranged to meet at the internal checkpoint to the DFAC. Montauk was there now, shooting the bull with the guard force, which today meant Fields and Kyriacou and a few Gurkhas. The Gurkhas were former British colonial troops from Nepal who were now basically mercenaries.

Tricia arrived alone. Khakis and a button-up. The hijab she wore outdoors lay around her shoulders.

"Lieutenant," she said. Her ID hung from a lanyard around her neck, government-worker style. She held it out expectantly toward Montauk.

He took it, flipped it around, and gave it the once-over. "You're good."

"Are you working right now?" she asked.

He raised an eyebrow. Fields raised one, too. "Technically, no."

"Technically, dinner?"

"The LT would be glad to keep you company, ma'am," Kyrie said. "Sir, me and the Gurkhas got it locked down, you're good to go." He flashed a grin and gave a double thumbs-up.

Tricia smiled and stepped through the gap in the sandbags, beckoning Montauk to follow.

"Sir!"

"Right . . ." Montauk hadn't cleared his weapon. SOP when entering US military buildings was to pop out your magazine, yank back the bolt to show the empty chamber, and then aim your rifle into the sand-filled clearing barrel and pull the trigger. Montauk pointed Molly Millions into the clearing barrel, but he yanked back the bolt *before* ejecting the magazine, which racked a round into the chamber.

"Oooh," said Kyrie.

"Shit." Montauk jacked the bolt back again, ejecting the rifle round, which he caught and popped back into the magazine. He pulled the bolt back a third time, then fired the empty weapon into the barrel.

"Good to go, sir!" chimed Kyrie.

"Thanks," Montauk muttered.

"Everything okay?" Tricia asked as they walked across the mosaic of Bush I's face.

"Everyone's already watching me because I'm an officer, and now I'm walking around with a hot American chick."

Tricia blushed. "Like it's fifth grade and you don't want to be the first guy with a girlfriend."

"Exactly."

"I see why you get along with Hal."

"I heard about a staff sergeant who got busted down like three ranks for getting blown by an interpreter."

"What? Why?"

"There's no sex in the Army."

"C'mon."

"No permissible sex."

"And what does that have to do with us getting dinner?"

They walked down the hall past the barbershop and one of the many stalls selling paintings and cheap watches and pocketknives. Montauk chuckled at himself.

"What?"

"It's just that my game's been sucking it through a glory hole."

"When did you become a frat guy?"

"I'm pretty sure I was dipping Kodiak and swigging High Life when we first met."

"That was when you were a blimp pilot."

"I still am, this is just a yearlong deployment."

She smiled at that. "Right."

"I'm serious—they have to hold my job for me at UAI. It's federal law."

"Let's just forget that, okay? You're not who I thought you were."

The track-lit buffet at the Al Rasheed spread out before them. Tonight was chicken Kiev, which here was basically a breaded fist-sized chunk of boneless chicken with a cream-cheese sauce injected inside. Montauk had no idea what chicken Kiev was supposed to be, but he'd wager money that it was totally different from what they served in the Al Rasheed.

They picked an empty table at the far end of the room.

"So how are you liking Baghdad?" he said.

"Let's get down to business," Tricia said. "You can get me leads on civilian casualties?"

"I get an intelligence brief on Karada every morning. It's like a police-blotter thing, except with stuff that's of interest to us. Mostly attacks and threats on their side, raids and other ops on our side, and tidbits of intel, like reports that we're going to get hit with a car bomb, which we seriously get every day."

"Car bombs?"

"Reports of car bombs. We haven't actually been blown up. Not my platoon, anyway."

"It'll have reports of civilian casualties, then?"

"No, it's just a bunch of incident reports, but it generally reports if one of our units has done an operation anywhere in the area, if they've done a raid or taken contact or whatever."

"And it has addresses?"

"More like grid squares. But they're accurate to about ten meters, if you have a GPS. Sometimes the reports mention which apartment building, plus maybe a street or an intersection. Mostly grid squares, though." The cheese sauce came oozing out of the chicken Kiev when he pushed on it with his fork. "Usually they won't mention if they hurt someone or trashed the place—it's an intelligence report. But if you know where an operation recently happened, you could roll over there and talk to people, see what they say."

"That's helpful. I think."

"I'm only giving it to you, not that other dude. Understood?"

"Okay . . ."

"And I'm not going to give you the whole thing. I'm going to write down the stuff that's relevant to you. I could get in serious shit for this. As in jail time, maybe."

"It's classified?"

"Tell people you got it from your translator friend."

"Okay. And what do you need from me?"

"You know," Montauk said, taking a bite of his entrée. "Just keep your ear to the street for rumors of insurgent activity. We get so many reports, and we can't pay attention to all of them. Even a hint about which ones to focus on, even if it's not hard intel, could be useful. Try your chicken Kiev. Not bad."

Tricia took an indifferent bite.

"So, really, how are you liking the city?" Montauk said.

"It's overwhelming. And incredible. Just . . ."

"Just your boyfriend's got his panties in a twist."

"He's not my boyfriend."

"Girls tend to say that around me."

"Stop it." She playfully slapped his arm. His frat-guy act was just thin enough to be funny. "But yeah, he's been kind of uptight. He chewed me out for going to observe the elections."

"I would have, too, Tricia. Jesus."

"Well, he doesn't explain anything. That's the real problem. I ask questions and he gets annoyed that I'm trying to figure out how to maneuver in this war zone. What you can do, what you can't. So I'm left just doing things and figuring out the consequences later."

"Now you know how the Army feels," Montauk said. "Ba-dum-tshh."

41

"Wooah, ho ho ho," said Jackson softly. "Worked *over*." He reached down to the Chinese walkie-talkie tied to his vest, and the news started wending its way through the platoon like word of some prodigal's return to a snowbound village.

"It's Ali Gorma?" Joh said into his walkie-talkie, resting in the shade of the Priority bunker behind the fifty.

Yeah. The voice wasn't quite identifiable through the cheap handset, but probably Ant.

What the fuck does he want? Thomas, over the talkie net.

Sergeant Nguyen is talking to him. Jackson again. *Looks like he got hit by a steamroller.*

Montauk stood on the lower lip of a T-wall, looking out over the traffic circle. He had his walkie-talkie switched on, the better to monitor the platoon chatter, although as a rule he responded only to official communications on the company net, which presently came alive with the voice of Staff Sergeant Nguyen.

Two-Six, Two-Two. Can you come down to Routine Search?

"Two-Two, Two-Six. On the way." Montauk spat out some dip and hopped down from the T-wall. The soles of his feet felt hot and tender in his boots, and he knew they'd be reeking when he pulled his socks off.

Ali Gorma was indeed worked over. He had on his usual baggy trousers and a button-up, but his cheek was covered in gauze, and a huge shiner spread across his eye up to his forehead. The tip of his nose was scabbed over, and his arm was in a sling and covered in more gauze from wrist to elbow. The gauze was crusted over with yellow fluid that had seeped through.

"Ali Gorma. What happened?"

Nguyen replied for him. "Says he got beat up by the AIF, sir."

Montauk led him up the lane toward the command post, walking slowly to accommodate Ali Gorma's new limp.

"Somebody attacked you?"

"Yes, they attack me."

"Do you know who it was?"

"Yes, I think so."

Montauk racked his brain for relevant episodes of *Law & Order*. Gorma had not been back to the checkpoint since Montauk had fired him last week. He was now coming in to report that he'd been attacked by terrorists, probably for working with Montauk's platoon. Did Gorma want protection? Montauk was fairly certain that 3rd Brigade was not in the witness protection business.

He felt like he was about to enter the familiar drill of listening to a local's grievance, saying he'd forward the concerns to his commander, and *Insha'Allah,* something would be done. He'd come to think of Baghdadi complaints as if they were complaints from girls—*stop trying to fix everything,* an ex once told him. *Just listen to me.* If Gorma really was attacked for (barely) working for Montauk, wasn't he taking another big risk by coming back to talk with soldiers? Aladdin's dead face materialized in Montauk's head. He threw it out of his thoughts, something he'd been getting better and better at.

Montauk pulled out a plastic chair for Ali Gorma in the CP. He laid his rifle on the desk's plywood top and fished a couple of cold Mr. Browns from the recycle bin. "So. First of all, I'm sorry you were injured. I hate to see you like this. Can you tell me what happened from the beginning?"

Gorma shifted in his chair and glanced at the satellite map of the checkpoint taped to the concrete wall. Sunlight passed through the city's haze and the CP's camouflage netting before settling on Gorma's bandaged face and oiled black hair. "I receive a note on my door, and it is from mujahideen, saying I work with Americans, and they kill me if I work with Americans."

"When did you get this note?"

"I get it last week."

"While you were still working here?"

"No, no, just after."

"Do you have the note?"

"What the note?"

"The note on your door? Do you have it?"

"No, no. I put in garbage."

From behind his desk, Montauk could see the apartment buildings across the street, with their crazy lattice of wires and rooftop satellite dishes. Electricity had become a free-for-all in occupied Baghdad; people regularly climbed telephone poles to splice wires into the power lines so they had extra sources of power during brownouts. Down on the street level, hidden from Montauk's view by T-walls, a ring of trash bags was stacked three high against the building like some putrescent buttress system. Montauk decided to play chief inspector, since he didn't really have a choice.

"You threw it out. Of course. Do you know where the trash bag is?"

"No, I don't know."

"It would help if you could find that note and bring it to us. It will help us to identify your attackers." A growing part of Montauk felt disassociated from the present moment and viewed the conversation from above. How absurd it sounded. Second Lieutenant Montauk asking former translator Ali Gorma to dig through trash bags to find a note from the AIF. It would never happen.

"Hmm, okay. I will look for it. *Insha'Allah, Insha'Allah,* I will bring it to you."

"Did they contact you again before the attack?"

They had not. Ali Gorma had been walking home after visiting one of his uncles in the neighborhood just southeast of the checkpoint when a car slowed down next to him, a revolver pointed out the window. Three men got out of the car and walked him into the alley and beat him and stuck the barrel of the revolver in his mouth. Montauk scribbled the details in his notebook with a ballpoint. His handwriting was like a personal encryption.

"It is the same men, I think," Gorma said. "The same who kill Aladdin."

Montauk stopped writing. After nailing his proverbial gold doubloon to the mast and slogging through that week of useless interviews, Montauk had done his best to quash any hope of finding Aladdin's killers. It wasn't going to happen. He knew that. And it distracted him from his job. But now it all came rushing back at him, that anger, that desire for black, metallic revenge. Holy Christ, if those motherfuckers had done a number on Gorma, then maybe he'd find them after all.

"Do you know them?" Montauk asked.

"Only one. His name Abdul Aziz."

"How do you know him?"

"He lives near to me."

"So he's not Al-Qaeda from Yemen or something. He's Baghdadi."

"Yes."

"Sunni or Shia?"

"I think he is Sunni."

"You think? You don't know?"

"I know. He is Sunni."

"Is he working for Zarqawi? Muqtada al-Sadr? Someone telling him what to do?"

"No, no. I don't know. Maybe Zarqawi, but—"

"Oh right, because Al-Sadr is Shia, but Abdul Aziz is Sunni."

"Yes, yes."

"So, where does Abdul Aziz live?"

"He live near Karada Kharidge."

"Near the middle traffic circle?"

"Yes."

"In an apartment?"

"Yes. Babil Apartments."

"What apartment number?"

"I think he is number eight."

"Abdul Aziz, Babil Apartments, number eight. Near Karada Kharidge."

"Yes."

"Can you point to where it is on the map?"

They walked a few steps to the T-wall, and Ali Gorma pointed to a spot on the satellite photo with his unbroken arm.

"Wow, that's close," Montauk said. And it was—a little over half a kilometer southeast of the checkpoint, in the Mansour neighborhood, nestled in a twisted knot of buildings and alleys that reminded him of a trip to Naples with Corderoy, the rooftops and upper alleys hung with wash, spidery electrical wires. Montauk began to calculate the number of troops he'd need and whether he could fit a Bradley down into that neighborhood.

"Yeah, it's really close," he said again.

———

Montauk sat across from Captain Byrd and handed him the photos of the building. He'd marked an X over the door that Ali Gorma had identified as the apartment of Abdul Aziz.

"You trust Gorma?" Byrd asked.

"He was lazy," Montauk said. "But I doubt he'd lie to my face. And someone clearly did a number on him. Gorma says it's the same guys who killed Aladdin. We have to do something, sir."

"I hear you. Can't lose any more translators. We oughta hit back."

"I asked Olaf to search the Connex for a battering ram," Montauk said.

"What's the scheme of maneuver?" Byrd asked.

"Third squad goes in, Second on perimeter security, First in reserve in the alley."

"Work up a full brief," Byrd said. "I'll approve it—*if* the intel is any good. I ate a mouthful of shit last month when Third Platoon booted a family out of their house at gunpoint—including Grandma and baby—because intelligence said they were AIF. I don't want to get burned again."

"Understood, sir," Montauk said.

"You find me some corroborating intel, and we'll do this, Montauk. Until then, no dice."

42

The barber brushed lather across the stubble on Luc's chin and upper lip.

"Mustache, no?" the barber asked. It took a few back-and-forths of pointing and head shaking to convince him. He gave a slight shake of his own head at the end and dutifully took the straight razor to the long stubble on Luc's upper lip, the barber's own luxurious mustache twitching slightly as he did so.

Tricia was transfixed by the music video playing on the barber's screen—in it, an Arab pop star in a flashy suit sang to rows of hot video-girls wearing hijabs and dancing on a set of stairs in a mansion. It was a weird combination of Biggie and Bryan Adams, but with an Arab/Islamic sensibility, or at least with girls who covered their heads (but not their midriffs).

"I heard back from my friend at the IPS," Luc said. "They loved the mortar piece and want to see more work from us."

Us? You mean from me? It was like he was pretending he'd never chastised her for visiting the polls, or for wanting to hear the military viewpoint at the press conference, without which her article would have been little more than a snapshot of a mortar in someone's back-yard. "That's great," Tricia said. She had been keeping one eye down the hall, where Bravo Company soldiers could be seen trooping across G. H. W. Bush on the way to the dining facility.

"And I found another lead this morning. A family that was booted out of their house by the Army. Bad intel, it seems. Thought they were insurgents. We'll try to track them down this afternoon."

She'd had a few false alarms when stocky young white men with short brown hair and Army uniforms passed through her field of vision. This one looked like him, though. Yes, it was him. "I'm going to the dining hall," she said. "Meet me in there."

She wandered past the vendors and fell into line a few people behind Mickey. He signed the roster in silence and continued toward the buffet. A moment later, she signed and was let through, wondering what kind of contract Halliburton had that they were feeding her for free. She caught up with him at the tray dispenser. "Hey, let's talk. I only have a couple of minutes."

For once he dispensed with arrogant witticisms and followed her straight back to a side table before hitting the buffet line.

"You get my e-mail?" Montauk asked.

"Yeah, so you think it's the same guys who killed your last translator?"

"Maybe. That's why I need your help."

"What can you tell me about him?"

"About Aladdin?"

"You know that's not his name."

"No, that's his name. Was, anyway. And that guy over there is Muhammad Ali. So is that guy. Seriously. Anyway. He was a student at Baghdad University."

Montauk handed Tricia a picture of Gorma and his injuries, then an image of Aladdin he'd printed off the black-and-white LaserJet in the TOC. It had been taken on his first day of work for the company database of possibly useful Iraqi portraiture. He was standing up against the T-wall of the CP with a bit of the checkpoint map jutting into the frame behind him. The grin he wore was not quite familiar to Montauk; it looked like his usual grin, but there was something more hesitant or tremulous about it around the eyes. Probably because it had been his first day.

"He looks nice. Why did they kill him?" Tricia asked.

"Because he was nice. Because he worked for me."

"That's it?"

"What? Yeah, that's it. I actually can't tell if you're fucking with me. You are aware of the insurgency, right? Car bombs? Dead bodies everywhere?"

"Excuse me for being curious," Tricia said. "And stop being a jerk. I can take these to Yasmin and see if she can ask around. You have a suspect?"

"We do."

"It would help if you gave me a name and address."

"Can't. I need an independent confirmation. If you give Iraqis some guy's name and ask them if he's a terrorist, they'll be like, 'Yeah, sure, whatever.' "

"That's what you think Iraqis are like?"

"Yeah."

"Aladdin, too?"

"Well, no. Look, if I give you a name and the confirmation comes back yes, I can't evaluate that. But if you can somehow get a name that independently matches the name I got, that suggests it's real."

"Okay."

"Independent confirmation."

"I got it."

"Obviously, I'm not counting on this. I just feel like you probably have more access to the locals than I do."

"Ya think?"

"Stop breaking my balls, all right? I'm fighting for justice here. That's not even a joke, I'm being serious. I'm fighting for fucking justice." As soon as he said it, he felt proud and moral in a way he hadn't until that moment. Maybe it was Tricia's presence. But he still wanted to drive a spike through the killer's eye socket. That was okay. Vengeance and justice weren't mutually exclusive.

Tricia was struck by his seriousness. When she'd met him in Boston, he'd seemed to be some sarcastic wit, bopping through life.

They noticed Luc's appearance at the table. Tricia slid the photos into her pocket. Luc said, "Tricia. And is it . . ."

"Mickey."

"That's right. And how do you know each other again?"

Tricia looked at Montauk. "He went to college with my roommate in Boston."

"So you went to university. And then you chose to come here."

"I was ordered to come here."

"I thought you were all volunteers."

"We volunteer for the military, in my case the reserves, but deployment orders are based on what unit you're in."

Tricia had also assumed that Mickey had volunteered for Iraq. She noticed his face beginning to darken and wondered if he disliked Luc because of a rivalry over her or because he was annoyed at the line of questioning. She felt fatigued and wanted nothing more than a long, cool shower followed by a long sleep in a cool, soft bed with the crisp New England night outside her walls. She'd lived like a princess back in Boston, in comparative terms. Her insulation and airflow and midshelf sheets and coffee press were items of luxury never seen or perhaps imagined by the vast majority of humans in history, and probably, no, definitely not by the majority of people in the world today. And yet that was her default, what she'd grown up in. Tricia forced herself to focus.

". . . I don't fight for Bush. We follow Bush's orders because he's the president. If Kerry won, we'd be under Kerry."

"And if he was elected unconstitutionally?"

"So we should all break out the UN Charter or whatever and give it a good read, and if we decide in our wisdom that the war is unlawful, then we should just turn in our stuff and go home?"

"Why not?"

"Gee, I never thought of that. I'll go ahead and spread the word, maybe we'll have a mass desertion. Then we can storm the White House, oust that charlatan cartoon villain, and install a military junta."

"This is a serious question. If the war isn't lawful—"

"Well, on that note, I'm gonna grab me some chicken parm or whatever they've got. When we get to D.C., I call the Lincoln Bedroom. Trish, a pleasure, as always."

Tricia gave him a quiet wave as he stalked off. Luc turned to her with a smile that was halfway sad. "I don't quite get it. Does he not understand these issues or does he just not care about them? I usually assume it's a little of both, but he's been to university."

"Maybe he thinks it's complicated."

"Oh, I don't think it's so complicated. I think people pretend that it's complicated so they don't have to make the hard choices."

It sounded like something she had said a dozen times. She still believed it, mostly.

———

Three days passed. The usual potshots. The usual VBIED scares. Another anonymous body in the river. Then, finally, Montauk received an e-mail from Tricia saying she had something for him. He hopped out of the Millennium Falcon after his shift and went straight to the Al Rasheed. He strode over Bush's face. The sheen of sweat exposed to the air was chilled far below his body temperature, though he was cooking sous vide inside his armor and fatigues. Molly Millions bounced gently against his chest as he walked past the elevators and barbershop and into the Al Rasheed's café.

He found Tricia sitting at a table sipping a Turkish coffee and smoking a Gauloise. "Pretty liberating, right? Smoking right here in the hotel?"

She exhaled. "You can do it in France."

"It's banned on dirigibles these days." He rested Molly against the booth and began taking off his armor. The Velcro made a loud tearing sound as he opened it up, and he actually felt a gust of hot air escaping as he slid out of it and exposed his soaked uniform blouse to the air-conditioning. She was wearing a tight tank top under a khaki safari-type jacket.

"How's everything going?" she asked.

"It's kind of dragging right now, to be honest. Pretty boring."

"That's good. Isn't it?"

"Found another body under the bridge, so that was something. It's getting harder and harder to get the cops to deal with the corpses. Maybe you and Luc could set up a side business in riverine corpse disposal."

She glared at him.

"Sorry."

"Is this a good place to do this?" she asked.

"No. There's a place upstairs. C'mon."

Tricia left five bucks on the table and followed him back down the hall to the elevator bank. Montauk looked around warily but didn't see anyone he knew. The door opened to an empty elevator, and he followed her inside, his nerves picking up at her proximity. He dropped his armor and hit the button for the seventh floor. He was acutely aware of how desperate he was for her and how easily that desperation could cause this whole operation to fall apart. Operation Horizontal Blonde. Operation Urgent Sex. Just the scent of her in the enclosed elevator was making his heart pump faster. The old tragicomic paradox about girls and action was that the more you needed it, the less likely you were to get it. A little tension was a good thing, though. The seventh floor was empty when the doors opened. Down the hall and to the left, to the infamous Room 710. It was unlocked and relatively clean. He ushered her in and locked the door behind them. Fly casual.

"Did this place get bombed or something?"

"It got hit with a rocket last year when the place was full of CPA types. It was kind of the opening salvo of the insurgency. There was an Air Force colonel in here at the time."

"Did he die?"

"Something like that." From what Montauk had heard, the Air Force colonel had been distributed across the walls and ceiling.

A tarp was duct-taped over the window where the rocket had come in and detonated at the foot of the bed. The wallpaper was torn up, but they'd replaced the bed for some reason. Montauk piled his gear against the wall and took out a green Army-issue notebook. Inside was a folded paper where he'd copied down several of the incident reports in the neighborhood. The sound of large truck engines wafted through the rippling window covering. Tricia sat down on the edge of the bed beside him and took the paper.

"I translated some of the Army-ese for you. It's probably a patois you should learn a little of, anyway. Do you get what the grid squares mean?"

"Hmm."

"Because the thing is, if you take a bunch of military grid squares and just give them to Luc, he'll probably assume I gave them to you. Or at least that you got them from some US Army source."

"Right."

"So I think our options are: one, you get ahold of your GPS, plot the points, and turn them into street intersections; or two, I could plot the points myself, but that will take me a while, and you might start getting day-old intel."

"And we have to stop meeting like this," she said.

"Of course." He looked at her lips, then back at her eyes. "It ain't free, though."

She shimmied out of the safari jacket and retrieved a scrap of paper from a front pocket. Montauk noted that it was not necessary to take off the jacket in order to reach that pocket. Her breasts were cupped snugly in the green tank top. He peeled his eyes away reluctantly to check the proffered paper.

Abdul Aziz, Babil Apartments, #8, Karada Kharidge. That was the place. He stared at it for a few seconds. Holy shit. The analytic side of his brain was in a brownout due to the power demands of the animal side. "So I just gave you the pictures and names of the translators, right?" Montauk asked.

"Yeah, that's what we went off of."

"So who came up with the info?"

"I went through Yasmin. She asked around. I didn't pry too much."

"Okay, wow."

"Is it right?" Tricia asked.

Independent confirmation. The raid was on. They were going to get that scumbag. He looked back at her. She was the picture of soft youth, a cool mind and driven spirit, padded out with just the right dimensions . . .

"Yeah," he said, and folded it back up, smoothed it out, and buttoned it into his own chest pocket.

"What are you going to do?" she asked, putting a hand on his chest.

He pushed some hair back from her forehead and slipped his hand behind her neck and kissed her. She gave a soft moan and kissed him back, draping her arms around his shoulders. "My God, you're soaking wet!" she said.

He laughed, unbuttoned his sodden uniform top, and threw it over his gear. He started unlacing his boots. "You know what? I'm going to give my dogs a rinse."

"What?"

"Sweat is one thing, boot sweat is another. Just give me a sec." Montauk's feet were absolutely swollen and soaked. He stumbled over to the bathroom, peeled off his socks, threw them in the corner, and quickly rinsed off his feet in the sink, balancing awkwardly on one foot and then another. He had some kind of tropical foot rot going on for sure. He turned around, and to his huge relief, there she was, on the edge of the bed, smiling at him.

Tricia wondered if this whole thing wasn't some elaborate plan to get her alone. She almost hoped it was. She peeled off his soaked undershirt and kissed him again. "Oh, you have these," she said, fingering his dog tags. "That's classic."

"Yeah, you're in a movie right now. It's black-and-white."

"It's more complex than that," she said as he pulled the tank top off her and kissed her along the lacy tops of her bra cups.

A knife edge of Arabian sunlight slid across the pillows from a gap in the tarp. They had followed each other to this place, and their previous drunken hookup was picked up and burnished to a shine and repackaged in a filigreed box of fate or kismet. Tricia looked up at the gouges in the ceiling where the insurgency began; below that, Montauk's face and muscled chest floated over her own, the warm steel of his dog tags sliding across the space between her breasts. They were making stories about themselves. Tricia knew this was happening even as it was happening, and realized that she didn't care.

43

After Montauk had provided independent confirmation of the address and name, Captain Byrd had given the go-ahead. From the halogen bath of the checkpoint's generators, the raid party walked into darkness. Baghdad was in a continuous brownout, and central Karada's streetlights had been mostly offline since the invasion. They spread out into the usual urban march formation—two columns, one on either side of the street, with about ten yards between each soldier. The apartments still had some juice, and a soft glow came from a few of the windows, although most of the city was long asleep. Each soldier did a quick swivel to either side every so often, scanning. Jackson pointed his muzzle at an upper story, and Montauk followed the line of sight to a silhouette in a dimly lit window: a middle-aged man, mostly bald on top, illuminated by a floor lamp with a red fringed shade. Montauk nodded to Jackson in acknowledgment. No one said a word. The man did not wave. When they had gone four blocks south, Jackson looked back and Montauk waved him left. Their column crossed the street to join the other column, and the raid party slipped into Mansour's alley network.

The temperature was in the high eighties Fahrenheit, and the air smelled of sweat and gun oil and smoke from homemade stoves and trash fires and something else, spicy and faintly putrid, that Montauk imagined as some kind of complex Iraqi stew. They fell silent as they approached the Babil Apartments. Montauk motioned for 3rd Squad to stack up along the front porch of number 8. Ant was at the front. Montauk took his position at the rear. He fingered the safety on Molly and ran a glove over her heat guard. If Abdul Aziz were waiting for them inside, there was a good chance Ant would catch some bullets. Montauk had told himself back in training that he'd never order troops into a building like this—he'd just call in an air strike and sift through the rubble. So much for that plan.

Fields stepped to the other side of the door from Ant, like they'd rehearsed, gripping the handles of a heavy SWAT-style door knocker that they'd borrowed from battalion. When Fields was in position, Ant reached behind him to Staff Sergeant Arroyo. Montauk, at the rear of the squad, received a tap a few seconds later, which signaled that the entire squad was cocked. Montauk gave a last glance around at the darkened shapes of the sleeping apartments and at the squads posted up on either corner of the target building. Not a sound from any living thing in the vicinity, only the throaty clanking of a private generator the next block over. Montauk returned the tap forward: the signal to execute passed back down the eight-man squad to Ant, who was breathing rapidly, the butt of his carbine jammed up in the meat of his shoulder, his elbows in, his gloved fingers opening and closing on the carbine's pistol grips like a gymnast's on a pommel horse. He felt the tap on his upper arm, then tightened his grip and nodded to Fields. The door gave way with a dry crack, and Ant felt himself shoved into the room, which was suddenly floodlit with four rifle-mounted white lights.

A second passed. No gunfire.

Montauk slowly exhaled and moved up to the open door to direct traffic through the house. He looked across the alley to see Captain Byrd and the company translator, Farouk, trotting toward him. Alarmed voices came from inside the apartment, and soon a paunchy, middle-aged man in a dishdasha was stepping fearfully outside.

"Is this his apartment?" Byrd asked. Farouk relayed the question; the answer was affirmative. He lived there with his wife and two sons.

"Tell him we're looking for Abdul Aziz," Byrd said. The man kept looking back into his house, where four soldiers were bunched up in the anteroom, the antithesis of a good tactical position. Fields gave the universal *what now?* signal to Montauk. Farouk was telling Byrd that Abdul Aziz was the man's oldest son. That he was not at home right now.

"Stand fast, I want this guy to lead us through the house," Montauk said. He turned to Byrd, who nodded.

In the neighboring buildings, candles and oil lamps were lighting up windows. Montauk turned aside and fingered his hand mike. "All Outlaw elements, this is Outlaw Six, be advised we've got the home owner here, and he's going to give us a tour."

The man walked back into his home. Montauk followed with Farouk, while Captain Byrd stood outside. The man slipped off his shoes in the anteroom and looked briefly at the feet of the soldiers crowded in there with him.

"Sorry we can't take our shoes off, it's against our rules," Montauk said. Farouk translated, then took off his own shoes. "It's not meant as an insult."

The man opened a door into a kitchen area lit by a Coleman-type propane lamp hung above the refrigerator. The room smelled faintly of spices and meat threatening to turn. Mom was almost exactly as short as Montauk's own mother. A boy of about thirteen stood beside her, impassive, which Montauk guessed meant he was furious. Montauk called for 1st Squad. Jackson sent in his Alpha team to search the bedrooms.

The younger son's room was covered in soccer posters, mostly eighties-looking team photos of different Arab and European clubs, although there was a large Nike poster of Baggio from the '94 World Cup. "This kid sure loves soccer," Phage said as he shone a flashlight into the darker recesses of the closet, the bulk of his weapon and body armor forcing him to bend in at an uncomfortable angle. Joh slid a stack of British *Maxims* out from under the bed. A Koran graced the bedside table.

Montauk found Captain Byrd standing by his Humvee with Captain Persons, the battalion intelligence officer. "How's it going, LT?"

Montauk sighed. "No sign of the target, sir. I was going to recommend we give them another five minutes, then call it a night."

"What's the rush?" asked Captain Byrd.

"Well, sir, I doubt the kid is AIF."

"We've been attacked by kids younger than him, LT," Persons said.

"Roger, sir, but the only reason we're searching this house is because one of our translators fingered it as the home of Abdul Aziz, the older son, who doesn't appear to be here." The mother was starting to yell.

"Go find out what's going on, Montauk," Byrd ordered.

The house was packed with people, which briefly reminded Montauk of the Encyclopaedists parties. All his soldiers had night optics on their helmets, so there was a weird alien vibe to the scene, almost comical. Like it was all part of the night's theme. Mom was barking heatedly at her son and, apparently, everyone else; the son sat on the edge of his bed in stony silence as Phage loomed over him.

"Tell her to quiet down," Montauk said.

Farouk gave her the command, but she simply raised her volume and tried to hit him. Ant jerked back to avoid touching her, as they'd been instructed in Montauk's operations order. But Fields hadn't retreated; he looked like he was about to smack the woman back.

"Fields," Montauk said. "Hey. Fields. Over here."

"She mad at her son. She crazy!" Farouk said.

"*Why* is she mad?" Montauk asked. The kid piped up from the edge of the bed, and the mother began raging at him again, her arms flapping in the loose dress. Ant stepped back from her along the counter, and a teapot slid off and burst across the kitchen floor.

"Hey, sir, I think she's mad because her kid had titty mags," Jackson shouted over the din. Captain Byrd's voice came through Montauk's radio, though he couldn't make out the words.

"*What?*" Montauk asked Jackson. The woman was yelling some hostile phrase repeatedly. Farouk looked stricken. Montauk gripped his sidearm, the one he'd promised his dad he'd lug around.

"We found some titty mags under his bed when we were looking for weapons, and she started flipping out," Jackson said.

"Hey, *shut up!*" Montauk bellowed at the woman. Silence filled the kitchen until the only sounds were an orchestra of breathing. The woman stared at Montauk's pistol, pointed at the ceiling, the glass lantern making the sheen of sweat on her plump face shine like glaze on a fresh donut.

Captain Byrd's voice through the radio again: *Two-Six, Six, acknowl-edge, over.*

"Six, Two-Six, say again?"

I say again we got him, one military-aged male on the fire escape, over.

Montauk ran outside and found Captain Byrd at the edge of the alleyway, where Staff Sergeant Nguyen and his squad were aiming their M4-mounted lights up at a shirtless man on the fire escape.

Thomas was yelling the Arabic word for *Get down!* while PFC Lo was yelling the Arabic for *Stop!* Nguyen silenced his squad and motioned for the guy to climb down the ladder. The light beams followed him down the dusty black metal, bits of paint flaking off underneath his bare feet as they touched the rungs.

"Abdul Aziz?" Montauk said.

The young man nodded.

Jackson appeared on the fire escape above and yelled down, "Sir." Montauk looked up. Jackson was holding an AK. "Found it in his closet."

Abdul Aziz began talking quickly and anxiously, and Montauk radioed to get Farouk back out to translate. Farouk arrived a moment later with Aziz's mother in tow.

"Ask him about the gun," Montauk said to Farouk. But Farouk could hardly be heard over the mother, who was berating her son with as much lingual dexterity as he was using to deny (apparently) any wrongdoing.

"LT," Captain Byrd said. "Contain the situation."

Montauk signaled to Thomas and Lo, who were on perimeter security. "Cuff this guy." Thomas moved in and forced Aziz into a prone position while Lo took his wrists and bound them with flex cuffs.

"Throw a hood on him and let's get the fuck out of here," Montauk said.

44

jenn_yi82: you think maybe you're attracted to him because it's illicit?

Tricia sat in her kitchen at a small circular table with a red-checkered tablecloth, the sort you might have found in a restaurant in Little Italy in 1970. Her laptop was connected to the only Ethernet connection in the hotel suite; she would have been cloistered in her room otherwise. She was alternately writing a long-overdue e-mail to her mother, chatting on AOL Instant Messenger with Jenny Yi, and taking drags from a Gauloise that sat smoldering in the chipped tea saucer they used as an ashtray. She could hear Luc in the shower.

tburner: It's not illicit for me.
tburner: But it is for him.

Tricia heard the shower shut off. A moment later, Luc left the bathroom with a towel wrapped around his waist and padded off to his room.

tburner: I find myself thinking about him all the time. And inventing scenarios in my head that are really just excuses to hook up again.
jenn_yi82: "hook up" huh? I thought you hated that phrase.
tburner: He could get in trouble. What if I'm helping him make a huge mistake?
jenn_yi82: you're horny, so what. That's normal.

Was Jenny even reading her messages? Luc walked into the kitchen wearing only a pair of shorts. His hair was wet, slightly mussed, and the towel was draped around his neck. "Ah, Tricia. Still clicking away."

"Yep." She took a drag without looking up at Luc and replied to Jenny's message.

tburner: That's not the point.

"Hard to pull yourself away from home, no?"

Tricia wanted to keep her head down and ignore Luc. "Home is my perspective," she said, glancing up at him. She turned back to her screen as if intently studying some treatise. She almost wanted to tell him about Mickey. Just to see how he'd react.

Luc walked over to the sink and filled a glass of water. As she heard him drinking only a few feet behind her, Tricia became acutely aware that he could now see her screen. She almost reached to close the laptop, but instead she pulled up a new browser window and quickly navigated to nytimes.com.

"I know the foreign news editor at the *Times*," Luc said.

"Do you?" Tricia said, turning to face him. That kind of name-dropping had impressed her back in Boston. Now she wondered if it was even true. At best, Luc had probably shaken the guy's hand once at a cocktail party, years ago.

Bing. Tricia could see the blinking chat window without even looking. And there was Luc's head tilting, his eyes refocusing . . .

She turned quickly with the intention of closing the chat window, but she couldn't resist reading it herself.

jenn_yi82: whatever. he's an adult. he can hook up with you if he wants to.

Tricia closed the chat window, blood tingling through the capillaries in her cheeks.

"I should send him the mortar piece," Luc said. "I bet he'd love it."

Tricia turned back to him. He was swiveling the corner of his towel in his ear. He wore a slight grin. "You refuse to simplify complex situations," he continued. "Why do you think I brought you along?"

Luc was never this forward with compliments. He thought the chat log was about him. "You know it's rude to read other people's conversations."

Luc's grin widened. He put a hand on the back of her chair. "We're all adults here . . ."

Tricia took a long final drag of her cigarette, inhaling the acrid taste of burning filter. "That wasn't even about you."

"Oh? Who, then? Your Army friend?"

"Yes, in fact. But it's not what you think."

His grin went slack. "Isn't it?"

"We're trading information."

"Are you serious? That's incredibly unprofessional."

"Don't lecture me on professionalism, Luc. It's like your prime concern is vilifying the military. We're supposed to be striving to get an unbiased picture of life in Baghdad. If we don't, then what's the point except to feel cool for being war-zone journalists."

"Tricia, you're fucking a soldier for information."

"No. I'm not. Those two things are separate."

Luc laughed in disbelief. "What information are you giving him?"

"Are we supposed to be hiding something?"

"Tricia, *what information did you give him?*"

"One of his translators was killed and another was beaten up, and I had Yasmin ask around to confirm the name of—"

"*Tricia!*"

"—of the person they *already* suspected. That's it."

"First off, you're endangering Yasmin's life, and who knows what they did to this so-called suspect? They might have killed him."

"No, they captured him."

"When?"

"Last night. They raided his apartment."

"You have the address? We're going. Right now."

"Luc, the guy they captured tortured and killed an Iraqi translator. We don't know who we're going to find there. You really think that's a good idea?"

"Are you saying you're not going to come?" he spat. "You waltzed right into the elections, ignoring the bomb threats."

She thought back to the video footage of Nick Berg's beheading. She'd forced herself to watch it after her little scare at the polling location. How meekly he knelt at their feet before they slit his throat, sawing through his vertebrae with a machete as if carving a turkey. She'd scrolled through the names of reporters killed in Iraq on the website of the Committee to Protect Journalists. Shot in the head at close range. Tortured and then strangled. But mostly it was the image of Nick Berg, his head held aloft like some cheesy Halloween prop, that had planted the seed of fear in her stomach. "This isn't a polling location," she said. "It's the house of a terrorist."

"Is it? Excuse me for not putting much faith in what your macho soldier tells you. We don't know who this guy was, Tricia. But now, thanks to you, we have an obligation to find out. I'll call Yasmin and have her meet us there. I hope you're right. I really do."

That was bullshit. Their entire trip thus far, Luc had gone for the easy story, the evocative but simple photo. He was doing this purely to spite her. Tricia lit another cigarette and watched Luc march into his room and pick up the phone.

She was afraid, but she could feel the inevitable victory of her pride. Her pride would always win that contest. She was going. She would prove him wrong.

———

The aluminum speaker on the earpiece of the Convention Center's public telephone vibrated with a reverb-heavy ringtone sounding from half a world away. After the fourth ring, Montauk heard the mechanical click of the receiver as if it were some old metal analog contraption from the forties.

"Hello?" said a hollow-sounding voice on the other end.

"Dad?"

"Mickey? Mickey. How are you, son?"

"We're making it through."

"Any word on your guy, the one who—"

"Urritia. He's back in the States now. They're stitching him up."

"That's good, that's good."

"So, you wanted to talk to me?"

"Well, yes." He paused. "Your mother and I. It's been hard working things out. We've been fighting. Mostly little things. But fighting, a lot. Too much. And although we love each other very much, and we certainly love you very much, too, we've decided it's time to make a change."

Montauk shifted on the phone booth stool so he could lean his back up against the chipping drywall and prop his boots on the sill of the booth.

"We didn't mention it when you were here on leave, but we've been living in different rooms of the house for a little over a year now. I don't know if you knew that."

"I guess I kind of suspected."

His father sighed. "I didn't want to bring it up during your deployment, but I didn't want to hide it from you, either. I hope you understand that. It seemed like you were doing all right, that your deployment's been pretty . . . straightforward."

"I haven't seen any real action, you mean."

"I mean you seem to be coming into your own. As a platoon leader. And I'm proud of you. I really am."

Ant's lanky figure floated tentatively outside of the window. He tapped on the glass. Montauk opened the door and held the receiver to his chest. "What's up?" he whispered.

"Sir, the CO wants you to come to his office."

"Be there in a minute."

Ant glided off.

"Hey, Dad. Company commander requires my presence."

"Okay, son. Let's talk some more soon. I love you."

"Love you, too, Dad."

Montauk placed the receiver back on its metal hook and exhaled through his nose. "Fuck," he muttered. He didn't want to move. Fields was waiting across the room, and he looked over when he heard the click of the hang-up. "Fuck," Montauk muttered again, pulling himself out of the chair.

"All yours," he said, slinging Molly over his shoulder and Walking With A Purpose toward Captain Byrd's quarters, trying his best to stamp out his irritation at himself. He should have just told Ant to hold on for a while because he was having an important conversation. With his father. And really, what could be so pressing? Montauk rapped on the door to the turret room that Byrd shared with the company first sergeant.

"C'mon in." Captain Byrd was sitting on his cot in the small office. He looked sleep-deprived but alert. "Shut the door. Have a seat." Byrd popped out a can of Copenhagen, stuffed a plug in, and held it out to Montauk.

"I'm good, thanks, sir."

Byrd was already leafing through his green Army-issue notepad. "All right, so. I stopped by Intel today at Warhorse. They've been putting the question to your guy from the raid."

Montauk blinked. "What'd he say?"

"Says he's never heard of Aladdin. But he does know Ali Gorma. He says—this is coming from the interrogators at Brigade, by the way—he's known Ali Gorma for a long time, and they've had differences. For a long time. That's what he says, that he was basically framed."

"Aziz could be lying, sir."

"Could be. But it's out of our hands now. Brigade's going to keep him detained for the time being to see if anything else pops up. They don't have their own detention facility, so your guy will be going to Abu Ghraib. They say they'll let me know if they learn anything, but I'm not holding my breath."

Montauk imagined himself bursting into tears.

Captain Byrd looked back down at his notebook for a moment. "Did your other source confirm the link to Aladdin?"

"No, sir. Just the name and address of the guy who assaulted Gorma."

"So all we know about Aladdin is that Gorma said it was the same dude. You know you need to take that shit with a grain of salt, right, Montauk? I mean, you've been here for a few months."

"Roger, sir. It's a pretty thin lead."

"Yeah, it is. Which leads me to another thing. Are you putting prices on people's heads?"

"Sir?"

"I heard you had a reward posted for the guys who smoked Aladdin. That true?"

"Yes, sir, it is. Probably a mistake, I realize now."

"How much?"

"Five hundred."

"Dollars US?"

"Roger."

Byrd spat thoughtfully into his plastic bottle. "That's an interesting choice," he said. "Do you think that's part of your mission?"

"Well, sir, force protection is part of our mission, as is nailing terrorists, so anything that would help accomplish those missions seems like an implied task. So finding Aladdin's killers is kind of part of the mission, yes."

"Montauk, let me tell you what your mission is. Your mission is to secure the southern entrance into the Green Zone. It's to ensure that the Green Zone doesn't get blown up by anything coming through your checkpoint. It's also to accomplish that while taking care of the troops in your platoon and following my orders. Which, by the way, means informing me when you intend to do something novel like post personal rewards for information leading to the death or capture of a terrorist."

"Yes, sir."

"I don't want to stifle your initiative. You're all about finding ways to accomplish the mission, and that's good. You'll be a good company commander someday. But this reward shit is dumb. It's just going to lead to a bunch of Iraqis coming up to try to get your cash." He spat in the bottle again. "But maybe the real issue is that it makes you look like a weirdo in front of your platoon. You know what most guys read around here? *Maxim*."

"Uh, hooah?"

"You've got a bunch of highbrow shit coming in, like your book review newspapers. And a big old copy of *The Canterbury Tales*. It's good that your troops think you're a smart guy. That's going to give them confidence. But you need to understand how you come off to your platoon. They need to know that you're not making decisions affecting their personal health and safety based on criteria from some cuckoo-cloud Montauk-land. And what I think is that your reward scheme comes across to your guys as a weirdo obsession. That you're thinking about revenge rather than your mission, or that you're somehow more attached to your translator than your men. Understand what I'm saying?"

"Roger, sir."

"So, with that in mind, shit-can the reward. Any questions?"

"No, sir."

"All right. Dismissed."

Montauk slung Molly over his shoulder and headed out the door.

"And go read a copy of *Men's Health* or *Low Rider* or something," Byrd said.

Thomas handed Montauk a letter as he reentered the FOB. Mani. He tossed it on his desk and collapsed in his cot. He couldn't imagine reading anything right now. Or ever. So Abdul Aziz had said he was framed—either he was lying or Gorma was. But Tricia's translator had confirmed Gorma's statement . . . He thought about sending Tricia a quick e-mail asking for more details. He should have asked back at the hotel. There were a thousand things he should have done, should be doing. His parents were getting divorced? It was all so exhausting. If he concentrated hard enough, maybe he could will his brain to liquefy itself and drain out his ear canals.

———

The Rabbit passed the flatbread shop and the miniature Eiffel Tower to the right. The ride was silent, save for Luc giving their driver, Adan, directions a few times. The machine-gun barrels in Mickey's towers gazed impassively out to the city, tracking neither the Rabbit nor anything else. Yasmin was meeting them at the house. Babil Apartments, number 8. If Tricia had given Mickey solid intel, then they were about to knock on the door of an insurgent stronghold, which was insane. That, or Luc's suspicions were right. Tricia desperately wanted to talk to Yasmin in private. But she wouldn't get the chance.

"Pull over here," Luc said. "This is it."

Yasmin was waiting for them out front. She had on her business face.

Tricia stood behind Luc as he knocked on the door. Yasmin introduced them when the door opened, and a woman nervously invited them inside. A soapy bucket was on the floor, which was still half covered in boot prints. Tricia had her pad open and was taking notes, but she was only half able to focus on what Yasmin was translating.

"She say they all come inside, all of them."

"How many?"

"Maybe ten." The mother was somewhat agitated, talking loudly. The husband stood in the corner of the kitchen, looking tense and vaguely embarrassed.

"She say they were yelling at her and spilling things in the house onto the floor. These were the black soldiers. They were saying that she and her family were terrorists, and the white soldier pointed his small gun into her face. Then they found her son. Her son is Abdul. Abdul was hiding and the soldiers found him and tied him up and took him away."

Luc took a photo of the younger son's ransacked bedroom. Tricia dutifully jotted the details in her notepad. She was skeptical about the whole gun-in-the-face thing. And the fact that it was only the black soldiers who were trashing the place.

"She say her son knows Ali Gorma."

"Who?" Luc said.

Tricia's mind swam to the surface as something sounded the alarm. She looked up to see Yasmin confusedly looking at her before looking back to Luc.

"Ali Gorma," Yasmin said, "the translator for the American check-point that was attacked. Ali Gorma say Abdul attack him up because Abdul is a terrorist. But she say Ali Gorma knew Abdul and that they not like each other, and this is why Ali Gorma say Abdul is a terrorist. She say Abdul is not a terrorist."

Luc's eyebrows were knitted together. "You're saying the reason that the Americans came in here and took her son is because their translator told them he was a terrorist?"

"They were trying to be careful, Luc. He asked me to help confirm the suspect before they went in," Tricia said. "Yasmin, tell him. She confirmed the name."

"Yes. I know Ali Gorma from Baghdad University. English depart-ment."

"Wait, you *know* Ali Gorma?" Tricia said. "Personally?"

"Go on." Luc's voice was flat.

"I ask Ali Gorma myself who attack him. He says Abdul Aziz."

Tricia dropped her pen. Oh God. Mickey had asked her to confirm the suspect Gorma had fingered, and Yasmin had just asked Gorma. They'd taken away this woman's son. Based on what? Someone who didn't like him had said he was a terrorist.

"Unbelievable," Luc said. He shook his head at the wreckage of the apartment.

Yasmin was speaking in soothing tones to the mother. Tricia covered her gaping mouth with her hand.

45

Montauk swung open the door to the commander's seat, heavy with makeshift steel plating, and squeezed into the Millennium Falcon. His mind was far away in time and space, at his old family home, a decade ago. His parents' home. Playing with his dog, Hadrian. Wrestling in the living room before dinner, dinner when Hadrian would lie at his feet, passively begging for a chunk of meat loaf. These memories were a tourniquet on his arterial rage—rage born of accumulated stress, the smell of death in his clothes. There were no answers here. Was Gorma lying or was Aziz? Had they sent an innocent kid to Abu Ghraib? How was he supposed to act around his parents now? Separate holiday visits? And that letter from Mani. Her and Corderoy. Seriously? Fuck, fuck, fuck. Hadrian did this funny thing where he'd lift one eyelid to see if you were watching him sleep or pretend to sleep. He'd died the summer Montauk was in Rome, the summer he met Corderoy.

No one in the truck said anything on the way out to the checkpoint. They unloaded as usual. He and Olaf got with 3rd Platoon's LT for the news of the day—there was supposedly a suicide VBIED threat against the checkpoint, the attack to take place in the next twelve hours. Montauk didn't really listen; this was a warning they'd heard about fifteen times now, each time being the time it would happen for real, except that it never happened.

He watched the traffic loop around the circle, sticking a plug of Kodiak in his mouth as his mind shot back to Tricia and her e-mail.

She was freaked out about something. Said she needed to meet soon. If it had to do with their intel exchange, which was likely, then it was probably bad. Maybe her translator was receiving death threats, too. Montauk had led her right into the sights of some demented terrorist serial killer, the Translator Eviscerator. He imagined laughing at that, but his face wouldn't comply. He reached under his eye pro and massaged his eyelids. Maybe it was nothing serious, nothing about Abdul Aziz. Maybe Tricia had just gotten some shit from her douchey photog for fucking Montauk instead of him. Maybe Luc had slapped her, really hit her, even. Given her a black eye. Montauk could make him answer for that. He imagined braining Luc with the grip of his pistol, making a nice red welt right where his widow's peak topped out.

The nine wouldn't do the best job, though: you really needed a rifle. The first hit probably wouldn't kill Luc; he'd collapse concussed on the ground, and Montauk would have to start bashing his skull in just like that, with the Karada blacktop as the anvil. He could almost see Luc's limbs flopping and twitching in their Benetton business casual as he brought the rifle down again and again, caving in his eyeholes, hitting him so hard that his skull split open lengthwise from the shock.

"LT!" Monkey's alto voice opened a door into Montauk's daydream. He hesitated at the portal as if half awakened. He smelled the air outside again.

"LT!" Monkey had skipped onto the lip of the T-wall and was approaching him with a paper bag.

"What? What do you want?" Montauk spat.

"I got it, man."

"You got what?"

"I got the head, LT."

"You got the . . ."

Monkey held up the shopping bag as if offering some kind of sacrifice or divine gift. Inside was a plastic paint bucket, and placed inside that, with some wadded tissue around it, was a human skull.

"Jesus." It was darker and yellower than Montauk would have thought. Green, almost. He supposed he was imagining skulls that had been bleached in some way. This one had not been bleached. He did not want to touch it, but he did anyway, lifting it a little out of the bag. Some of the surface of the interior, he could see, had dark gunk clinging in the crevices and rough parts, like old dried barbecue sauce in a pocked wooden bowl.

"Where did you get this? Don't answer that. Did they search you?"

"What, man?"

"Did the guys on Routine Lane see this?" He looked up and over toward the entrance of Routine Lane. They were busy mirroring a car.

Montauk peeked into the bag again. There it was. A human skull. He'd heard about a guy from 1st Cavalry who'd gotten in deep shit for keeping a toe he'd found a block away from the wreckage of a blown-up Opel. Rumor had it, he'd tried to hide it from his CO, but he couldn't keep his mouth shut. A skull would be a lot harder to conceal than a toe, and a lot harder to keep quiet about. But it was the ultimate souvenir.

"Look, kid. I'm not taking this. I don't need this. I've got enough fucking problems right now. Seriously." He dropped the bag at Monkey's feet.

"One hundred bucks, man. You said, LT."

"I don't have a hundred bucks on me."

Monkey's face screwed up. "You don't have it?"

"I don't have it on me. Look. I'll bring it tomorrow. But I'm not taking the skull."

"I give you the head, you give me one hundred bucks, man!" The kid was almost whining. He looked like he was about to cry, which was a shock considering he mostly acted like an eleven-year-old warlord.

"All right, Christ! I'll take the damn skull. Just shut the fuck up!" Montauk snatched up the bag.

Monkey recoiled as if he'd been smacked by an abusive father. "Hundred bucks, man," he whimpered.

"Tomorrow. I promise. I'm sorry, Monk. Didn't mean to yell at you."

"Why you so mad, LT?"

"A lot of reasons, buddy."

" 'Cause Ali Gorma lie to you?"

"What? When did Ali Gorma lie to me?"

"He fall off his motorcycle, man. He break his arm, and, his arm. And his face." Monkey dragged his hand across his face, where Gorma had the bruising and lacerations. Holy shit. Gorma's injuries did look a lot like road rash.

"Yeah, man," Monkey went on. "He fall off his motorcycle in Dora. Now he want his job back. Everybody knows."

"He said he got beaten up by terrorists," Montauk said lamely.

Monkey shrugged. "He a liar, man. He Ali Baba."

Montauk could feel it coming. He was going to rage on someone, and he didn't want it to be Monkey. "Leave," he said. "Right now."

———

As soon as he walked into the Al Rasheed, Tricia could tell he was furious, almost maniacally furious. He didn't say a word. The elevator doors closed. He leaned back against the wall as they began ascending. He did not look at her except out of the corner of his eye. When the door opened, Montauk stepped out and began walking down the hall toward the death room. Tricia hesitated, then followed him, having to almost jog to keep up. "Mickey," she said after him. He looked back and held up a *wait* finger, then opened the door, beckoning her inside.

She had asked to meet, thinking she would apologize, hoping he would comfort her—as horrified as she'd been with herself, Luc had been even angrier. He'd said he was sending her home. A huge overreaction, all because she'd been tangentially involved in providing information that had led to a US military "atrocity." More like a "fiasco," and hopefully one they could remedy. But it was pointless to argue with Luc. He was probably e-mailing her degree advisers at Harvard right now to cancel her independent study. She had imagined meeting with Mickey and having a sensible discussion about how to fix this. But when she saw him standing there, breathing through flared nostrils, all she could summon was anger. Anger toward him for being angry with her, for not admitting that he'd fucked up, too.

"You have to let that kid go!" she said.

"I would love nothing more than to let him go. But I can't."

"He's innocent."

"Yeah. I know!" Montauk spat on the floor. "Ali Gorma fell off his motorcycle. He was lying to me when he fingered Abdul Aziz. You confirmed that name."

"We're not the secret police. What did you expect?"

"Where did you get your information?"

"I told you, I had Yasmin ask around."

"Tricia! Who told Yasmin that kid was a terrorist?"

"How was I supposed to know that Yasmin would just ask Ali Gorma?"

"Are you fucking kidding me? I told you why I needed confirmation. Because *I didn't trust my translator*! Yasmin's as stupid as you are."

"Don't you dare blame her for this! You were the one crashing into that family's apartment, sticking a gun in that woman's face. You were the one who abducted their son."

"I didn't stick my gun in anyone's face."

"No? You didn't pull your pistol out? Why would she say you did?"

"I pulled it out, but—"

"You pulled it out and waved it at her. Did *she* have a gun?"

"No. If she did, we probably would have shot her."

"Why are you doing this to me?"

"Doing what?"

"Acting like you hate me!"

"I don't hate you."

"Because you failed in your little revenge mission?"

"Yeah, I was trying to nail the guys who killed my fucking translator. Crucify me! I've got like three months to find them and shoot them in the head before I board a plane for Seattle."

"Jesus, what's wrong with you? Just get the kid back to his family and stay safe until—"

"The kid is in Abu Ghraib! I can't just bring him back."

She had to grab on to the wall to steady herself. Her fingers poked into one of the shrapnel holes, and she pulled her hand away. "You took him to Abu Ghraib?"

"No, Battalion took him. It's the same thing they do with all detainees they suspect will have intelligence value."

"Oh, God, that's horrible."

"It's not like he's going off to get raped in a human pyramid. They just sent those idiot soldiers to prison for like ten years. That doesn't happen anymore."

"So you only sent an innocent kid to a normal Iraqi prison. No big deal."

"I was just doing my fucking job," Montauk said.

"Well, good job, then. You gonna get a promotion, an award for throwing this kid in Abu Ghraib?"

"He wouldn't be there if you hadn't given me bullshit information!"

"Fine. I'm sorry, okay? I fucked up." Mickey had fucked up, too, but she didn't have the strength to keep fighting. She was desperate for comfort, for affection, and it made her feel pathetic.

"Sorry doesn't do much, does it?" Montauk opened and closed his hands. This wasn't justice. This wasn't about Aladdin's killers. He wanted someone to pay, and seeing Tricia squirm was perversely cathartic. Why was it so hard to stop himself?

"You're not a nice person," she said. Her lips were compressed into a thin, flat line.

Montauk counted out three even breaths. "I'm having a bad week," he said. "My parents are getting divorced."

"I'm sorry to hear that," Tricia said. "But I have to go."

"Wait, wait, wait."

"Don't touch me. Good luck shooting terrorists."

"Wait, just wait for a second, I'm sorry."

But she was already out the door and moving down the hall.

Montauk sat on the bed, then lay back and closed his eyes. When he opened them, a full minute later, he stared at the mottled ceiling. The blood splatter from the rocket attack didn't seem to make sense. There were flecks of blood up there, even though the rocket would have appeared in the room above the colonel's head. Did his blood somehow splash upward from the impact of the blast?

♟ Log in

article   discussion   edit this page   history

The Encyclopaedists   [edit]

The Encyclopaedists are a fantasy stepped into when the storm is at its worst, an armor of formal diction and analytical calm.

Contents [hide]
1 Precursors of the Encyclopaedists
2 Motivations of the Encyclopaedists
3 Ice
4 Used goods
5 Things that don't exist
6 War
7 Betrayal
8 Human remains
9 The first-person plural

Precursors of the Encyclopaedists   [edit]

As Borges said while discussing Kafka, we all create our own precursors. This is especially true of the Encyclopaedists who have consciously constructed the past versions of themselves necessary for their present selves to exist. You tell yourself a story with explanatory power—you were here, she was there, I was gone—and it legitimizes your present, makes your wordless, formless future bearable.

Motivations of the Encyclopaedists   [edit]

Is it pretentious or absurd to suggest that what drives one is simply a need to accept the general shittiness and wonder of being a human?

Ice   [edit]

No thanks.

Used goods   [edit]

If being used is an objective quality, it's conceivable that you might be aware of the moment you yourself become a used good. It can't be a fun moment. If being used is a subjective quality (see: trash v. treasure), then it's possible to periodically reinvent yourself in the eyes of someone new, someone whose past is inconceivable to you, someone who did not exist until you met her.

Things that don't exist   [edit]

It is curious how much time and energy can be expended pursuing things that don't exist. Locating a phantom insurgent, cultivating an emotional intimacy that was never there to begin with.

War   [edit]

War, what is it good for? Many things, turns out. It's good for business. It's good for character-building. It raises the stakes and makes otherwise lackluster narratives compelling.

Betrayal   [edit]

Don't even talk to me about betrayal, son. Try reinterpreting your own past villainies. Consider, if you will, that betrayal can act as glue, it can yoke the destinies of nations and peoples in diaspora. It can do the same for individuals.

Human remains [edit]

From *re* + *manere,* to leave behind. The word itself assumes the personality went somewhere.

If a person survives an explosion that causes loss of limbs, the amputated flesh is considered medical waste rather than human remains. Medical waste, however important it was in life to its surviving host, does not rate funeral treatment or other ceremony; it is disposed of as a biohazard along with used medical equipment such as bloodied gauze and hypodermic needles.

Victims of punitive amputation, especially manual amputation, have been known to carry around the amputated piece (typically only the cleaned skeletal remains, after decomposition has taken its course). In these cases, the carried body part is properly classified as neither remains nor waste (in etymological terms) but, rather, as a human relic.

If one person vows to eat his friend's brain after his death—to gain his power—then human remains will be converted into human waste.

The first-person plural [edit]

The head is a hotel, complete with a resident manager, a crew of bellhops, a suite owned by a wealthy investment banker, another by a rap mogul, a rotating cast of wide-eyed visitors from flyover states, teen couples blowing their wads on saccharine one-year anniversaries, addicts, escorts, and people under assumed names, hiding from the authorities or hiding from themselves. Sometimes there are conventions. Sometimes, during a fire drill, only the manager remains inside. During an actual fire, everyone exits the head, gathers in the parking lot, fretting over what they left inside.

We are accustomed to thinking that the central question, *How can I be happy?,* is a difficult one because of that complicated word, *happy,* but the true Gordian knot is that slippery pronoun, *I.* The first person, which is already plural, can form yet further pluralities.

There is the theoretical *we.* There is the former *we.* The *we* that needs to talk. The *we* that doesn't speak because it doesn't need to. The *we* that holds these truths to be self-evident. The *we* that is few and happy. The *we* that by its existence excludes and annihilates a prior *we.* (One molecular bond breaks so another can form, leaving a lone atom adrift.) It is a strange truth of the human world that four or more is many, and such *wes* composed of many can persist in time as individuals assimilate and separate, that two is a *we* that is fragile and fragile and fragile until one day it is unbreakable, but three, three is a seemingly impossible *we,* an unstable compound not found in nature, synthesized in the laboratory.

External links [edit]

1. ^ "The Encyclopaedists of Capitol Hill."
www.thestranger.com/apr04/encyclopaedists.htm

2. ^ "C. PLINII NATVRALIS HISTORIAE PRAEFATIO."
www.thelatinlibrary.com/pliny.nhpr.html

3. ^ "Stanford Encyclopedia of Philosophy entry on 'War.' "
plato.stanford.edu/entries/war/

4. ^ "Project Gutenberg Bible, King James, Book 42: Luke."
www.gutenberg.org/dirs/etext05/bib4210h.htm

WAKING IN
THE BLUE

46

A flurry of snow swept across the windowpanes on the tenth floor, whiting the outside world—the Charles River disappeared. After a moment, the wind subsided and Corderoy could see it again in the distance, wending through Boston. It had frozen over sometime in January and was still covered in a sheet of ice.

He'd told Mani he was at school. Why he had lied was complicated. There was Mani's ongoing lie to her parents, which Corderoy took as a moral context to excuse his own lies. There was his fear that if Mani knew he had dropped out of BU, she'd see him as a pitiful mooch, and he desperately wanted her to see him as a person going places. Then there was the fact that Mani had to paint, he wanted her to paint, and she needed space, which meant he had to leave the house. He had to go somewhere. And so he had come here, to Massachusetts General Hospital, to do some cocaine.

Corderoy had saved up what he considered a fair chunk of money in Seattle, but most of that had gone to paying rent to Tricia over the last five months. He couldn't depend on his parents anymore, and he couldn't take out loans because he hadn't registered for classes. Mani was already graciously giving him shelter. At the least, he felt obligated to buy food and booze for the two of them. He'd briefly considered getting an actual job, teaching ESL or tutoring for the SAT, but he didn't want to reprise his life in Seattle. Initially, he'd gone to the blood bank. Montauk had always said, *There are only two ways to be more drunk: drink more alcohol, or have less blood.* Unfortunately for Corderoy, this principle led inevitably to the direct transformation of fifty dollars' worth of blood to fifty dollars' worth of booze. Thus, he had responded eagerly to an ad for a medical study paying six hundred dollars and requiring only a small amount of his time, provided he had previously used cocaine. And now here he was, on the tenth floor of MGH, reading an anthology of confessional poetry, waiting to meet a Dr. Hernandez.

Though he hadn't enrolled for the spring semester, he had bought a few books that were on the syllabi for classes he might have taken. It helped keep up the illusion, for himself, that his current situation was temporary, that he'd catch right back up when he figured things out. It also allowed him to more effectively lie to Mani.

He read a few lines of Robert Lowell's "Waking in the Blue."

Absence! My heart grows tense
as though a harpoon were sparring for the kill.
(This is the house for the "mentally ill.")

He looked away and tried to remember what was next. He'd memorized that poem for a class some years back but could remember only scraps of it.

Dr. Hernandez opened the door and introduced herself as Antonia. "There's a dressing gown behind the door," she said, handing him a clipboard. "I'll be back."

Corderoy changed into the paper gown and sat down with the questionnaire. It focused mostly on his past drug use. One of the questions asked if he'd ever used crack cocaine. He was pretty sure the answer was no. About a year ago, he and Montauk had been out drinking on Capitol Hill and had gone down to Broadway to buy some coke. They'd dropped fifty bucks and walked away with a bag of something white. When they'd examined it back at the Encyclopad, it wasn't powder, as they'd expected, but hard crystals. They'd had difficulty cutting it up enough to snort it. So they'd called up Johnny, their resident drug expert.

"Sounds like you bought crack," Johnny said. The question then was, "How do we smoke it?" Following Johnny's instructions, they cut

the metal nub off of a lightbulb with a bread knife, extracted the fila-
ment, and shook salt around inside to remove the white coating.

They rotated the bulb slowly over a lighter while the crystals inside
began to melt and give off vapor trails that they inhaled through a
straw they'd made from a Bic pen. Their mouths numbed and they felt
light-headed. According to Johnny, it should have hit them with more
intensity and less duration than coke. This was more akin to licking
the bag at the end of the night. Or leaving the dentist.

Was it crack? Corderoy figured it was just the shittiest coke he'd
ever bought. It got them high, that was true. But it didn't smoke like it
was supposed to. And having tried to smoke crack or been willing to
smoke crack wasn't the same as actually having smoked it. He checked
the box for *no,* then quickly finished the rest of the forms.

A nurse arrived and escorted Corderoy to the MRI room, where
Dr. Hernandez was waiting. They laid him down on the extended bed
and put an IV in his arm.

"We'll be injecting you with intravenous cocaine," Dr. Hernandez
said. "Then we'll slide you into the MRI and ask you questions while
we capture images of your brain. When you're done, we'll give you
some food and you'll stay here until the cocaine is out of your system.
Then you're free to go. Ready?" She held up a large syringe.

"What percent solution is it?" Corderoy asked.

"Sorry?"

"Sherlock Holmes injected himself with a seven percent solution of
cocaine. There was a story about it. Just curious."

Dr. Hernandez began injecting the cocaine. "I'm not sure," she said,
looking at Corderoy as if he were an addict who might break into the
hospital later that night.

The cocaine surged up his arm, hit his heart, and sent it into a
drumroll, building to a fearsome cymbal crash, then took the off-ramp
and hit the expressway aorta to his brain—the windows of the house
were flung open and spring drafts leapt in and swept out the stale aro-
mas of private consciousness.

The doctor hit a button, and the bed slowly brought Corderoy into
the maw of the MRI like the tongue of a huge beast, languid and sure
of its catch. He became aware of the inside of the tube, the seams in

the metal, the guard strapped over his head. The cocaine had hit him hard, and he was clenching his jaw several times a second, about every fourth beat of his heart.

"All right, Mr. Corderoy. Can you rate your intoxication level on a scale from one to ten? Ten being the most intoxicated you've ever felt and one being the least."

"I don't feel intoxicated," Corderoy said. "I feel sober. More than sober." He remembered the first time he'd tried cocaine—he'd been seven beers deep at five in the afternoon, and he could suddenly converse, walk, and drive with a miraculous sobriety.

"Just choose a number."

"Can it be negative?"

"No."

"Fine, then. Zero." Corderoy thought he heard Dr. Hernandez sigh, but it was hard to hear above the pulsing of his blood in his ears—or was that the MRI spinning around him—did it spin?

"And how euphoric do you feel?"

"Twelve. Just kidding. Ten."

"Your desire for more?"

"Ten."

After a few more questions, she told him to lie still while the MRI finished its work. He was twitching his leg and arm muscles, grinding his teeth, trying to channel all his nervous energy away from the top of his head, where the giant magnet was focused, focused not on his head but on his brain, which he now realized was a meat computer.

Lie still. Lie still. What kind of craziness was that? This is cocaine. No weed, Quaaludes, mushrooms, no whoa trippy man, no sit on the couch with a beer and watch the game alcohol bullshit I need to do something. Fuck on coke. Skydive on coke. Say hello to my little friend and go out with a grenade launcher on coke. Flex your toes. This is the house of the mentally ill. Absence. That was backward. Go in for the kill. Lowell. Fuck confessional Lowell. Pound. There was a motherfucker who probably did some coke. This is the house of bedlam. The man that lies in the house. What was the line? This is a Jew in a newspaper hat. Hated Jews, Pound. How long has it been? Went to the madhouse. The boy that pats the floor to see if the world is there, is flat . . . creaking sea of board . . . dances weeping. That wasn't Pound. It was Bishop, about Pound. Some god got hold of me. I sizzled in his blue volts. That was Plath. How long has it been? Some god got hold of me. Stop whispering. Hold still. Blue volts like a desert prophet. And then? And then? The nights snapped out of sight like a lizard's eyelid. But what about Pound. These thoroughbred mental cases. Lowell again. Fucking Lowell will not leave. Twice my age and half my weight. All old-timers, each of us holds a locked razor. Yes. Fuck. How long has it been? Flex your toes, hands, toes, hands. Who puts a man on coke, says be a statue. Count to twenty. Again. Number four, I know you heard this before: never get high on your own supply. Stop grinning, grinding. Not my supply. Where do you get coke this good? Ten months in this gut, what the fuck. I wish Moms'd hurry up. Biggie. Yes yes. Umbilical cord's wrapped around my neck, I'm seeing my death and I ain't even took my first step. Breathe, breathe. The MRI is whirring down, whirring worrying to silence out, out into the open, praise be to the open.

By the time he'd returned to the exam room and changed back into his clothes, the edge of the cocaine had worn off. He was still clenching his jaw every thirty seconds, and his heart rate was above normal, but he was no longer thinking in double time. They'd given him a sandwich.

When Dr. Hernandez came in twenty minutes later, she handed him a CD. "Thought you might like to have this," she said. "FMRI images of succeeding slices of your brain."

"My brain on drugs," Corderoy said.

"That's right."

"When is my next appointment?"

Dr. Hernandez gave an inaudible sigh. "Dr. Bradley and I have to discuss the results of this visit before we schedule another. You'll hear from us in the next week or so."

Outside, he walked toward the T. Would they call him back? He'd fucked up, being so difficult with their questions. And why did he have to ask about Holmes and the Seven-Per-Cent solution? A damn fool thing to do. No, they weren't going to call him back. Which meant he'd have to find something else to do each day, when Mani thought he was hard at work, earning his degree.

———

When Corderoy walked in the door, Mani was holding a small brush and worrying the curling loop of a palm frond in the corner of a paint-ing. "How was class?" she asked over her shoulder.

"Good. Good. Plath, you know." He wanted to sound excited, but the comedown had hit him so hard that the world felt muted. He slumped down onto her mattress. "Take a break," he said.

Mani turned and set her brush down. "Chinese food?" She wiped her hands on her paint-splattered jeans and leaned dangerously close over Corderoy to reach for her phone on the windowsill.

They ate their kung pao chicken and vegetable moo shu sitting up in Mani's bed, watching old episodes of *Buffy the Vampire Slayer* on her laptop. This was more or less what they'd done for the past week, although it wasn't always Chinese food, and it wasn't always *Buffy*. It was always three to five beers, maybe some whiskey, and then a shoul-der rub—but that was all. This time, though, after working the knots out of Mani's neck, Corderoy ventured a hand onto her upper thigh; he kissed her behind the ear.

It took all of two minutes for them to get completely naked.

Mani had climbed on top of him, but she pulled back and said, "Do you have a condom?"

Corderoy shook his head.

She slumped, but her weight was still pressed against his erect penis. "We shouldn't, right?" she said.

"Yeah," Corderoy said. "We shouldn't."

So they did. Mani came with controlled violence, curling her pelvis into him like she was sanding a piece of wood, and as she breathed against his neck, Corderoy lost control, pulled out abruptly, and ejacu-lated on his stomach.

She lay back on the mattress next to him, breathing fast. Corderoy stared at the peeling paint on the studio ceiling, his chest rising rapidly in time with hers, his hand resting again on her upper thigh.

"You pulled out in time, right?"

"I think so, yeah."

"You think—"

"Yes, I did. We're fine."

"You know," Mani said, "this doesn't—"

"I know," Corderoy said. "You want to sleep head to toe again?"

"Shut up," Mani said. And they went to sleep naked, spooning for warmth in the drafty airspace of her loft.

47

There is no definitive moment when two people become a couple. Elements of intimacy accumulate, and what makes a couple a couple is the gradual recognition of this accumulated intimacy. In the weeks since Corderoy had moved in with Mani, they had fallen into a rhythm: Mani hated doing dishes and Corderoy loathed taking out the trash, so a symbiosis had developed around these household chores; Corderoy left during the days (for "school") and Mani painted; Mani rolled joints, Corderoy cracked beers. And though the idea that they were nothing more than intimate friends was becoming a fiction, they had yet to admit it to themselves. Without that critical admission, they were not a couple, but merely two people who lived together, ate together, traded chores, fucked each other, and each night left their bodies, vulnerable and asleep, in the shared space of a single bed.

Until you find a place, Mani had said. And she had meant it at the time. Whether she still did or not, Corderoy wasn't sure. He hoped not, but that hope was fragile, bearing the weight of his conviction that he deserved nothing from her, not even a smile. It was a hope that would collapse immediately if Mani thought for a second that he was leeching off her. There was no way she'd let him stay, given the fact that he'd left her on the street, if he wasn't contributing. He needed money. He hadn't been called back for the cocaine study. He'd donated blood once, but that was only fifty dollars. He needed a miracle, and he found one.

Do You Have What It Takes to Be a California Cryobank Sperm

Donor? Corderoy went through the checklist on the pamphlet. He was *at least 5'9".* He was *between 19 and 38 years old.* He *already held a bachelor's degree.* He was *in good health.* And he was *legally allowed to work in the US.* Yes. Of course he had what it fucking took. How hard could it be? And for a hundred dollars per donation, up to three times a week! You could give blood only once every two months. Plasma, twice a week, but at only twenty bucks a pop. And it left your arm bruised and tender.

Comparatively, this was the jackpot. Three hundred bucks a week for whacking it into a cup! He did that anyway, minus the cup. It was a stroke of luck that he'd come across this pamphlet, splayed on the cement in front of the CVS. The thought of millions of little Corderoys swimming their way through the world was, if anything, pleasing. Better his seed than some other idiot's. And if some kid approached him eighteen years later?

You're my father.

No, your mom was my customer. I sold her the seed—through a middleman, of course—and she grew a plant. And that's you. Glad to be of service.

But—

Come back anytime, kid, if you need more seed—but cash on the barrelhead! Now get lost.

He called and made an appointment.

———

The California Cryobank was located on the ground floor of the large red-brick Bay Square condominium building. Six or seven floors above, large multibalconied condos with spired roofs looked over Central Square. It was ten a.m. on Monday morning, a rare sunny day in late February, almost T-shirt weather; both car and foot traffic were light, and birds chirped in the barren birch trees, exactly as you would expect.

Inside, the receptionist handed Corderoy a clipboard with a stack of forms to sign. He sat down and began reading:

The quality of our donors is the foundation of our service, with less than 1% of all applicants making it through the selection process. Potential donors are subjected to an extensive medical, genetic, and psychological blah blah

He stopped reading, flipped the page, and signed. His sample, according to the next form, would be tested for *sperm count, motility, progression, morphology, and freezing traits.* Flip, sign, flip, sign, sign, initial, sign. *Compensation will not be provided for this specimen as it is used only for analysis.* Balls. Sign.

After handing the sheaf across the counter, Corderoy was conducted through the security door down a hallway and into a room about the size of most doctors' examination rooms. The solid metal door clicked shut behind him. He turned the lock and felt the heavy bolt slide into place, then he surveyed the room. There were the usual pastel prints of plants and lakes on the wall. In the center of the room, a green pleather chair. Next to it, a sink with hand soap and a paper towel dispenser. The only giveaway that this was a masturbatorium was the large cabinet in the corner with a TV, a DVD player, and stacks of DVDs and magazines. He set down the collection cup he'd been given, then shuffled through the DVDs. *Score Island, Latin Sexfiesta, Sorority Sluts 5 . . .*

He was accustomed to short preview clips and freebies on the Internet. Actual porn *movies?* He didn't want to have to fast-forward through ridiculous plots to get to the good stuff. And the thought that someone passing in the hallway might hear the moans and genital sloshings and flappings. He would have to do this the old-fashioned way.

He picked up a stack of magazines: *Club, Penthouse, Playboy, Juggs, Leg Show, Naughty Neighbors, Asian Fever.* He flipped through *Penthouse.* How many other donors had held this rag in their hairy palms? None of the featured sections aroused his interest, and soon he had reached the end of the official content, leaving only pages and pages of advertisements. It brought him back to his first pornographic magazine.

He'd found it half covered in a pile of leaves near a park bench somewhere in New York City while on a family vacation when he was fourteen. He'd rolled it up and tucked it next to his hip, cinching his belt tight enough to keep it from slipping down his leg. He walked around all day like that, several times claiming an injured ankle. His mother very nearly got him into a doctor's office.

The best stuff in the magazine had been the advertisements for 900

numbers in the back. Variety! Lesbians, spankings, blow jobs, orgies—
it was all there, small but plentiful, a cornucopia of options. It never
bothered him that some homeless guy had probably jerked off on that
park bench while holding the same glossy pages. Why did it bother
him now? Perhaps that was the power of one's first pornographic possession—all previous owners were erased.

Corderoy's dick was in his hand, but it was half-limp. He had to concentrate. He found a suitable image of a black-haired girl licking the
head of a penis and struggled toward completion, readying the sample
cup in his left hand. But the magazine kept slipping off his leg, and he
had to downshift, readjust, and begin accelerating again. After two failed
attempts, he managed to dribble a small pool into the collection cup. It
certainly wasn't porn-star volume, but he really had no idea what a typical volume of ejaculate was. He'd have to look it up when he got home.

Out at the desk, he hesitantly handed the cup to one of the nurses.
They were wearing gloves, but the cup was warm, and they would feel
that. Then again, they must be used to warm cups.

The receptionist thanked him, handed him a pamphlet that
described the next phase of the process, and told him he'd hear back
soon. On his walk home, he flipped through it. It seemed to be for prospective buyers. Rich infertile couples. They must have handed him
the wrong pamphlet. There was a list of information one could acquire
from different donors, for a price:

Short Donor Profile	FREE
Staff Impressions Report	FREE
Donor Essay	FREE
Facial Features Report	$15
Long Donor Profile	$17
Keirsey Report	$19
Donor Baby Photo	$24
Donor Audio Interview	$30
Handwriting Analysis	$25

They'd been analyzing his handwriting? Writing down their impres-
sions of him? He didn't remember reading that on the consent forms,

but he had skimmed them. He looked down at his clothes. There was a burrito stain on his T-shirt. From last week.

Mani was sitting near the window, smoking next to an overstuffed ashtray, when Corderoy walked through the door.

"You okay?" he asked.

"Fine," she said.

"You look, I don't know."

"Late? Because I'm late."

"For what?"

He was clueless. She leaned forward and raised her eyebrows. "Late."

"Oh . . . late."

"Yeah. Late."

"So we get a pregnancy test."

"Will you do it? I can't leave the house right now."

"Why not?"

"Hal."

"Okay. I'm sure it's nothing. I'll run down to CVS."

He left and she inhaled the last quarter inch of her hand-rolled cigarette, burning her fingers. It was probably nothing. It was nothing last time. Maybe it would always be nothing.

Corderoy stood in an aisle of drugs, under fluorescent lights, soft Muzak bleeding from everywhere and nowhere, examining box after box after box, each claiming to be 99 percent accurate, easy to use, and better than the tests in all the other boxes, each doing exactly the same thing.

He didn't have a great track record at avoiding pregnancy. He'd split the cost of Plan B several times with his college girlfriend. Worse, he'd knocked up his high school girlfriend despite regular condom use. And he'd thought long and hard about what to say to her: *I want you to know that whatever happens, I respect your decision and I'll be here in whatever capacity you need me to be. That said, I also want you to know that I think it's in everyone's best interest, yours, mine, the potential child's, to not go through with it. We're broke, inexperienced, and we'd make great parents someday, but now's not that day. It's your decision. And I'll live by it. I mean that, I'm here for you, blah blah blah.* He found out later that half his friends had given nearly identical speeches to distraught girlfriends at one time or another. Corderoy liked to believe that he would have kept his word and been the best father he could have been. His high school girlfriend ended up miscarrying.

The cheapest option was the CVS-brand pregnancy test for nine dollars. It made identical claims to the leading brands, Clearblue and First Response. Clearblue was fifteen dollars for the standard version. A stick that you pee on. A plus sign in the presence of hCG (human chorionic gonadotropin). Though the CVS brand was nearly identical, he didn't want to walk back into that apartment and hand Mani an off-brand test. This wasn't a thing you were allowed to skimp on. But which Clearblue? There were several varieties. The digital version (more than twice as expensive) boasted extreme ease of use. No symbols or lines to read. It provided the results in words: *Pregnant* or *Not Pregnant*. P or not P. It was a logical proposition with a simple truth table.

Pregnant	Not Pregnant
True	False
False	True

But it could easily be more complicated, depending on the truth value of P→A (If "Pregnant" then "Abortion") and of the corresponding truth value of "Happy."

Pregnant	Not Pregnant	P→A	Birth	Happy
True	False	True	False	True
True	False	False	True	False
False	True	True	False	True
False	True	False	False	True

But he could just as easily imagine the same truth table with reversed H values.

Pregnant	Not Pregnant	P→A	Birth	Happy
True	False	True	False	False
True	False	False	True	True
False	True	True	False	False
False	True	False	False	False

The problem here was that given P or –P, and hence B or –B, he was arriving at both H and –H. Therefore, by reductio ad absurdum, he ought to infer –P. That meant he didn't even need to buy a test. By the law of noncontradiction, there was logically no way that Mani was pregnant. The only scenario for which he could imagine a definitive H value was if Pregnant was false and Birth true, which made sense only when you were talking about Mary mother of God, the virgin birth, the virgin abortion. Corderoy's head hurt.

He chose the standard nondigital Clearblue test. He pretended to be checking a text message as the cashier rang him up.

"Well, what does it say?" Corderoy asked through the door.

Mani often peed with the door open, knowing Corderoy wouldn't care. But this wasn't just peeing. It was peeing with additional hardware, and she'd opted for privacy. "I don't know," she said. "It's like half a line or something."

"Pee on it more."

"I'm out of pee," Mani said.

"You're just not forcing it out," Corderoy said. A minute passed. Corderoy heard some tinkling. "Mani?" Another minute.

The door opened. She held the plastic strip up, her face expressionless. There was a big plus sign in the test window. "I'll just get rid of it," she said.

"Whoa. Okay. Have you done that before?"

"What? No!"

"Sorry."

"That's the best thing to do, right?"

"Definitely."

And it went on like that for a half an hour. Mani sitting in bed, her legs tucked into her arms, Corderoy sitting on the edge of the bed. He didn't have to convince her. She had convinced herself, but for some reason, they both felt compelled to reiterate what a correct decision it was, how obviously right they were to make it, how it was not only the best choice but the only choice, right? Right, of course. Do you even have to ask?

48

Mani spent the next week not painting and not smoking cigarettes and not drinking and not smoking weed and not calling Planned Parenthood. Corderoy left for "school" during the days, so she had prodigious blocks of time in which to do nothing. She couldn't even watch TV. She could only think about what she wasn't doing. The many things she wasn't doing. Which included writing a letter to her Wartime Husband. She could do that. She should.

It was an incredible feat of will to climb out of bed and grab a sheet of paper and a pen, but once she had written *Dear Mickey* at the top of the page, the words came freely.

Dear Mickey,

I suddenly find myself with child. I never understood that phrase until now. It's so honest and blameless, that "with." It's not heavy like "pregnant" or crass like "knocked up." It has none of the hand-wringing denial of "I'm three weeks late." Late for what? "With child." It has weight without judgment. It's a soft and full acknowledgment of fact.

You know who the father is. I make myself say that to remember gravity. It's so easy to go walking on the moon when you have life-altering decisions to make on earth. And there's really only one option. Right? The pros of doing it are great, the cons of not doing it are enormous. I'm sure at some point you gave some girl the speech that all boys think we've never heard before, the speech we start giving ourselves in our own heads—on continuous loop—the moment we find out.

I don't know exactly why I'm writing you, Wartime Husband, except that it seems like a thing you should know. I'm not asking for advice. The whole thing will be over by the time you even get this letter. And so it seems a little fucked up to send it to you. I don't want to freak you out or give you extra things to worry about. Maybe writing to you is like flipping a coin. That always helps me make decisions. Not because it tells me what to do, taking away the burden of thinking it through, but because it helps me figure out how I really feel once some outside force pressures me to act one way or another. So, I'm going to the clinic soon. Can you imagine what it feels like to write those words to you right now? I hope you can. I hope you're safe. Thanks for being my coin.

xoxo

mani

Less than a day after sending the letter, things began to crystallize inside her psyche, and not in the way she had expected. She began to imagine ways it could all work out. Hal's parents had some money. So did her own. They could help. Who knew what artistic and personal wisdoms she would gain from bringing a life into the world? There would still be time to paint. With babysitters. *Baby.* She said that word and it sounded so warm, so vulnerable and worth protecting. She remembered that moment in the hospital, her need for morphine, her fear of what it might harm. Baby. A small portrait of herself and Hal together. She was confused and excited about her confusion, and it was overheating her. For the first time in days, she needed to move, to really move.

It was the last day of February and the air was cold and empty of life. The people on the street shambled like animatronic piles of scarves and gloves and coats. Mani cruised past them on her bicycle, wearing only a light jacket, unzipped, letting the violent air caress her. She had been angry that her own biology could trap her in such a way, limiting her future options. She had wanted to rebel against that. But now she was beginning to feel that it was her culture, her friends, her family, her ambitions that were limiting her future options. Raising a child would give her energy, it would redefine time, it would become her art. And wouldn't that be the true act of rebellion, to say: *Fuck it! I know it's not practical, I know the world doesn't need another ego, but I'm doing it anyway. And I will love that thing and the person it will become and it will make me an immeasurably wiser, kinder, better human.* A baby was, perhaps, the biggest opportunity she would ever have. How could she so easily pass it up?

Her fingers felt like brittle and useless twigs as she tried to lock her bike up to a pole on Brighton Avenue, across the street from her loft. When she stood up, she breathed hot air onto her fingers and found herself staring into the window of the local dive bar, the Silhouette Lounge. And there, past the Sam Adams sign and the Bruins logo, there was Hal, playing Big Buck Hunter. She went inside.

He had just finished his game and he plopped down at a table, seemingly unaware that Mani was standing ten feet away. He had a tallboy PBR in his hand and several empties on the table. It was five p.m.

"Hello?" Mani said.

"Hey!" Corderoy exclaimed. "You want a drink?"

"What are you doing here?" Mani asked. "I thought you didn't get out of class until five-thirty." She noticed that he had a bandage in the crook of his left elbow. He looked pale. "Did you give blood or something?"

"Plasma. What are you having? I'm buying."

"We need to talk."

"Let's talk."

Mani looked around the bar. It wasn't a dive so much as a wreck. There were a few sullen construction-worker types at the bar top. Some hipsters playing pool, darts. Megadeth was on just loud enough to be annoying. "No," she said. "Let's go back to the apartment."

"I'm half-full here," Corderoy said, taking a swig of beer.

Mani gave a weary grunt, then sat down across from him. She took a moment to compose herself. "I've been thinking a lot about this," she said.

"About what?"

She stared at him, unblinking.

"When is the appointment?"

"I didn't make it yet."

"What?"

"I will. I just want to be sure. Consider every option."

"We did that already."

"My parents have some money. So do yours, right? And I have money from the Army, through Mickey. It would be tough, but I think we could do it."

"I don't want Mickey's money," Corderoy said. "And my parents are broke. And you know what it would do to our lives. You think you'll have time to paint?"

"We could figure out sitters or something."

"You think I'll have time to study once I go back?"

"Go back where?"

"I mean." Corderoy chugged the rest of his PBR. "I dropped out," he said.

"What?"

"But I'm gonna go back. I just need to earn some money—my parents can't help with tuition anymore."

"What the fuck! Where do you go every day?"

Corderoy looked down at the bandage on his arm. "I've been doing medical studies."

"That's your plan?"

"Well, it sucks to be stuck with needles and shit, and the pay is inconsistent, but I could make three hundred dollars a week as a sperm donor. I'm waiting to hear back about my sample."

"What is wrong with you?"

Corderoy looked like a teenager called on unexpectedly in English class. "Nothing . . . I hope?"

"You didn't think that was something you should tell me?"

"I didn't think—"

"Yeah, you didn't think." Mani swiped his empty cans off the table and left. Corderoy stood to follow her but stopped himself and thudded back into his seat. There was a way to fix all this. There had to be, he just had to think harder, a lot harder, and maybe drink a few more beers.

Corderoy stumbled in an hour later after taking a brisk and coat-less walk down to the Charles. Mani was standing in the middle of the room, facing the door, like a villain in an action movie. *I've been expecting you. Prepare to die.*

"Maybe it would be," Corderoy said. "Good, to have it."

Her face softened. "What makes you say that?"

"Sometimes you just have to jump in the river with your clothes on," he said.

Mani cocked her head at him.

"You know, when you don't know what to do. You might as well go big, do something drastic. At least it will be exciting."

"And then what. Raise it? Adoption?"

Corderoy shrugged. "Do we have to figure that part out now?"

"I should call," she said. "I'm calling."

"Sit down," Corderoy said. And he went over to her bed and patted the mattress next to him. She slumped over and joined him.

"Is that what you want?" he said.

"Fuck," she said softly, lying back on the bed.

"Fuck," he said, lying down next to her.

"How can you know?" she said.

"Me?"

"Not you, the general you."

"So, you."

"Yes. Me. How can I know if I want to go through with it until I'm going through with it?"

"You can't, I guess."

Mani sighed.

"But you can always walk out."

"Can I?"

"Why not? Talk to the doctor, see how comfortable you are in that room. And if you're in that chair or whatever and you want to leave, just get up and walk out."

"I can't figure out which choice is more exciting," she said.

"Maybe that means you're lucky?"

49

The waiting room at the Planned Parenthood had light blue walls, blue chairs, blue Kleenex boxes. Mani squeezed Corderoy's hand, hard and rhythmically. Across the room from them were two other women, sitting several seats apart. One looked like a middle-aged career woman in her dressy pantsuit. The other was a teenager who looked bored. Corderoy thought that perhaps it was a defense mechanism, an unwillingness to face the fear and uncertainty of what this room represented.

"Are you okay?" he whispered. "Do you need some water or anything?"

Mani squeezed his hand again. "I'm okay," she said.

A door opened and a woman said, "Ms. Saheli?"

Mani stood, still holding Corderoy's hand.

"I'll be right here," he said. "Just get up and walk out if you need to."

Mani nodded and followed the woman in back.

There was a rack of pamphlets on the end table, and Corderoy plucked out the one that said, *Thinking about getting a vasectomy?*

Apparently he could get one for as little as three hundred dollars. The amount he'd be paid for a donation at the sperm bank. The awkwardness of the donation process had faded in the last week, and Corderoy had found himself getting strangely excited about being a donor. This was due largely to the fact that his waking and his sleeping thoughts had been sucked into the vortex of Mani's pregnancy, and perhaps partially because, for a sense of balance, one act of destruction suggested an act of creation. And here he was, waiting for Mani to emerge unburdened. So why not donate? He wasn't perfect, but he had desirable traits. He was even wearing a clean shirt today. They could analyze his handwriting all they wanted; he had nothing to hide. He hadn't understood earlier why they called it a donation if you were getting paid, but it was clear to him now—it was an act of charity, potentially helping some infertile couple to conceive. It felt good.

The door swung open and the older woman was called in; he had an odd feeling of envy, like he was sitting in coach near enough to first class to catch a glimpse of their luxury when the flight attendant passed through the curtain. Of course, it wasn't luxury behind that door. Or if it was, it was the luxury of being burdened with weighty moral decisions. He had nothing important to decide. There was nothing he could do that would damn him, nothing that would bless him.

Mani was led to a small room where she was instructed to remove her clothing and put on a paper slit-backed robe. She felt embarrassed getting naked under the fluorescent light, so she did it quickly, then climbed up on the examination table, feeling her thighs stick to the parchment paper. And she waited. She counted out a minute. Another. She reached for a pamphlet on the counter next to the table and flipped through it. It was a description of the vacuum aspiration procedure.

> Once the cervix has been numbed and dilated, a sterile cannula is inserted into the uterus and attached to an electric pump. The pump creates a vacuum which empties the uterine contents.
>
> After the procedure, the tissue removed is examined. Expected contents include the embryo or fetus as well as the decidua, chorionic villi, amniotic fluid, amniotic membrane, and other tissue.

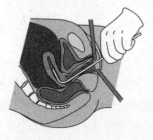

There was a clinical diagram of the cannula being inserted into the uterus. Mani was fixating on it when a woman walked in.

"Hi. I'm Vanessa. I'm the head clinician here." She was in her late thirties. Her dark brown hair was pulled back in a ponytail, and she wore tortoiseshell glasses. She was on the heavier side, with a roundish face. Mani thought she looked like someone who could bake a great pie.

"You've read through the pamphlet, I see," the clinician said. "Any questions?"

Mani shook her head. Get up and walk out?

"Are you sure?"

Yes, she was sure. She had no questions. "Will it hurt?" she asked.

"There will likely be some uterine cramping," the clinician said. "But no worse than typical menstrual cramps. We'll apply a local anesthetic to your cervix, so there won't be any direct pain from contact with the speculum or dilators."

"How long does it take?"

"No more than fifteen minutes. But we ask you to wait in our recovery area for a while afterward."

Get up and walk out?

"Are you ready to begin?"

Mani nodded.

"Okay, lean back on the table and put your legs in the stirrups."

Mani lay back and stared at the perforated ceiling while the clinician took the metal speculum and ran it under warm water to heat it up. She tried to conjure the diagram from the pamphlet, but it had become an abstract jumble of colors in her mind.

The clinician turned the water off and began applying grease to the speculum. Get up and walk out? Mani felt the metal slip into her, widen her.

"I'm applying the anesthetic now," the clinician said. Get up.

"Okay," Mani said. And something snaked its way into her, past the metal clamps, and stabbed at her soft and untouched inside, piercing until it began tingling outward. Walk out of here.

She was no longer seeing the diagram—it had become a flower, or a dancer, or an explosion. Get up and walk out.

"We'll give that a minute to take effect," the clinician said.

"I'm going to dilate your cervix now," the clinician said. "You'll feel this a bit, but it shouldn't hurt." Walk out.

"Halfway there," the clinician said. "All we have to do now—"

"I don't need to know everything," Mani said. I'm getting up and walking out. Okay?

"Okay, just let me know if you have any concerns."
And then something hooked its way to her hollow.

Her hollow, which was a mushroom cloud. The pump wheezed to life and Mani got up and walked out as the vacuum collapsed her dimensions, drawing everything in, her center buckling with cramps, a system-wide dry-heaving that moved up through her chest and into her head, where her consciousness imploded.

But she was fine, for she had gotten up and walked out. She wasn't even here. She was nowhere. There was a black tear in the fabric of the universe and she had slipped through it to a place of uncompromising silence.

"All done," the clinician said.

Corderoy sat in the waiting room, tapping his foot, angling his neck to look through the small vertical slit of a window in the door to the back area, as if that would allow him to see Mani. His phone rang. Unknown number.

"Hello," he said quietly.

"Hi, this is Melissa calling from California Cryobank. I'm calling for Halifax Corderoy."

"Speaking."

"Mr. Corderoy, I regret to inform you that your donor application has been declined, as your sample does not meet our needs at present. We thank you for your interest in California Cryobank."

"What do you mean, *does not meet your needs*?"

"We do not disclose that information. I apologize."

"Does that . . ." Shit. Did he have a low sperm count? Poor motility? That couldn't be it, or he wouldn't be in Planned Parenthood right now.

"Mr. Corderoy?"

"Hi, sorry. Do I have an STD? I mean, if I did, you'd tell me, right?"

"Yes."

"I have an STD? What is it?"

"Yes, I would tell you, Mr. Corderoy. You do not."

"Great."

"Have a nice day."

"Thanks."

So he wasn't HIV-positive or syphilitic. He was just deficient for completely natural reasons. Good to know.

When Mani walked back into the waiting room, she looked nauseated and defeated. Corderoy assumed she had gone through with it. It had been almost forty-five minutes. But *Did you?* didn't seem like a good question to ask right then. He grabbed Mani's bag, held the door for her, and they walked out into the cold.

————

Mani spent the next few days in bed with a heat pad, both because of the cramps and because of a general spiritual malaise. They hadn't talked about her experience in the clinic, and they were operating under the tacit agreement that everything was fine, that Mani was completely capable, both physically and emotionally, of helping herself. Corderoy took care of her as if she were an aging matriarch, which meant he excused the helpful things he did as mere acts of convenience; Mani could have gotten her own cup of tea, but if Corderoy was just about to make some for himself anyway, well, it was no trouble to pour a second cup.

Getting *it* taken care of hadn't solved anything. Corderoy didn't want to leave, and Mani didn't want him to, either, but he thought she did, and she feared he wanted to. It was probably best to air the place out, anyway. So Corderoy started looking for solutions. The most immediate one was liquor. He brought home a handle of Jim Beam. Then he turned to Craigslist. He spent two drunken days looking for jobs, trying not to let it bother him when Mani declined a pour, when she asked how many drinks he'd had that day. He didn't find a job, but he did find a solution: two thousand dollars for a two-week inpatient sleep study at Mass General Hospital.

He would live in a small windowless room for two weeks, doctors and scientists observing his routines, and when he emerged, well—it would be later, and hopefully he and Mani would have a real talk about everything that needed talking about. He showed her the advertisement.

"It says here you won't be able to consume any substances. No caffeine, no nicotine, no alcohol."

"I think I could use a detox anyway," Corderoy said.

"Maybe that would be best."

"So I should do it?"

"I didn't say that."

If he couldn't start making his own decisions, he'd drink himself to death. "I think I'll do it," he said.

"Okay."

"Will you miss me?" he said.

She had to start protecting herself. "I don't know," she said.

"Let's find out."

SLEEP

SUBJECTIVE STUDY RECORD, PARTICIPANT H. CORDEROY

———

Day 1 of my captivity.

I counted out a minute, then five, then ten, and then an hour, letting my body get a sense of that time, trying to incorporate the span of a day into the rhythms of my viscera. But there are no windows. The lights are kept dim and steady. White walls. A white bathroom. A white metal door, the hospital kind with the handle lower than you expect. There is no TV, no bookshelf. There is a small desk with a computer, but it only turns on when they activate it from somewhere outside the room. And then it is locked into the testing program. A camera watches me from the upper-right corner. My clothes are in storage. There is no clock.

I entered the room at eight a.m. and have eaten two meals since then. Good, as far as hospital food goes. After each, they had me fill a cup with urine, and after the second, they drew blood. The first meal consisted of a dinner roll, slice of ham, steamed broccoli, hash browns, apple, small milk. The second meal: biscuit, sausage, steamed carrots, mashed potatoes, apple, small milk. I don't like milk, so I didn't drink it the first time. I told them not to bring it again, but they did anyway. I tried to save the apple for later; they said I had to eat it now. I'm beginning to suspect they design each meal to contain the same basic ingredients but in varied forms, and that these ingredients are specifically chosen so the meals cannot be identified as breakfast, lunch, or dinner. Hard to complain, though. I've lived on ramen and beer for weeks at a time.

I'm reminded of the beginning of Robinson Crusoe's journal. I must have read that book a dozen times when I was a kid. Something like, *September, 1659. I, poor miserable Robinson Crusoe, being shipwrecked in a dreadful storm, came on shore on this dismal island, the rest of the ship's company drowned. In despair of any relief, I saw noth-*

ing but death before me. Only Crusoe's journal was voluntary—I write because they tell me to write. Though I did volunteer for the study, so I guess that means I've shipwrecked myself. Which is kind of what Defoe did in choosing to inhabit that character. Right? Maybe I'm talking out my ass.

————

Day 2 of my captivity.

Garret's voice on the intercom. *Test time, Hal.* So I get out of bed and sit down at the computer. Today's test is the same as yesterday's. They call it the PVT—the psychomotor vigilance task. Basically, the screen is black and every few seconds a small white light flashes in the middle, about the size of an icon. And I have to press the space bar right when it happens. It is so fucking boring. I guess they're trying to quantify my sleepiness by reaction time or something. Garret calls me to the computer for a ten-to-fifteen-minute session once every hour or two. You're probably going to read this, aren't you, Garret?

Garret is kind of a dick—he's about my age, grad student at MIT, studying computational psychology, which I guess means he's on his way to some combination of computer programmer and neuroscientist. Garret was the guy I first talked to on the phone. He said they'd be looking at genes linked with circadian rhythms to see if they're different for early birds and night owls. And to make sure there are no other factors, I had to abstain from all foreign substances. No caffeine, no nicotine, no prescription drugs, no over-the-counter, no "street drugs," no vitamins. No alcohol. One day and I already feel off balance, chemically vacant.

Last night—already that doesn't sound right—just before the first sleep time, Garret came in with one of the nurses, and they said it would be lights-out in five minutes—they ordain when to sleep, when to wake, when to shower, when to eat—and so they had to connect me to the EEG. They put on the electrode cap and began poking through it with wooden sticks, scraping the dead skin cells from my scalp and pulling my hair out of the way. Then they squeezed in this weird gel. It's like having nineteen ticks attached to your scalp, slowly engorging themselves. And they expect me to sleep this way. I wasn't tired. I wanted to keep reading *Endurance*. They allowed me a single book and that's what I brought, figuring it would be appropriate when isolated in a white room. But they wouldn't let me read. It was lights-out. I lay there with those wires coming out of my head until my body figured out how to shut itself off without the help of booze.

———

Day 3 of my captivity.

Get up, Hal. It's shower time. Shower time seems irregularly spaced. I tried to expect it the first two days, but I've given up on that. It reminds me of when my dad used to wake me up for school in junior high. I was never ready. I'd turn the shower on, lie down in the tub, and get fifteen more minutes of sleep.

Garret came in a little later, after the first round of tests for the day. He was reeking of cigarettes and I wanted one so bad. He stood above me while I sat at the computer, explaining the day's test, and his breath washed over me with the smell of used-up nicotine.

When Garret left, they brought in my meal: blueberry muffin, lemon chicken, peas, sweet potatoes, apple, small milk. WTF? I'm sure they're keeping a record of what I choose to eat and how much I eat. I know they're paying me, and they're all really nice, mostly, but I feel angry. I want to screw up the experiment. I ate the blueberry muffin and the chicken, didn't touch the rest. What do you make of that, Garret?

———

Day 4 of my captivity.

The test is different today. The screen has a constant parade of random capital letters moving from right to left,

←KUSOCIGHQISKDEBHC [S] XPTLFKRFHGASLQIRP←

and I have to hit the space bar every time an *S* passes through the brackets in the center. This goes on for fifteen minutes. I want to just hit the space bar randomly, but I feel this stupid need to score well.

At least the tests, which happen eight to ten times a day, feel like work. Work I can deal with. But after twenty-odd years of eating food, I've come to associate it with relaxation and enjoyment. So you can imagine how frustrating it is that the meals take on this same repetitive tasklike quality. After days of the same basic things switched around— bread, meat, veggie, starch—I've found myself combining the food in strange ways. Today's meal: toast with jam, scoop of tuna salad, pickled beets, oatmeal, apple, small milk. I slid the beets over the lip of the tray trough and into the oatmeal. I spread the tuna on the jammed toast. That was quite good, actually—reminded me of a cranberry turkey sandwich. The beets in oatmeal were harder to swallow but interesting—the creaminess of the oatmeal and the sugar seemed to repel the flavor of the vinegary, salty beets. I took one bite of the apple. I didn't touch the milk.

When Shackleton's ship was crushed by the pack ice, and they were stranded on the featureless white floes of the Antarctic, they ate meals of bannock and seal hoosh, whatever those are. They were each rationed a cube of sugar, a mug of powdered milk. Once, they ate dog pemmican, baked beans, canned cauliflower, and beets cooked together in an empty gasoline can.

———

Day 5 of my captivity.

Wake. Shower. Test. Eat. I wrote about my day, Garret!

———

Day 6 of my captivity.

Didn't sleep well last sleep time. I had finally adjusted to the EEG cap prickling my scalp. But I started thinking about my brain waves being recorded, and then I thought, My brain waves must be different when I'm waking and when I'm sleeping, and do they change depending on what I'm thinking about and how hard I'm thinking? And if I'm thinking about my own brain waves, will that throw the electroencephalograph into some sort of recursive feedback loop until the machine explodes?

The lights went back up sometime later. I took out *Endurance* and tried reading. I've been going through it slowly, rereading paragraphs, even whole chapters sometimes, lingering, savoring the experience of that world. It's my only book in here and it feels like the last book in the universe. The waking-period light is sufficient for reading but not comfortably so. It's never bright, never like sunlight or even like cafeteria lighting. More like restaurant lighting at dinnertime, soft yellow, never energizing or oppressive—like twilight—that hour of the day when you can't tell if it's just after dawn or just before sundown. As Lansing describes it, *a hazy, deceiving half-light remained . . . But it was difficult to perceive distances. Even the ice underfoot grew strangely indistinct so that walking became hazardous.*

But I found a way, Garret. I found a way to tell the time. You came in late in the waking period—shoulders slouched, eyelids a quarter closed, hair mussed, strong cologne covering a hint of booze—a hungover dude if I've ever seen one. It must be late morning. Out in the real world. In Boston, where Mani is. Which means it must be late afternoon, I think, in Baghdad.

———

Day 7 of my captivity.

Wasn't hungry today, but found myself craving milk for the first time in my life. I took a bite of my dinner roll and washed it down with 2 percent. It was so cold I had to stop halfway through the carton. I wiped the milk off my mustache and realized how long it was, projecting out over my lip like an awning. I haven't trimmed my beard in over a week. There are no mirrors in here. I finished the milk in one long series of gulps. The sliminess, stickiness of it in the back of the throat.

They took the tray away and I saw Garret note something down on his clipboard. He left, and a minute or two later, his voice on the intercom announced that it was test time. But I couldn't focus. Mani drinks milk. Not like her cereal milk, or dipping cookies or anything, but she'll just pour herself a glass of milk. I never understood it before. But I do now. I think it reminds you that you're human—the way it lingers in your esophagus, it makes you conscious of the whole process, the fact of your biology.

———

Day 8–9 of my captivity.

I've been up for who knows how many hours. This is the part Garret warned me about—a double-length waking period. I can't leave the bed. The lights are on. They stay on. The room is hazy and featureless and everything is white. Even I'm white. I was already vitamin D–deficient.

They put the computer on a wheeled cart and brought it next to the bed. I sit here with the keyboard on my lap, waiting for the letter *S*, waiting for the flashing light. My scalp is wired and itching and wet. I make my way slowly through *Endurance*. *One looks forward to meals, not for what one will get, but as definite breaks in the day. All around us we have day after day the same unbroken whiteness, unrelieved by anything at all.* I picked the right fucking book. The same apple, the same milk, dinner roll, slice of ham, steamed carrots. I've had five meals already, which means, I think, that I might get to sleep soon.

I need to sleep soon. I can't take any more tests. My legs ache. Bedsores? I've begun counting again, like on day 1. *A tally sheet of infinity. Every individual minute had to be noted, then lived through and finally checked off. There was not even a crisis to relieve the tortured monotony.*

Have had my last meal—I think—and they've got to shut the lights off soon. I'm nearly done with *Endurance*. The lights are on. The EEG is reading my brain waves. Writing keeps me awake—sort of. It would be so easy—I've slept under brighter lights than this—to just doze off. Shackleton leaves twenty-two men stranded on Elephant Island and goes for help. He takes the small lifeboat, the *James Caird*, and after crossing seven hundred miles of the deadliest waters on the planet, he and five others arrive at South Georgia. But they arrive on the wrong side of the island. He hasn't slept in days. But there's nothing else to be done. He and two other men prepare to cross the uncrossable glacier that covers South Georgia, riddled with uncharted chasms and crevices. They've only got fifty feet of rope and a carpenter's adze—the woodscrews from their boat extracted and driven through the soles of their tattered boots. And they make it to the top of a crest, but they're exhausted, and night is falling, and if they camp up here they'll freeze to death. And so they slide two thousand feet down and incredibly, they live. And they continue marching, with no time for rest and only small breaks for seal hoosh. And after several wrong turns and hours of wasted exertion, they're very nearly across the island and they've been traveling for over two days without rest. And they are so close to salvation but so near utter ruin.

Almost at once Worsley and Crean fell asleep, and Shackleton, too, caught himself nodding. Suddenly, he jerked his head upright. All the years of Antarctic experience told him that this was the danger sign—the fatal sleep that trails off into freezing death.

———

~~Day 10 of my captivity.~~ *Waking Period 10 of my captivity.*

I cannot describe how soundly I have slept. The dark is gone again and I'm back in the low light of not *day* . . . from now on, I'll use the phrase "waking period."

Meals and tests. A shower. Blood sample. Saliva sample. Urine sample. After giving me the daily alertness questionnaire, Garret sat down to review his notes. I asked how long. He smiled and left.

———

Waking Period 11 of my captivity.

What an invaluable resource this book has been to me. I finished and started over yesterday and am now reading so fast I am almost halfway through it again. *Day after day after day dragged by in a gray, monotonous haze. Each day became so much like the one before that any unusual occurrence, however small, generated enormous interest.* I've taken to observing Garret, and the nurse, Barbara, and any other doctors who come into my room on rare occasions. When people ask, "Who watches the watchers?," why do they always leave out the possibility that the watched can watch as well?

There was a small but strange incident earlier. Barbara was draw-ing my blood after the second meal of the waking period. She's in her mid-thirties, black hair in a bun, wears lots of makeup, smoker's voice, has a big rack. Not really my type, but Mickey would certainly bang her. Garret came in just after she had stuck the syringe into the IV in my right arm. I was holding my book in front of me, but I was actually looking out of the corner of my eye at Garret.

GARRET: (walking in) Hey, how goes it?

NURSE BARBARA: (not turning away from my arm) All right.

GARRET: (affecting a shit-eating grin) He's not giving you any trouble, is he?

NURSE BARBARA: (not turning away from my arm) No.

GARRET: (shit-eating grin disappearing) Oh.

I couldn't believe it. Garret had been trying to flirt. And he'd failed his fucking nuts off. Nurse Barbara finished drawing my blood and left without so much as a word to Garret. Then Garret left, as if his walk-ing into the room had been an innocent mistake. And I was alone. It felt like it should have been test time, or shower time, or mealtime, but it was nothing time. I lay in bed. I thought about picking up *Endur-ance* again. I thought about Mani at Swedish Hospital, unable to move, trapped in the gray monotony of her own unconscious mind. I look back at the person who left her there. He is so desperate for forgive-ness. I wish I could give it to him.

———

W.P. 12 of my captivity.

Had a small breakdown this waking period. I finished *Endurance* again early in the day and couldn't bring myself to flip back to page one a third time. I didn't feel like writing. There was nothing to pass the time but the fucking PVT and meals. Garret's voice on the intercom: *Test time, Hal.* And the PVT had cycled back to the simple flashing light from the initial waking period. See light → hit space bar. See light → hit space bar. I began whapping my thumb down with a slight rotation of my wrist, like how you strike a snare drum, and the causation seemed to flip. Whap! → Light, whap! → Light. I began striking the keyboard harder and the space bar stuck—it didn't pop back up. But the lights went on flashing in their inscrutable pattern—which didn't make any sense, because if my whaps were causing the lights to flash, then how—unless it was like winding a crank engine on an old-timey car, and once you got it going, it just kept on. Even if that was true, they weren't judging me by the efficiency of the motor, but by the rhythms that I turned the crank handle in, and the handle—the space bar—was broken!

So I did what anyone would do in that situation. I freaked the fuck out. I stood up from the PVT, I pulled my hair, Garret's voice on the intercom: *What's wrong, Hal? The test isn't over. Hal?* I went into the shower and turned the water on and stood there with my gown on until Garret came in and shut the water off.

"I've got to get out of this room," I said. "I can't do it anymore. Let me out. Garret, please, let me out." He handed me a towel and stood there while I dried my head. I kept my face against the terry cloth for a good thirty seconds, and when I looked up, Garret was sitting down on top of the toilet lid. He looked up at me at said, "Don't do this, Hal. Please. We've had two other participants quit early." He was earnest and exhausted. "Please," he said. "Please just stick it out, Hal. I need this."

I wanted to ask him why he needed it—if he had to write a paper or something, or if he'd get in trouble with whoever was funding the study, but instead I asked him how many days were left and he said he couldn't tell me but that it wasn't much longer. He left and I lay down on my bed on top of the sheets.

I was wrong about Garret the whole time. He's not an asshole. He's just socially awkward. If he looked like your average dungeon master, it would be obvious that his social skills were lacking, but since he's handsome—curly hair, scraggly beard, a strong jawline—and dresses well, he seems like an elitist dick. But his reserve isn't reserving anything! He's even more socially inept than I am. This realization is oddly comforting, and hopefully it will get me through another battery of PVTs and blood and urine samples and interchangeable meals. It's got to be over soon. Please let it be over soon.

———

W.P. 13 of my captivity.

Another body in the river today. Ho-hum. Meals and tests. How can they expect us to walk through the rubble of this city like ballerinas when we're so bagged down with ammo and armor, which we couldn't even remove if we wanted to. At my easel today, my mind is a riot of color and shape. Substances course through my body. THC. Alcohol. Naproxin. Images bloom on the canvas: Hal in a white room. White sheets, white walls, everything stark. His thoughts taking shape above his wired skull: Mickey, ice floes, explosions, and most prominently, me, the woman stuck in the back of his brain, painting his likeness, half-awake and dreaming.

———

W.P. 14 of my captivity.

I awoke to the slow plucking of wires from my scalp, as I awake every waking period—but it wasn't Nurse Barbara. It was Mani leaning over me, nipping out even through her thick lab coat, carefully removing the engorged ticks and eating them like a monkey. And Mickey came in with his clipboard and said, "Sorry I'm late—you know how it is leaving your mom's house." And he was huge—his arms were as big as my thighs—and he was bald, dog tags the size of playing cards hung down to his sternum. And once the EEG was off, Mani sat cross-legged on the bed and began knitting the wires into a little blanket and Mickey sat me down at the PVT and said, "Test time, Hal." And I worked that PVT like I was pumping the holds of the *Endurance, all night, working with closed eyes, like dead men attached to some evil contrivance which would not let them rest,* and I asked Mickey how I was doing and he said it was all subjective anyway, and Mani was gone, buried in a pile of blanket, pulsing with my brain waves. I could smell it in the air, the world was ending, one second at a time.

50

A wave of nicotine washed over Corderoy's brain. His body was still adjusting to the ball-freezing air of Boston in early March, his eyes still relearning daylight. Mani had rolled him a cigarette. They stamped out their butts on the cobbled walkway of Winthrop Street and ducked into the basement hideaway that was Grendel's Den. Corderoy grabbed a table in the corner and proceeded to wobble it intentionally while Mani took her seat. None of the furniture in the hospital had any wobble to it; how he had missed these imperfections.

"You okay?" she asked.

Corderoy transferred the task of nervous movement to his knee. "Yeah. I like the light in here." There were low incandescents, a little daylight through street-level windows. The waitress came and left with their drink orders.

Corderoy stood abruptly and said, "I think I'm gonna hurl."

He ran to the bathroom, hunched over a toilet, and began dry-heaving.

A minute passed.

His nausea ebbed.

He washed his face.

He felt fine, didn't he? He did.

"Nicotine hit me hard," he said, sitting back down across from Mani.

"What was it like it in there?"

"It was. There were a lot of things it was. But mostly it was lonely."

The waitress returned and set a Tom Collins in front of Mani. In front of Corderoy: a cup of coffee, a glass of milk, and a pint of Guinness. Mani ordered a burger, Corderoy a Reuben. As the waitress left, Corderoy lifted the coffee to his lips and carefully sipped, then slurped, then slugged the whole cup back like a shot. He savored the milk a bit longer, letting the slime linger on his tongue, and when it was drained, he settled into his Guinness, letting the foam froth over his mustache. His facial muscles began twitching from the caffeine.

"You sure you're okay?" Mani said.

Corderoy smiled and gulped down the cold black of his Guinness. "How are you?" he said. "What have you been up to?"

Mani stared at him as if he were an art object, a favorite sculpture she hadn't seen in years. "I finished the last two paintings in the Seuss series," she said. "I have to drop them off at the gallery next Friday."

"That's incredible. Are you excited?"

"They're not good enough yet."

"They never will be."

"The fuck does that mean?"

"You have high standards is all."

"Hal," Mani said, reaching out to touch his arm.

But the waitress returned with their orders, and Mani drew back to make room for the plates.

The waitress left, and Corderoy snatched up his Reuben to take a huge bite. "Hot sauce," he said. "How have I lived without hot sauce?" He half stood, holding the dripping sandwich.

"Sit down, dork," Mani said.

As she walked away, Corderoy followed her ass, the way his eyes sometimes latched on to a railroad tie from the train window.

He was still holding his sandwich when Mani returned. He opened it up and she dashed some Tabasco on it. Corderoy bit in. He chewed and chewed and just kept on chewing that first bite—the meat was fatty and moist and delicious. He barely said a word as he devoured the rest of the sandwich. Mani had eaten only half her burger.

"Did they feed you in there?" she asked.

"Hospital food," Corderoy said. "But hey, can't complain. They paid me two grand. That's enough to put first and last month's on an apartment." He had been waiting to say those exact words and was now carefully observing Mani's reaction.

"It is," Mani said.

Something tiny snuffed out in Corderoy's chest. After a moment, he said, "Where should I look?"

Mani finished off her Tom Collins, then stared enigmatically at him. "Don't look," she said.

"Why not?"

"Right now, I mean. Close your eyes."

Corderoy did so, and the pub became a soundscape of clinking silverware and chaotic chatter, laughter, indie music.

"Open your hand," Mani said.

Corderoy felt the object. It was cold, jagged. It was metal. "Can I look?"

"You can't tell what it is?"

"It's a key," Corderoy said.

Mani said nothing.

Corderoy opened his eyes and found hers, still and attentive.

"I missed you," she said. "But that's not a good enough reason."

"Is there one?"

"Don't know."

"So." He looked down at the key and rubbed it between his fingers like an old coin.

"That key is for tonight."

"And tomorrow?"

"Maybe I change the locks tomorrow."

A weakness rippled through Corderoy's being but quickly passed.

"And maybe I don't," she said. "That's the best I can offer you."

"I fucking love you," he said.

It was dark when they left Grendel's Den. Mani lit up a joint in the alley, and when Corderoy took a hit, his mind bloomed like a bud opening after weeks of night. They made out against the wall for a moment, then stumbled back to what had been Mani's home, what was, for tonight at least, their home.

Corderoy slung his body into what had been Mani's bed—tonight, their bed—and exhaustion clocked him in the head. Mani crawled in beside him and fitted her body against his. His face was numb with oncoming sleep, and his last thought felt like the last thought he would have before his soul—if he had a soul—slipped from the husk of his harrowed body. It was a thought aware of itself as a weed-and-booze quintessence: all of Boston, and his months of floating through grad school, of giving away his blood, his urine, his semen, his sleep—it was a voyage in a lifeboat in the Weddell Sea, dodging floes and slowly dying of thirst, and now, after a winter on the treacherous ice, he'd found solid, unsinkable land, right where he'd left it, land at the end of the known world, a rocky inhospitable island leagues from civilization, but land, immovable, magnificent land. Corderoy melted into a dead and dreamless unconsciousness and slept as he had never slept before.

Mani lay awake for a moment, staring at his child's face. In the two weeks since her visit to the clinic, she had come to think about her life in a new way. You make decisions; some are reversible and some are not; and they have consequences that are both bad and good. Nothing is pure. Nothing easy. When she settled into sleep, she did so uncertain of what her world would be like upon waking, her mind circling the suspicion that there was a deep relationship between uncertainty and beauty.

article | discussion | edit this page | history

The Encyclopaedists [edit]

It seems so obvious and moralistic and wrong to say that we are all the Encyclopaedists. But fuck it, we say it anyway.

Contents [hide]

1 Precursors of the Encyclopaedists
2 Motivations of the Encyclopaedists
3 Ice
4 Used goods
5 Things that don't exist
6 War
7 Betrayal
8 Human remains
9 The first person plural
10 Sleep
11 Fuel

Precursors of the Encyclopaedists [edit]

How arrogant it seems to talk of precursors, a form of false humility, as if one were even important enough to belong to a lineage, real or imagined.

Motivations of the Encyclopaedists [edit]

To have none, the master said.

Ice [edit]

Not a substance but a state, the way loneliness or violence can be states of the human substance, states that are, by definition, temporary, though they sometimes seem immutable; even a monolithic glacier of loneliness melts.

Used goods [edit]

But used "for what" or "by whom." Those are the important qualifiers. Used "how often"? Used "with love"? Used "like a blow-up doll" or "like a violin"? It sucks to be used "like a hammer" unless one is built like a hammer. No matter how one is built, it is better to be "used well" than to sit unused, collecting the dark.

Things that don't exist [edit]

Did the dodo or the steam engine have a moment, the way a dying man has a moment, the way two lovers or two friends can have a moment, where they saw their looming nonexistence, a moment when they were disappearing but still solid enough to see their disappearance?

War [edit]

When the unforgivable happens, when the Punisher's family is killed by the mob, when the Japanese bomb Pearl Harbor, one often hears the phrase "This means war." Historically understood to mean: "We will destroy the fuck out of you even if we have to destroy ourselves." But when Al-Qaeda remodeled lower Manhattan, the ensuing action gave the phrase a new meaning: "Let's all get some guns and build a swamp in the desert and never leave. We'll play Scrabble to the death in a language with no fixed words."

Betrayal

[edit]

I'm sorry, someone says, and betrayal becomes indelibly certain, ontologically false.

Human remains

[edit]

One of the most damning claims against the existence of Bigfoot is the absence of any Bigfoot remains. In present times, it is not unusual for a person in his early twenties never to have seen a dead human, never to have been to an open-casket funeral. Is it not then reasonable for this person to conclude that Humans don't exist? That sightings, blurry videos, and photos are all the result of wishful thinking and a vast constellation of independent hoaxes? Only the soft of mind believe in Humanity.

The first person plural

[edit]

The grammar assumes that in the evolution of thought, man became aware of his own person first. "You" is the second person. This seems wrong. The number 1 is unnecessary until there are two or more things. "I" and "you" are differentiating terms. Before there is a "you," there is no need for either term. The plural is surely the embryonic conception. The Zeroeth person, "we," something "you" and "I" learn to forget. It should be no wonder that a true "we" has a womblike security that feels eternal though it must always be terminal.

Sleep

[edit]

Scientists are still debating the function of sleep (wound healing, the solidification and organization of memories?) because for centuries they have ignored the fact that sleep is awesome for its nullity, for its voiding of the stress of constant sensory input.

And dreams, however real they seem, are not sensory input. For you might feel totally at ease while dreaming of, for example, riding through the desert in a Humvee, weighed down by body armor, iPod ear buds snaking up into your helmet, playing some haunting aria you feel culturally guilty for not being able to identify. Your buddy sitting behind you puts you in a headlock and you start elbowing him in the ribs, playfully but with force, and then the Humvee is flying through the air, spinning, and you and your buddy both point your M4s, you're holding M4s now, through the small windows and begin firing your infinite clips at the fiery, rotating world.

Death is often confused with sleep ("to die, to sleep") though even an endless sleep is not death. In sleep, the void surrounds you. In death, you are the void. And endless sleep would be a form of bliss, moving in and out of REM for eternity, with that unwanted waking waiting patiently at infinity. John Keats, a man well acquainted with death, writes:

> Can death be sleep, when life is but a dream,
> And scenes of bliss pass as a phantom by?
> The transient pleasures as a vision seem,
> And yet we think the greatest pain's to die.

To Keats, the greater pain is not death but waking. There is no apathy involved in this equation. There is only inevitability and the praise of unreality.

Fuel

[edit]

Imagine yourself in a cold, dark vein of crude oil beneath a layer of ocean floor. You are a volume of methane gas and you live in darkness until the vein is lanced, then the crude swims up lengths of riveted steel pipe, ever upward, filling enormous cauldrons, and you swim with it to final escape from the earth's bowels, there above you, the coffee can–sized aperture at the top of the well tower through which you can actually *see* the outside air and flecks of cloud and beyond—on a moonless night in the Norwegian Sea, straight through the atmosphere, itself gas, like you—into the star fields, the light-art of distances beyond distance. Those are your cousins out there, burning away. Fuel beyond imagining.

What appear from a distance to be the glowing embers of the birth of the universe are, up close, the nth order of magnitude of fire—a hellish heat of a scale only vaguely imagined by earthly fire-wielders. The rage of a star being newly born into the race of a trillion suns. You can almost feel it, racing up through the depths, through steel, the pressure from the swells of crude below you so great the transition from undersea pipe to surface pipe is imperceptible, the night sky and star fields newly visible to you as the crude is sucked into its holding tanks, your celestial family all beckoning you with their own plumes of self-immolation while you race upward through the scaffolded pipe, the aperture becoming a window, the smell of the night sky present, the suggestion of the dark outline of a sea bird at the edge of a flock floating across the window, the pilot light merely a foreground detail to the vast oiled landscape until you touch it and then, poof.

External links   [edit]

1. ^ "The Encyclopaedists of Capitol Hill."
www.thestranger.com/apr04/encyclopaedists.htm

2. ^ "C. PLINII NATVRALIS HISTORIAE PRAEFATIO."
www.thelatinlibrary.com/pliny.nhpr.html

3. ^ "Stanford Encyclopedia of Philosophy entry on 'War.' "
plato.stanford.edu/entries/war/

4. ^ "Project Gutenberg Bible, King James, Book 42: Luke."
www.gutenberg.org/dirs/etext05/bib4210h.htm

5. ^ "Dreams & Sleep—National Sleep Foundation."
sleepfoundation.org/sleep-topics/dream-and-sleep

BOOM

51

Montauk awoke, covered in sweat. He hit the illuminator button on his Casio: 3:12 a.m. He'd been dreaming about the skull, the skull that Monkey had brought him. A skull in a paper bag. He slid out of his cot, opened his footlocker, and lifted out a pile of shirts and socks. There it was, barely visible in the dim light from the exit signs and the small glowing dots from sleeping electronics. A smell of damp earth. A smell he'd grown fond of over the past week, taking intermittent peeks at his prize, picturing it sitting on the mantel of the fireplace in the house he would have one day, making enigmatic comments about its origin to a dinner guest over a glass of brandy.

He'd obsessively researched Army regulation on penalties for possession of prohibited items, in this case, war trophies. Human remains, whether enemy or civilian, were certainly contraband. Who knew what they would do to him if they found out. There'd probably be a 15-6 investigation. He could get an other-than-honorable or possibly even jail time. Mostly he worried what his platoon would think.

He'd read about soldiers in World War II taking the ears, teeth, and even full skulls of Japanese dead in the Pacific theater. It was contraband then, too, but regulations must have been a lot more lax. From what he'd seen here, even snapping a photo of yourself with a hajji corpse would, at the very least, expose you to the salival spray of Greywolf Six.

Montauk had thought of a dozen different methods to smuggle the skull back. There were thousands of packages and crates that left the country every day. He could ensconce it in dirty clothes in his duffel. He could build a false bottom in one of the electronics crates to be shipped back to Fort Lewis at the end of the deployment. He could buy a soccer ball and carefully slice it open.

But as he looked at the skull for the tenth time this week, at what was now surely three-fifteen a.m., the smell made him retch. Montauk shoved the skull in his backpack, laced up his boots, and left.

Outside, he passed a soldier from 1st Platoon who was standing guard. "Everything all right, sir?" he asked after taking a drag from his cigarette.

"Couldn't sleep," Montauk said. He walked on, then turned abruptly and asked the soldier for a smoke.

The nicotine washed through his blood and brought a sense of calm to him as he stood on the bridge and leaned out over the Tigris. He was far enough from the BOB crew that no one would notice if he did it quickly. He fished out the skull. He moved to his left a little to avoid the mud pit around the pilings where Aladdin had gotten stuck. But he couldn't just drop it at an instant. He found himself staring at it wistfully. He or she might have been one of Saddam's victims— where could a kid like Monkey get a skull except from some mass grave? Mysteries piled on mysteries, but the mystery of death itself was surely at the top of the SecDef's known unknowns. Depending on the answer to that mystery, even murder could be a blessing. Some half-remembered and malformed version of Hamlet's "poor Yorick" speech fluttered through Montauk's head, then he kissed the skull on its bony forehead and gave it a reverent toss into the water below.

———

Sodium Joh was hunched over in the backseat of the Millennium Falcon, trying to get his dick into the mouth of an empty plastic water bottle.

"What the . . . Are you jacking off back there?" demanded Ant from the driver's seat.

"I'm taking a leak, dude. Piss bottle," yelled Joh. Thomas sat on the other side of the backseat, encased like a sweating sausage in his battle rattle. Sergeant Fields's feet dangled between them as he reclined in the sling attached to the gunner's turret.

"Oh, dude, I gotta piss, too," Ant said. "Hey, sir, could you find a bottle for me? I gotta piss."

"I'll hold the wheel. I'm not holding your dick, though," Montauk said.

Ant was chewing gum in a way that would have been loud if you could hear it over the roar of the Millennium Falcon moving over the highway. They had to keep a maximum speed of forty mph due to the extremely slow fuel trucks they were escorting, which was nerve-racking, as the trucks were fat and slow targets in one of the main IED alleys in central Iraq.

Montauk had fallen into that passenger's state of mind where, once you hit a certain speed, you perceive yourself as motionless, the world scrolling past you. And with the soft assurance of the pensive child he was when riding home on the yellow bus after a long day at school, he began to daydream. He daydreamed mostly of Tricia Burnham. He thought of her in Boston, which was probably cool and crisp right now. He thought of her reclining in a large, soft bed with puffy white sheets. Sipping tea and intelligently discussing the arts at a dinner party with her college friends. He'd been too harsh with her. She'd made a mistake, a big mistake, but what the fuck was he doing gathering his own intel through civilian sources anyway. He'd been an outright asshole, unwilling to admit his own fault in the Gorma shitstorm. It was calming to recognize that character flaw. He felt cleansed, as if admitting a sin. Knowing was half the battle.

"Hey, Joh," Fields said, leaning down from the turret. "Hand me that bottle. I need to piss, too."

"It's full, Sergeant," Joh said.

"Thomas," Fields said, "finish your bottle and hand it to me."

"You kidding?" Thomas said. "Your crotch is right in our faces. Gunner's gotta hold it."

"Drink your fucking water or pour it on your stupid face or whatever and hand it to me."

"Okay, okay."

"Okay, *what*?"

"Okay, *Sergeant.*" Thomas drained his water bottle, then handed it to Fields. "One more thing, Sergeant," he said. "How long exactly should we look at your dick?"

There was a slight pause, then Ant burst out laughing. Then Joh, then Fields as well.

At just that moment, a bomb dug under the highway exploded directly beneath the Millennium Falcon. Montauk's view of the central Iraqi landscape skewed as the Falcon transformed into its namesake and the roll axis was introduced to its passengers. The altitude and roll became more pronounced as it picked up speed, and the landscape cut across Montauk's field of vision. His tympanic membranes ruptured from the overpressurized blast wave, and his brain, reacting belatedly to the new direction, sitting as it was in a liquid-filled chamber, misfired as it pushed up against the bottom of his skull. He did not feel the metal biting into him as his brain slipped a gear and the image of Tricia Burnham that had been framed in his imagination became a memory; a memory of her with conditioned hair in a cool New England morning, looking at him and smiling, her chin propped up in her hand, a gift from Tricia, a portrait of how she wanted him to remember her, a sepia tone in a tasteful pewter frame to be placed next to a computer in an office cubicle and gazed at every so often during decades of a unique but not especially noteworthy twenty-first-century middle-class American life.

FOOLS

52

"I'm looking for Mrs. Montauk. Is that you?"

Mani went blank.

In the hallway outside her loft, the soldier stood impossibly erect in his green dress uniform, bedazzled with an assortment of abstruse patches, insignia, and pins that glinted in the afternoon light.

"What is this about?" she asked. Had they somehow discovered their marriage was . . .

"Your husband, ma'am. We apologize for the delay in bringing you this news. We had trouble locating your contact information."

How could she be so stupid. Of course it wasn't that. Her internal monologue trembled past her lips. "No, no no. He's not. He's not."

"No, he's not," the soldier said. "He's been wounded in action."

"Oh my God." Mani took a few quick deep breaths. "Is he okay?"

"He's at the Walter Reed Army Medical Center. He was admitted with a compound fracture to his femur and cerebral edema due to . . ." The soldier's eyes broke Mani's gaze and looked past her into the room. "Traumatic brain injury."

Mani turned and saw Corderoy standing there, shirtless, in his boxer shorts, looking like he'd just been startled out of a postcoital nap, which he had. They both had. Oh God. "Mickey . . . ?" Corderoy said.

The soldier looked back at Mani, a new sadness in his face. He sighed. Mani ran her hand through her mussed hair, knowing it didn't matter, that there was nothing she could do to look more put together, dressed as she was in a torn pair of leggings and one of Hal's T-shirts.

"What happened?" Corderoy said.

The soldier continued to address Mani. "His Humvee hit an IED while on a convoy into Diyala Province."

"What does that mean, cerebral, whatever you called it?"

He glanced at Corderoy again. "I'm not a doctor, ma'am. They'll have more information for you at Walter Reed." He handed her an envelope.

"This isn't what you think," Mani said. "It's—"

"It's none of my business, ma'am. Is there anything else I can do for you in this time of need?" The words were so polite, and so dead, so rehearsed.

"I guess not," Mani said.

As the soldier left, Mani closed the door and fell back against it. She surveyed her loft, her home, the Montauk family home. Dirty dishes near the wash sink, open tubes of paint on the windowsill, beer bottles overflowing with cigarette butts. And a man who was decidedly not her husband standing in the middle of the room, half-naked, staring back at her.

"We have to go to D.C.," he said.

Mani heard the words but not their meaning. She walked over to the unmade bed as if she were going to collapse into it and drown in the comforter, but she merely stood there, looking down at her feet. There was a torn condom wrapper on the floor. She turned around and swiped it toward the middle of the room with her foot. "Clean this shit up," she said.

"What the fuck," Corderoy said. "He's my best friend."

———

The exterior of the Walter Reed Army Medical Center, with its rooftop cupola and its colonnaded portico, looked more like a mansion in the English countryside than a trauma center. Corderoy and Mani passed a circular fountain big enough to swim in. On the landscaped East Lawn, ranks of soldiers did sit-ups while others knelt beside them with clipboards. Your everyday fitness test, except many of the soldiers were double amputees.

"What if he's . . . different?" Corderoy asked.

"Don't say that?" Mani said. "Whatever he's gone through—"

Corderoy grabbed Mani's hand as they ascended the steps. They passed soldiers on crutches, in wheelchairs, and soldiers who looked perfectly healthy. Were they staff? Were they visitors? Or had they been wounded in some invisible way? Corderoy felt a gnawing anxiety in his gut that every normal-looking person they passed was either mentally crippled or missing his genitalia.

"I haven't stayed in touch like you have," he said. "I'm not his best friend anymore."

"Stop it," Mani said.

But that statement had a mental momentum that carried him forward. He and Montauk had an intense connection, they'd become friends overnight, but it lacked the stability of a childhood friendship. Maybe it had already withered, maybe it had snapped the night of the last Encyclopaedists party. How would he know? What would he even say to Montauk? "Our relationship," he said, "it was never really characterized by emotional disclosure."

"Who *are* you?" Mani said.

"What?"

"Did you consider that maybe you've changed, too?"

They reached Montauk's room, but before Mani could open the door, Corderoy reached forward to ward her off. "I have to," he said. "I have to ask."

Mani turned toward him expectantly.

Corderoy hesitated. "Did you two hook up?"

"No," Mani said flatly. "Can we go in now?"

Corderoy sighed. "Not at all?"

Mani's shoulders slumped as if she couldn't muster the energy for anything but the unadorned truth. "We kissed," she said. "And honestly, I would have. But Mickey's a good guy. He's a good friend to you." As she said the words, though they felt true, they also felt hollow. She had been proud, those months ago, that her relationship with Mickey had not become sexual. Perhaps, on the threshold of witnessing Montauk's injuries, she needed to see him in a heroic light. Or perhaps, as messed up as it was, she wanted to see how this new Corderoy would react to that sting. "I'm sorry," she said.

"No, you're right. He's a good friend. Much better—"

"Let's go in already."

Montauk was asleep when they walked into his room. His left leg was in a cast, and his ear was covered with a gauze bandage that left a piece of sutured flesh visible. "Ohhhh, Mickey," Mani said. She walked to him while Corderoy stood back, surveying the room. There were cards, books, flowers on the side table. Montauk's parents had obviously visited. Venetian blinds on the windows, one of them twisted the wrong way. Something ugly breathed inside Corderoy, an oppressive guilt centered on the unconscious body of his friend. But then Montauk stirred. He blinked a few times, inhabiting the silence, taking in the presence of his friends. Corderoy pushed the feeling away. "It's good to see your face," he said.

Montauk blinked a few more times. "Hi," he said.

"Tell us what happened," Mani said, squeezing his right hand.

Montauk took a moment to process the question. "I got blown up," he said.

"Duh," Corderoy said. "But how?"

"The usual, dude. IED." Montauk seemed to finally recognize the expression on Corderoy's face and he returned a tentative smile of his own. "Thanks for coming," he said.

"What about your head, Mickey?"

"It's fine," Montauk said.

"They said you had cerebral edema."

"I'm okay."

"I looked it up. You—"

"I'm fine, all right? Jesus. I just got my bell rung. I'm healing up. I'm really lucky."

"Lucky?" Corderoy said.

"Yeah. Lucky. I'm not dead and my face isn't melted off."

"Did someone die?" Corderoy asked.

"Yeah, my gunner died. Fields. A really good guy. Just a really nice guy. Evan Fields. His girl was pregnant."

"Oh . . . shit. Shit, dude."

"Yeah. Do you know Ant? Maybe I told you about him, I don't know. I'm a little drugged out right now. He's here, too."

Mani and Corderoy looked at each other. "We're just worried," Mani said.

"I get it. I'm fine, though. Everything's fine except that my parents are pissed. They found out from the Army about our, that we . . ." Montauk glanced at Corderoy, then back at Mani.

"He knows," Mani said.

"I know," Corderoy said.

"Oh, shit, they sent someone to your house, too, didn't they?"

"Yeah," Mani said. "At first we thought you were . . ."

"God, I'm sorry," Montauk said.

"Don't be," Corderoy said. "We're just glad you're okay."

"Stop it, already. I'm fine. I've still got my face. Dick's still attached, so your mom will be relieved, bro."

"My dad will be, too. They called last week. They were worried about you. So was I."

Montauk glared at Corderoy as though his unflinching sincerity were some kind of trick. "It was just a fucking roadside bomb," he said. "I don't really remember getting blown up, just getting medevaced. Whatever. Like I said. Nothing to complain about. I mean, the cast sucks, but I'm getting paid. I feel kind of guilty about it, honestly. Ant is down the hall with his fucking face burned off."

Mani stroked his forearm. "Well, I'm glad it's not you," she said.

"What?" Montauk pulled his arm out from under her fingers.

"She didn't mean it that way," Corderoy said. "We're just glad you're back. We should celebrate. We should throw an Encyclopaedists party. In Boston."

"I don't know, man," Montauk said.

"We can do it at Mani's loft. When do they release you?"

"I'll be outpatient soon, but I have to be in and out of here every week for rehab for like months."

"But you can get a pass or something, just for the weekend."

"I guess. Maybe."

"Hal's right," Mani said. She linked arms with him and took Montauk's hand at the same time. "It would be good for you. Let's throw a party."

Montauk sighed and turned toward the window. It was good to see his friends, but they would leave in a moment, and it would be even better for them to leave now. He hated feeling that way, but hating the feeling didn't make it go away.

———

"Light the candles," Ant said. Thanks to some industrial pain meds, his speech was slurred and slowed.

"I don't know how," Montauk said. "Oh, wait. I found the menu. They're lit."

"All right, hooah. Do you see the stereo? I think it's by the couch."

Montauk clicked the action menu, and the stereo began pumping out eighties-sounding R&B. He was sitting in a wheelchair with Ant's laptop resting on his legs.

"Yeah," Ant said. "Everything we've worked for is coming to fruition. The neighbor lady should be just outside. Go invite her in."

Montauk navigated Ant's Sim outside. There was the neighbor lady. "Wow, she's smoking," Montauk said.

"What's she wearing? I forget."

"A blue midriff and Daisy Dukes."

The entire left side of Ant's body was covered in bandages, and most of his face, including both of his eyes, was hidden behind gauze. "Not for long," Ant said.

Montauk looked over at him and imagined that Ant was making the slight narrowing of the eyes that conveyed satisfied recognition. Of course, he was doing no such thing. Ant was in such constant pain that he probably wouldn't dare move any more facial muscles than necessary. Worse, he might never again be able to narrow his eyes. Montauk had seen the doctors change the bandages and reapply a salve. Most of Ant's eyelids had been burned off.

"Well?"

"There's no invite button," Montauk said.

"Just click on her and make her walk in the house."

Montauk did so. "Wait, her name is Hotass Neighborlady?"

"Yeah. I named her that when I created her."

"You created Hotass Neighborlady just so your Sim would have someone to bone?"

"Hooah."

"Hooah." Montauk navigated the two Sims to the table. "Now what?"

"Click on her. What romantic interactions do we got?"

"Flirt. Hold Hands. Whisper In Ear. There's a bunch, I don't know."

"Definitely Whisper In Ear."

Montauk selected that, and Ant's Sim leaned in for a sweet nothing.

"Check again. We have any kiss interactions?"

"I'm pleased to announce that Make Out is now available. Proceeding," Montauk said.

A few minutes later, Montauk had guided Ant's Sim and Hotass Neighborlady out to the back patio, where Ant had previously installed a hot tub. The Sims threw off their clothes, revealing shimmering pixels of obscured nudity, and leapt in.

"Sit next to her," Ant said.

"We got an option for WooHoo," Montauk said. "You ready?"

"Wait. Check the relationship menu. Are both their hearts red?"

"Hers is pink."

"Don't WooHoo yet or we'll get rejected, sir. Go for Cuddle."

Ant's Sim sidled up next to Hotass Neighborlady, and Montauk watched her heart symbol deepen in color. When it was finally time to engage in WooHoo, he counted down from T-minus ten before clicking the button. The Sims embraced each other, splashed, dove underwater, resurfaced, dove again, and one could only imagine how those pixelated genitals were interacting.

"How does it feel to tap that neighbor lady?" Montauk asked.

"Awesome," Ant said.

Silence descended on the room.

Montauk looked away, both from the game and from Ant, as he began imagining Ant's future romantic prospects. "What now?" he asked.

"I don't know. Go into Buy Mode? Maybe get a new couch?"

Montauk navigated through the options.

"You know, there was this girl back in Seattle that I was huge into," Ant said. "We had a philosophy class together."

"Yeah? There's a red leather couch here. Looks pretty nice."

"Sure," Ant said. "She invited me to this house party, was supposed to be a rager."

"Looks like you don't have enough cash for that couch," Montauk said.

"Ah, fuck it, then."

"So tell me about this party."

"Couldn't go. It was the weekend after we shipped out."

"Sucks."

"I think I coulda tapped that. I mean, it could have been something. Maybe."

Montauk looked out the window at a small patch of bluish D.C. sky. "My buddy wants to throw a big house party, like we used to."

"You should."

"Yeah, I don't know."

"What? Come on, sir, you gotta go. I'll tell you how to get the chicks into the hot tub."

"I've still got a broken femur."

"Whatever. Chicks dig that shit. I'd kill to go to a party right now."

"I'm also pissed at my buddy. He's banging my wife."

"Oh, shit."

"Well, she's not really my wife."

"Wait, did you get a PFC marriage for money?"

"That's in the vault, Private."

"Sir, yes, sir." Ant chuckled as much as the bandages and pain would allow. "Didn't think officers did that."

"Neither did I."

"So why are you pissed at your buddy?"

"I don't know. Maybe I'm not. Maybe I just want to be."

"Punch him in the face," Ant said.

"What?"

"Then you'll know. If you're mad or not."

Montauk laughed. "Your bandage is soaking through," he said. "I'll call the nurse."

53

No one knew how to react. Were they supposed to look or not? Was it an art piece? A tasteless joke? Was Mickey just fucking with everyone? They felt like fools. That was the party's theme, but still. He wore a peacoat and had a fake harpoon sticking out of his wheelchair. Mani was pushing him through the crowd. The fucked-up part was that Mickey was carrying a laptop on his legs and introducing people, via webcam, to Antonin Ant, whose bandages had been freshly removed: his eyes were lidless, and his forehead and left cheek were a corrugated and spongelike swath of moist pink, stretched taut toward his ear.

It was a point of extreme gravity moving through a lighthearted and ridiculous party. Hal wore a pair of tights and a ragged floral shirt that drooped down to his thighs in Renaissance fashion. He had a bindle over his shoulder and a rose in his hand. He was straight out of a tarot deck. His contribution to the art on display was a small cairn of golden nuggets on a pedestal with a sign that read: TOTALLY REALLY REAL. It wasn't real gold, but it was real pyrite. There was a sadness in his eyes that night, watching his best friend and the woman he loved at the center of so many conversations, not a sadness that life wasn't turning out the way he'd hoped, but a sadness that sadness would be a routine part of his life. One day, perhaps, he would be able to speak about these things without the safety of intellectual abstraction. Until that day, they would remain unverifiable, neither true nor false.

The loft space was really done up. Down the middle of the room, Mani had painted the double yellow lines of a road which ran into the wall and continued into a painted tunnel, à la Wile E. Coyote. Hal's old professor and some handyman guy, they were standing close to it, deep in a discussion of the metaphysical implications.

The thing about a Wile E. Coyote tunnel was that, to the outside viewer, the Road Runner, it was real enough to run right through, but to its maker, the Coyote, it remained an illusion he could never enter, always hitting the rock wall of his own artifice. There was some important idea in there about the nature of art, and Mani had painted this piece in order to help herself articulate it.

That was the kind of night it was. Ridiculous and theoretical. And always circling back to Mickey and the laptop, Ant directing him (*Hey, introduce me to that girl.* Or *I wanna say something to that buddy of yours that's banging your wife*). Ant seemed happy, meeting Mickey's friends, though it was difficult to tell, through his fresh scars, whether he was smiling or scowling. Could it be both? Nearly everyone at the party took a moment to say hi. No two reactions were the same. A bashful *Thank you for your service.* A willfully casual *Nice to meet you.* An awkward *Hello.* Even uncomprehending laughter.

When Tricia arrived—there were doubts all around that she'd show—she and Hal got into it about Mickey. She was wearing a bow tie and a green top hat with a card in the band that read *10/6. The thing about Mickey holding that laptop,* she said, *sure, maybe it's an attempt to puncture the civilian art bubble, which is good, but it's still vulgar. Even if it was Ant's idea, like you say. It's exploitive.*

On returning from Baghdad, prematurely, Tricia had been shocked and unwilling to look at the mess she'd made. That had given way to a wellspring of guilt and confusion. She'd failed to keep her professional and romantic lives separate. And Abdul Aziz had paid for that failure. That small bit of specificity, that boy's name, made it ten times worse. The night of the party, she was trying her best to smile right through her mind's preferred grimace. Fake it till you make it. Maybe that's exactly what Ant was doing.

The pug that Jenny Yi had brought crashed through the room,

chasing the red dot from a laser pointer being passed around. They laughed and refilled their drinks.

If we owe our wounded anything, Hal said, *it's that we face them with a certain disposition, a disposition that makes no assumptions. Take it at face value even when—no, especially when—the face is horribly disfigured.*

That's nice, Tricia told him. She looked with admiration at Mani, pushing Mickey's wheelchair through the crowd. Mani had rubbed acrylic paint all over her skin and clothes, darkening her shadows, more strongly limning her facial features. Her costume was an impressionistic portrait, the canvas was her body, and her subject was the fool she knew best: herself.

No one knew what was going to happen between her and Hal. She caught the soft focus of his eyes and smiled back at him—the poor, sweet idiot wasn't as much of an asshole as he liked to think. Hal thought he needed her. Maybe he really did. Whatever Mani had been through, it had left her more self-possessed; there was a nascent warmth emanating from her, a lone but not a lonely warmth, as if she had glimpsed her heart's thermostat and knew she couldn't reach the knob while wearing so many layers, so many sweaters and jackets of other people. There she was, pushing Mickey's wheelchair, but he didn't need her to, and soon she wouldn't be. She had been so reactive, it had made her art reactive, art bent on sorting out the messy dynamics she shared with the people in her life. Perhaps she was ready now to make art not in relation to anyone, art that was causal, not caused.

Then Hal asked Tricia about Mickey, if she was going to talk to him. And she said, *Do I have to?* And he said, *Yes,* and she said, *Why?* and Hal got all rom-com and said, *Because that idiot's in love with you!*

Tricia denied it, then demanded to know what Mickey had said about the two of them. Hal just raised his eyebrows.

Everyone watched her and Mickey talk in the corner of the room once he'd handed Ant off to Hal. They tried to make out the conversation, just based on the body language: *Didn't think you would come. / Here I am. / Guess you can't hate me now that I'm in a wheelchair. / Hal said that . . . / He said what? / I don't know. I forgot what your smile looked like.*

And then Mickey examined her face. What was he thinking? That he'd been angry, yes, but not *at* her, not at anyone or anything. Anger had become a feature of his existence. A feature that, for some reason, that night, seemed to have retreated into a burrow in the back of his mind. Maybe it was thanks to Ant. No one knew what to make of the two of them at a hipster art party. Were they really wounded? Were they really soldiers? The easy definitional categories had fallen away. Maybe that's what allowed Mickey to see himself outside of the roles he was accustomed to filling. A naked version of himself that had no use for anger, no relationship with it. It was still there, probably, hibernating.

Then Mickey's face took on an unfamiliar earnestness, a hint of fear. He was about to take a risk: *Come get dinner with me. Next weekend.*

It could have been something like that, judging by how Tricia tilted her head, dwelling in that space between *yes* and *no*. *What's he saying now?* someone asked. Another chimed in to supply the answer in Mickey's voice: *I'll pick you up in my blimp.*

But perhaps that's far too optimistic. Perhaps they were talking about Abdul Aziz. *I tried to get him released.* Then Tricia tilting her head, dwelling in that space between guilt and hope. *They'll let him out, eventually. / Eventually. / I know. / And there's nothing we can do? / I fucked up. / Gorma lied. / We fucked up. / Where does that leave us? / Free. Rich, relatively. / Whole lives ahead of us.*

It almost doesn't make sense to ask what they were really saying in that moment, across the room. They were saying what everyone assumed they were saying. Supposition became fact.

Later in the evening, when all the guests had gone home, when Ant had retired to the cold fluorescent light of his hospital room, Mani and Tricia went up to the rooftop, leaving Hal and Mickey to speak to each other for the first time all evening.

So what's the deal with Mani? Mickey asks. *You back together? Not exactly,* Hal says. *But you're living together,* Mickey says. *Today,* Hal says. *I think she's gonna ask me to leave. Sometime soon.* Hal's voice is strangely calm. *Shit,* Mickey says. *Just have that feeling,* Hal says, *like when you spin a coin and it starts to wobble out of control.*

Sad. Why does it have to be that way? Perhaps it's too difficult to suspend the disbelief that everything can work out in the end—no, not *in the end*; there is no end, or life is just a string of ends, none of them simple, all of them seeds.

Where does it go from here? Mickey says, *I've been thinking about punching you in the face. Just to see. If it's something I want to do. To have done.* Hal says, *Do it. Naw. I'm weak,* Mickey says. *And I can't reach you from here. I'd have to get up on my crutches.* And Hal leans down close and presents the side of his face. *Do it.* And Mickey socks him in the jaw and Hal falls backward. *Fuck. Ouch. Fucking Fuck.*

Sorry, dude, Mickey says as Hal groans. Look at his face. It's so obvious, that creeping smile, he feels closer to Mickey than he has in a long time, perhaps ever. *This is it, isn't it?* Hal says. *The last Encyclopaedists party. Probably,* Mickey says. And he looks up to the ceiling. *What do you think they're talking about up there?* And Hal rubs his jaw, settling into the pain. *Not a fucking clue.*

It almost doesn't make sense to ask what Mani and Tricia were saying at that exact moment. They would recall it later; they were saying what they would remember saying. Consensus would become fact.

Mani speaks to Tricia without looking at her. *You ever wish you could want to be a doctor?* She takes a hit of a joint, staring out at the city, then passes it to Tricia. She takes a hit herself, contemplating. *I wish I could want to be a consumer,* she says. *A professional consumer. God, can you imagine? If all you had to do to be fulfilled was buy shit and watch TV and read novels, to feed and feed yourself until your heart gave out?*

Fools, all of us. Glorious fools born into a vacuum of need, told we could be anything, flailing in a sea of possibility, thinking it a curse, having to design our lives from scratch, forever skeptical of what we create, forever revising, no idea of who we are or what we will make of ourselves—everyone a creator, everyone a voice in the universal knowledge—how lonely, with every mouth moving, no one actually listening, truth constantly in flux. That very same day, in Rio de Janeiro, a death squad gunned down thirty people. Across the world, 350,000 infants inhaled for the very first time. Over the next five years, we would all become different people. We couldn't help ourselves. We needed to know the truth, and no one would give it to us, so we made it up as we went. We authored our lives in real time. We became invisible and everywhere. Over the next billion years, the sun would grow more luminous, and surface temperatures on the earth would rise until all the water on the planet evaporated into space, a sublime obliterating ascension worthy of humanity, though no human would live to see it.*

* Not in person, anyway.

♟ Log in

article | discussion | edit this page | history

The Encyclopaedists

[edit]

This page has been deleted. The deletion and move log for the page are provided below for reference.

- 20:11, 01 April 2005 Carbon (talk | contribs) deleted "The Encyclopaedists" *(G1: Patent nonsense, meaningless, or incomprehensible; & A7: No explanation of the subject's significance.)*

Wikipedia does not have an article with this exact name. Please search for *The Encyclopaedists* in Wikipedia to check for alternative titles or spellings.

- Search for "*The Encyclopaedists*" in existing articles.
- Look for pages within Wikipedia that link to this title.

Other reasons this message may be displayed:

- If a page was recently created here, it may not yet be visible because of a delay in updating the database; wait a few minutes and try the purge function.
- Titles on Wikipedia are **case sensitive** except for the first character; please check alternative capitalizations and consider adding a redirect here to the correct title.
- If the page has been deleted, check the **deletion log**, and see Why was my page deleted?.

WIKIPEDIA
The Free Encyclopedia

navigation

- Main Page
- Community portal
- Current events
- Recent changes
- Random page
- Help
- Donations

search

[Go] [Search]

toolbox

- What links here
- Related changes
- Special pages

ACKNOWLEDGMENTS

Dear Reader,

You allowed this book to hijack your mind for a significant number of hours, hours you could have spent skydiving or mastering the Rubik's Cube. If you are now regretting that decision, please direct all hate mail to us. Should you feel otherwise—fingers crossed—we would like to remind you that this book could not exist without the help of dozens of brilliant and generous fools.

We are deeply indebted to Phil Klay, who read draft after draft of this book and pushed us to make hard decisions, removing the vampires, having Montauk deploy to Baghdad instead of an exoplanet orbiting Tau Ceti, and changing Corderoy's wizardry school into an MA lit program.

Many others gave us editorial feedback along the way; these insightful readers include: Richard Armstrong, Carmiel Banasky, Jeffrey Coffin, Melissa Falcon Field, Stephanie Kese, Molly Wallace Kovite, Clare Needham, Erin Pollock, Jason Sack, and Katie Vane.

Thanks to our astounding agent, Eric Simonoff, who somehow manages to be as nice as he is shrewd. Thanks also to the rest of the WME team, including Cathryn Summerhayes, Kate Barry, Eve Atterman, and Kathleen Nishimoto.

Liese Mayer, our sharp and judicious editor, was instrumental in streamlining the plot and heightening the emotive impact throughout. And to everyone else at Scribner: our publicist, Katherine Monaghan, our designer, Jill Putorti, our production editor, Dan Cuddy, and our copy editor, Beth Thomas—brilliant work, all of you. And to Nan Graham, for believing in this book and helping it become a reality.

We'd also like to thank Simon Prosser at Hamish Hamilton and Oscar van Gelderen at Lebowski for their early support in bringing this book to international readers.

And of course, countless hours of research were spent combing the near infinite well of knowledge that is Wikipedia. So, thank you to Jimmy Wales and the entire Wikipedia community.

———

Christopher would like to thank:

My parents for not pressuring their vagabond son to get a real job during the five years in which *War of the Encyclopaedists* was written. I'm also grateful to my recently deceased grandfather for raising a family of journalists, songwriters, and poets, including my uncle Mike, who helped me find my bearings in the world of poetry at the age of twenty-one.

I would not be the writer I am today without my time at the University of Washington, and in the MFA programs at Boston University and Hunter College, where a host of professors pushed me to fail better. They include: Richard Kenney, Heather McHugh, Linda Bierds, Louise Glück, Robert Pinsky, David Ferry, Rosanna Warren, Jean Paul Riquelme, Derek Walcott, Tom Sleigh, Donna Masini, and Jan Heller Levi.

I'm also in debt to the following organizations for supporting me over the last five years: Bread Loaf, the Djerassi Resident Artists Program, the Kimmel Harding Nelson Center for the Arts, the Lanesboro Arts Center, the MacDowell Colony, the Millay Colony for the Arts, the Santa Fe Art Institute, and the Virginia Center for the Creative Arts.

Much of this book was also written while house- or pet-sitting for a number of people who were incredibly gracious in sharing their space: Doug and Gretchen Stewart, Steve and Mimi Johnson, Simone Kearney and her father, Richard, Donna Masini, and Nina Budabin McQuown.

Thanks to my Djerassi pals for the moral support during the beginning of this publishing journey, and in particular to Susanna Sonnenberg for the invaluable advice.

And my undying gratitude to Mary Karr, who kept me clothed and fed and writing, who showed me the way up the crags of Parnassus, and who kicked my ass when I needed it most.

————

Gavin would like to thank:

My wife, Molly. And to my parents: thanks for a childhood full of books and everything else. Thanks to Nicole, for being who she is. Thanks to the 5035 and Spaceship Excellent for all the characters. Thanks to those who taught me to be a soldier and a leader, especially Dave Carr and Craig Hanson. To Mike Starbuck and the 4th Platoon Mad Dogs: you guys do Riverside proud. I hope you like the book. Thanks to Vinne Lichvar for the story—you know which one. To the 555 legal team: thanks for keeping my head above water while I put the finishing touches on this thing.

To Aladdin, Mohammed, and Monkey: for your friendship, wit, and courage, you have my undying respect and gratitude. I hope you're safe.

ABOUT THE AUTHORS

Christopher Robinson, a Boston University and Hunter College MFA graduate, is a MacDowell Colony fellow and a Yale Younger Poets prize finalist. His writing has appeared in many publications, including *The Kenyon Review* and *McSweeney's*.

Gavin Kovite was an infantry platoon leader in Baghdad from 2004 to 2005. He attended NYU Law and is now an Army lawyer. His writing has appeared in literary magazines and in *Fire and Forget,* an anthology of war fiction.